Juliette lay beneath Roger, aware only of the fire he lit when he touched her body. She had felt shame when she disrobed, but she lost it now under his caresses. A moan escaped her lips, and she felt a heat move from her thighs through her abdomen.

He made no protests of love—spoke no words of endearment. But his body said more to her than words ever could. Before the night was over, he held her close to him, cradled against his body, united with her as Dumont had been. But this time there was no hint of pain. This time there was only delight—and a surprising, wonderful, mind-destroying ecstasy.

SHE HAD NEVER BEFORE KNOWN . . .

So Wild A Rapture

by Andrea Layton

PLAYBOY PRESS
PAPERBACKS

Published simultaneously in the United States and Canada by Playboy Press, Chicago, Illinois. Printed in the United States of America. Library of Congress Catalog Card Number: 78-59974. First edition.

This book is available at quantity discounts for promotional and industrial use. For further information, write our sales-promotion agency: Ventura Associates, 40 East 49th Street, New York, New York 10017.

ISBN: 0-872-16489-6

CHAPTER ONE

"Juliette! Juliette de Condillac! You'd better come home! It's almost time for your dinner!"

Impatiently, Juliette rose, brushing the loose blades of grass from her skirt. Far in the distance she could see the red-tiled roof of her home, but Hermione Bouchard, whose voice carried easily over the hills, was nowhere in sight.

"Do you have to go?" François du Quesnay sat up and brushed his hair with a slender hand. "I haven't finished telling you about my studies."

Juliette cocked her head, alert for any indication that Hermione intended to demand obedience. The call was not repeated. "I don't think so. She isn't mad enough yet." She looked up at the sky. The sun rode high above the horizon. It would be a long time before dinner. "No! I think she's just yelling to impress Papa. It makes him think she's watching me!"

Spreading her skirt, she dropped to the ground. This wasn't the first time Hermione had called her with no reason, nor would it be the last; of that she was certain. Madam Bouchard had been mother and nurse to her from the moment she had been taken as a squalling infant from the arms of her dying mother.

The sharp-tongued woman had been father as well, much of the time, for Jean de Condillac had never quite recovered from his wife's death. His occasional excursions into parenthood had at first confused

Juliette. Now, a young lady of 16, she understood them as his way and accepted them without question.

"You're not going right away, are you?" François frowned up at the sky.

"No, of course not!" Juliette hoped the interruption would cause François to change the subject. He'd talked of the plebeian revolution in America and had explained in detail how important it was for France to change as well. "It's 1789, Juliette!"—his voice reflected his impatience—"1789. And France still has serfs! Everywhere else in the world laborers are free!"

Actually, she resented his preoccupation with politics and his education. They had romped together as small children. She'd watched him as he learned to ride and had been taught on his abandoned pony when he graduated to a horse. In fact, they'd done everything together—until he began to grow up and was sent away to school.

Taking a long blade of grass, she knelt close to him. "You're the one who's going away. Couldn't you get a longer vacation? After all, I won't have another birthday until next year!" Deliberately, she began to tickle his nose.

He sneezed, brushed the grass from his face, and sat up beside her. "I only got away now because it was your sixteenth birthday, and your father convinced mine it was important! I'm going to have to work hard to catch up!" His expression changed. "Juliette, you know I love you, don't you?"

His sudden seriousness filled her with a vague disquiet. Dropping to the grass, she lowered her gaze, avoiding his eyes. "Of course I know. But we don't have to talk about it, do we?"

He stretched his long legs and then, with a quick leap, he was on his feet. He grasped her arm and pulled her up beside him. "Yes! We do have to talk about it! For one thing, you owe me a kiss! I didn't get one last night at your party."

Impishly, she twisted in his arms, her black curls bobbing enticingly as she tilted her face toward his. Wide sensuous lips parted as he moved closer. Her tongue emerged, flicking lightly over her white teeth. Their eyes met. His were dead serious, deep and brown, filled with an urgent emotion she hesitated to acknowledge. He had said it before, but she had always refused to listen. He was eighteen. A man. He could not go on forever pretending he was still a child.

She felt a tremor of fright. She wasn't ready. Not yet. With a cry of delight, she ducked from his arms. "Catch me! See if you can catch me!" She was off, running down the hill like a sprite chasing the will-o'-the-wisp.

He stood unmoving. Skipping now, she circled around the grass, a mischievous laugh on her lips. "Come on, try to catch me! If you want a kiss, you have to catch me!"

Quickly he covered the distance between them with long, easy strides. "Got you!" He held her in his arms more firmly than before. She felt his long body press against hers, and once more his lips drew close.

Holding her breath, she gently moved her arms upward toward his shoulders. They paused on his chest and then, before he could stop her, they were buried in his armpits, her fingers twitching rapidly.

"Juliette! Stop it! You're tickling me!" Doubling up convulsively, he tried to break away.

She moved with him, her fingers keeping him in a state of helpless laughter. Then, with a lunge, he attacked. Startled, she fell to the grass. They dropped together, rolling and tumbling down the hill onto a bed of grass that bordered a small stream. Juliette loved such play. She always had. But, somehow, she felt that it soon would be ended.

As quickly as she had started, she stopped. Panting with laughter, they lay together, staring up at the willow tree above them. "Do you have to go tomorrow?" Her voice was petulant, as if by acting the child she could talk him into staying.

"You know I do. But that's tomorrow. Right now, I still want a kiss."

She gave it to him without further teasing. He didn't kiss her often, though she sensed it was not from lack of desire. At times, thinking about him, she knew he was waiting. She knew he had long ago outgrown her childish games. But never before had she felt it as strongly as she did now.

At first his kiss was light, as all of them had been in the past. Then, slowly, she felt a change. Nervously, she rolled out of his arms and propped herself up on one hand. "What makes you think I owed you a kiss?"

With a sigh, he looked up into her face. "You have, you know, ever since last night." His mouth twitched, but he resisted the impulse to smile. "Everyone else at your party got to kiss the birthday girl. Everyone but me."

Her lips formed into a delightful pout. "And why didn't you get to kiss me?"

He made no attempt to answer. Instead, he raised his shoulders and tried, vainly, to bring his mouth once more to hers.

She pulled away, her eyes flashing. "Tell me! Why weren't you there when all the other boys kissed me?"

Still he did not respond. Her hands sought his sides and she sent him once more into helpless paroxysms of laughter. "Why?" Her fingers moved faster. "Answer me, or I'll keep this up all afternoon!"

Gasping for breath, he tried to speak. Immediately, she settled back on the grass, her eyes on his face. "Are you going to tell me now?"

"You're being silly, Juliette! You know why as well as I do!"

"I don't care. You still have to say it! Otherwise I'll never let you kiss me again."

He raised himself into a sitting position beside her. "If you insist! I didn't get to kiss you on your birthday because I was dancing with Gladys." Before she had a chance to interrupt him, he hurried on. "But I had to. It isn't my fault my cousin is such a leech! Anyway, she's gone back home already, so I don't have to cater to her any more. If she weren't, she'd be bothering us again, as she was yesterday." With a sudden motion he pinned Juliette to the ground. "Now you have to give me another kiss."

When he did not immediately release her, Juliette squirmed uneasily. He made her nervous when he acted this way. Slowly, her hands moved upward until they rested against his shoulders and then, with a sudden shove, she was out of his arms and he lay sprawled on the grass.

She tried to stand, but his legs shot out and circled hers. His hands touched her sides. He was his old self again, teasing back the way he used to. Delightedly, she burst into laughter. Then, with a shout of pleasure, she rolled over, momentarily pinning him beneath her spread legs.

He grabbed her arms, and once more they were rolling together, tumbling over each other in hilarious abandon. She shrieked with surprise when they hit the water, but she didn't stop her tickling. It was François who, suddenly serious, rose and helped her to her feet.

Immediately, her mood changed. The water was cold. She was cold! "François! Now see what you've done! I'm all wet. What will I tell Bouchy?"

He laughed loudly. "You little vixen! You can't blame this on me!" Holding her about the waist, he guided her to the bank. Her soft cotton dress, green as the grass they had rolled on, was soaking wet. He had fared no better than she. His rust-colored wool breeches were dripping, his simple white shirt clung to his chest, outlining the strong muscles of his arms and shoulders. Even his hair was wet, sending a small stream of water over his nose, where it fell with a splash to the grass.

When they reached the bank, she held her arms up before his face. "Look at me! I'm freezing! I can't go home to Hermione looking like this! She's a regular Medusa. One angry look from her and I'll turn to stone!"

He was already pulling his shirt over his head. "Take off your dress. Quick! It'll dry in the sun in no time."

She hesitated for a moment. She had not taken her clothes off during play with François since she was a child of four and Hermione had caught them splashing each other in the stream, naked as two elves. Her nurse had been furious. Juliette could still remember the thrashing she had received, and she knew François had fared no better. "Oh, no. Hermione will be angry."

"At what? Your getting wet or your drying off? Don't be silly! It won't take any time at all for your clothes to dry in the sun."

Still, she hesitated. She was uncomfortable, of that

there was no doubt. But to take off her clothes in broad
daylight? She didn't even do that at night, when she
went to sleep!

Something changed in François' face. He was
watching her with a new intensity, as if it was terribly
important that she do as he asked. ''See?'' He dropped
to the grass and began to remove his boots. ''I'm
doing it, too.'' Rising, he slipped his breeches down
over his bare hips. Then, without glancing in her
direction, he hung them over a low branch.

Juliette stood as if mesmerized. She was a farm girl,
and she knew the difference between male and female.
But never in her life had she seen a grown man so intimately. She gasped. ''François! You're—'' She did
not finish. Instead, driven by an impulse she made no
attempt to understand, she stepped out of her wet
clothes, letting the warm sun kiss her naked body.
''Please, François. Hang these up, too.''

She was blushing, but she didn't retreat. He took
her dress and draped it over one of the main branches
of the willow, stepping aside as the wind puffed it out
like a balloon. He hung her chemise beside it. Then,
his eyes lowered, he turned toward her. She said nothing. She was aware that this was not at all like that first
time. They had been children then, frolicking in the
stream in innocent play.

Now, even her body did not feel the same. The
warm breeze touched her skin and brought a flush to
her cheeks. She was terribly aware of his eyes, yet she
made no attempt to hide. She stood proudly before
him, pleased that her young breasts were round and
full, that her nipples jutted out before her. She had
been slow to bloom, and for a time she had feared she
would never become a woman. But under the warmth

of his eyes, she knew she had worried needlessly.

He took a step forward. "Juliette!" It was more than her name. It was a prayer.

With a rush they were together, his arms encircling her body and drawing her close. She felt the strange hardness of his body against her soft stomach, and she knew she would not be content until she could hold him closer. Until—

"François—" He lifted his head and drew back, but she moved with him. "You're not a boy anymore, are you? I mean, you're a man, and—" She blushed. Why was it so difficult for her to speak?

"No, Juliette. I'm not a boy anymore, and you aren't a little girl." His voice sounded deeper than it had ever been. "What I mean is—Juliette, I want to marry you! I—"

Her laugh was like crystal, like the song of a soaring bird. "Silly! Of course! I've always known we would be married someday!" She slipped from his arms like a feather and floated around him, settling, at last, on the grass. "François, is this the way a—man—looks when he wants to—?" Again the strange difficulty, as if she didn't know all about the act of mating.

She reached out and touched him, a timid smile on her lips. "It's beautiful!" Suddenly she giggled. "I thought you would look like a stallion when you grew up! I didn't know you would be so smooth and strong!"

His laugh was hearty. "You little simpleton! Really?"

A frown creased her forehead. "Well, not altogether. But I didn't know it would look like this!"

Suddenly, his laughter was gone. "Juliette—" He sat down on the soft grass.

An unfamiliar shyness overcame her. He had not

said it, but she knew what he wanted. "Will it hurt? Your cousin Gladys said it would."

A startled laugh broke his serious mien. "Gladys? Did she say she had—?"

"Yes." Juliette was more confident now. "And she said it hurt."

He touched her stomach with his fingers, sending a shiver of pure sensation through her body. "If it hurts, will you stop loving me?"

She laughed impishly. "You didn't ask what she said next! I told her I'd never do it if it just hurt, and she said it was fun, later. So I guess I have to endure the hurt." Her smile vanished. "And I won't blame you. I'll still love you, anyway."

He touched his lips to hers, starting a trembling in her body that she could not control. Everything was different. Even his kiss was not the same as kisses they had shared when they were dressed.

Again he drew back. "Are you afraid?"

Still shaking, she gazed up into his face. "No." She struggled to quiet her agitation. "I don't know what's the matter. I can't stop trembling." Resolutely, she braced herself against his arms. "I'll be all right soon, I'm sure. Please, I want you to do it."

Gently, he pulled her backward onto the cushion of green. "It'll be fine. I know why you're trembling, and I know what to do. I've known for a long time. But I wanted to wait until you were ready."

Her lips quivered, but her eyes were steady. "I'm ready now, François. Tell me what I must do."

He moved then. Touching her knees, he spread her thighs until the dark curls were exposed to his view. His fingers found the center of her maidenhood and then, with a sigh, he rose and settled himself above her, his legs forcing hers farther apart.

She lay beneath him, tense with anticipation of pain, but none came. The warmth of his body stretching over hers brought relief from her trembling. She felt his breath against her cheek. Then his mouth touched hers and, with a suddenness that caught her unawares, he thrust forward. A cry escaped her lips, a cry that was picked up by a bird overhead and echoed again and again in the trees. Once more they lay quiet.

She looked into his face. "Is that all? Is that all there is to being a woman?" Even as she spoke, she knew there had to be more. She felt a warm moisture spread over her thighs.

"Did it hurt?"

"Not very much! I've had toothaches that were more painful!"

"Does it hurt now?"

"No. It feels good now." She shifted beneath him. "We'd better go. Hermione——"

She didn't finish her sentence. He moved slowly, holding her body loosely so she could respond without inhibition. Imperceptibly, she began to stir. Her body was suddenly hot, her temples pounding. She reached up and tried to grasp his hips so she could hold him still, but her fingers seemed detached from her body.

The movement of her hips increased, following the surge of passion that welled up within her. She forgot the pain, forgot that she was naked, forgot that moments before she had thought there was nothing more to be done. Forcefully, she pressed against him, meeting his thrusts with a desire she had not known she possessed. A pressure grew within her body that wiped all thoughts from her mind. Nothing mattered any more. Nothing but François.

A tingling sensation began in her feet, moving upward until she was lost in a sea of emotion. The trem-

bling was gone, replaced by surging waves that rose
and crested, each higher than the one that came before
it. She was filled with a fever, a fever that was born of
her growing passion.

Clutching his bare shoulders, she writhed and
moaned beneath him. Closer, deeper, she pressed
against him with all her strength.

The trembling began again, different now. It came
in great spasms that shook her limbs and tore at her
consciousness. Helplessly, she felt herself fall, as if a
great pit had opened below her. But she had no fear,
only an awareness that he was still near, that his arms
still held her, that his lips still were close to her own.

"François! Oh, François!"

She floated gently, once more growing aware of the
grass beneath her, of the call of the birds in the tree
above. The breeze ruffled her hair and she brushed a
lock away from her face. His body was heavy on hers,
yet she felt no desire to escape the weight.

He moved then, rolling onto the grass beside her.
The playful breeze tickled her damp stomach and
lapped up the moisture their closeness had left. She
pressed her forehead against his chest. "Oh, François,
Gladys didn't tell me it would be like this!"

His voice was thick. "I love you, Juliette. I meant
what I said before. I want to marry you, this fall, as
soon as I'm through with college."

Again, she smiled. "I want to marry you, too."
The girlishness was returning. Sitting up, she let her
hair cascade over his bare chest. "Let's get married
now! Right away! Do we have to wait?" Suddenly
embarrassed by her aggressiveness, she lowered her
eyes.

He raised himself up. "Yes, silly! Of course we do!
It won't be long, though. Only six more months." He

stood above her, staring down. "Juliette, we should be going. Come. We must wash your legs so Madam Bouchard doesn't know what we've been doing."

Juliette felt a glow of pride as the stream carried the red blood of her maidenhood away. She was a woman at last! Her party had been fun, but it had had little meaning. This was the ultimate proof of her maturity.

"Juliette! Juliette de Condillac! Hurry now! This time I mean it!" The shrill voice of Hermione brought Juliette to her feet. "Answer me, girl, or I'll come and get you!"

Juliette stepped from the stream, stripping the water from her skin. "I hear you, Bouchy! I'll be there in a minute!" She burst into irrepressible laughter. "Wouldn't she be mad if she came and caught us like this!"

François was already tucking his shirt into his breeches. He seemed suddenly nervous. "She won't come, will she?"

"Of course not! She never has, has she? She's too fat to climb the hills!"

He began to laugh. "She can yell, can't she? Maybe she should have been in charge of the pigs instead of you! Just think how she could call them!"

Juliette slipped into her chemise. It was new—Bouchy's gift to show her she was no longer a child. She had been so proud of it when she first put it on. Now it had lost its importance.

Her dress was dry, except for a dampness about the hem. Thankfully, she pulled it over her head. How fortunate that she had put on this particular garment with its loose weave. It was her runabout dress, made specifically for a child who tumbled about in the grass, and always had a wrinkled appearance. As she pulled it down about her shoulders, she looked up into François' face. The thought of the portly Madam Bouchard calling hogs was too funny! A small titter burst through her closely pressed lips, and then she convulsed with laughter. "Oh, François! What a thought! She could yell louder than any pig in the sty!"

Once more the sharp voice cut through the peace of the meadow, drowning out the murmur of the stream. "Juliette! Are you coming?"

The last buttons were closed. Standing on her toes, Juliette planted a kiss on François' lips. "Tomorrow?"

He flushed. "No. I'm afraid not. Remember? I have to leave for school in the morning." She frowned. "But I'll be back soon," he said.

"Juliette! Your papa's waiting!"

Impulsively, Juliette unlatched a tiny locket that hung around her neck. "Here." She dropped it into François' hand. "This will make you remember me!"

He cupped the tiny heart and fine chain. "Won't your father wonder what happened to it?"

"I'll tell him I lost it. He thinks I'm careless, anyway!" She turned and started up the hill.

"Wait!" He slipped a heavy ring from his finger. Opening the chain, he removed the heart and replaced it with the ring. "Here. Wear this. I want you to have it while I'm gone."

She giggled gleefully. "It's so heavy!"

Once more his face was serious. "It's important. Don't lose the ring, and don't show it to—people like your father—and Bouchard. They won't understand. It could save your life, maybe."

She laughed excitedly. "Oh, François! A real mystery! Does it have magical powers?"

His smile was that of an indulgent adult toward a much-loved child. "No, not at all. But—well, just be careful who sees it."

"Juliette! I'm coming to find you!" Madam Bouchard's voice boomed.

Juliette threw herself into François' arms. Then, before she could let herself think of the months of loneliness that lay ahead, she turned and ran up the hill. At the top she paused. "Good-bye! I'll be waiting for you!"

Her last view of François was one she would not soon forget. He was looking up, balancing on one foot, his other struggling to fit into a boot that seemed somehow unwilling to obey his command. Then, with a shout of surprise, he fell onto the grass and rolled on his back.

She laughed all the way back to the house.

CHAPTER TWO

"Just look at you, Juliette! When will you grow up? Your dress is all covered with grass!" Hermione shook her head, a look of mock despair on her round face.

Juliette tossed her head impudently. "Oh, Bouchy! Stop treating me like a baby! You told me yourself I was a young lady now, but you forget it more than anyone else!"

"You'll be a young lady when you learn to act like one! And I'll treat you exactly the way you deserve to be treated." As usual, Bouchard's smile belied her angry tone. "Were you playing in the meadow again?"

Juliette felt a warmth creep into her cheeks. Quickly, she turned toward the rolling hills. She didn't want Bouchard to begin to wonder about things that were none of her business. "Of course. François and I were wrestling."

Hermione rested her hands on her ample hips. "Child, you must realize you're getting too old for that kind of nonsense!" She stared off in the direction of the du Quesnay estate. "If you aren't, François certainly is! He's a grown man, not a child. You shouldn't be teasing him that way anymore."

Juliette brushed past her nurse. This was a subject she'd just as soon abandon. "Bouchy, I saw one of the rioters this morning."

19

Immediately, Bouchard's blustering ceased. Suddenly pale, she stared intently at Juliette's smiling face. "You should have come and told your papa right away! You know that he doesn't want them on his property!"

"He wasn't doing anything bad, Bouchy! He was just walking across the meadow, looking at the horses." Juliette felt strangely mature, but she dared not let her nurse notice a change in her behavior. Following her habit, she spun like a top, her arms extended, careening to an unsteady halt at Bouchard's side. When the sky stopped whirling, she felt a strange relief. After she and François were married, she could stop pretending to be a child! "I think they're stupid! Imagine peasants thinking they can farm by themselves! Papa's told me they want him to divide the land into little pieces and give it to them."

Bouchard's lips grew tight. "Poor creatures! They're hungry, and they don't seem to have the sense to know they can't eat if they don't work! It was better in the old days, when everyone knew his place and peasants didn't dream of becoming squires." She patted Juliette on the back. "Serfs are serfs, whether they call themselves slaves or freemen! They're free, all right. Free to starve!" Her voice was disparaging. "They were better off before."

Juliette leaned back against the railing that separated the barnyard from the lawn and garden. "What I don't understand, Bouchy, is why they hate the meadow so much! The horses have to eat, and so do the cows! If we gave them all the pastureland to make into their little farms, they still wouldn't have enough, would they? And then where would the horses pasture?"

"Don't try to understand them, Juliette! They're irrational, that's all.'' Bouchard began to walk slowly toward the house. ''It's sad, though. If it weren't for those terrible *philosophes*—if educated men would pay attention to their studies and leave politics alone, the poor would still be content. It's the colleges that do it. How often have you heard the good Father tell us that the Lord Himself decreed that we would always have the poor with us. It's God's way to keep the wealthy humble.'' She shook her head. ''Nothing good ever comes from questioning the will of the Lord.''

Juliette skipped lightly ahead of her nurse. ''Bouchy, why do boys have to go to school? If it's so bad and makes people do foolish things, why send them at all?''

Bouchard smiled indulgently. ''You do ask questions!'' Juliette stopped directly before her, halting her progress toward the house. ''Oh, we've gone through it all before. You know as well as anyone!''

''Tell me, anyway. Please, Bouchy!''

''I don't know why you like to hear it. There are a lot more things a man has to know, that's all! He has to be able to manage his estate. He has to learn to deal with his underlings—and his superiors.'' Her face was still, her voice monotonous. ''He must be able to understand business these days, though God only knows why. I'm sure it's better left to the bourgeoisie!''

Pestering Bouchy with questions had always been one of Juliette's favorite routines. Fearing that a sudden abandonment of it would arouse Bouchard's suspicions, she decided to keep it up. Besides, Bouchy always got so annoyed when she spoke of modern problems and modern education! ''Now tell me what a woman has to know.''

''Oh, Juliette! You're such a bother!'' Bouchard

smiled indulgently. Once more she recited, as if by rote: "A woman has a far better life. She must learn the arts, be able to dance, sing, paint, even embroider a bit. Some, who are especially talented, even learn to play the harpsichord." She smiled with a sudden show of warmth. "You, young lady, are doing very well for yourself! If only you'd stop running about like a tomboy!"

"Oh, Bouchy, I'll stop—someday." She wanted to tell what had happened, but she felt certain Bouchard wouldn't approve. With a teasing glance at her nurse, she broke spontaneously into a minuet. Through her half-closed eyes, the green carpet of grass became the smooth floor of the ballroom of the palace at Versailles. "When I get married, Bouchy, I'll live at court. And I'll be the most popular lady there. Maybe the king will dance with me more than he does with his Austrian princess."

Bouchard smacked her lips. "Juliette! You mustn't talk like that about Queen Marie Antoinette! It's disrespectful!" She increased her pace across the lawn. "Hurry now, child. I have instructions to get you cleaned and dressed right away. Your papa has a surprise for you."

Despite her newfound maturity, Juliette felt a thrill of delight. "A surprise? What is it, Bouchy? Please tell me! What is it?"

A smile softened the usually severe features. "Oh, child, don't be so impatient. You'll find out soon enough." Her voice lowered conspiratorially. "I can tell you that I've been instructed to make you look your most grown-up—like a real lady."

A glow of pleasure suffused Juliette's mind. "You mean I can wear my party dress again? And all my slips? Oh, Bouchy! You have to tell me why! You just have to!"

"It isn't my place to tell you what your father has planned. I have my duties. Each of us has his God-given place in life. And yours is to do as you're told, like a good girl." Hermione hurried up the walk, swaying from side to side with each step.

Juliette turned away, her attention deceptively directed toward the distant hills. It wouldn't do for her to be too obedient, no matter how much Bouchy fussed, especially when the crabby old thing had referred to her as a child.

Hermione had disappeared into the house. Juliette turned and followed, her curiosity overcoming the desire to show her independence.

As she stepped into her room, Juliette was aware of a new sensation. The room was the same—but she was different. The love she had shared with François had, indeed, given her a new sense of identity. The room was that of a young girl—a child. But the child would never return to it again. "I'm a woman now," she whispered as she patted the blanket on her feather bed. "I'm a woman, and I'm in love."

She paused, leaning over the bed to gaze directly into the portrait of her mother. Had her mother and father loved each other the way she and François did? With a sudden realization of lost innocence, she leaned closer to the smiling face. Of course they had! She had never thought of that part of her parents' lives before. Now, at last, the door was opened. She knew that, as severe and unemotional as her father seemed now, he and her mother had at one time shared the same kind of closeness François and she had tasted in the meadow.

Pensively, Juliette settled on the bed. She loved to visit with this one proof of her mother's reality. Often, before she fell asleep, she would stare up into the kindly eyes and recount her day's pleasures. Though she had never said anything to Bouchard, she had always felt a love and understanding when she spoke to the portrait that she could not seem to establish with her crusty nurse. She smiled secretly. "I know, Mother. I know now. And, oh, I love him so much!"

"Juliette, stop daydreaming! It's time to move! Come, I have your bath ready."

Juliette leaped up, her skirt billowing about her legs. "Bouchy, you have to tell me what Papa is going to give me or I won't get into the tub. After all, I'm sixteen! I'm not a child anymore. And you're not my nurse anymore, either. You're just my companion."

Madam Bouchard sighed. "Please, Juliette, don't try to force me. I've been told by your father under no circumstances to tell you his plan." A shadow seemed to float over her face, replaced, immediately, by a forced smile. "But I can assure you he has your good at heart! How could it be otherwise? You're his only child. When you were born, his dear wife, your *maman,* went to heaven!" She crossed herself piously.

Juliette, mindful of the seriousness of her nurse's words, also made the sign of the cross over her chest. Then, with a loud sigh, she stamped her way toward the dressing room. Bouchard followed close behind.

At the door, Juliette stopped. "I can get in by myself! Bouchy, I'm a lady now, remember? If I have to take a bath, I'll do it by myself." She lifted her chin haughtily. "I'll call you when I'm ready to have my back scrubbed."

When she was certain that Bouchard had left the room, Juliette stepped out of her clothes, examining each piece before she dropped it to the floor. There was no blood on her chemise. She sighed with relief. Her monthly bleeding was still somewhat irregular, but Bouchy would not have been fooled. She had washed out the last rags only a week ago.

Her concern over chemise and dress satisfied, Juliette gazed at her body. A large mirror covered one wall of the room. Standing close to it, she turned slowly about, searching for telltale stains. She was safe. Her legs were as clean as her chemise. Relieved, she stepped gingerly into the hot water. "Bouchy!" Her voice echoed in the empty room.

Madam Bouchard appeared in the doorway. "Ready so soon? You can't have scrubbed yourself properly, then!" She paused when she saw that Juliette stood knee deep in the water, gazing at herself in the mirror.

"Bouchy, I'm beautiful, aren't I? Am I beautiful enough to be a lady at the court of Versailles?"

Hermione blushed, her eyes lowered, but not before Juliette had caught a look of admiration in their shadowed depths. "Juliette! What a thing to say! You show none of the modesty I taught you! Where's your sense of decency?"

Juliette laughed and abruptly sat down, her hand "accidentally" hitting the edge, sending a spray into the face of her critic. Then, as if she had no thought of anything but proper obedience, she meekly submitted to the scrubbing.

"You didn't answer me, Bouchy. Am I?"

"Are you what?"

"Beautiful."

Bouchard's jaw tightened. "You're too young to be beautiful. Your *maman* was beautiful, God rest her soul! You are pretty. If you ever learn to control your-

self, you may, eventually, become a true beauty."
Juliette cried out as Hermione grabbed her hair and
began to scrub a spot of grass from the back of her
neck.

Suddenly the rubbing stopped. "Juliette! What is
this?" Hermione was pointing at the ring that hung between the firm young breasts. "Where is the heart
your father gave you?"

Juliette blushed. "I—" She looked up into Hermione's flushed face. There was no way out. She
might as well tell the truth. "I gave it to François. And
he gave me this in return."

Hermione was silent for a moment. Juliette stared
up at her belligerently. If she began to scold— Well,
she'd just better not!

When the scrubbing was resumed, Juliette felt
strangely disappointed. She had almost been looking
forward to a fight with her motherly nurse. It wasn't
like Bouchy to miss an opportunity to scold. Something was not the same, and Juliette felt a tremor of
concern.

Hermione sponged the soap away from Juliette's
shoulders. "We haven't time for arguments now.
Your papa's waiting."

Convinced at last that she would get no information
from her nurse, Juliette became amazingly docile.
When she was instructed to step out, she did so with
only a mild splattering of water on the floor. And
when Bouchard rubbed her with a towel until her skin
felt warm, she did not complain. She stood quietly,
staring at herself in the mirror as the old woman scurried to a cabinet and drew out a clean chemise.

While Juliette pulled on the soft, delicate garment,
Bouchard rushed back into the bedroom. With one
final glance at her image, Juliette followed. Again she

stood patiently as, one by one, Bouchard pulled crisp new slips over her head. Clearly, this was to be a very special occasion.

At last Bouchard left her charge and headed toward the wardrobe, from which she drew Juliette's newest dress, a lovely, light-green garment, made of the best Irish linen and trimmed in lace she herself had knitted. Juliette gasped with delight. "Oh, Bouchy! I thought you were only fooling when you said I was to put on my party dress! What *is* it Papa has for me? Is it another present?" She twisted around so as to look into Hermione's round eyes. "Please tell me! Please!"

Bouchard shook her head. Smoothing the dress over the full slips, she began to button it up the back. "You'll find out soon enough. You know you can't expect me to disobey your papa. Now," she smiled into the frowning young face, "sit down and let me comb your hair. We've taken too much time already."

Despite Hermione's complaint, not much more than a half hour had passed from the time of Juliette's arrival in her room to the moment when she was ready to leave for her father's study. As she opened the door, Hermione touched her arm. "Now, remember, Juliette. You're a young lady! Walk like one!"

Juliette nodded obediently. She had heard that warning before and heeded it only when necessity demanded. How, she wondered, could a girl, even a girl who was a young lady, be sedate at a time like this?

In the distance, she could hear the voices of two men, though the words they spoke were as yet indistinguishable. She wondered what was so special about this particular guest. Why was she decked out in her finest garments and sent to join her father while he had company? Usually, when someone visited, her father was glad to have her away somewhere. He was one who believed that young girls should not be privy to man's business.

Juliette glanced back at the door to her suite. Bouchard had closed it when she returned to dispose of the bathwater. With a smile of delight, Juliette broke into a pirouette. Once more she was the newest member of the court, walking—no, dancing—past a row of admirers. Ahead, his gaze riveted on her glowing face, was Louis himself. She paused, grasped her skirt in her hands, and bent low in a deep curtsy. Then, rising, she covered all but her sparkling eyes with a make-believe fan.

"Ah, Your Majesty, you're too kind! I'm but a country lass, unaccustomed to the ways of the court!" Her dark eyes flashed as she looked into the invisible face of her fantasy monarch. She laughed lightly. "Oh, Your Majesty! Her Royal Highness-Princess will hear you!"

A door opened. Behind her, Madam Bouchard cleared her throat. Immediately, Juliette resumed her normal pace, increasing it slightly when she heard an impatient tapping on the wall. "Juliette, your father is not accustomed to waiting!"

Juliette began to run. When she reached the library door, she glanced back to see if Bouchard was still watching. She was. With a stamp of her slippered foot, Juliette drew herself up, her head high. Then, without another backward glance, she rapped lightly on the heavy oak panel.

"Come in! Come in!" The voice was muffled, but she recognized the annoyance in her father's tone. Bracing herself against the weight, she pulled the door open and stepped inside, pausing only to recover the poise she had lost in the effort. So she was to receive a scolding!

"Ah, Juliette! Come in, my dear. Hurry! I want to present you to a very important gentleman."

Juliette looked into her father's face. Something was wrong. Never before had he passed up an opportunity to correct her for improper behavior. When she was late, as she was today, he made certain she knew it. Why was he smiling now?

Suddenly frightened, she moved slowly across the room. Even his smile was wrong! Always, if he was pleased with her, his smile showed it. If he was angry, he didn't conceal his irritation. It was not his nature to dissemble in his dealings with her. What had happened to change him now? Why a smile, when she could sense he was overcome with sorrow—and anger?

Unsure as to what she should expect, yet forewarned to expect the worst, she positioned herself close to her father's side. When she felt his hand touch hers, she started. Then, with increasing apprehension, she held fast to his strong fingers.

She could not keep her eyes from the stranger whose presence accounted for her having been called from play. He was sitting cross-legged on her father's favorite chair, one arm hanging loosely by his side. His other elbow rested close to his body, his hand extended, palm up.

Juliette felt a pang of jealousy. That was the chair she shared with her papa on those rare occasions when he permitted her to enter his study and touch the mementos of her mother's brief life. That man had no right to sit there! None at all!

Still, he showed no discomfort. He looked at her

with an intensity that made her nervous. As if he were evaluating her. With a feeling of awkwardness, she met his gaze. She had not seen a man like him before. He was tall, with a slender body that looked almost feminine. His hair was blond, gathered at the back in a long curl, as was the fashion, with a large bow at the nape of his neck.

His features drooped, as if he were unwilling to exert the energy needed for a smile, or even to open his eyes fully. His mouth was broad, with thin lips that seemed to vanish at the corners. His nose was long, with flared nostrils, its rosy hue overshadowing his sallow cheeks.

He was dressed in blue brocade, in breeches that left nothing to the imagination, and a jacket that gave him the appearance of a peacock in full spread. He wore slippers, not boots, and his stockings were a creamy white that had never seen dirt. In his outstretched hand he held a long cigar, its tip glowing brightly. Above the glow, a thin line of smoke snaked its way to the ceiling.

Juliette looked down, unwilling to risk eye-to-eye contact. So that was a dandy! Why, they were funny! She had heard Bouchard use other words to describe court gentlemen. *Dissipated* was one. *Fop* was another. The thought made her feel better. Wouldn't she have fun telling François about this meeting! She smiled.

"Your daughter is beautiful when she smiles! She will be an asset to me in the court."

The court? Juliette had the strange feeling that the words had been said to excite her, but she felt only a growing uneasiness. Why did this stranger speak of her in such a manner? Confused, she turned to her father. "Papa?"

He didn't meet her glance. Instead, he looked down at her hand, which he still held tightly. His voice, when he spoke, was forced.

"My dear, this is Roger duDeffand. The *Baron* duDeffand. He has bestowed a great honor upon you—upon us. He has asked for your hand in marriage."

Her face froze. Marriage! How could her father even consider such an offer when he knew how she felt about François? With a rising panic, she searched his lowered face for some sign that this was all a joke, that he and his guest were teasing her.

"Come here, my child, and kiss your bridegroom."

She shuddered. The voice, like the face, was foppish. She was to kiss him? Never! Instinctively, her grip on her father's hand tightened. "No." Her voice was little more than a whisper, but it sounded through the room like a shout. Her father's head snapped up, and she found herself staring into his troubled eyes.

"My dear, you must not disobey. It's settled. You are to marry him within the year."

Her first reaction was to his words. How could he command her to approach—to kiss—a man such as this? Then, welling up in his darkened eyes, she saw tears.

She felt a momentary shock. Tears? Her father? He was her strength, the pillar to whom she turned for comfort and support! Never, except when he spoke of her mother, had she seen him look so sad. She felt trapped by his distress. Hateful though it was, she had to obey. More than just a kiss lay in the balance.

She turned and stared into the face of Baron duDeffand. He looked at her soberly, a slight frown marring his smooth brow. Still, his eyes held no antagonism. Clearly, he was not the type who would permit a child's thoughtless remark to upset him unduly.

Slowly, she pulled her hand from her father's grasp. As she moved forward, her fists clenched in determination. Her jaw was tight, her lips pressed together. Her solemn eyes showed no sign of the youthful glee that usually bubbled irrepressibly, even when she tried to be sober. They were opened wide now, and she was watching duDeffand's face with unconcealed revulsion.

Like a child taking her first steps, she began to move across the space that separated her from her suitor. She paused once, looking back at her father, her eyes pleading for release from this horror. But he refused to meet her glance.

By the time she reached him, Roger duDeffand was on his feet, his arms extended. She felt the smooth silk of his jacket brush her arm. Then she was held lightly against his body. Her skirt pressed the front of her legs, and she felt a sudden thankfulness for the many petticoats Hermione had tied around her waist. They kept him away. She didn't have to feel the hard pressure of the bulge that spoiled the smoothness of his breeches.

She closed her eyes when he brought his face close to hers. It would be over soon, and she could scrub the taint away. But he was in no hurry to let her go. His first kiss was on her cheek, and when he pulled away, she breathed a sigh of relief. Then, to her horror, he reached up and clasped her head in his hands, turning her face directly toward his own.

His second kiss was deliberately placed. She felt his broad mouth engulf hers, felt his tongue press against her closed lips. Tightening her jaw, she resisted his efforts, but he persisted until, suddenly, her lips gave way. His tongue probed her mouth, forcing itself into her with a demand she could not fail to recognize.

She began to tremble. He wanted what she could give only to François! The thought cast a shadow on her memory of the glorious afternoon she had shared with her lover. Never! Never would she let duDeffand penetrate her! Never would she give herself to him! She belonged, now and always, to François!

She could not pull free from his hold. She remained helpless in his hands, held against his chest, pressed so tightly she could hardly breathe. She couldn't even pull her face away from his, for he held her too tightly. Angrily, she held her breath. Maybe, if she held it long enough, she would faint, and then he would have to let her go.

Before she lost consciousness, he released his hold. Stepping back, he took her right hand into his own and brought it to his lips. Then, his eyes fastened on her face, he held her at arm's length. "You're right, Jean. She's everything you said she was. However," a small line appeared between his eyes, "she does seem a bit frail. She is in good health, isn't she?"

From somewhere her father found a voice, but Juliette did not recognize it as his own. "Yes. She has even survived the pox without scarring. She's in excellent health and will remain so, God willing."

Her father's words reminded Juliette of that terrible winter when her older sister, always the lady, had contracted the pox and, despite constant care provided by Hermione, had passed quietly into heaven. Juliette had been mildly sick that year herself, but she hadn't shown any signs of the terrible malady that robbed old and young of life. At the time, small as she had been, Juliette had felt guilty because she had lived and her sister had died. Now she had an even stronger reason to regret her survival.

Abruptly, as if he had tired of her closeness, Roger

duDeffand dropped his arms and began to pace the room. "You can have her ready? She has much to learn if she is to bring me honor in the court."

Her father spoke quickly. "We can have her ready. Don't upset yourself. She's very quick to learn." Silently, Juliette vowed she would become the poorest student any teacher had ever encountered. "We'll have everything prepared for the wedding, as well. I would be most pleased to have my daughter married here, where her mother bore her."

DuDeffand's mouth twisted in a grimace, but he did not speak. Gently, almost apologetically, Jean de Condillac took his daughter's hand once more into his own. "Juliette, you may go now. I'll speak to you later. Go back to Madam Bouchard."

She turned at his touch, searching his face one last time for an explanation of his perfidy. He knew of her love for François! He knew that, despite her talk of court life, she loved the farm and wanted nothing more than to spend the rest of her life near her father and her family home, as the wife of François du Quesnay.

He refused to meet her searching eyes. When it was clear he would say no more, she turned and fled from the room. She couldn't wipe the vision of her father's face from her mind. He'd betrayed her. He knew it. He'd betrayed her, and he didn't dare look her in the eyes.

She didn't stop running until she was back in her room, wrapped in the comforting arms of Madam Bouchard. Gently, the kindly woman led her to a chaise and sat beside her. "Come, my little darling, come now! You must stop crying! Surely things aren't as bad as all that!"

Juliette raised her head, her eyes red, tears stream-

ing down her cheeks. "D—do you know wh—
what—?" She couldn't continue.

Bouchard nodded her head. "Yes, my love, I
know. But you must think of it from your papa's point
of view. He loves you too much to have you left penni-
less, the mistress of a vanishing estate."

A frown creased Juliette's brow. Her voice was
thick with tears. "What do you mean, vanishing?
Papa has the best farm in the province!"

Hermione's smile was gentle. "My dear, how long
has it been since you rode with him to the far ends of
the estate?" Juliette looked up. "You've been busy
with the animals and your lessons—and with François.
You've been surrounded by old, familiar people and
things. You've been too occupied to notice that things
aren't as they used to be."

"But— But, I can see for miles from the top of the
hill!"

"How often have you seen the peasants at work?
You know about the rioters. How many of them do
you think there are?"

Juliette thought for a moment. "There can't be
many. Most of the de Condillac people are too
smart!"

"You're wrong, little one. The only loyal people
we have live within sight of the house. The stableboys
are all members of one family. The others are filling
their minds with fighting and rebellion."

"But if they don't work, they'll starve!"

"And so will you, my darling! And *that* is why your
father has consented to your marriage to duDeffand!
That, and——"

"And?"

"Nothing! Nothing at all!"

The tears were forgotten. Juliette sat up, her attention focused on the flushed face of Bouchard.

"Bouchy! You can't lie to me! Besides, it's a sin to lie. You must tell me what it was you were going to say."

"Nothing! I tell you, it was nothing."

With a leap, Juliette was across the room. Her hands pulled the crucifix from where it hung over her bed. She held it close to Bouchard's face. "Swear before the crucifix of Christ that there's nothing else! Swear it!"

Bouchard lowered her head. "Please, Juliette, don't!"

"Bouchy, swear! If you can't, then tell me. I have a right to know, don't I?"

"Your father will lose the land unless he can get some money—" she hurried on before Juliette could interrupt, "—but I'm sure that isn't the reason for his accept——"

"Why will he lose the land?"

"I know little about finances. I only know that money, like food, has become scarce. These are troubled times. Nothing is safe. I heard your father speak of a wish to hire soldiers to protect his manor from the rioters, and of his lack of money with which to pay them. He and Seigneur du Quesnay face the same problem."

"Oh, no! François' papa has lots of money!"

"And yours does, too?"

Juliette stopped, her hands at her sides, the crucifix hanging close to the floor.

"Put the holy crucifix away, my dear. You don't want to desecrate it by letting it fall!"

Slowly, Juliette walked back to her bed. Kneeling over it, she returned the crucifix to its place. Then, turning, she stared across the room. "But I can't marry that—creature! I just can't! Oh, Bouchy, what am I to do?"

There was a tap on the door. Bouchard rose. "You'll wait until I see who's knocking, that's what you'll do. And then— Well, then you'll obey your father, like the good girl you are."

Bouchard reached the door and pushed it open. Immediately, Jean de Condillac stepped inside. He appeared crushed, as if he hated to face what lay ahead. But he walked directly to his daughter, his hands extended. "Juliette, my darling child! I can't explain more than to say that were there any other way out of our dilemma, I would take it!"

He smiled tremulously. "You're a proud girl, and a strong one. You'll make a place of honor for yourself at the court, I'm sure you will. As Madam duDeffand, you'll receive the noble and cultured in your salon. You'll learn to love your life at court as much as you now love the country! Believe me, my dear, I know."

"But, Papa—"

He spoke compulsively, paying no attention to her interruption. "You'll not immediately head for the court, however. The baron has duties that take him far away. He'll return within the year to claim his bride. In the meantime, he's provided for your education in the ways of the court. You'll leave within the week for the Abbey Villeurbanne. Your Uncle Henry is the abbé there, and duDeffand has a suite reserved for you at the guest cottage. You'll be taught all you need to know to fit into court life. My dear, you actually are a very fortunate child. You'll realize your dream of living in Versailles." He tried to smile as he spoke, but he could not force his face to show a cheer he didn't feel.

"But, Papa, I can't marry that man! I just can't! I—You know I've always wanted to marry François!"

He shook his head. "A child's dream, my dear. You would live your life in poverty, no better than a peasant." He looked wearily into Bouchard's mournful face. "I suppose I was wrong to hide the truth from the child. But I wanted her to have a happy childhood, free from the worries that lay ahead. Yet, if by giving her a few carefree days I have destroyed her ability to accept the world as it is, I have done her no service."

Bouchard forced a smile. "Don't worry, seigneur, our Juliette is a de Condillac through and through! She has all the spunk you would want in a woman, even though she's still young. Just give her a little time. She'll come around to realizing everything has happened for the best."

"I hope so." He took Juliette's chin in his hand and turned her face up toward his. "Do you understand, my dear? It *is* for the best. I didn't arrange your betrothal for the benefit of the estate, though duDeffand. has promised to use his influence to assign soldiers to this area. I thought only of you. I know how you have dreamed of the court, how you have pretended you were speaking with the king. This seemed the best way to help you realize your goal."

She looked into his eyes, trying to think of the words that would tell him how unhappy she was. But, before she could speak, he turned and left the room. Throwing her hands in the air, she turned to Bouchard. "Bouchy, what shall I do? I love François!"

Bouchard put an arm about the girl's shoulders and pulled her back to the chaise. "My sweet, it's time you learned the ways of the world. If you go to live in Versailles, you'll have to live as others do. You can take François as a lover! It's the sophisticated way! If you marry duDeffand, you'll have both wealth and love. If you refuse and insist upon marrying François, you'll have only poverty."

Juliette stared at her nurse, her mind in a turmoil. "Did Mother have a lover?"

"Of course not! How can you speak so of the dead?" Her face red with embarrassment, Bouchard quickly crossed herself.

"Then how can you speak of *me* in that manner? How can you say that such a life will be good for me when you consider it a shame to even speak of it in the same breath with my mother's name?"

Madam Bouchard lowered her head. "I speak only of what *is*. Everyone knows the morals at the court are not those of the countryside. It's the way life is. Who am I to criticize the king?"

"Bouchy! You're—" Juliette leaped to her feet. "Oh, Bouchy, isn't there anyone I can trust?" She pulled away when Bouchard tried to comfort her. Turning, she threw herself onto her bed, her body racked with sobs.

For a time, Madam Bouchard hovered over the bed, muttering words of comfort that fell on deaf ears. At last, when she realized Juliette wouldn't permit herself to be placated, she moved quietly to the windows. One by one, she drew the drapes. When the room was dark, she slipped silently into the hallway. At the door, she paused and looked back. Juliette's sobs had subsided. Her shoulders were still. Her head buried in her arms, she was breathing steadily.

"That's good." Bouchard's voice was gentle. "Rest, little angel. You'll feel better about everything in the morning."

CHAPTER THREE

Juliette awoke with a start. For a moment she lay still, trying to remember what had happened. Why was she sleeping in her best gown? Why was she not tucked properly under the covers? Then the events of the night returned, bringing with them the weight of her new commitment.

She sat up. What time was it? She had planned to be at the gate early, so she could wave to François as he went by. Now, she was certain, it was too late.

She started to call Bouchard, and then, suddenly reserved, held her tongue. Right now she didn't wish to talk to anyone. Except, maybe, her mother.

Kneeling, she gazed up into the portrait. "Mama, what shall I do?" The gentle eyes did not change. The lips smiled back at her troubled face.

"You can't help me, can you?" Juliette's voice was bitter. "No one can help me! Not even God!"

Shocked at her own audacity, she reached for her rosary. It wouldn't hurt to pray, especially after such heresy. Maybe, this time, she would receive an answer.

She rose quickly to her feet when she heard a sound at the door separating her room from Bouchard's. "Open the drapes, Bouchy, I'm up." She slipped to the floor.

Bouchard looked at her without speaking. Then, as if aware there was nothing they could say that would

change things, she opened the drapes and set about
unbuttoning Juliette's party dress, which now was
badly in need of the iron. She didn't fuss, as she nor-
mally would have, nor did she question Juliette's demand for one of her old runabout dresses.

When the slips were hanging up and the green gown
spread carefully over the bed, she turned to her mistress. ''Breakfast is waiting.''

''I don't want it now!'' Juliette felt a small satisfaction when Bouchard's face fell. ''I'll eat it later!''
Without looking back, she strode from the room. It
felt good to be back in her playclothes. Suddenly, she
didn't want to be a lady. She took the steps two at a
time, landing with a jump on the path.

''I don't ever want to wear that dress again! Ever!''
She ran to the fence. Climbing on the railing, she balanced expertly as she removed her shoes. They fell
unheeded onto the grass. Then, smiling, she lowered
herself into the mud of the pigsty. It oozed up between
her toes and spread over the tops of her feet.

She half slid, half walked across the barnyard, playfully slapping the back of one of the pigs that got in
her way. Then she was over the fence and into the
meadow. As her feet touched the grass, she began to
run. There was only one place where she would be
safe, only one place where the unpleasantness of last
night could be forgotten.

When she reached the grassy knoll where she had
rolled playfully with François, she stopped. Was it at
this spot where they had made love? No. She moved a
bit to her right. She was sure it had started right here,
where the willow tree shaded the grass in the late
afternoon.

Satisfied that she had found the right place, she
dropped to the ground and lay back, her knees bent.

Closing her eyes, she pressed her heels into the dirt, lifting her hips up and rolling them gently. The motion brought back the memory. A warmth engulfed her body.

Then, suddenly, she lay quiet. "Oh, François! What will I do?"

She turned onto her stomach and lay staring into the stream. François! Of course! She had felt alone the night before, but she wasn't alone at all! She had François! He'd never let her be forced into a marriage with duDeffant!

But where was François? Never, in the years since he had started school, had she bothered to find out where he went. Now, suddenly, it was important. Tears welled in her eyes. "François! How will I ever find you?"

The breeze rose, whispering through the tall tree. The long branches bobbed gently, stroking her shoulder. She sat up and looked about her. A cow wandering along the ridge of the hill paused and gazed down toward the stream, its jaws working steadily. With a shout, Juliette was on her feet. Leaping across the stream, she raced up the hill, yelling and clapping loudly. Frightened, the beast lumbered off, its full teats bouncing as it ran.

Juliette watched until the cow rejoined the herd where the stream ran level with the meadow. She wanted no interlopers in her private hideaway. It belonged to her—and to François.

"Mademoiselle Juliette!" The voice was timid but quite clearly masculine. Juliette spun around, her face lit with a smile. Maybe François had not gone after all! Maybe he was back, playing one of his usual games.

The lad who stood before her bobbed slightly as she turned. Michel had been François' personal servant since he reached the age of 14, and he showed the same pride in his position he had evidenced when first he took the assignment. His clothes were of coarser material than those of a gentleman, but they were neat, and scrupulously clean. His face was pleasant, though lacking in brilliance. His features were even and entirely unremarkable. A hint of the boy that still hid within him shone through his sparkling eyes. "Miss—pardon me, miss. I have a note for you from François. He told me I'd probably find you here."

The excitement of the chase was over. A lady once more, Juliette held out her hand. "Give it to me."

Michel extended the note, but he didn't leave when she took it from his hand. "He left early this morning, with his father. Just before he climbed into the carriage, he gave me this message. He said it was very important."

Juliette looked at him sharply. Had he read it? Was he, like so many other menials, assuming rights he didn't deserve? "Well?" Her voice was cold.

The lad stood silent for a moment, a faint smile touching the corner of his mouth. "I—you run very"—he hesitated again—"fast, mademoiselle."

She didn't allow herself to respond to his familiarity. Slowly, his eyes dropped. Once more his head bobbed. "Will that be all, miss?"

"Yes. You may go."

He turned and ran up the hill. Juliette felt a wave of annoyance. It didn't please her that a servant had seen her in a playful mood—especially now, when she had so little to be happy about. When he was out of sight she tore open the letter.

My dearest Juliette,
I couldn't leave without telling you how much yes-
terday meant to me, and how it pains me to leave you

*again. Hopefully, this will be the last time I will go. I
expect to get my degree very soon, for I have com-
pleted all of my qualifications. Wait for me, my love.
Next time we meet, I'll speak to your father.*

> *All my love,*
> *François*

A tear fell from her cheek onto the ink, making a
purple streak across the page. Carefully, she blotted it
with her dress. She read the letter once more. He said
nothing about where he had gone. She stamped her
foot impatiently. Places hadn't mattered to her before.
Now this one was of the utmost importance.

Pensively, she climbed the hill. She was feeling
hungry now. Hungry—and curious. Hermione could
answer the question that burned in her thoughts. She
began to run, the letter clutched tightly in her hand.
Just before she reached the gate to the garden, she
folded the paper and shoved it under the bodice of her
dress.

Bouchard greeted her at the door to her room.
"Juliette! I'm glad you're feeling better. Come in, my
dear, you must eat."

Juliette slowed her pace. "Well," her voice was deliberately free of emotion, "only if you don't try to
feed me cold eggs."

Bouchard smiled. "Of course not! I gave them to
the stableboy." Gently, she rested her hand on the delicate shoulder. "I'm glad to see you've come around.
The games of childhood must end eventually."

Juliette pulled away. "Don't touch me! And don't
talk like that about François. We are—were going to
get married when he finished school!"

Bouchard laughed awkwardly. "Ah, child, those
are the dreams of children! We all have had them. But

time passes and reality moves in. We show our breeding by the way we adjust to what has to be. A true aristocrat puts aside childish things and accepts life as it really is.''

''Don't tell me how an aristocrat acts! How do you know? You're only a servant!'' Her face red, Juliette stared into Hermione's eyes.

Bouchard seemed not the least ready to take offense at the angry words. Her arms opened, as they so often had in the past. ''Oh, my little girl! My poor, broken-hearted little girl!''

With a sob, Juliette let herself be pulled into Bouchard's embrace. Her head rested against her ample bosom. The tears that she had held back since waking suddenly flowed down her cheeks.

Bouchard patted the dark head. ''Don't fret too much, little sweetheart. Maybe you'll get to see François while you're at the abbey.''

Juliette lifted her head. ''Is he near the abbey? Will you help me? I have to see him!''

A shadow passed over Bouchard's face. ''I don't know. I'm not sure I'll be with you at all.''

Immediately, Juliette pulled away from the comforting arms. Stamping angrily, she tossed her head. ''Not going with me? Why not?''

A hesitancy not familiar to Juliette held Bouchard immobile. Her face twisted oddly. ''Oh, little one, everything will be just fine for you! The baron has made arrangements for some of his family retainers to meet you at the abbey on Thursday next. You'll have a suite of your own in a cottage that has belonged to the duDeffand family for generations. You'll live right next to the abbey, and you'll have everything your heart desires!'' Her face worked. ''You'll have lessons in all the graces I could never teach you. When the baron returns to take you with him to Versailles, you'll be polished like a magnificent diamond!"

"I don't want to be a diamond! And I don't want any of duDeffand's retainers! I want you! How dare he tell me you can't go with me!"

"Oh, but I'll journey down there with you! But then"—her voice broke—"then I'll return here, to stay with your poor father."

Juliette was silent. She hadn't thought of her father. Then the memory of his betrayal gave her strength. Pulling herself erect, she listed her head. "No, you won't! You're going to stay with me!" She hoped, passionately, that Bouchard wouldn't see her trembling. "Will the baron be at the abbey to greet us?"

"Oh, no. He's already on his way to India!"

"Well, then, he'll find out when he returns. We won't even have to ask his permission."

"But who'll take care of your poor papa?"

Juliette's face hardened. "Have you attended him in the past?"

Hermione shook her head. "No—but he'll be all alone."

"It's his choice, isn't it?" There was only a small quiver in Juliette's voice.

The days that followed were busy ones. Juliette and Bouchard went through her wardrobe, separating out those dresses she felt worthy of her new estate. The runabout dresses she had worn in the meadow she gave to the servants. It was a difficult task. The loose dresses were bound in her memory with her love for François.

Her father, who had ignored her most of her child-hood years, suddenly seemed dependent on her company. The first time he called her in to sit with him, Juliette felt resentful—and angry. She was convinced all he wanted was to ease his conscience.

She quickly learned otherwise. The decision to wed her to duDeffand had been a difficult one for him to make. So difficult, in fact, that he seemed to have changed completely.

They spent most of the evenings browsing through the memorabilia that cluttered his desk and all the surfaces in the dusty room. Despite her depression, this delighted Juliette, for she loved to look at and touch things that had belonged to her mother. Each item had a story, and Jean de Condillac seemed never to tire of the telling.

On her third visit Juliette received a shock.

Her father was speaking about Madeline, Juliette's sister who had died of the pox, when Juliette realized he was speaking not of the past but of the present. "She's such a lady, my Madeline is! Juliette, you must tell her to come and see me more often. The house isn't the same since she went away."

A cold chill ran up Juliette's back. "Papa! What are you saying? Madeline is dead. Don't you remember? She died when I was just a little girl." She stopped speaking and stared in horror as his face underwent a series of changes.

Anger at her words replaced the calm that had characterized his expression throughout much of the evening. Before he could speak, however, the anger was gone, and he gazed about in pitiful confusion. Then, as if a hand had wiped the indecision from his eyes, the pain and hurt returned. Tears coursed down his cheeks. "Yes." His voice was weak. "I forgot for a moment. I forgot, that's all."

Juliette clutched his hands in helpless pity. "Oh,

Papa! What will happen to you when I'm gone?''

Once more his eyes were shielded. His expression grew calm. He was again the father she knew so well. She stared at his face with growing understanding. It had been there all along: the pain, the hurt, the loneliness. It had been there as long as she could remember. But only now had it broken through. His strength, his calm—it had all been for her benefit.

Everything had been done for her! The appearance of wealth—it was only a façade. Bouchard was right. The estate was suffering from the riots. Her father had protected her from everything that might have spoiled her childhood! He'd borne it all—alone. It was time she shouldered her share of the burden. She squeezed his hands gently. ''Papa, who will take care of you after I'm gone?''

Their eyes met, equal for the first time in her life. Equal—and honest. ''Don't worry about me, my dear. I'll be all right. I have the servants, and, fortunately, some of them are faithful. And the du Quesnays are close. When I need companionship, I'll visit them.'' He chewed on his lip. ''Why, I might even show up at the abbey! I couldn't let an entire summer go by without seeing my only daughter!''

She sat silent, staring into his face. He was old. Old—and very tired. She thought of François' animated expression, and her heart fell. Was this what would happen to him, now that she was marrying duDeffand? Would he be lonely like this, too? Gently, she leaned forward and kissed her father's damp cheek. Throughout all of her life, she had thought of her mother's death as her private, personal loss. Now she knew. Her father had missed her mother with all the agony of bereft love. The sixteen years of her life had been to him sixteen centuries of loneliness.

"Oh, Papa, I didn't know! I never thought. I never knew how strong you were."

His voice was thick with pain. "Can you forgive me? Can you ever forgive me?"

He didn't have to say more. She knew. As the realization grew, she watched the child within her vanish.

Once more she touched her father's cheek with her lips. He knew of her love for François. He knew—and he still had betrothed her to another. But he hadn't acted from selfishness, nor from lack of understanding. He'd done it to free her from the decay that was destroying the country. He had done it because he loved her. His voice broke as he explained.

She clutched his hand. "I understand, Papa. I didn't before. Oh, Papa!" Her eyes were so filled with tears she couldn't see his face. "I love François so very much! I don't know if I can stand to let him go!" Her voice grew quiet. "But I do understand. You wanted me to be safe."

They looked at no more mementos that night. But when she left for her bed, Juliette felt closer to her father than ever before in her life.

In the days that followed, the memory of her father's loneliness haunted her. At last, she decided to speak to Bouchard. She sat before her mirror, watching as Hermione combed through her dark curls, preparing her for sleep.

"Bouchy, will Papa be all right?" She bit her lip as she thought of his lapse of memory. "The other night he talked as if Madeline were still alive."

Bouchard shook her head. Tugging at the long hair, she gently teased it into a braid. "He'll be as good as possible. He's just growing old. And he's lonely. But he would be most upset if his problems interfered with your happiness.''

Juliette shook her head. "He knows marrying duDeffand won't make me happy. Don't talk like that!"

Bouchard pressed her lips together. "You're going to live at court, aren't you? You'll no longer be a simple country girl with no future. You'll be a companion to the queen! I've seen how often you pretend to dance with the king. And all that bowing and scraping! How could anyone not see what you want?"

"He knows what I want! He knows I—" Juliette stopped short. There was no point in talking about François to Bouchard. She didn't understand. She never would. "Bouchy, did you ever get married?"

The round, calm face showed no emotion. "No, of course not. I've been in service all of my life. I've always had others to care for. Your sister—and then you—and others before that. I didn't have time for such nonsense."

Juliette stared into the mirror. How much understanding was coming to her, now that she was a woman! Her father recognized her love for François, but he couldn't acknowledge it fully without questioning his decision to marry her to duDeffand. Hermione thought of it as nothing but the infatuation of a child. Well, she would learn that she was wrong.

Bouchard patted the braid and let it fall on Juliette's shoulder. "We're almost ready. Tomorrow I'll hem up the dress I started last week. You'll have to get more, probably while you're at the abbey. But we can't have you leaving home like a pauper!"

Juliette smiled. There was no need to quarrel further with Bouchard. It didn't really matter what the old woman thought. Let her be happy with her fussing and mothering. She was a servant. Nothing more. She would accept whatever her mistress decided. For the time being, it was just as wise to let her think everything was settled.

But only for the time. Long before the Baron duDeffand tried to hold her to her father's promise, Juliette would have François by her side. She would be his lawfully married wife. Then the baron couldn't get her. She'd return to the farm and care for her father. It would be that simple. Soon, very soon, all her troubles would be over.

The final visit with the du Quesnays was far from happy. Madam du Quesnay was close to tears, for it was clear she had fancied her son married to Juliette. Still, like the lady she had always been, she listened patiently to Juliette's farewell.

"I'll drop by often to see your father, my dear," Madam du Quesnay's voice was gentle, "though I find it difficult to forgive him for what he's done to you—and to my François. But, if you wish it—" She stared past her young visitor to the meadow. "We all do what we must, especially in these hard times. Your father is right, I suppose. There's no future in the country. The estates are falling apart as the feudal system collapses."

Juliette stared at her hostess. Where had she heard talk such as that?

"François has told me of the condition in the countryside. We're like your papa. We never leave the estate, except to visit our neighbors. But François—" She caught sight of the tear that trickled down Juliette's cheek and stopped. "I'm sorry. I shouldn't remind you of him—not now."

"It's all right. I—I like to speak of him."

Madam du Quesnay put a lean arm around Juliette's shoulder. She was taller than Juliette, but she had none of Bouchard's peasant looks. François' mother was a lady, the daughter of a duke. When Juliette was small, she had often found comfort in Madam du Quesnay's arms. She even had fancied that her own mother, had she lived, would have been as cheerful and full of *joie de vivre* as Madam du Quesnay always seemed to be.

But now there was a wall between them. Juliette spoke gently. "Madam, please. It's all right. I love to speak of François."

"He'll be heartbroken! Can your father possibly know what he is doing to you two young people?" Her eyes flashed. "Men!" Her voice was scornful. "Nothing is as important to them as finances—and security! They don't seem to know what matters to young people! Why, when they get old, do men forget what it is to love?"

Juliette thought of her father. No, he hadn't forgotten. He had just learned to bottle it up.

"Where is François' school?"

"Why, in Lyon, of course! Hasn't he told you?"

"Yes, I guess so. But I didn't really concern myself with it before. But now—"

"But of course, my dear. He's studying at the Cathedral University in Lyon." Her expression brightened. "He's such a brilliant student! Oh, Juliette, my dear, I've always been so proud of him, so happy that—" Her voice broke. "I wonder, sometimes, that he bothers to talk to me at all. I'm sure I must bore him."

Juliette decided to ignore the break. Nothing could be gained by letting François' mother know of her plans. "Papa speaks of my wedding taking place at home. But I can't see him going to all that trouble. I'm not sure what will happen now."

Madam du Quesnay gasped. "Don't speak so! You'll be back to see your father—and to visit with us! Why, I love you as if you were my own daughter."

Juliette felt the tears pressing against her eyes. Despite her plans of escape with François, she had an ominous feeling that these were her final farewells.

François' father remained locked in his study. Juliette felt the slight, yet she couldn't help but understand. There was nothing to be said between them. Her father had broken an unspoken agreement between the two families. Their closeness had been destroyed. Nothing was left except to say good-bye.

The day of her departure was cloudy, and by the time the carriage was loaded, a light drizzle was wetting the ground. Juliette, dressed in a new gown sent by the baron, had spent the morning saying her farewells to the house and the farm.

She started with the attic, where she and Madeline had played hide-and-seek when they were children. It was much as it had been then: long, high-ceilinged, dusty, filled with trunks and large wooden boxes in which the many fragile memories of an old established family lay buried. She and her sister had played with the brittle dresses and the broken fans, imagining what life must have been like in their grandparents' day.

Then, her mind stuffed with poignant memories, she had wandered about the upstairs rooms. Without telling her father, she had unlocked the door to her mother's room, a door that had been sealed after her birth. She stood for a long time just inside the portal, looking, for the first time, at the bed in which she had been born—and in which her mother had died.

Many of the larger rooms in the manor had also been closed all of Juliette's life, for her father had done little entertaining after her mother's death and even less after Madeline succumbed to the pox. But now Juliette visited every one. Finally, with a feeling of emptiness, she returned to her room. She stood gazing at her mother's portrait. Nothing seemed to lighten her despair. Why did she feel as if each farewell was final?

Bouchard entered the room, a cape draped over her arm. "It's time to go, my dear. The farm hands have expressed a wish to bid you good-bye."

Juliette smiled. She had spent many hours playing among the animals. Of all the people on the estate, John and Emil and George and Paul—and—She could name each one and tell how he felt by the way he greeted her. She would miss them all, almost as much as she would miss her father. She nodded to Bouchard. "Meet me at the carriage. I'll be there shortly."

The men were lined up, waiting for her. Quickly, she kissed each one on the cheek. As she left the barn, Paul began to herd the horses toward the door, his palm extended to test the strength of the rain. Turning, she called out, "Let them stay in today, Paul. It's raining too hard!"

He nodded and closed the doors. She was alone once more.

She wanted to caution him so that, in the days to come, he would keep the animals away from her private valley. She wanted to tell him to be sure they didn't dig up the grass that grew under the willow tree at the edge of the stream, but she said nothing. The cool rain wet her face, concealing the tears that ran from her eyes. She was thankful for the shower. It had helped her conceal her weakness. She didn't want to expose herself to the pity of the peasants.

Quickly, she turned and ran to the carriage. She had said all her farewells except one. Her father stood in the rain, waiting to assist her into her seat. Impulsively, she threw her arms around his neck and kissed his damp cheek. "Good-bye, Papa."

He tried to speak, but his voice wouldn't obey him. Silently, he kissed her cheeks and then, a forced smile on his face, waited as she settled into the carriage. The horses pawed the ground. The whip cracked above their heads. Slowly, the carriage began to move. Leaning forward, Juliette pulled back the curtain and stared as her home receded in the distance. Her father had not moved. He stood alone in the middle of the driveway, his old black cape clinging to his body, his dark hat tilted to protect his eyes from the rain.

"Good-bye." Juliette's voice was a whisper. "Good-bye, Papa." She settled back again, adjusting her skirts so they didn't overlap Hermione's. Her childhood was over. No matter how much she wished, she would never be able to go back.

CHAPTER FOUR

They reached Chalon sur Saone by nightfall, pulling into the courtyard of the best inn in town well before the shadows deepened and the night grew dangerous. Bouchard climbed down first, the carriage tilting far to the right as she placed her high-buttoned shoe on the tiny step. Laughing, Juliette held onto the supports and waited patiently until the carriage stopped its swaying. Then, daintily, she followed her maid into the general room.

The coachman rushed to her side. "Ma'am, I've been seeing to the rooms. It'll be a few minutes while they put up the bed for your maid. I expect you're hungry. Shall I order you some food?"

Juliette nodded. "I'll sit in the corner, over there, out of the way. Tell them to hurry. I'm very tired." She turned to Bouchard. "Come, let's eat before we retire."

As they seated themselves, Juliette realized Bouchard was grumbling angrily, ". . . no place for a lady to eat! Only a streetwoman would dine with the rabble!"

Juliette smiled disarmingly. "Then this is where I belong. That's exactly what I am, isn't it? I'm selling my body for money. Though, of course, being a lady, I'll never see any of it!"

Bouchard sputtered, her hands floating nervously before her face. "Juliette! What a thing to say!"

Juliette looked up at the approaching waiter. He held two large bowls before him and a long loaf of bread under one arm. The fragrance of the stew beckoned her invitingly. When the bowls were placed on the table, she picked up her spoon and began to eat.

The coachman appeared with a jug of wine and two glasses. Gratefully, Juliette rinsed her mouth with the ruby liquid. She ordered her glass refilled without glancing at Bouchard. In the past, she would have asked permission. Now she didn't bother. A lady did what she wanted—except where it truly mattered. Then she did what she had to do, and usually what she had to do was unpleasant.

As soon as Bouchard was snoring, Juliette crept from her bed, pulled on her gown, and slipped across the room. As she opened the door, she paused. Raucous voices soared up from the common room. Startled, she glanced back toward the bed where Bouchard lay. The woman hadn't moved. A faint ray of moonlight illuminated her features. She was sound asleep, her nostrils flaring with each intake of breath.

Swiftly, Juliette stepped into the hall and closed the door behind her. She paused at the top of the stairs. Did she dare to descend? Did she really want to?

She wanted something. She was restless, tired from hours of sitting in the coach. What she truly desired was a chance to walk. With a reluctance as foreign to her as the hall in which she stood, she hesitated, listening to a voice that floated up the stairs.

". . . they fought for freedom—and they won! A new country, governed by the people, for the people! And what have we? Nothing! We settle for vandalism! We suffer under the same burdens that destroyed our parents, yet we do nothing to change our lives!"

The voice stopped, as if the speaker might be imbibing a draft of wine. Immediately, the cry was taken up by many other voices, most of them male. Then the shrill voice resumed. "As long as we stand by and let the aristocracy bleed us, our children will continue to die of starvation and our women will go to early graves, worn out from labor!"

A deep voice broke in, angry and raw. "The price of bread rose again today. Will there be no end to profit-taking at the expense of the workers?"

Again the shrill leader spoke. "It will end in revolt, if you are men! Have you seen any land broken for planting? Is any water carried from the river to the parched fields? Even the heavens are protesting! Where will your bread come from when this summer is over?"

Now a third voice rose above the murmuring of the crowd. "There's bread in the manors!"

The leader spoke once more. "Aye, there's much food in the manors. And there's much waste. While your children starve, the children of the landowners grow fat."

Timidly, Juliette crept down the stairs. She no longer wanted to descend for a walk or a goblet of wine, but she felt a curiosity regarding the speaker. He didn't sound like a peasant. His tone was gentle—and somehow familiar.

She reached a position that gave her a view of the common room. The thought of what might happen were she seen made her tremble, but she didn't retreat. She had to see. The speaker, a tall, youthful man, stood on a table, his back to the stairs. His brown hair was unruly, his clothes rags. She stared at him fixedly. He sounded like François!

She pulled back. What was she thinking? François a revolutionary? Impossible!

The voice continued. "God, in his infinite wisdom, created all men with equal needs. We all have to eat. We all have to feed our children. But the aristocracy has taken control away from God! They make their own rules and force us to live by them! Well, it's time for a change. It's time we returned to the laws of God!" As he spoke, the young man turned, his fist shaking violently.

Juliette stared at the ragged figure. When he became still, she felt a wave of disappointment. She could not see his face. Angrily, she addressed her doubts. How could she even think that François would speak in that manner? How could she be so disloyal? François was in Lyon—in school.

She turned and crept back up the stairs. As much as she had wanted to escape the monotony of her room a few moments before, she now wanted to reach its safety. Below were the rioters, dangerous men who scared her. Below, too, was a young man whose appearance filled her with confusion.

She had no reason, however, to hurry. The men were far too busy with their own complaints to worry about her, or, for that matter, to notice her presence on the stairs.

Juliette closed the door gently. Bouchard stirred. "Juliette?" Her voice was heavy with sleep.

"It's all right, Bouchy. I just got up to use the chamber pot. I'll be in bed in a moment."

As she climbed between the covers, Juliette realized she was trembling. It wasn't easy to wipe the vision of the young rabble rouser from her memory, nor, for that matter, was it possible for her to forget that, for one terrible moment, she had thought he was François.

For the remainder of the journey, Juliette became increasingly aware of the horrors of the drought. The

Saone River was low on its banks. When they embarked on the barge that would take them to Lyon, they had to be rowed out to the center of the stream, where water was still deep enough for passage.

Once, as they floated downstream, she saw a cow buried up to its flanks in mud, its owner frantically struggling to work it loose. She watched as both man and beast sank deeper and deeper into the slime.

Juliette was silent for a time. She wished, fervently, that she could close her eyes to the suffering around her. The words of the speaker still rang in her ears. Was all this really her fault?

At last, in desperation, she began to recite some of the light-hearted rhymes she had learned as a child. Bouchard joined in, an understanding smile on her face. Each rhyme she remembered was funnier than the last. Finally, they were both laughing, the horrors about them forgotten.

A raucous voice cut through their merriment. "Heartless! You're worse than the Austrian queen! Laughing at others' miseries!"

Startled, Juliette turned in the direction of the voice. There, standing in the lengthening shadows, was a gaunt woman, one thin arm holding a baby while the other hung at her side, resting on the shoulder of a boy who looked to be about three. Both children were pot-bellied, with legs and arms that were little more than skin and bones.

By the time Juliette regained her composure, the boat had drifted on, leaving the angry woman far behind. Her humor gone, Juliette turned to Bouchard. "I wasn't laughing at her, really I wasn't."

"I know that, my dear! But— Don't let yourself become upset over a few starving peasants. It isn't your fault they have no bread."

Juliette didn't answer. Maybe it was. If any of the words she had heard the night before were right, she was not as innocent as Bouchard claimed.

It was close to sunset when the barge tied up at a rocky bank on the outskirts of Lyon. The two lackeys grasped Bouchard between them and, with much grunting and shouting, carried her to the shore. Then they returned to assist Juliette.

But the girl was too fast for them. She leaped over the side of the boat, landing lightly on the rocks. Quickly, she balanced herself and ran from rock to rock until she stood beside her nurse. As she passed the men, she gestured toward the deck. "Bring our bags. And hurry. I want to see Lyon before all the light is gone."

Bouchard shook her head. "What do you want to see of Lyon you haven't already seen as we approached it? It's a big city, much larger than Chalon, with many tall spires. And it's built all of stone!"

"Is it really?"

"Oh, Juliette, of course I don't know! Why do you ask so many foolish questions?"

Juliette decided not to answer. "Where are we going now?"

"I hope to another inn. I'm far too exhausted to travel all the way to Villeurbanne tonight. Besides, curious as you are, you'll want to see the abbey as we approach it. I understand it's a magnificent structure."

"Have you seen it before?"

"No." Bouchard sighed. "Questions! Always questions!"

Juliette was silent. She didn't feel like games, anyway. They didn't help her forget the angry woman's curses or the man floundering in the mud.

When she was safely in her room at the inn, with a steaming dinner spread before her, she felt no desire to eat. She stared at her plate with a new sense of understanding. "Bouchy, it isn't fair!"

"What isn't fair, dear?"

"It isn't fair that we have so much food and—those children so little."

"It's God's will."

"Then he's a cruel God!"

"Juliette! Pray to the Lord that He forgives you for such blasphemy! You must learn to look on all the works of the Lord with the proper appreciation. He's done it all for the good of our souls. The poor suffer so they'll find rest and reward in heaven."

Juliette frowned, slamming her fork on her plate. "Well, then, we should suffer when we die, since we have so much that is good here on earth!"

Bouchard stared at her in horror. Then, crossing herself, she resumed her meal. "It's good you're going to live in the abbey. Your religious education has been seriously neglected."

Biting her lip, Juliette stared at her companion. Then, taking up her fork, she began to eat. Bouchard smiled smugly.

Suddenly, Juliette slammed her fork back onto the plate. "Isn't Uncle Henry the same one who profaned the Holy Virgin when he was visiting Papa? Didn't Papa get into a fight with him because he said Our Blessed Savior couldn't have been born of a virgin?"

Bouchard stared at Juliette. "How did you learn such things?"

"I—well—" Suddenly Juliette was blushing. "I listened at the study door when Uncle Henry visited."

Bouchard looked into the girl's face, her frown replaced by a slight smile. "You couldn't have been at the study door——"

"Because *you* were there!" Juliette burst into laughter.

"—because I would have seen you from your room had you been." Bouchard wouldn't acknowledge so impertinent a remark.

"You're right, as usual, Bouchy." Juliette decided not to argue. "I was hiding in Papa's closet. I had planned to surprise them both, and then, when they began to fight, I didn't dare come out."

Juliette finished her meal in better humor. Somehow, the thought of old Bouchy crouching outside the study door was too funny to be ignored. And she was certain that was just what Bouchard had done. Otherwise, she mused, how did Bouchard know of her uncle's heresy?

When she had said her prayers and climbed into bed, Juliette lay staring into the darkness. She was in Lyon, but she wasn't sure how she should go about finding François. She tried to remember the parts of the town they had passed on their way from the river, but she couldn't recall seeing a cathedral.

Bouchard, who had retired as soon as her charge was settled, began to snore lightly. Juliette lifted her head. "Bouchy!"

"Huh?"

"Bouchy, stop snoring!" The breathing resumed, this time more lightly. Relieved, Juliette felt herself slip into unconsciousness.

A sudden noise brought her back to wakefulness. Startled, she leaped to her feet. Someone was shouting loudly outside her window. Terrified, she pulled on a robe and rushed to the casement. She loosened the latch, then pushed it open.

The moon cast a silver glow on the scene below, giving it the appearance of an ancient painting. But the subject was far from classical. The narrow street below her was filled from one side to the other with struggling men, all shouting and pushing in anger. Many, she could see, held sticks or large stones.

Her heart beating furiously, Juliette stared at the angry crowd. Were they trying to reach her? Frightened at the thought, she pulled back, half closing the window behind her.

The cries of the men didn't change. They hadn't noticed her at all. Their anger was directed at some other enemy.

She felt a hand on her shoulder. Bouchard's voice was gentle. "What's the matter, child? Close the window, the night air is bad for the lungs!"

"Oh, Bouchy! You frightened me!" Juliette pushed the casement open once more. "Look. What are they doing?"

Suddenly, a roar went up from the street below and the crowd began to shift uneasily. Some of the men, those farthest to Juliette's left, were still pushing forward, but the others, who had obviously found some reason for retreat, were trying to retrace their steps. The result was a press that only served to increase the general uproar.

Juliette watched in horror. From the far right, she could see a line of soldiers moving inexorably forward. She leaned out over the mob. "Go back! Please, go back!"

No one listened to her cries. When the soldiers were equally spaced across the intersection to her right, they raised their rifles to their shoulders. Immediately, the men closest to the guns began to push back, shouting for retreat.

The call rang out over the rumbling of the mob. "Ready, aim, fire!"

The sound of the explosion tore through the air, ripping at Juliette's consciousness. She felt herself shake with fright. But now the shrieks and cries of the wounded men filled the night. Juliette screamed, but she could not turn away from the scene.

Once more the men farthest to the left, who were only vaguely aware of the tragedy that had occurred, pushed forward, forcing the entire crowd to move ahead. Injured men fell beneath the onslaught of the mob, their cries muffled as they were crushed to the earth.

Then, again, the guns exploded. This time, even the last men in the mob were aware of the explosion. But they didn't behave as Juliette expected. Instead of dropping their sticks and fleeing, they pushed forward with added vigor, their cries of rage equaling the roar of the rifles. To her surprise, the soldiers were the ones who ran. Whoever had given the order to fire wasn't willing to stand his ground.

The crowd surged forward at an increased rate, trampling the bodies of fallen comrades. As suddenly as they had appeared, they were gone. All that were left were the injured—and the dead.

Juliette turned from the window. "Bouchy, hurry, we have to help them."

"Help them? Are you insane? Those men were destroying property. They were killing one another! I pray to God the soldiers can stop them soon."

"Bouchy, they're dying!"

"Then it's the priests' duty to help them. Believe me, my dear, the street is no place for a child like you!"

There was a knock on the door. Bouchard reached out and pulled Juliette into her arms. "Who's there?"

"It's me, ma'am. The coachman. I thought you might be awake. It's only about an hour till morning, and I—we— Well, we thought it might be best if we left now, while the crowd is gone.''

Bouchard was silent for a moment. Then, with a sudden rush, she began to gather her clothes. "You're right. We'll be ready as soon as possible.''

Juliette stood halfway between the still-open casement and the beds. "Bouchy! How can you let them order us that way? We can't go now!''

"We must. The coachman is entrusted with your safety. If he feels it's dangerous to stay, we must leave.''

Juliette groaned. But there was nothing she could do to change the decision. Bouchard proceeded with the packing and, as soon as they both were dressed, led the way to the general room. The coachman and the two lackeys were waiting at the door.

"Well,'' Bouchard swept toward them like a ship in full sail. "Where's the carriage?''

The coachman stepped forward. "Begging your pardon, ma'am, it's around the corner. There was no way we could drive it through the crowd.''

Now that she was closer to the street, Juliette felt a wave of fear. The thought of walking past those dead bodies made her cringe.

Bouchard put one arm around the girl's shoulder.

"Now, now, Juliette, don't worry. We'll get you to the carriage safely.''

Immediately, Juliette pulled away, her face red with embarrassment. How could Bouchard see her fright so easily?

One lackey pushed the door open and stepped into the street. "It's clear now, ma'am. Please hurry.''

Bouchard stepped forward. Gritting her teeth, Juliette followed. Before she had a chance for second thoughts, she was through the door.

The street was empty of all but the fallen. Gingerly, her skirts held off the ground, Juliette moved after Bouchard. She wanted only to pass through this horror as quickly as possible.

She felt a pull on her cape. Panic overwhelmed her. Jerking abruptly, she tried to pull loose without looking back. The tug was repeated. Grasping her cape more firmly, she pulled away, fearful that if she glanced down, she would find herself staring into the face of death.

"Please, ma'am, please help me!" The voice was high and ragged with tears. A woman! Surprised, Juliette turned.

The creature who crouched before her was small, no taller than Juliette herself. Her features were those of a woman not long out of childhood. But the eyes that met Juliette's were not those of a child. They were filled with despair.

She spoke again, her voice full of pleading. "Help me! Help me move my man before they come back!"

Juliette stared at the woman, unable to move.

"Please!"

The word stirred Juliette into action. She moved toward the fallen figure with a swiftness that took Bouchard by surprise. While the woman bent to grasp the shoulder of a male figure lying nearby, Juliette lifted his feet. Then, slowly, the heavy body slipping from their hands more than once, they moved toward the shelter of a nearby building. The third time they dropped the body, Juliette stood erect. "Lackey! Come here!"

Slowly, one of the men moved to her side.

"Pick him up!"

"Oh, no, ma'am! We have to hurry!"

Juliette's voice rose. "Do as you're told!"

Silently, the man obeyed. For him the corpse was light, more like that of a child than a full-grown man. Nevertheless, he carried it gingerly, as if he feared it might wake up and attack him. The other lackey and the coachman followed close behind.

The woman moved ahead, leading the way from the street. They turned a corner and she paused. "Thank you, ma'am!"

"Do you live here?"

"Oh, no, ma'am. I live down the street a bit."

"Well, then, lead us there! You can't carry him alone!"

Once more the woman took the lead. They passed the carriage and turned into one of the narrow alleys that branched off from the main thoroughfare. When they turned another corner, Juliette began to feel uneasy. Would they be able to find their way back through the maze of streets?

Pushing the fear aside, she hurried on. She was determined that she wouldn't abandon the poor widow. Resolutely, she followed her lackey, trying not to look at the head that fell back over his arm.

Just when she began to regret her eagerness to help a stranger, they stopped before a tall building. With obvious relief, the woman pushed open a door and led the way inside.

"God save us! Is it the plague?" The shrill voice came from above, and when Juliette looked up, she realized that every window in the street held at least one face, all of them staring down at her.

Juliette stared back. "No. He was killed in a riot!"

"Shot by soldiers, eh? See?" The angular face turned sideways. "See, I told you they wouldn't help!"

Now, suddenly, all the watchers were shouting angrily. A bucket of water was emptied above her, and Juliette leaped quickly aside. Bouchard caught her hand. "Come, my dear, it's dangerous for us to stay here."

Juliette frowned. "Why? We're only trying to help!"

The lackey stepped from the dark room, blinking furiously at the sun, a look of disgust on his face. Gingerly, he brushed at a stain on his sleeve. "Miss, we have to go."

The coachman took her arm. "We must go, ma'am. I can't be responsible for your safety if you continue to be so foolhardy. The master will have me killed if any harm comes to you."

Juliette turned toward the open doorway. "The widow—is she all right?"

"Yes, ma'am. Please, we must go."

Pulling away from the coachman, Juliette followed him through the crowd that had gathered around them in the street. She realized, as she looked into the angry faces, that indeed there was reason for fright.

A voice called out. "Mademoiselle!"

Juliette turned. The widow stood at her door, her hand upraised. "Thank you, mademoiselle! Thank you!" She was running now, clutching at Juliette's cape.

The coachman turned, his arm raised, but Juliette held him back. She looked down at the pinched face. "What's your name?"

"Marie, ma'am. Marie Frougard."

Juliette smiled. "I'm Juliette d— Condillac. I come from Chalon sur Saone."

The widow smiled awkwardly. Then, with a quick curtsy, she turned and ran back into the crowd. Immediately, Juliette felt her arm grasped by firm hands.

She was half led, half pushed down the alley.

When they reached the carriage, the horses were stamping restlessly. Quickly, Bouchard hustled Juliette into the safety of the cab. Juliette settled down with a sigh. She held one hand up before Bouchard's face. "Look, Bouchy, I'm trembling!"

"No wonder! I began to shake the moment you picked up that flea-bitten—the minute you committed us to carrying that body from the street. My dear, you mustn't do that sort of thing again! We could have been murdered."

"But—" Juliette stared out through the small window. She couldn't deny she was happy to be safe in the coach. The threat of the mob had been real. Then she remembered. François! She had to find François. "Bouchy, are we going to pass by the cathedral?"

Bouchard smiled. "You want to say a prayer of thanks that we were saved. Yes, that's a good idea." She hammered on the carriage wall. "Coachman!"

There was no reply.

"You there! Coachman!"

"Yes, ma'am?" The voice was muffled.

"Do we pass the cathedral?"

"Yes, ma'am. It'll be to the right when we reach the river."

"Stop when you reach it. Mademoiselle Juliette wishes to give thanks for our safety." There was no answer. "Do you hear me?"

"Yes, ma'am."

Bouchard settled back once more in her seat.

It was difficult for Juliette to keep her head bowed or even to give the impression she was praying. To her delight, the cathedral was filled with a crowd of young men, obviously students at the school who, like her, were saying their rosaries. Fortunately, Bouchard paid them no heed. She closed her eyes and began to mumble her prayers as soon as she found a spot in which to settle. Juliette raised her head and studied the orderly lines of identically dressed young men.

She had never visualized François as part of a large class. Nevertheless, she did find him and, from that moment on, she fastened her eyes, her entire attention, on the back of his neck. When the men rose to leave, her heart leaped. Soon, very soon, he would be passing the spot where she knelt. She would have to attract his attention before he was out of sight.

To her consternation, the men filed past in almost military order. Each one was within range of vision for no more than a second. Frantically, she cast about for some way to make the one man who mattered to her notice her presence. Then, with a smile, she rose to her feet. He could not fail to notice her when she towered above the kneeling supplicants.

She heard a gasp, and she turned. He was beside her.

"François, oh, François!" Her voice was little more than a breath.

He hesitated for one moment, and then, responding to pressure from the man behind him, began to move on. His head turned in her direction, and his eyes frantically held onto hers.

Roughly, Juliette climbed over Bouchard and stepped into the aisle. He was moving so swiftly! If she didn't hurry, she'd lose him altogether! Quickly she ran to his side. "François!"

"Juliette! What are you doing here?"

"Oh, François, my dear François!"

"Hurry! I can't leave the column!"

"I—I'm going to the Abbey Villeurbanne."

"Why? Is your father dead?"

"No—" As she spoke, they reached the narthex, and the column moved toward an open doorway that led into the monastery gardens. François, straining to keep her in sight, moved slowly with it. Once more she ran to his side. "Please, come and see me."

The men were vanishing through the doorway. François paused at the opening. "I can't. Not now! Why are you there?"

The student behind him pushed him roughly. "Hurry, François. Do you want the father to use his whip on every one of us?"

François started to step out of line, but someone grabbed his shoulders and pushed him through the doorway. Juliette stood immobile, staring at the open doorway until the last man entered it and slammed it shut. Then, not bothering to wipe the tears from her eyes, she moved back toward the basilica. Bouchard met her at the entranceway. "Juliette, hurry! Had I known why you wished to stop here, I wouldn't have permitted it! I only hope the baron never learns of this!"

Closing her ears against the angry scolding, Juliette moved back toward the carriage. Why had she been unable to speak? What curse held her tongue when she should have told François about duDeffand?

She didn't look at Bouchard when they were, at last, seated together in the carriage. She didn't dare. Her tears were too close to spilling over. She had tried to get François' help, and she had failed. She couldn't even be sure he would try to find her.

CHAPTER FIVE

The abbey was beautiful, just as Hermione had promised. Constructed mostly of granite, it looked like an ancient castle, standing proudly on a hilltop overlooking a neat row of large cottages, a number of stables, and rows and rows of grapevines. It seemed to reach out to embrace the tired travelers. Juliette felt her body relax for the first time since leaving Lyon. Everything was as it had always been at the abbey. The Church, as vigorous as ever, appeared to be above the trials of the secular world.

Juliette's quarters weren't at all what she had expected. She was surrounded by luxury and slept on a feather bed draped in rich brocades. Her feet never touched stone, for carpets from the Orient were everywhere. The food was designed to please the gourmet. She breakfasted on quail, ate fresh-caught trout for lunch, and dined in the evening on roast pig or beef.

The guilt she felt when she first saw the sumptuousness around her faded as the days passed. The peasant floundering in the muck with his cow was forgotten. The angry woman with her starving children grew less formidable, less reproachful. She even forgot the dead lying in the street of Lyon. This was the life her father had pretended to live in order to shelter her from the troubles of the world. But it was not a fantasy, as Bouchard had led her to believe. It was real—and she was a part of it.

Her uncle, Henry de Condillac, the abbé of Villeurbanne, was a total surprise. There was no doubt he
was her father's brother, though their bodies seemed
to have been poured from different molds. Her father
had always been lean. Henry had grown paunchy,
with a round face that seemed always to be smiling.
His only concession to his orders was the style of his
hair. He no longer wore the robes she had remembered
as his constant habit.

She found him immediately attractive—and friendly. He hovered around her for the entire first day of her
stay, leaving only when he was certain she had found
companions closer to her own age. Then he seemed
content to remain in the background, ready, at a
moment's notice, to step to her side. By the end of the
second week, she saw him hardly at all, except when
all of the group were together. She had lost her
novelty. He was far too busy with those feminine
members of his tiny court who could provide him with
more earthly pleasures than just good company.

As the week progressed, Juliette's urgent desire to
see François diminished. With a full year before Roger
duDeffand was to return, Juliette began to enjoy her
position as his affianced. There would be, she decided, plenty of time to run away after her period of
pleasant training was over.

Her lessons were simplicity itself. She rose when
she wished, was dressed, not by Bouchard but by
Annette and Anabel, both at least half the age of her
aging nurse, who had been trained as maids by Madam
duDeffand herself. Despite her determination to remain aloof from all that happened to her, Juliette was
impressed. Even her father had shown respect for the
old dame whose salons had been, in their time, the talk
of cultured France.

Once dressed, Juliette spent hours sitting quietly in the garden, listening to ballads, reading books, reciting poetry. Much was made of her talent for memorizing, and she was given long passages to learn. She felt vaguely superior when she was told that the king was impressed by anyone who had a good memory. Of her own accord, she picked out particularly sensuous poems from the ancient books she found in the library, repeating them until she could recall them on demand.

Bouchard seemed totally out of place. At first, she tried to restrain Juliette when others enticed her into frivolity, but Juliette quickly put a stop to such arrogant behavior. Still, she couldn't quite get herself to send the motherly old woman back to the farm. She settled the matter by avoiding Bouchard as much as she could.

Whether alone or relaxing with her new companions, Juliette was free to acknowledge that she actually enjoyed her new life. Roger sent her gifts regularly, many of which had been left with Annette to dole out each day. Juliette felt like a queen. Her gowns were made by the best seamstresses in the district. Jewelry that had belonged in the duDeffand family for centuries hung around her neck.

Anabel insisted that she wear a small beauty spot just below her right eye, and the touch filled Juliette with delight. How wonderful it was to be a woman—a beautiful woman! If the court at Versailles was even better than this, as some of her companions insisted, then maybe marriage to duDeffand would not be as terrible as she had thought. Surely, she decided, she could endure his attentions once in a while, if her reward continued to be so gratifying.

The dresses Hermione had sewn before they left the manor hung neglected in the back of her closet.

Juliette ignored them, choosing, instead, gowns that made her look more mature. When one of the monks came looking for clothing to give to the poor, she had Hermione pull them out. "I won't wear them again." She ignored Bouchard's pained expression and the fact that many of the dresses had never been worn. "They're just going to waste! Bouchy, you've always told me we should think of the poor!"

Bouchard nodded, her eyes still shadowed with hurt. "Yes, Juliette. All of them?"

At the last minute, Juliette relented. Throwing the others aside, she picked up her birthday dress. "Not this one. See if you can work the lace into one of my other gowns. Don't forget I'm not a child anymore."

Her eyes brimming with tears, Bouchard took the dress and left the room. When the others were packed away, Juliette stood gazing at herself in the mirror. It was true, she wasn't a child now.

The ring hanging around her neck caught the light, and the memory of her afternoon with François tumbled back. Not a child? She had been a child then, even though she hadn't thought she was. And now it was time for her to put aside childish things. Her dream of marrying François was no longer possible. In the cruel light of reality, she knew she had to go through with the pledge her father had made to duDeffand. Reluctantly, she took the chain from around her neck. She gazed nostalgically at it for a moment and then dropped it carefully into her jewel box. She couldn't throw it away, as she had the dresses. But she couldn't wear it, either. Her future lay in another direction.

Across the garden from her cottage was the chapel of the abbey. In it, monks went about their daily routines, devoted to prayer and hard labor. Of them all, only her uncle was free of the vows. For him, the Abbey Villeurbanne was a small court, of which he was the center. Everything pivoted around him. He organized hunts in the morning, croquet on the lawn in the afternoon, balls and festivities in the evening. As his niece, and as Roger's affianced, Juliette was in the position of a princess. She never lacked for companionship, nor was she ever allowed to forget that soon she would be the Baroness duDeffand, the mother of Roger's children.

Of the ladies who attended the abbey functions, Juliette found Helene Suison to be particularly interesting. A red-haired firesprite with ivory skin, Helene was the only remaining member of an ancient Lyonnais family. Her estate bordered on that of the abbey, so she didn't bother to live within its protective walls.

Each morning, when Henry de Condillac changed from his priestly robes into his hunting jacket, she was on hand. She stayed all afternoon, frolicking merrily on the lawn in a game of croquet or blindman's buff. When evening came, she usually returned home to dress, and then, resplendent in a new gown, appeared for the evening celebration. Juliette recognized her as the only important competition around. Her fire and enthusiasm inspired everyone to increased enjoyment of what appeared to be an idyllic life.

Two days after her arrival, Juliette was flattered when Helene paused beside her to remark on the beauty of her necklace. By the end of the first week, the two were inseparable companions. Helene always seemed to find something about Juliette worthy of a compliment. If it wasn't a new bauble that brought forth her praise, it was a new hairstyle—or a gown.

Juliette began to seek Helene's little flatteries. She ignored Hermione's warning that such a woman had her reasons for cultivating a young, relatively innocent companion. As far as Juliette was concerned, Helene was above any dissembling. She refused to seek any ulterior motive in Helene's friendly behavior.

June arrived amid a profusion of flowers. In honor of the glorious month, Henry de Condillac declared the first a day of celebration. The entire 24 hours would be spent in play. There would be a hunt and a horse race, followed by contests in croquet, in singing, in every activity requiring the smallest amount of skill.

For Juliette, it was like a second birthday. As soon as she was finished with her breakfast, she called her maids and had them dress her in her riding gown. Of all her new dresses, it was one of her favorites. A golden color, it was from heavy silk threads, with a pattern of green and blue tastefully woven in. The skirt was full in back, with a rather flat area in front that allowed her leg to hang comfortably over the saddle.

Her hat, sewn of the same material, was decked in a magnificent ostrich feather, the green and blue of its plume emphasizing the shades of her gown. She stood admiring her own beauty as her maids put finishing touches on her hair. Then, with a smart crack of her whip against her dress, she was off. Her uncle would be waiting.

As she reached the door, there was a light tap. Helene stood in the hall, flanked by two buxom maids. "Juliette, my dear, please forgive me for surprising you like this. I'd hoped to arrive sooner."

"That's all right!" Juliette, as always, preened under the admiring gaze of her friend. "Can I be of any help to you?"

Helene smiled sweetly. "Yes, if you would be so

kind. In light of your uncle's announcement last night,
I decided to bring my gown and remain here all day.
I'm sure he'd provide me with a changing room if I
asked. But I'd much prefer if I could share yours for
the day. I feel we're almost like sisters.''

Juliette beamed. ''Why, of course.'' She turned to
her maids. ''Annette, Anabel! Hurry. Help Mademoiselle Soison's servants get settled. We're late
for the hunt.'' Linking arms with Helene, Juliette hurried down the hall. Behind her, the voices of the four
women blended into a musical rhythm. She had no
doubt that when they returned, the boxes Helene had
brought would be stowed away.

The hunt was particularly successful. Flushed with
victory, the huntsmen stormed back into the stables,
laughing wildly over the frantic efforts of the fox to
outwit the yelping dogs. Juliette didn't allow herself to
remember that there had been a time when hunting
upset her. Such concerns were fine for children. But
she was a lady now.

Helene returned with Juliette for a short rest before
lunch. When they entered the room, the four maids
rose and stood at attention. Helene waved her hand.
''Go! We won't need you for at least two hours. And
knock when you return. We might be busy.'' The four
women looked knowingly into one another's eyes and
then, silently, left the room.

With a laugh, Helene tossed her hat onto a chair and
sprawled gracefully on the bed. Then, as if on impulse, she rose and removed her gown. Tossing it after
her hat, she slid out of her slips and, clothed only in
her chemise, climbed into bed. ''Resting time,
Juliette.'' She looked into Juliette's face and chuckled. ''Come! We're going to have a big night tonight.
We might as well get some sleep.''

Juliette removed her dress and hung it carefully in

the closet. Her slips she spread out on a chair. When she turned toward the bed, she was startled to see Helene propped up on a pillow, her eyes bright, a strange flush on her cheeks.

Suddenly embarrassed, Juliette stood looking at her friend. Never before had she felt uncomfortable undressing in the presence of a woman. But Helene was different. Her mouth was partially open, and her tongue moved restlessly around her lips. Her eyes seemed to burn holes in Juliette's thin chemise.

"Take it off!" Helene's voice was husky.

Juliette stared at her in surprise.

"Take it off. Look. I've slipped out of mine!" Helene dropped the blanket, exposing a white body almost as perfect as Juliette's.

Juliette hesitated. Then, with a sudden motion, she slipped the straps from her shoulders and let her last protection drop to the floor. With an uneasy excitement, she moved toward the bed.

Helene threw back the covers. "Lie down, little goose! I'm not going to hurt you!"

Sitting gingerly on the edge of the bed, Juliette waited for her blush to subside. Helene was right, of course! Why was she being so foolish? Carefully avoiding the eager eyes of her companion, Juliette lifted her legs onto the bed and lay quietly, her body tense. When Helene didn't move, she turned and gazed at her face. Helene's eyes were coals of fire, and her mouth worked sensuously. Suddenly, Juliette wished she were still safely dressed and sitting on a chair.

"Relax, little sister." Helene's voice was still husky. "I promise I won't hurt you!"

Juliette didn't answer. She lay with her legs pressed close together. She could feel a trembling beginning in her abdomen, and its presence increased her feeling of panic. What was happening? Why was Helene acting so strangely?

Helene smiled, and suddenly the tension was gone. "What's the matter, little goose? Are you so virginal you haven't even felt the thrill of your own hand?"

Juliette felt herself growing red. Sometimes, in the privacy of her own bed, she had enjoyed her own touch on her private parts. But never had she thought of speaking of her acts to others!

Helene kicked the covers down to the foot of the bed. The two girls lay side by side, two white, firm feminine bodies. Despite her uneasiness, Juliette felt suddenly curious. She had never seen another naked woman before.

Helen brought her fingers down to the mound of red hair that crowned her thighs. "Look if you like. You really ought to know more about other women. We all react very much the same." With a quick movement her thighs parted, and Juliette was staring at the moist curly ringlets and the pink convolutions of flesh beneath them. Helene's fingers began to move. "Come, you do it, too. It's fun when two women do it together."

Juliette stirred uneasily. This wasn't something two friends should do together! Before she could move away, she felt Helene's hand on her nearer leg. A finger came perilously close to Juliette's private parts.

Still working her finger on her own body, Helene smiled languorously. "Come on! Look! We're very much alike!"

Blushing, Juliette let her leg be pulled to the side. She didn't want to follow Helene's directions, but she lacked the strength to say no to her older companion. She was incapable of resisting. The hand on her thigh was burning like a hot coal.

Slowly it moved up, slipping gently to the inside of

the leg until, with a motion that seemed directed from afar, it came to rest just below the dark curls. Then, suddenly, it was removed. Helene leaned forward, her face close to Juliette's breast. "You've a beautiful body, Juliette. You'll give Roger some happy moments."

Juliette didn't answer. Somehow, she knew Helene's thoughts weren't on Roger at all. Certainly her own were not. She was trembling again, and her thigh still felt as if Helene's hand rested on it.

Most of all, Juliette felt a rising panic. This was wrong! "Helene"—her voice trembled—"what are you doing?"

Helene ignored her question. Taking Juliette's hand in hers, she lifted it from the bed and moved it upward until it rested on the white firm skin. "Look, Juliette"—her voice was soft—"my breasts are almost as firm as yours. Feel them." Juliette felt her fingers touch the soft mound nearest her and then Helene's hand was over hers, pressing it close.

A weakness invaded Juliette's limbs. She wanted to pull away, wanted to jump from the bed. But somehow she couldn't move. In that instant of indecision, Helene lifted up and, with a sudden lunge, positioned herself face down over Juliette's body. Her legs pushed between the tight thighs. Then, with a sigh, she pressed her most intimate parts firmly over Juliette's. Her long red hair trailed over the pillow. Their lips met.

Juliette lay absolutely still, unable to believe what was happening to her. But when Helene began to grind her hips in an ever more demanding circle, Juliette suddenly came to life. Crying out, she pushed with both hands at the face above her.

Caught by surprise, Helene fell to her side. In that

instant, Juliette was on her feet. Ripping her chemise from the chair, she pulled it over her nakedness. Her eyes flashed in anger. "Go away! Leave me alone!"

Helene sat up. "Come now, Juliette. Don't be provincial! There's nothing wrong with two women sharing a bit of pleasure! Everyone at court who's at all sophisticated does it! Why, watching two women together is one of Roger's favorite sports! I've put on more than one show for him when he visited the abbey. On his way to India, just a few weeks ago, he enjoyed a whole afternoon of entertainment with me and some of my friends!" Her face hardened. "Don't be a fool! You won't keep Roger's interest very long if you play the prude!"

Juliette was trembling. She wasn't certain she could control the tears that welled in her eyes. "I don't care! I don't want to marry Roger, anyway!" She was moving now, frantically pulling on the slips she had abandoned. She had to get dressed. She had to stop those eyes from burning into her body.

Helene shrugged carelessly and rose to her feet. "As you will! I can't imagine why Roger, of all people, would choose an ignoramus like you for a wife!" Still moving seductively, she pulled on her chemise. "I guess he really does mean to keep you for breeding stock."

Juliette's jaw tightened. "I don't care what Roger plans for me. I have plans of my own. And I don't want this!" She felt the tears come, but she was too upset to stop them. "I don't want this sort of thing at all!" Sobbing, she threw herself down on the bed. Behind her, she could hear Helene moving about. Then, finally, the door opened and closed.

Holding her fingers before her face, Juliette peeked around the room. Helene was gone. She was alone. Impulsively, she rose and ran to her jewelry case. Gently, she removed the ring François had given her. She needed it now. As she fastened it around her neck, she jerked the bellpull that hung at the far end of the room that summoned Hermione. She hadn't bothered with it for weeks, but she wanted her nurse now. More than anything, she wanted a hot bath. Maybe that would wash the memory of Helene's burning fingers from her body.

CHAPTER SIX

There was no hunt on the day following the ball, but the next morning, bright and early, everyone appeared dressed for the ride, in answer to the call of Henry's horn. Henry, dressed in a new red outfit made especially for the occasion, greeted each new arrival and then turned his attention back to his immediate favorite, a dainty blonde girl who, Helene informed Juliette, came from Germany.

Helene seemed determined to regain Juliette's confidence—and friendship. She had not returned to her estate, though she had moved to another apartment in the cottage. When they mounted, she insisted that they ride side by side, though Juliette would have preferred otherwise. She even showed a willingness to restrict her repartee, so Juliette couldn't complain that she was being secretly reproached for what had been, in any terms, an open rejection. Juliette felt no desire to discuss that terrible afternoon. The farther into the back of her mind she could push it, the happier she would be. When Helene showed the same reluctance to mention what had happened, she felt a great relief. Maybe she wouldn't have to hurry away quite as quickly as she had first thought.

Immediately, as if to reassure herself that she hadn't weakened in her resolve, Juliette brought her hand up to her neck. Beneath the heavy brocade of her riding dress, she felt the hardness of François ring. She wouldn't be foolish enough to take it off again.

Helene glanced slyly in Juliette's direction. "What do you have there, Juliette?"

Juliette grasped the reins with both hands. "Nothing! It's nothing!"

The horn was sounding again, and the hounds were being released. Conversation could wait until later.

Juliette felt a surge of pleasure as her horse sprang into action. Leaning forward, she urged him on until she was up beside her uncle. Side by side, they bounded over the small fence that edged the stables and then, in a mass, the riders moved down the road after the yapping dogs.

Juliette was familiar with the path. Henry had long ago decreed that the hunts should take place on public land so as to avoid damage to the monastery grapes. With whoops of delight, the riders spurred their horses past the vineyards to a fork in the road. To the left lay Lyon. To the right, the Soison estates. Henry crossed the road, leaped the fence, and thundered across the open fields.

Juliette galloped close behind. Then, with much laughing and calling out, the others followed. Recklessly, they rode through the few remaining plants that had weathered their earlier assaults. No one, including Juliette, looked down at the ground as they passed.

As they careened toward another fence, Juliette glanced back at the other riders. Their faces, like hers, were flushed with the excitement of the chase. With a pull on her reins, she urged her horse over the railing that separated two fields. This time they were in new territory. Tall stalks brushed against her legs and she pulled them up in annoyance.

The discomfort didn't last. Another fence was be-

SO WILD A RAPTURE   87

hind them, and the fox was in view. The kill came quickly.

The dead fox held triumphantly aloft, the hunters turned their horses toward the abbey. Still flushed from the run, Juliette leaned across her saddle toward Helene. "Great hunt, wasn't it?"

"The best! I swear, your uncle must have his foxes trained to run a good chase." She leaned forward and quieted her horse with a gentle pat. Then, suddenly, her voice rose. "Say, everyone! Listen! I have an idea." She waited as the riders settled their mounts and stopped their voices. "We're close to my estate, and most of you've never seen it! Instead of riding back to the abbey right away, let's take a detour. I have some very special wine cooled and waiting to be tasted."

Juliette's first reaction was to refuse. It was another ploy the woman was using simply to reestablish herself as a harmless companion. But Helene wasn't looking at Juliette. Her eyes were sweeping the entire group, searching for assent to her invitation.

Henry was the first to agree. "Great idea!" His voice was hearty. "I happen to know that Helene has more than just good wine to offer. She has one of the best mazes in all of southern France." He glanced at his young companion, and Juliette realized with a shock that he anticipated losing himself and his friend in the circuitous hedges.

Once the abbé showed his interest in Helene's offer, none of the others dared refuse. Even Juliette, reluctant as she was to spend additional time with Helene, had to consent to accompany the others. Still, she determined under no circumstances to permit herself to be enticed into the garden.

With a shout, Helene pulled her horse to the right.

She was off with a leap, racing over the fields as if the fox still was loose. Cheering loudly, the others followed. The wind blew Juliette's hair over her face as she swerved to avoid a pig that was wandering through the field, and then she was off again. Over hill and vale the huntsmen galloped until, at last, Helene signaled a stop.

"You've got to see the old place before you hurry into the stables. It really is quite a magnificent old home! Built by my grandfather, I believe." She laughed. "But truly enjoyed, for the only time in history, by me!" She dug her heel into her horse's flank and sedately led the way up the hill.

At the crest she stopped, a cry of alarm on her lips. Juliette, riding close behind, could not repress a gasp of surprise. No tall, stately building stood before them, nestled beneath the trees. Black fingers of burned wood reached up from the ground where the house had stood. Ashes lay where chimneys had been. Facing them stood a stone staircase, leading to a narrow shelf of blackened wood.

"They did it! They actually did it!" Helene's voice was heavy, as if she were speaking in a dream. She didn't move as the others rushed past her to form a half circle in front of the cold ashes.

Juliette moved up with them, and then, with a sudden rush of pity for Helene, pulled her mount back. "Helene, who are they? What do you mean, they actually did it?"

Helene didn't respond. A gurgling sound tore its way through her throat and she sagged in her saddle.

"Help!" Juliette reached for the falling woman. "Help! Helene's fainting!"

They were back immediately. Strong arms lifted Helene from her saddle and laid her gently on the ground. When she opened her eyes, they were filled with bewilderment. Twisting her body, she stared at the ruins.

Juliette felt a surge of compassion. Brittle and sophisticated as Helene seemed to be, she had a softer side. Juliette stared at the pale face. It gave her no comfort to see the strong face broken and confused.

"It really was very beautiful!" Helene's voice was hoarse. "And all—all— It's all gone. How could they?"

One by one the riders mounted their horses and rode away. There was nothing for them to do. Nothing remained. The barns were open and empty. The farmyard held no lowing cows or squealing pigs. An unholy quiet hung over the burned remains of the mansion.

The wind stirred, blowing the acrid odor of smoke into Juliette's nostrils. With a feeling of overwhelming depression, she let her eyes wander over the desolation. Even the leaves above the remains of the house were charred from heat and smoke. Had the house remained aflame much longer, the woods, too, would have been ablaze.

Helene sat up and Henry de Condillac rose to his feet. Juliette looked helplessly into his face. "Why would anyone do something as terrible as this? What did they have against Helene?"

The abbé shook his head. "My dear, innocent little niece, didn't you see what was going on as you came down from Chalon? The whole country is in turmoil. These peasants had nothing against Helene except that her house held the feudal lists by which taxation is determined. They've lost all perspective. They lash out in anger in an attempt to free themselves from a life God has decreed to be theirs. I have no doubt as to what lies ahead. The Lord will smite them with a bitter sword! They can't disobey the will of God without being punished.''

Juliette felt momentarily confused. She looked down at Helene. The red head bobbed gently below her. Startled, she bent down, her face level with the wild eyes of her friend. Helene paid no attention to her movement. In a voice that bore little resemblance to her usual tone, she was singing a song. Juliette listened carefully, straining to hear the words. *"Sur le pont, d'Avignon———"*

''Helene!'' Despite her desire to remain calm, a tremor crept into Juliette's voice. ''Helene!''

The song stopped. Her eyes blank, Helene gazed into Juliette's face. Then, with a tiny smile, she returned to her singing.

Juliette looked up at Henry. ''Uncle! What'll we do? What's happened to Helene?''

Henry crouched beside Juliette. ''Her mind has broken. The shock.'' He reached out and took Helene's hand. It lay still in his, as if she had lost the power to move. His voice grew gentle. ''Have you any place to go, child?'' Helene went on with her song.

He rose to his feet. ''Juliette, can you watch her for a while? I'll be back for you both. I don't believe she should be asked to ride.'' He moved toward his waiting horse. ''I'll bring a carriage.''

Juliette stared at her uncle and then down at Helene. ''Will she stay quiet?''

''I don't know. Probably. She's had quite a shock.'' He swung into the saddle. ''Try not to let her wander too far if she becomes active. I'll be back here in less than a half hour.''

He was gone before Juliette had a chance to protest.

It wasn't that she was afraid of Helene any longer. There was nothing left in the blank, childlike face to frighten her. What Juliette feared was a return of the rioters.

Nervously, she gazed about. Were they hiding? Would they now leap out and kill both Helene and her? A soft, whispering sound brought her around, her eyes wide. There was nothing behind her but a few bushes moving gently in the wind.

Abruptly, Helene rose to her feet. Stumbling over the bits of rock and burned wood that littered the driveway, she approached the charred remains of her home. Juliette extended a hand to hold her back.

She tried to pull away when her fingers were grasped in a firm grip. Had Helene been pretending? Was her act of being overcome by shock just her way of getting Juliette alone once more?

Prepared to fight, Juliette looked directly into Helene's eyes. She was met by a clear, childlike stare. "Let's play hide and seek!" Helene's voice was high-pitched, lacking in any subleties.

Startled, Juliette shook her head. "No! Please, let's just stay here and wait for the abbé."

"There isn't anything for us to do here! I don't want to stay here! I want to go home!" Helene's voice grew frantic.

Nervously, Juliette strengthened her grip on Helene's fingers. She was frightened enough at remaining alone in the middle of the destruction. She certainly didn't want to chase a childlike woman around the ghost of her burned-out home.

Suddenly, her face brightened. "Helene, let's start walking to the abbey. I think I hear someone calling us!"

Helene giggled, holding her fingers loosely before

her mouth. "You're funny! You can't hear people at the abbey from here!" Once more her expression changed. "But you can see it from the top of the hill!"

Juliette had a sudden picture of herself, laughing and teasing with François. Had he been as frustrated by her foolishness as she now felt with Helene's infantile behavior? Maybe he had. At least, up until the last time they were together. That time, she had finally stopped acting like a child.

Unconsciously, her hand went to the ring. It had pulled out from under her dress and was hanging in plain sight. When she touched it, Helene looked up. Her hand went out and touched the bauble. "Pretty!"

She held it up, bending down to gaze directly at the design. Then, suddenly, it fell from her hand. With a cry, she was running down the road toward the abbey. "You're one of them! I've seen that before! You're one of them!"

Startled, Juliette sprang into action. Leaping on her horse, she set off in pursuit.

When Helene saw her coming, she swerved into a dry field and stumbled when her foot landed on a hard clod of dirt. Then she fell to the ground. Quickly, Juliette dismounted. Tying her reins to the broken fence, she climbed into the field. "Helene, please don't run away! I won't hurt you!"

Helene tried to regain her balance as Juliette approached. She rose, swaying perilously. Her first step was steady and then, with a cry of despair, she rolled back onto the ground. When Juliette reached her, she was weeping helplessly.

Juliette stood over her until the carriage arrived. Helene had begun to sing again, but this time the tune was one Juliette didn't recognize.

The two men who arrived in the carriage hardly

looked at Juliette, though she greeted them with obvious relief. One of them was Jacque, a regular at Henry's affairs. The other was a stranger.

Jacque bent down and lifted Helene in his arms. "I'm glad you were able to keep her near the road." His eyes refused to meet Juliette's, and she felt apprehensive. Suddenly, he turned to his companion. "Andre, why don't you walk up and get Helene's horse. No point in letting it run."

Without answering, Andre strode up the hill. Juliette stared at him, aware that things weren't right, even in the carriage that had come to rescue her. There was no coachman or lackey. Jacque was driving the horses like a common servant. She turned to Jacque. "What's happened? Where's my uncle? I thought he was——"

"Juliette, please! Helene's house isn't the only one that's burned."

Now a new terror gripped Juliette's heart. Not the only fire? Had her little cottage been destroyed while the hunt was on? And did Bouchy lie dead among the ashes?

She released the reins of her horse from the fence and leaped into the saddle. Immediately, Jacque's hand was on the bridle. "Juliette, where are you going?"

She pulled her horse free. "Where should I go? To the abbey, of course!" Bending forward, she urged her horse to a gallop. In her mind was a vision of her nurse lying dead in the rubble of a blackened cottage.

CHAPTER SEVEN

When Juliette reached the fork in the road, she swerved quickly, turning her horse toward the billowing black cloud that had already darkened most of the sky. As she slowed down, she realized the vineyards were uprooted as far as she could see. The peasants had taken their revenge on everything that belonged to the abbey.

For the first time since her arrival, Juliette thought about what she had been doing. Each day on the hunt, she had thundered through someone else's fields. Still, it hurt to think of plants being deliberately destroyed. Averting her gaze from the drying vines, she hurried up the hill.

She was so certain Bouchy was dead that she didn't respond when her nurse hurried toward her. But Hermione blocked her passage, her hands upraised. Quickly, Juliette leaped to the ground. "It's all right! I'm so glad you're alive! We can replace everything else!"

Hermione's hands were shaking. Tears coursed down the pale, wrinkled cheeks. "Oh, Juliette! My dear baby!" She began to moan, rocking her body back and forth like a mourner at a funeral.

Impatiently, Juliette pulled away from her outstretched arms. "Hermione Bouchard! Stop it! Crying doesn't help!"

But Hermione made no attempt to restrain her weeping. She waved one arm in the direction of the house. Then, with a loud cry, she buried her face in her hands.

Not knowing what to do with her maid, Juliette hurried toward the flaming building. She came to a halt when she almost stumbled over a gray robe that lay on the grass. She glanced down impatiently—and then dropped to her knees. The robe covered a body—a body dressed in a red suit.

"Uncle! My God! What happened?" She stared up. "How could he be dead? He was fine when he left me with Helene!"

A man she didn't know knelt beside her. Gently, he took her shoulders and pulled her to her feet. "It's best you not look at his face." The voice was deep. "He was badly burned. He died trying to save your two maids."

"Annette? Anabel?" Juliette looked about as if she expected to see them.

"They were killed in the fire, too." The voice was gentle. "We heard them scream as we came up the hill. Before any of us could think what to do, the abbé was off his horse. He ran into the fire, screaming for them to wait." The man lowered his gaze to the corpse. "But we could tell it was too late. They'd been at a window, shouting as we came up the hill. But long before he reached the door, they'd fallen inside. The heat—it was unimaginable!"

Juliette looked at the smoldering ruins. There was little left in the cottage to burn, though the smoke continued to rise, dark and ominous against the morning sky. She wondered dully if the fire had been an attack against duDeffand, who owned the building, or the abbé. It didn't matter, of course. Whoever the peasants were trying to hurt, they had succeeded in killing her uncle.

She looked up, suddenly aware that she was almost alone. Hermione stood a distance away. There were two men beside Henry de Condillac's body. All the others were gone. None of the huntsmen had made any attempt to put out the fire. They had abandoned their host the first time he needed them.

Hermione stumbled across the lawn and knelt beside the corpse. Her lips moved steadily; her fingers flew swiftly over the beads of her rosary.

Juliette crossed herself. What had she been thinking? He was her uncle! She couldn't leave him lying on the ground like an animal. She looked at the two remaining hunters. "Help me! We have to carry him into the abbey."

The men didn't immediately respond. Her fingers tightened into fists. "Please, do as I say! We can't leave him here!"

Slowly, they bent and lifted the body into their arms, carefully shifting the robe so the face couldn't be seen. Hermione rose, her rosary dangling in her hands.

The two men stood, staring dully toward the chapel. Then the one who had spoken before turned. "Most of the monks are gone. They must have run off when the rioters came. I don't know if there are any left."

Juliette stared across the garden. She had to summon the monks, if there were any, to come and assist her. She shouted once, but there was no response. Then she remembered that her uncle had called his followers to worship with an old bell. It stood now half buried in the ashes.

As she approached it, her feet stirred up the dust.

The acrid odor of burned wood and flesh filled her nostrils. Momentarily she paused. This was no time for her to get sick. When she recovered, she lifted the knocker and swung it firmly.

In response to the bell, a door opened at the side of the chapel. Five monks emerged, grouped together as if for self-defense. They stood at the door for a moment, gazing at the devastated garden.

Juliette's companions had already begun to move. She watched with a strange feeling of detachment, as if she were observing a morality play. The body of her uncle hung loosely between the two men, one arm dragging along the ground. There was something bizarre about the brightness of his sleeve, as if he had forgotten to put on the proper costume for the performance.

Now the monks left the shelter of the chapel, like the chorus in a theater, moving slowly toward the gaudily dressed hunters. All five had their hoods up, as if to protect themselves from the brightness of the sun, and their hands were tucked into their sleeves. She had seen drawings of death that looked as they did. Involuntarily, she shuddered.

The scene before her reached its conclusion. The two groups of actors met and stood, for a moment, facing each other. Then they merged, and the hunters were lost in a cloud of gray. Now, at last, the chant began. Deliberately, the five monks separated themselves from the hunters, but now the body of her uncle was held aloft, like the corpse of a hero returned from the wars. His robe had been slipped over his brilliant riding suit, its hood pulled down over his head so that, even now, his face wasn't visible.

As the chanting monks vanished through the narrow doorway, one arm slipped from its resting place on her uncle's chest. It flopped down, the red sleeve flashing in the sunlight, as if he were waving a final farewell. Then he was gone. The play was ended.

The two men who had borne the corpse turned and walked back to where Juliette waited. Hermione, who had paused during the transfer of the body, knelt on the grass. Her face turned toward the cold walls of the chapel, she silently continued her prayers.

When the men reached her side, Juliette tore her gaze from the heavy wooden door that had swallowed the body of her uncle. She took a step forward, and then her arms fell helplessly to her sides. There was nothing she could do inside those forbidding walls.

She mumbled a prayer and crossed herself again. There was something more she had to do. Her eyes rested on Hermione and then flitted across the garden to the rubble that had been her home. That was it! She had to decide where she was going. Even if she was welcome at the chapel, she didn't want to stay.

A rattling drew her eyes to the road. At last, Jacque was returning with the carriage! Then, dully, she realized there was no help to be found in its dark recesses. It carried more problems—but no solutions.

She stood idly staring at its approach. First the horses appeared, pulling firmly as they mounted the steep hill. Then the top of the dark carriage came into view. Sitting in the coachman's seat was Jacque, his bright riding habit looking like some exotic livery. Now the full carriage was in view, and Juliette could see Andre sitting near the window, his arm around Helene. Her horse trotted behind, its stirrup flopping loosely at its side. It whinnied as it approached, and its call was taken up by the other horses that wandered about, munching on flowers.

Jacque pulled the team to a halt and leaped to the

ground. He reached Juliette's side and took her by the arm. "Are you all right?"

She stared at him blankly. Was she all right? How could she answer that question? "I— I'm fine. I mean—" Jacque nodded, and she let her voice trail into silence.

Helene leaned through the carriage door. Andre was helping her out. At the sight of the pale face, Juliette felt her spirits rise. Something in Helene's face was different. She looked brighter—as if some of the shock had passed.

Juliette stepped toward the carriage. "Helene! I'm so glad you're better!"

Helene turned slowly. "Oh, Juliette! How pleasant to see you again!" She paused dramatically, a small smile on her face. "I've been thinking, my dear. I'm bored with hunting. I do believe I'd like to visit my cousin. You know my cousin, don't you?"

Juliette nodded. This was no time to ask for long explanations. "Does he—your cousin live nearby?"

Helene nodded. "Yes, he lives in Lyon! He keeps pestering me to visit. Well, I think I'll go!" She turned toward Jacque, no sign of recognition on her face. "Coachman! Come along! You've had a long-enough rest! It's time we go! My cousin is expecting me!"

Jacque turned to Juliette. "She's better—but far from well." He didn't move toward the carriage. "I might as well go. It isn't too long a ride to Lyon, only about five hours, and if she has a cousin there, that's where she belongs. Where are you going? I don't imagine you want to stay in the abbey."

She shook her head. "No. I suppose the monks would let me, if I wanted to. But I can't. Not after—this."

Jacque turned toward the two men who had moved Henry's body. "George, Jean, where are you off to?" He turned back to Juliette. "You might go with one of them, if they live nearby."

George had already mounted his horse. "I'm heading for Avignon. If I leave now, I might get past the dangerous area before nightfall." He looked down at Juliette. "You're welcome to come with me, but I warn you, I must ride hard."

Juliette shook her head. "No, thank you. I have to get back to Chalon. I'm sure that's where Roger will expect me to go."

Jean took her hand and kissed it. "I go the wrong way too, then. My home is due east, about twenty miles past the Soison estate. If I'm lucky, I'll find it still standing."

Andre had left Helene's side and mounted his horse. "George! I'll ride by your side. I, too, live near Avignon. If we go due south from here, we'll cut some hours from the journey." He looked down at Juliette. "You're sure you won't come?"

Juliette shook her head. "No. I have Hermione to think of. She can't travel too fast."

The three men left then, racing down the hill as if their lives depended on their speed. Juliette wondered if they would have difficulty on their journeys. Probably not. Surely the rioters had had enough carnage for one day.

Jacque touched her arm. "I'll wait. You can ride to Lyon with Helene."

But when Juliette approached the carriage, Helene pointed at her throat and began to scream. "She's one of them. I saw! Coachman! Come! Quickly! We must escape before she kills us, too."

Juliette touched the ring. Suddenly, she didn't want

to be near Helene again. She turned to Jacque. "Go ahead, please. If necessary, I'll stay in the chapel tonight. Don't worry. We'll be all right."

Jacque climbed to his seat. The whip cracked and the horses moved away. Just before he disappeared behind the hill, he turned. "Get the monks to go with you when you leave. Don't travel alone, whatever you do!"

The task of finding the bodies of the two maids was assumed by the monks. Juliette and Hermione watched helplessly as the five hooded figures sifted through the rubble. For Juliette, the ordeal was frightening. Her imagination filled in what she hadn't seen. Hermione refused to look. She kept her eyes lowered, fastened on the rosary she continued to hold.

When the monks located the bodies, Juliette resisted the impulse to rush to their assistance. She waited as they lifted the remains onto a board, and then found she could not look as they passed her on their way to the chapel. When they were out of sight behind the wall of the small cemetery, she led Hermione into the place of worship.

They prayed first for her uncle. Then, with tears streaming down her cheeks, Juliette prayed for Anabel and Annette. When she was finished, she said one more prayer. She begged for guidance in finding François.

In the sunshine again, she took Bouchard's hand. "Bouchy, is there another carriage in the stables?"

Bouchard shook her head. "No. They were burned, too. Didn't you see? They would have burned the chapel if it hadn't been made of stone!"

Juliette looked into the frightened eyes. "How did you escape?"

"I hid in the cemetery. I tried to get Annette and Anabel to come with me, but they insisted they were safer from the rioters in the building." Her voice broke. "It was terrible! They were calling for help, and I could do nothing."

"Thank God you didn't try. You'd have been killed, too, and then I would have been all alone." Juliette stared at her horse. "Bouchy, can you ride?"

Bouchard nodded, her round chins shaking. "Not well. But I can stay on."

Juliette took Bouchard's hand and led the way to a low wall. "Good. My horse is strong enough to carry us both. It's early enough so we can make Lyon before dark. Let's go, Bouchy. I don't want to stay here. We can get a carriage when we reach Lyon. I want to go home."

When they were safely mounted, she turned the horse toward the road. There was no need to say farewell to the monks. She had hardly seen any of them during her entire stay.

Just before the horse turned on the road to Lyon, Juliette looked back at the stone chapel. She had thought the abbey was safe, that in the court society she was protected from the dangers that surrounded her. Now she knew she had been wrong. Her uncle had not been strong enough to save himself and his abbey from destruction.

Now she had to find François. He would help her reach Chalon. In her need to find him, she refused to face the one question that remained unanswered. She had told him where she was going. Why, in the month she had been at the abbey, had he made no attempt to seek her out?

CHAPTER EIGHT

"Bouchy! Hold onto the reins! Don't let him get too close to the underbrush!" Juliette felt suddenly uneasy. They had been moving slowly, the horse picking his way carefully over the ruts in the road. But they were approaching a heavily forested area, and the sight of the thick trees filled Juliette with fear. This would be a perfect place for the rioters to hide.

She looked apprehensively at the sky. They'd been traveling for some time, but she was suddenly aware that they'd covered very little distance. She hadn't noticed the passage of time. Her thoughts had been on the past, and on how fortunate she was to have Bouchard alive and with her still.

Bouchard tugged at the reins, but the horse paid no heed. He whinnied nervously, moving closer to the left of the road with each step. They reached a turn. Ten yards ahead, Juliette saw what had startled the animal. A coach stood in the ruts in the center of the road. It was abandoned. No horses pawed the ground before it, and no coachman sat high above the roof. An unearthly silence surrounded the vehicle. She recognized it immediately.

There was little doubt what had happened. Jacque and Helene had been waylaid. A log lay stretched across the road blocking the front wheels. The horses must have cleared it with ease. Maybe Jacque hadn't even noticed it in his hurry to reach Lyon.

The impact of the front wheels against the log had

broken them, and the carriage must have stopped abruptly. Jacque had been thrown forward with tremendous force. His body had landed crossways on the sharp ornamental decorations that marked all of the abbey carriages, and one of them had cut through his neck, severing it completely. His head had rolled forward, like a ball. It lay in the center of the road, its eyes wide and frightened.

With a cry of horror, Juliette was on her feet. "Bouchy! Wait for me up ahead. You mustn't look at this!"

But Bouchard had already begun to slip from the saddle. She landed on the ground with a thud, her legs buckling beneath her. Her face was white, and her eyes were wide with fear.

Juliette followed her gaze. At first she couldn't believe what she saw. It looked as if a life-sized rag doll had been draped over the floor of the carriage, its skirts pulled up to expose bare legs to the afternoon sun. Hermione reached up and pulled at Juliette's dress. "Don't go near her! You're too young to see——"

Despite her fear, Juliette began to laugh hysterically. "Bouchy, don't! We can't both be protected. I know what's happened. She's been raped."

Bouchard nodded. She was breathing heavily, and her skin was a bright red. For a moment, Juliette looked down at the frightened face. Then, pulling loose, she walked toward the carriage. She moved slowly. Fear had robbed her of her strength. She felt certain that at any moment the attack would be renewed and that this time she would be the victim. But she had no control over her actions. She felt compelled to approach the fearful sight. She couldn't leave Helene so terribly exposed.

Swiftly, she reached into the carriage and grasped cloth. Tugging frantically, she brought slip after slip down over the white legs. When she covered the top slip with the skirt, she began to tremble. Helene's eyes were wide open, staring directly into her face.

"Helene!" Her voice shook. There was no answer. Timidly, Juliette touched the pasty skin. It was firm in a way live flesh never is. Her hand jerked back and she crossed herself nervously. Then overcome by weakness, she leaned against the coach door. She had never looked directly into the face of death before.

A bird chirped overhead. Gradually, she became aware of crickets singing loudly in the bushes. Yet, despite the sounds of nature, she felt an unholy hush around her.

She glanced forward, and her eyes fell once more on Jacque's head. Her stomach convulsed.

As she regained her control, she glanced toward her mount. Something was the matter with Bouchard. Never, in Juliette's entire life, had she been sick without having her nurse hurry to her side.

She stood up with a cry of alarm. "Bouchy! What's the matter? Are you ill?" Her own sickness forgotten, she rushed to her nurse's side. Bouchard's heavy body lay in a heap, like a bag that had been dropped to the ground. Her head drooped to one side, its mouth hanging open grotesquely. Gently, Juliette settled beside her, her arms supporting the sagging body.

"Bouchy, speak to me! Please!" Panic directed her words—and her actions. Roughly, she shook the unresisting shoulders. Suddenly, the eyes popped open. With a sigh of relief, Juliette kissed the sagging cheeks. "Oh, Bouchy, thank God!"

Bouchard's mouth closed convulsively. Then, slowly, it opened again. She was gasping for breath.

Helplessly, Juliette held the pale face against her breasts. Hermione's hand came up, as if to give a blessing, and then, silently, it fell to the ground.

Terrified, Juliette bent low, her ear pressed against her nurse's matronly chest. She could hear nothing. The steady heartbeat that had comforted her so often when, as a child, she had come to Bouchard with her sorrows, was still.

Frantically, Juliette pulled at the unresisting hands. "No! Bouchy, don't die! You can't leave me now!" Letting the body drop to the ground, she rose to her knees. "Dear God, please don't take her from me! Can't you see how much I need her?"

The crickets chirped rhythmically. A nightingale began to sing loudly above her head. Slowly, Juliette let her hands fall to her sides. She was alone, terribly alone. Even God had deserted her!

Rising, she looked about, carefully avoiding the terrible head that stared at her from the road. She wanted to bury them all. How could she leave them as they were, spread out over the road for the vultures to claim? But as she contemplated the task, she knew it was beyond her. Even if she could dig three holes, she would never be able to move the bodies. Hermione was too heavy. And Jacque— She felt her stomach turn again and brushed the thought from her mind.

Once more she bent over Bouchard. Maybe she had been wrong. Maybe Hermione wasn't dead after all! Maybe she had just fainted.

Gently, she took the gray head into her arms and began to rock back and forth. At first she moved silently. Then, slowly, she began to hum. Soon she was singing a lullaby, crooning softly, as Hermione had so often done in the past. She lost her awareness of the dirt in which she sat. She even forgot the horror that lay in front of the carriage and the brutalized body that lay within.

When the song ended, she bent down once more and listened for some sound of breathing, for the faintest hint that the faithful heart still beat. There was nothing. Hermione lay as dead as the two who had been direct victims of the rioters.

Trembling, Juliette rose to her feet. She stood gazing down at the soft, still face and then, impulsively, she bent down and closed the open eyes. Tugging the dark cape from around the dead shoulders, she pulled it up to cover the face.

She knelt once·more, this time with her rosary in her hands. Her first prayers were for Hermione. Then, quickly, she repeated one for each of the other victims. She was beginning to feel uneasy again. The sun was dropping lower in the sky, and the shadows made by the trees and bushes were darkening. She couldn't remain much longer.

She stood up and turned toward her mount. Then, quickly, she ran back to the carriage. Climbing lightly over the still form, she pulled the eyelids down over the wide eyes. She was breathing heavily when she returned to where Bouchard lay.

Again, she stared down at the ponderous body. "Good-bye, Bouchy. I'll never forget you." Her voice broke. "Oh, Bouchy, I'll miss you so!" She bent down and planted a kiss on the still cheek. Then, with tears streaming from her eyes, she leaped into the saddle.

She didn't look down as she passed the body of Jacque. The sight was too horrible. The thought came as she pulled the reins and returned to the center of the road. Her voice frightened her when she spoke. "I should have closed Jacque's eyes, too." But she knew she couldn't possibly have touched that frightful head. As it was, it would haunt her dreams—and her waking thoughts—for many years to come.

There was nothing now to slow Juliette's progress. Leaning forward in the saddle, she spurred her horse, her eyes sweeping the landscape for signs of danger. The horse's hoofs pounded loudly on the hard dirt road. The sun was far too low for comfort. Anxiously, she stared up at the sky. An hour, maybe a little more, and darkness would be upon her. She tried frantically to determine how many miles she had already traveled. One? Ten? She didn't know.

"Faster!" She leaned toward the horse's ears. "Faster!"

The rhythm of the hoofbeats increased. Again, she looked at the darkening sky. Would she make it in time? She dared not look behind her. The demon of terror was close on her heels, grasping at her skirt as it flapped in the wind. "Dear God"—her prayer came from her heart—"if I get to Lyon safely, I'll never doubt you again!"

The wind rustled through the dry fields, rattling the brittle leaves. A low-hanging branch tugged at her hair as she passed. Gasping, she lay closer to the horse's strong neck.

The long evening shadows stretched across the road, hiding ruts that had been visible in the afternoon light. Juliette's horse stumbled, but she held on tightly until he regained his balance. Time was running out.

The dying sun loomed red on the horizon, its blood flowing over the helpless clouds. The sight sent a shiver of fear through her. Was it an omen? Juliette tried to swallow. Her throat was parched, her lips stuck together. Had she seen help in the distance, she wouldn't have been able to call out.

Then she saw the town, a faint speck on the horizon, a few wisps of smoke spiraling their way into the red sky. She jabbed her heels into the horse's side and he sprang forward. She would make it after all! She was almost there!

Suddenly, a figure detached itself from the darkness that edged the road. Juliette felt a sob catch in her throat. So close! Why did they have to catch her when she was so close!

As she neared the figure, her fear vanished. It wasn't a rioter, after all! It was only a woman. A woman, alone, asking for help. A feeling of faintness threatened to overcome her, but she held tight to the reins, deliberately pulling her horse to a stop. She was beside the woman now, and the thin arms reached up pleadingly. "Help me! My baby's sick!"

Without pausing to think, Juliette slipped from her saddle. "Where is it? Show me. I'll do what I can."

The scrawny hands were on the bridle now, and she felt the horse being pulled away. Suddenly frightened, she turned and tried to leap again onto the safety of his back. From beside the road, more figures appeared. Men! Strong men with angry faces surrounded her, their eyes filled with wild excitement—and lust.

The horse was led into the bushes. The evening glow colored the faces around Juliette with a reddish tint. She felt hands fumble at her skirts, and then she was thrown to the ground. "Let me go! Stop it!" The faces showed no interest in her cries. "Please! Let me go! You can keep my horse. Just let me reach Lyon!" The red lips smiled, the red eyes gleamed.

She was held down now, her arms pinned to the ground by heavy bodies. Two men sat on her legs, holding them apart. Her skirts were around her waist. She could feel the cool of the night air as it touched her naked abdomen. Her legs jerked convulsively, but she couldn't break loose.

One man stood above her. From her position on the ground he seemed monstrously tall, like a giant towering over her helpless body. The men were laughing now, shouting obscenely to each other. Juliette shuddered.

"What a juicy bitch!" The voice came from the monolith that stood between her legs. "She'll keep us warm through this night, won't she, my friends?"

She tried to pull her hand free. Immediately, she felt an arm press against her wrist. A voice spoke close to her ear. "She fights, too. We'll have a bit of fun with this one."

The man above her began to untie the sash that circled his waist. She felt herself grow faint. The violence that had killed Helene was about to be inflicted on her.

Suddenly a hand reached toward her neck. One tug, and the fragile chain that held François' ring was torn away. Anger replaced her fear. "That's mine! Give it back!"

The only response was coarse laughter.

Once more the tall man stepped forward, his hand extended. "Let's see the precious gem the wench fights for so furiously."

The man who had pulled it off turned away, his hand closed over his prize. A hand cuffed his cheek. "Give it to me! I want to see it!"

There was an exchange, and the tall man brought his hand close to his face. For the moment, Juliette was safe. A hush came over the crowd of men. Even the grip on her arms relaxed.

Suddenly, the tall man glared into her face. "Where did you find this?"

She hesitated for a moment. It was none of his business where it came from! Then she felt a tug on her arm. She was in no position to argue. "I got it from a friend."

"What's his name, lass!" The voice was impatient.

"François. He told me it might save my life."

The men burst into raucous laughter. As it subsided, the tall man spoke again. "He said that, did he?"

Juliette felt foolish. That had been an impetuous remark made to a foolish child! What had made her remember it now? And why, at a time like this, did she speak of it?

The tall man extended his hand. "Let her up." His eyes met hers. "Take it. Your friend François was right."

She was too stunned to respond. She felt herself lifted to her feet, and then her hand was forced open and the ring dropped into her palm.

She stood unmoving as, one by one, the men vanished into the shadows. She was alone again.

A foot scraped on the dirt. The woman was back, the horse's reins in her hand. "Mademoiselle?"

Juliette turned. "Yes?"

"Were you in Lyon about a month ago? Did you help a woman carry her dead husband to her home?"

The memory rushed back. Juliette nodded. The woman lifted her face toward the fading light. "Don't you remember me? I'm that woman. Marie Frougard."

Juliette stared at the woman in silence. The face before her wasn't the same as it had been that terrible night. It was hard now and lined with bitterness.

Marie put the reins in Juliette's hand. "You plan to go to Lyon?"

"Yes."

"You mustn't. Lyon is filled with danger. Soldiers guard all the roads. They'll shoot anyone who approaches."

Juliette looked in the direction of the city. "But they won't shoot me! I'm not a rioter!"

"How will they know? Have you a flag you can wave before you? Can your voice travel faster than bullets from their muskets? They'll kill you first and ask questions later."

"What should I do, then? I can't stay here."

"But you can. The men won't hurt you now that they know you are under François' protection. You can sleep beside me, and I will direct you to François in the morning."

When Juliette hesitated, Marie took her hand. "Come. It's too late for you to travel now." She led the way into the woods.

Juliette followed, too stunned by the turn of events to argue. François? A friend of these vicious peasants? Surely, there must be some mistake! François was a common enough name. They had just misunderstood.

When Marie directed her to lie on a pile of branches, she obeyed. The terrors of the day at last took their toll. She lay back, watching as Marie tethered the horse and settled beside her.

There was nothing she could do now to correct their error, nor did she wish to. It was best that these people believe she was a friend of the François who carried so much weight in controlling their actions. In the morning, she would listen to Marie's instructions, but she wouldn't heed them. Her goal still was the cathedral at Lyon. There was where her François waited. And only when she reached his side would she again feel safe.

CHAPTER NINE

Marie woke Juliette at dawn, fed her some dry bread, and directed her to the road. "François will be somewhere between here and Lyon. Most of the men don't know him. They only see his signature on the letters he sends. But I know him well." Her voice was filled with pride. "I deliver the letters." Her eyes were alight. "He's a brave man, and a very smart one. Without him and others like him, our cause would be hopeless."

"Letters? There are men among you who can read?"

"Pitifully few. Most of the letters are read to us by students who have left the académie." Marie looked into Juliette's face. "Can you read?"

"Of course!" As soon as she spoke, Juliette regretted her tone. Embarrassed, she lowered her voice. "My father made me learn. Many women today have taken up reading. It's quite the fashion."

Marie nodded. She had lost interest in the conversation. Pointing toward the road, she indicated a figure that was trudging up the hill from Lyon. "Look! That must be François." She turned back to Juliette. "The ring. You still have it?" Juliette nodded. "You mustn't lose it." She looked again at the figure on the road. "Where do you want to go?"

"To Chalon sur Saone. I—my father's house is near there."

113

"You must ask François to go with you. I'm sure it'll be all right with him. He's gone there before. The road— Even your ring might not protect you that far north. He's best known near Lyon."

Juliette shook her head. "I'm sure I'll be all right by myself. I can get into the city during the day, when the soldiers can recognize me. Then I can take a carriage. I have friends there, too." She was thinking of the duDeffand family. Surely they would have connections in such a big city. "Thank you for your help— and your advice. But I don't think I'll need your François for a guide." She pictured François du Quesnay sitting beside her in duDeffand's carriage, and she smiled. She had her own François.

With a sense of joy, she leaped onto her horse, pulled on the reins, and spurred him to a gallop. The sun had cleared the horizon, covering the land with a golden light. Everything was better now that it was morning!

Her horse's hoofs pounded loudly on the hard dirt road, as if he shared her exuberance. Yesterday, with all its terrors, was past. Today things would be different. Today she would find François in Lyon, and she would be safe.

The figure before her grew more distinct. At first it was only the walk that seemed familiar. Then, gradually, she began to pick out features that stirred her heart and set it beating furiously. Marie had been wrong! The man who moved up the road ahead of her was François du Quesnay, not François the revolutionary!

Juliette didn't bother to question why he was on the highway. Her heart, so torn and bruised from the tragedies of the past day, leaped in recognition. Pulling on her reins, she brought her horse to a halt. Her voice was high with excitement and delight. "François! Oh, François!"

He looked up in surprise. "Juliette? What are you doing here? It isn't safe for you on the road!"

She hardly heard his words. With a smile of pleasure, she slid from her horse. As her feet touched the ground, her arms went around his shoulders. Her face pressed close to his. Her own delight blinded her to his reluctance. When she felt his arms encircle her body, she planted her lips firmly against his.

He lifted her from the ground, pulling her body close against his. Then, slowly, he let her slide down until she was standing before him. His voice was thick with emotion. "Juliette? Answer me! What are you doing on the road—all alone? Doesn't your uncle care for your safety at all?"

Her eyes lowered. "My uncle's dead. And oh, François, so is Bouchy! They killed them both. Those people killed them both!"

The story burst out, jumbled and confused. Yet, with judicious questioning, François finally got it all—including the fact that she was engaged to Roger duDeffand. When Juliette reached the part about Marie, she paused. She glanced up the road. No other figure had appeared. "François—" A new realization forced itself into her mind. "She said—" Her eyes pleaded with him to disagree. "Are you the one she spoke of? Are you?"

He stepped back and looked into her eyes. His face was solemn. "Yes, Juliette, I am. I was on my way to join them now. But, of course, I won't. I'll take you to Chalon, where you'll be safe."

She stared at him in disbelief. "You're teasing me! Please, say you're teasing me! You, a rioter? Impossible! You wouldn't kill my uncle! You wouldn't kill anyone!'' She saw no twinkle in his eyes, no sign that he had been playing one of their old games. Her voice began to shake. "François? Please! Don't play with me now! I can't stand it! Please tell me you're just fooling!''

He shook his head. "No, Juliette. I'm not fooling. I'm the François she told you about. But I didn't kill your uncle. You're right. And I didn't kill your friends, or burn down the abbey and the farmhouses. I had no idea they were going to do something like that.''

Juliette sighed with relief. "So you aren't one of them. You just misunderstood! Now that you know——''

His voice was harsh. "Juliette, don't! I can't desert them now, just because they've gone too far. They need guidance. They need leaders who will help them. Of course they'll make mistakes! But without leaders, they'll be crushed!''

She stared at him in horror. "She said you wrote letters that kept them going! She said they— She said you gave them courage.'' Her eyes were wide with anger. "François, you urged them on! You've kept them fighting when they were ready to give up! If it wasn't for you, my uncle would be alive! And so would Bouchy!'' She was backing away from him, trying to keep him from touching her again. "Even if you weren't there, François, you did it! They listen to what you write, and they're stirred up! François! You're to blame!''

With one stride he covered the space between them. Grasping her shoulders, he shook her roughly. "Juliette! Stop it! That isn't true at all! I'm not to blame for what they do when I'm not even around!''

"But you are!'' Her voice was high with frenzy.

"You're a traitor to your own class! You killed my uncle! I hate you! I hate you!" Pulling from his grasp, she burst into tears.

He was beside her again, his arms around her waist. Angrily, she pushed away again, pressing her hands over her eyes. Her breast was seared with agony. He had done it! Her François had done it all! Her heart cried out for him to prove her wrong, begged him to tell her it was all a mistake. But in her mind she knew that what he said was true. He was part of them. She had reason to hate him. She had reason to never wish to see his face again.

"Well"—his voice was controlled—"you'll listen to me anyway. While your friends were being molested, a hundred workers were being shot in Lyon! A hundred people, Juliette! There's suffering on both sides of us." His eyes caught hers and held them fast. "Did your friends have children?"

She flushed. "No! They were—" The memory of Helene's character silenced her. "No." Her voice was subdued. "They had no families."

"Well, the workers did. There are hundreds of children in Lyon who go hungry today because their fathers were shot. There is no one to feed them, no one to care for them at all!"

"They have their mothers, don't they? And, besides, those men wouldn't be dead if they'd stayed on their jobs!" She remembered her uncle's words. "They want more than God has allotted to them. They show no acceptance of the will of God!"

"Nonsense!" François' voice was full of anger. "It isn't God who gives to the rich and steals from the poor! It's the system of government under which we live! And it's wrong, Juliette, it's wrong! No man needs the kind of wealth the aristocrats in France enjoy! And no one should be allowed to starve as the poor do all over our country! It isn't fair!''

"Well, what they're doing isn't fair, either! Helene never hurt them! She didn't even know them! Neither did poor Jacque! And my uncle—he was a man of God!'' She ignored the small voice that reminded her of his profligate behavior. "And my maids. Who have they injured?''

Her hand closed around the ring. A sudden wave of fury shook her body. Pulling the chain from her neck, she threw it on the ground. "Take your old ring! I don't want your protection! I'd be better off dead than indebted to you!''

With a sob, she turned and began to run. She had to get away from him before her foolish heart took control. He was a traitor. She didn't want to see him— ever again.

When he didn't follow, she felt a wave of fear. Was he going to let her go? Her heart was torn with pain. Yet, she was determined not to return, not even for her horse. He could have the beast! She would get a new one from the duDeffands when she reached Lyon!

Despite her anger, she was unable to maintain her pace. She hadn't slept well on the hard dirt, and she was still exhausted. Yet, it was not her fatigue that caused her to slow down. Her heart was not willing to let her lover go so easily. It had to give François a chance to show he still cared. Her ears were tuned to his step, but they heard no sound behind her.

Then his footsteps sent her heart soaring. She felt her breath coming quickly. He still loved her! He still cared! He wouldn't leave her alone in the middle of such dangerous country!

Immediately, her anger returned. He was one of the dangerous ones! He was as much the enemy as they were. If he showed concern for her safety now, it was just to salve his own conscience. By the time he reached her side, she once more had her emotions under control.

He swung lightly beside her, adjusting his step to hers. "Juliette, I understand how you feel. I never intended you should learn of—all this. But you have now, and there's nothing I can do about it." He tried to take her arm, but she jerked away. "Whether you believe me or not, I want you to know I still love you. I've never loved anyone else!"

She averted her eyes. "It isn't a question of who you love! I haven't asked you that! It's your lack of loyalty that shocks me! I can't believe anything you say!"

She sensed, more than she saw, the shrug of his shoulders. "Well, I suppose it doesn't matter any more. You're engaged to duDeffand." His voice sounded bitter. "But I still can't let you run into danger without trying to protect you."

Her voice was heavy with sarcasm. "You protect me? How? By turning me over to your friends for safekeeping?"

He grasped her by the shoulder, shaking her forcefully. His face was dark, and he scowled as he at last released her. "You won't see, will you! You refuse to believe! Juliette, my ring saved you last night, didn't it?"

She nodded. It outraged her that he would handle her so roughly.

"Now I'll make it clear to you. You must wear my ring where it can be seen at all times—or you're in danger." He paused, his eyes focused behind her, on the distant city. "Even that might not be enough. There're too many men out of work. That's why you must travel with me—so I can protect you. Otherwise, you might not live to enjoy the honor of marriage into the duDeffand family."

Her eyes widened in fear. Never had she seen François so angry. There was a fire in his face that sent tremors through her body. This wasn't the gentle boy she knew. Not at all! He was an angry man—like the peasants. A violent man! She didn't dare to contemplate what he might do were she to refuse his assistance.

When she didn't respond, François took the ring and, tying the chain at its break, fixed it around her neck. Then he stepped back, studying her carefully. When he spoke again, his words came as a surprise. "Are you wearing petticoats?" She nodded. "Well, take them off!"

She glared at him balefully. Was he going to force himself on her now—in broad daylight? In the middle of the road? Her anger overcame her fright. Stubbornly, she made no move to obey his orders.

He seemed not to notice her delay. Pulling at the pins that held her curls in a crown on her head, he let them drop to the ground. When she tried to escape, he gripped her tightly with one hand as he continued working with the other. He didn't release her until her hair hung loosely about her shoulders.

Her horse nickered restlessly. François lifted his hand as if to send the beast on his way back to the abbey.

With a cry, Juliette grasped the reins. "How dare you? Why should I obey you?" She felt the tears again, but this time she made no attempt to hide them. Her voice rose. "I hate you! Oh, why do you torment me?"

A look of unhappiness flitted over François' face

and then, once more, he was calm. "It doesn't matter what you think of me. I can't let you endanger yourself. Your full skirt, your hair piled on your head, and that horse—all identify you as an aristocrat. I've no desire to fight our way up to Chalon. If you're just another peasant woman traveling with her man, you'll attract less attention."

Juliette turned away, her face cold with anger. François grabbed her shoulders and spun her around. "Don't you want to see your father again?"

Her expression softened. "Oh, yes!"

"Then do as I tell you!"

Still, she hesitated. She'd never been afraid to walk. As a child, she'd run around the meadow like a serf, her legs growing strong from the exercise. But to walk all the way to Chalon? It seemed a terrible journey!

A distant noise drew her attention. Another mob was moving toward them from Lyon. She stared at the mass of people. Were they peasants? Or were they, maybe, some of her own kind, come out to rescue her?

The figures grew more distinct. Their clothes were ragged—and they were walking. These were no aristocrats. They were marauders, like the gang she had left behind in the woods.

Without further argument, she stepped from the road. Hiding behind a bush, she pulled off her petticoats. For a moment, she gazed at them, thinking of her torn chemise. Maybe she could keep just one—for comfort. She glanced up at François. He would object. She was sure of it. With a feeling of despair, she dropped them all to the ground.

When she returned to the highway, her horse was gone. A trail of dust on the road told her he was on his way back to the abbey. She wondered, forlornly, whether he would succeed in reaching his destination.

Once more François forced her to look into his eyes. "Juliette, we have a long journey ahead of us. I want no foolish attempts to get away. It's hard to tell who's friend and who's enemy." Her face showed her disbelief. "You told me many of the monks were gone from the abbey. Do you know where any of them are now?"

Before she could answer, he continued, "I'm sure some of them have joined the gang you left this morning." She shook her head. "So you think I'm lying? Well, you'll see. There have been desertions from the monastery before, and I know. It's the same with soldiers. Some have left their posts and joined the peasants. It's growing, Juliette. His Majesty will soon have to accept the revolution for what it is!"

Juliette still didn't speak. Silently, she decided she'd remain with François for the present. She lacked the courage to travel alone. But when they reached Lyon, she would break away and seek help from a noble family within its gates. They'd give her a carriage—and liverymen—to see her safely home. Then, when Roger duDeffand would learn that the abbey was destroyed, he'd come searching for her, and she would be waiting for him.

When they reached the lowlands near Lyon, François drew her off the road into the shelter of the fields. A line of soldiers lolled across the road. Juliette struggled to break free of François' grasp. Freedom lay just ahead. All she had to do was return to the road and call out for assistance. The soldiers would protect her from being recaptured.

A bead of sweat trickled down her temple. As she wiped it back, she looked at her gown. It had been one of her favorites. Now it was smudged with dirt and stained with perspiration. She'd caught the skirt on a branch, somewhere during the night, and a small tear marred its smooth design.

Automatically, she patted her hair, feeling startled when her fingers didn't encounter the big curls to which she had grown accustomed. Then she remembered. François had pulled down the curls. All the signs of her station in life had been removed!

A growing sense of despair overcame her. She could expect no help from the soldiers! They'd take her for a peasant—and they'd shoot her before she had a chance to explain. François had seen to that!

The soldiers turned their attention to the fields, and François pulled her quickly to the ground. "Stay still!" His voice was a whisper. "They won't come out here unless they're sure of where we are. We won't have long to wait. They'll go back to where it's more comfortable in a few minutes."

They settled side by side on the dirt, their heads low. Suddenly, Juliette was overcome by an irrational desire. François was so close! She began to tremble. She could feel his breath against her hair.

Then, mustering all her strength, she forced the thought out of her mind. "Never!"

"Quiet!" François' lips were close to her ear. "They'll hear you!"

She felt a sudden lightness. Maybe, if she screamed for help first, the soldiers would listen. Then, when they saw her, they'd understand why she was so disheveled. She opened her mouth to call out, but no sound escaped her throat. His lips were over hers, his breath warm against her cheek. His arms tightened around her, pulling her close.

She struggled at first. How did he dare to take such advantage of her? But when the pressure of his lips against hers increased, she felt herself weaken. The hatred she had felt drained away. Say what she might, vow whatever she would, she couldn't refuse his love. If he wanted her, she was his. There was nothing she could do to change it.

As suddenly as he had kissed her, his lips were gone. Rising, he pulled her to her feet. ''They've gone back into the city. It's safe now. We can move again.''

She stood beside him, shaking with anger. How could he treat her so meanly? She had been ready to give in to any demand he might make, and he had brushed her aside. His only concern was for the soldiers! Silently, she allowed herself to be pulled back on the road. Her face was burning. How humiliating! ''I hate him!'' She spoke under her breath. ''I hate him!'' With a dull awareness that her words were lies, she let herself be led northward, away from the town.

CHAPTER TEN

"Liberty! Equality! Fraternity!" The cries of the mob swelled around Juliette like waves cresting on a mighty ocean. Deep within her heart, she felt a response. They were noble words! Meaningful words! If only the men and women who shrieked them listened to what they were saying!

She felt herself moved along by the crowd, propelled through the streets helplessly, like a boat in the middle of a rapids. She looked around frantically for François, but he was nowhere to be seen.

The mob had come upon them suddenly, as they passed through the small mill town. François had tried to pull her out of its way, but his grip on her hand had been broken, and she had been swept off down a narrow street. Now she was alone—separated from him by a stream of screaming rioters.

The street ahead narrowed. Juliette felt herself lifted from her feet, propelled upward by the forward pressure of the mob. For one moment, her head was above the others. She stared ahead curiously, and then, with a shriek, she began to claw her way back to the ground. Lined across the road at the next intersection were soldiers, their muskets braced against their shoulders.

She was living through a repeat of her night in Lyon, when the mob had met soldiers below her window. Only this time it was different. She was helpless in the line of fire.

Screams that threatened to deafen her came from nearby. Startled, she looked about her. Everyone was charging forward. Everyone but herself. The screams came from her own mouth. Scratching and clawing, she forced her way toward the shelter of a nearby house. If she could reach it in time, she had a chance to survive the calamity that lay ahead. Voices cursed at her as she pushed her way through the mob. An elbow smashed into her ear, but she ignored the pain. Her only thought was to reach the protection before the guns were fired.

The first volley sounded as she pushed her way past a toothless woman carrying a small child on her shoulders. Juliette saw the child's body jerk, and then it fell limp in its mother's arms, its head smashed by the impact of the shot.

When the second round was fired, Juliette was under the stone lintel of an ancient building, pressing herself as close to the door as she possibly could. She had seen all this before. There was as much danger of death from trampling as from the guns.

Another roar of muskets reverberated down the narrow street. The retreat had begun. Screaming, men and women who had miraculously escaped death from the shots began to run for safety. Juliette cried out as a scrawny man approached. He stretched a lean arm out toward her, its hand clutching madly. Then, with a cry, he fell at her feet. He was lost immediately under the rush of frightened people. Juliette closed her eyes. It was too much! Horror like this should never happen!

A hand gripped her wrist. François! Opening her eyes, she found herself staring into the face of a burly man, almost as tall as François, but carrying more than twice his weight. His hair was black streaked with gray, his face rugged and tanned. He had a sharp nose that bent down toward his mouth like the beak of some exotic bird.

Shrieking loudly, she tried to pull away, but the fist tightened. She was caught. And she was being dragged back into the rushing mob.

Her assailant veered into a narrow alley, pulling her through a pile of rubble and into an open doorway. As she was pushed into the dark interior of the building, Juliette tugged hard, but she could not free herself. Frantically, she bent down and bit the fingers that held her captive. Her captor let out a shout of anger. And in that instant, she broke loose.

With a leap, she was through the door and back into the sunshine. She had to run! She had to get away! Somewhere, she had to find François!

She had reached the street when her path was blocked by two ugly creatures. One stared at her solemnly. The other grinned evilly into her frightened face. He had a long slash over one eye, and his smile was toothless, except for one blackened point that extended from his upper jaw like a fang. He caught her around the waist and held her against his body. "What's the hurry?" His leer was horrible to see. "You ain't leavin' before we can show our hospitality, are you?"

"Let me go!" She beat furiously against his chest. "Let me go!"

He laughed, his fetid breath threatening to overwhelm her. Sick from the odor, she felt her stomach heave. With a scream, he pushed her back into the garbage that lined the alley. "Bitch! We don't need no sick ones! We got problems enough!"

His momentary reaction gave her the opportunity. Lowering her head, she tried to run, but her stomach wouldn't allow her to move. Bending helplessly, she waited for the unpleasantness to pass. Maybe, when she was feeling better, she'd still be able to get away.

But there was no escape. She stood staring at the row of men who blocked her exit, and then, overcome with terror, she screamed. "François! Help me! François!"

She had little hope her cry would be heard. François had been pushed in another direction by the mob. He might even be among those who lay dead on the street, trampled by the last fleeing rioters.

The men circled around her, their hands plucking at her dress, at her bobbing curls. She kicked the first one who reached for the buttons of her dress, and he swore angrily. Then another pair of hands grabbed her around the waist. She was held close against a malodorous body.

Hands fumbled at the buttons of her gown, and she felt the warm sun hit her bare back. With a jerk, her dress was pulled from her shoulders. She stood in the circle of her attackers, her naked body gleaming like ivory. The fear that had driven her to try to escape drained away. Despair, total, overwhelming despair took its place.

She stood unmoving. There was nothing she could do. François had not heard her, and there were too many of them, anyway. He would be helpless against such a mob.

Now that they had her naked, the men seemed suddenly to become quiet. They stood gazing at her as if dumfounded at her beauty. Not one made a move in her direction. But she knew the attack would come. Soon they would be swarming over her body like rats, prodding and crushing her to the ground.

Why, oh why, had she and François come into Macon? They'd avoided all the other towns! He'd spoken of friends, of food, of a place to rest. He hadn't expected a riot.

A rough hand touched her shoulder. It was beginning. Closing her eyes, Juliette waited for the inevitable attack. Her prayer was simple. "Dear God, don't make me endure too much. Let me die quickly." It was then she remembered François' ring.

Suddenly, a cry broke out. The man nearest her pushed her to the ground. With one gesture, he released his trousers, and then he was above her. Frantically, she held the ring before his face, but he turned away, as if he were unwilling to acknowledge its presence. She felt him push against her, felt his legs spread hers apart.

A hand grasped his shoulder and pushed him to one side. Startled, Juliette stared into another face, just as evil as the first. But her new assailant was looking at the ring. He glared at it intently. Then, with a curse, he turned to the crowd. "It's his ring, all right! She's not to be touched."

The first man had recovered his balance. Swearing loudly, he pushed his way above her. "The hell she ain't! Where's he, if he wants her to himself? How come he ain't with her? He's dead, that's why! That ring don't mean nothing no more! He's dead, and she's up for grabs!" Triumphantly, he settled himself between her legs.

A man standing behind him grasped him by the shoulders and swung him to his feet. Surprised at the sudden release, Juliette pulled herself into a crouching position. The next man who attacked her would be greeted with a kick in the groin.

But no one took her assailant's place. Angry voices rose around her. The men were fighting one another! She stared about her in amazement. Each one of the men wanted her first! All were determined no one else would have that privilege.

With growing hope, she backed toward the wall. Her dress lay at her feet, half buried in the garbage. She grabbed the skirt and held on, pulling a bit more free every time the mob shifted. When, at last, she held it in her arms, she rose to her feet. Maybe she would be able to escape, after all!

Then a cry went up from the edge of the circle. At first, Juliette feared it might be soldiers—or more rioters who might pay no heed to the significance of her ring. Her eyes wide with terror, she stared in the direction of the new disturbance. It was then she saw him. François!

With a cry, she began to push through the still-fighting mob. She was screaming shrilly. "François! François! Here I am!" She forgot she held her gown in her hands, forgot she was naked. All that mattered was that he had come. She was safe, at last.

As if by magic, the rioters vanished until only a few were left. The one who had identified her ring greeted François with a small, almost imperceptible bow. "I tried to stop them, François. But it wasn't easy. Most of them never saw the ring before. They're new. They weren't part of the first ones, like we were."

François nodded, his eyes on Juliette. Gently, he lifted her in his arms. She was trembling, and her lips quivered as she spoke. "Oh, François, I was— It was terrible!"

He pulled her dress from her grasp and draped it over her body. "It's all right, my dearest, it's all right. It's all over." Cradling her tenderly, he carried her across the street and pushed his way through a battered doorway.

The room they entered was empty—and dark. Like

most of the hovels, it had no windows and only a bare dirt floor. As her eyes grew accustomed to the darkness, Juliette saw a mattress in one corner. François carried her to it and placed her gently on its rough covering.

He knelt above her, gazing into her face. Then he bent over and kissed her lips. She realized that nothing mattered except his nearness. He was alive—and he had saved her from the ravages of the mob. Her hands fumbling at his breeches, she pulled him down beside her.

The touch of his fingers on her breasts set her body afire. She forgot her vows of hatred. How could she reject the only man who had ever loved her? His body was familiar—and yet somehow strange and new. Lying beneath him, she knew she could never turn his love away.

When they at last lay back exhausted, Juliette stroked François' dark, curly hair. "Oh, François, I love you so!"

He kissed her lips gently. "I love you, Juliette. And I promise never to let you out of my sight again!"

They reached Chalon as the sun was setting behind a row of trees that lined the Saone River. Juliette gazed about her with growing excitement. She was almost home! Soon she would be in her father's arms, safe at last.

She hadn't spoken of the love she had shared with François since that terrible day. Her mind was in far too great a turmoil. She couldn't deny she had given herself to him voluntarily. It had been her desire as much as his own. Yet, once they resumed their journey, she found herself resenting what had happened.

He hadn't been fair. He had taken advantage of her

fear, of the terror she had experienced. If he had been a gentleman, he would have brought her to a safe hiding place—and then he would have left her alone. Gradually, as the days passed, she built up her anger until, once more, her hatred for what he stood for overcame her love for him. She refused to allow him to touch her except when it was absolutely necessary. He had taken her once, when she was weak. She wouldn't let it happen again.

At the fork in the road she paused. One path led to her home; the other ended at the duQuesnay estate. Coldly, she held out her hand. "Goody-bye, François. Thank you for helping me reach safety." She paused. This was no time to let her emotions get the better of her. "I imagine we won't see each other again." Once more she paused. What should she say to a man she both loved and hated?

"I can't wish you good fortune, not anymore, for it would mean I wished the rioters success. I don't. I'll pray every day that they're destroyed, that they're driven back to work. I'll pray the world returns to normal." Her voice broke. "And I'll pray their leaders are punished—as they deserve."

A grim smile touched his lips. "Good-bye, Juliette. I hope you never regret your decision to marry duDeffand."

He was gone then, running up the road. She stood for a moment watching him. She could hear her heart crying to him, begging him to return, to not leave her alone. Then, with a resolute expression, she began to walk to her home.

Before she could see the grove of trees that shaded her roof, her nostrils were assailed by a familiar odor. Smoke! It was too warm for her father to have a fire in the fireplace! Frightened, she began to run. She knew long before she reached the ancient building that she was too late. There was no fire burning in the ruins. Only the acrid odor of burned wood hung like a cloud over the remnants of her home.

A figure detached itself from the one remaining structure. With a cry, she ran toward it. "Papa! Oh, Papa!"

She stopped abruptly. It wasn't her father at all! It was Paul, the stableboy. They stood facing each other awkwardly. Then Paul bobbed his head. "Mademoiselle Juliette!"

She nodded. "My father! Where's my father?"

He shuffled slowly, like an old man, around the ruins to where four bare mounds of dirt rose above the lawn. Silently, he pointed at the grave that had a small marker. "He's here, ma'am. He died before they set the fire. He was trying to keep them away from the house, and he just fell. God had mercy on him, taking him before he saw the worst of it. I'm thankful for that!"

She felt the strength flow from her body. What was the use of all her fighting? The world was falling apart around her, and she was pretending there was a normal place to which she could return! She stared at the ashes of her home. Was this normal? Was it right that an old man who had always been kind to his servants should be murdered by his own people?

The memory of his face came before her, and she felt the tears begin to flow. Her father was dead! Never again would she be able to cuddle in his arms, protected from her small fears by his strength! She was truly alone now.

Then the memory of his own loss returned. He had been deprived of his love for over sixteen years! Ever since her mother died at her birth! Sixteen years! He couldn't have gone to his death with too much regret. He was in heaven now, reunited with his wife at last.

Slowly, she regained her composure. She looked up into Paul's anxious face. "Bouchard is dead, too. And my uncle! Oh, Paul, people are so cruel!"

He didn't answer. His youthful face was gray with sorrow. She turned to the three remaining mounds. "Your brothers?"

He nodded. "They tried to stop them. They tried to reason with them. We knew them all! People we had worked with ever since I can remember!"

She touched his shoulder gently. "They were good men, your brothers. I loved them all."

A faint smile lit his face. "Emil made me promise to stay here until you came back. He said we couldn't just let you find—these!" He gestured toward the graves.

They were standing side by side when François appeared. Barely glancing at the remains of her home, he stood looking at her bowed head. Juliette was reciting a prayer for the dead.

When she lifted her head, he stepped over one of the mounds and stood beside her. "Juliette, what are you going to do?"

She looked into his face. She'd thought he would be gone, that, safe in his home, he wouldn't think of her again.

He seemed to sense her surprise at his sudden appearance. His voice was low. "My home was gone, too. When I realized what had happened, I suspected you'd find—what you found." He looked at Paul. "No one was left at my place. Do you know what happened there?"

Paul nodded. "They were all killed. I buried them myself, after—" He glanced at the four mounds.

François' face grew grim. His voice was angry. "And all because no one listens! If only they'd stop fighting and listen!"

Juliette looked up. "You mean the peasants? They've been listening—to people like you! It's your fault! You killed my father—and your own. François, you murdered your own mother!"

François shook his head. "No! No I didn't! I've never advocated violence like this! This is done because the landowners won't listen. The king pretends the riots are nothing more than a few starving beggars hunting for bread. The landowners insist it'll all pass away. No one pays any attention to the cry of the poor for surcease from their miseries. If only someone would listen, the violence would stop!"

Juliette stared at him in disbelief. "François—your own parents! Don't you care for them at all?"

For one moment the pain in his heart reached his face. Then, setting his jaw, he pushed back his private agony. "Of course I mourn for my mother and father. You know how much I loved them! But I've seen so many die needlessly that death means less to me now than it did in the past. My parents are only two more sacrifices on the altar of greed—the king's greed! The day will come when we'll triumph. Then, and only then, will my parents' blood—and that of your father and Bouchy—be justified!"

"Justified! They can never be justified! What justice lies in the murder of innocent people like them?" Juliette turned away, disappointment overshadowing her sorrow. Nothing of what François said made any sense to her. He was blind! He couldn't see the riots for the terrible things they were. When she turned again to face him, her voice was low and intense. "And in the meantime, people will go on dying?

While you're hunting about for someone to listen to you, more children will lose their parents, more loyal servants like your Michel and Paul's brothers, will die defending their masters? François, can't you see? It's impossible! It must be stopped! Nothing good can come from such terror! It's an outrage against God!''

He shook his head. ''It seems that way, sometimes, doesn't it?'' She saw his jaw tighten. ''But it isn't! It can't be! We must go on! If men in America can have freedom, we can have it here! The common man deserves the right to live in honor!''

Juliette shook her head. ''The common man? Who is the common man? The beasts who killed my uncle and raped Helene? The monster who almost raped me in the woods? The creatures who stripped me of my clothes in Macon? Are those the sort of men you call common? Do they deserve anything except the gallows? Do the people who killed your parents and my father deserve your understanding—or do they deserve to be imprisoned for murder? François! Think what you're saying! Surely you can't any longer defend people as violent as this!''

François reached into his shirt and withdrew a roll of papers. Carefully, he held them out before her. ''Read this. This is that I've written. This is my *philosophe*. Read it, and see if you can find cause for violence within its pages.''

Without taking the papers from his hand, she began to study them. The language was beautiful, filled with all the words she had heard him say when they used to meet in the meadow. He spoke of human dignity, of the need of all living creatures for food and the freedom to defend their loved ones. He spoke of the mistreatment of the serfs in the past, and of the terrible way in which they had been abandoned to starve after they had been freed.

When she was through, Juliette gazed back at the ashes. François was right. He hadn't urged violence—or mayhem. But his words had aroused them, nevertheless. She looked again into his face. "François, what you write isn't real. Reality lies in the fire there, in the graves at our feet! Reality is murder and rape—and hatred. There are no honorable peasants. There are only angry beasts raging out at the world. There's no human dignity in the streets of Lyon—or Macon—or Chalon. There's only hatred—and violence."

He didn't answer. Silently, he stuffed the papers back into his shirt. When he spoke again, his voice was steady. "I'm going to Paris. I see now the only solution is to bring the cause to the king. The government must take the suffering of the people into account. And they'll only do it when educated men speak up in the defense of liberty and equality." He looked into her flushed face. "Do you want to go with me?"

She turned to Paul. "What are you going to do?"

Paul spoke hesitatingly. "I think, mademoiselle, there's nothing else but to join them. I'm sorry, ma'am. I'd like to have stayed here and served your father—and you—until I died. But—" His voice trailed off in a hopeless sigh.

"Do you want to come with us?"

"Oh, no, ma'am. I belong here. I can't leave—" He made a helpless gesture over the graves.

Solemnly, she held out her hand. "Well, then, I'll go to Paris with François. I must find my affianced. You're sure you'll be all right?"

He bobbed his head. "Thank you, ma'am, I think so. It doesn't matter, anyhow. Not now." He raised his head. "Well, since you've come, and you don't need me, I'll be going." Bobbing once more, he turned and stepped into the half-destroyed barn. When he came out, he was carrying a small kerchief in his hand. He held it out. "Ma'am, I saved a bit of food. It might help you on your travels."

She started to take it, and then she drew back her hand. "No, Paul, you keep it. We've managed so far; we can go on the same way. That bit of food is the least I can give you after all your love and loyalty."

He bobbed again and turned onto the road. She watched silently as he disappeared from view.

CHAPTER ELEVEN

François placed himself before Juliette, his body shielding hers, his legs planted firmly apart, his arms raised. "This woman is mine! Haven't you anything better to do than to steal another man's possessions?"

The massive man grinned wickedly. His eyes swept the circle of onlookers. "Comrades! What a little rooster! A bantam chanticleer trying to protect his mate from a lion!" His words brought a roar of laughter from the crowd. He convulsed at the brilliance of his own wit, but his eyes never left François' tense face.

Juliette watched in horror. How had they let themselves fall into such a trap? Frantically, she thought back on the journey. It had been quiet for the most part. They had traveled alone, avoiding any groups they encountered. But now they were close to Paris, and François' attitude had changed. Instead of shunning others, he seemed to seek their companionship. His explanation was that he wanted information on what was happening. Juliette could not dissuade him, no matter how strong her arguments.

They had joined this group of travelers two days before, and everything had seemed to go very smoothly. Most of their companions were too tired to quarrel and too hungry to think of anything except food. But then the first group had been joined by a small band of marauders who had raided a nearby abbey. They poured down the road, ladened with food and wine.

And with their arrival, the entire character of the mob altered.

The leader of the small band, Armand, was liberal with his booty, taking obvious pleasure in acting the generous lord. Soon everyone was eating and drinking with a gusto that left Juliette thoroughly disgusted. Roasted chickens were torn apart and demolished by the ravenous people. Bones were tossed to the ground. Watching them, Juliette was certain more food was wasted than was actually eaten.

Yet, it was the drinking that caused the problem. Soon men and women were pairing off, taking their pleasure near the edges of the group, with no seeming hesitation or show of modesty. Armand's gaze fell on Juliette, and he staggered to her side. With a leer, he grabbed her by the shoulders and planted a kiss on her lips. It was then the fight had started.

François had thrown himself at Armand with a roar, pulling his arms away from Juliette's shoulders. Immediately the cry went up. "A fight! Hey! A fight!" The expressions on the glutted faces brightened. Shouting and pushing, a circle was formed. The arena was ready. The battle could begin.

A shout rang out behind François and he glanced around. "Here, mate!" One of the men in the original party threw him a knife. He caught it deftly and held it before him. But Juliette could see that equalizing the weapons didn't balance the fight. Armand was far stronger than François. His shoulders were broader. How could François stand up against such a massive man?

Juliette backed up until she rested against a bare tree. She knew she ought to run now, while no one noticed her. It was only a matter of time before François would lie dead and Armand would come to take her. Yet, she couldn't leave her lover as long as there was any possibility that he might need her. Eyes wide with fear, she watched what she was sure would be François' execution.

"Aha!" With a roar, Armand leaped toward his prey. Juliette gasped, but François sidestepped calmly, leaving Armand to jab his knife into empty air. The monster chortled wickedly. "Keep it up, little cock! Keep it up! We'll see how long it takes you to grow tired!"

François didn't answer. Lightly, he circled around, his eyes holding steady on the giant hand. He held his own knife casually, as if he had no intention of using it. Juliette crossed herself and began to pray, though she had little faith in the effectiveness of her supplications. François was doomed. How could he hope to win? He had learned swordsmanship as a child, that she remembered, but it had been only a game. A gentleman had little use for such weapons, unless he entered a military career. And François had decided to become a scholar.

Armand, on the contrary, showed a thorough knowledge of street fighting. He crept after François like a panther stalking his prey. He attacked and feinted with a force that, when he made a connection, Juliette could see would destroy his opponent. François' only recourse was to keep out of the way.

Juliette began to tremble. It was clear what would happen. The constant running would exhaust François. He would grow tired—or careless—and that would be the end.

A deep sense of regret brought a flush to Juliette's cheeks. She had rejected all of François' advances during the weeks of their journeying. The argument that had erupted over her father's grave burned in her memory, driving all love away. Aware as she was of the importance of François protection, she had accepted his companionship without protest. But she had kept him at arm's length. Now she wished she had been more affectionate. The thought of losing him made her suddenly long for his touch.

When she realized where her thoughts were leading her, she tried to force her mind to focus on other things, but she didn't succeed. François' safety loomed before her as the most important thing in the world.

The rabble that surrounded her cheered boisterously each time Armand lunged. They were crying for blood now, encouraging the massive man in his ruthless attack. "That's the way, Armand!" "He's getting tired, Armand. Hit him now!" "Kill! Kill! Kill!" It grew like advancing artillery, and with each repetition, Juliette felt her terror increase.

She wondered if any of the shouting people remembered François' thoughtfulness during the days they had traveled together. Looking about the circle of bloodthirsty beggars, she decided no one cared for kindness. Power was all that mattered. And Armand was well endowed with brute strength.

Once more the big man lunged toward François, his blade extended. "François! Look out!" Juliette's scream startled her lover into movement. The blade caught his jacket and tore a gash across one pocket. Juliette held her hands, palms together, before her face.. "Dear God, save him!"

She remembered, then, how much she disliked everything François stood for. Uneasily, she questioned the efficacy of a prayer for the protection of an avowed revolutionary. Quickly, she continued her plea. "Please, dear Mother of God, I need him to protect me. Don't let him be killed."

Once more, Armand missed François, and a shout rose from the mob. Juliette inhaled nervously. Her worries about why she wanted François safe were forgotten. The next prayer came straight from her heart. "Dear Mary, save him. I love him so!"

It was clear that heavenly intervention would be needed if François were to live. He seemed totally inept at handling a knife. He held it loosely in his fist, its blade pointed upward. What was worse, he seemed unwilling to use it, even when the opportunity presented itself. Despite his handicap, his blade did connect with Armand once, forcefully enough to draw blood.

As a line of red appeared on Armand's arm, the crowd roared with pleasure. Juliette stared about her in surprise. What had happened to their loyalty to their hero? Looking at their animated faces, she understood. Most of them cared very little who won the fight. They cheered the game. They were excited when someone—anyone—made a good hit.

Nevertheless, Juliette was encouraged. The fight had at first appeared to be one-sided. She had expected Armand to win quickly, to kill François, and then to rush over to take her as his prize. That wasn't at all what was happening. More than 15 minutes had passed, and François remained on his feet. Armand lunged again—and once more François leaped lightly aside. When Armand recovered his balance, Juliette reached a surprising conclusion. It was he who was growing tired, not François!

Again and again came an attack that never reached its goal. Now Armand was visibly exhausted. He was breathing heavily. His face was red with exertion.

A faint smile appeared on François' face as he responded to his opponent's fatigue with a new tactic. The next time Armand dove toward him, François stepped lightly aside and then, at the last moment, kicked swiftly into the air. His foot contacted Armand's shoulder, throwing the big man across the circle to an ignominious collapse on the ground. The crowd roared its pleasure. Now their shouts were for François. "Kill him!" "What's the matter, François? Kill him!"

François paid no attention to the angry calls. He waited patiently as Armand rose unsteadily to his feet. Then he shifted his body, ready for the next attack. Juliette stamped her foot in anger. What was the matter with him? Didn't he realize this was a battle to the death? Had he been the one on the ground, Armand's knife would have slashed his throat before he had a chance to recover his senses.

Still François waited. Armand moved heavily now, his breath labored. When he passed Juliette, she realized he was groaning with each exhalation. The crowd was screaming in frenzy. This was a show they had never expected. They were going to get more than just a quick kill. This fight would last until the defeated man acknowledged the victor. Then, and only then, would the death blow be struck.

There were no cheers now for Armand. He panted about the circle, a look of desperation on his face. But when he glanced at the onlookers, he was greeted with jeers and catcalls.

Juliette could see that his only hope lay in overwhelming François with his strength. He lumbered about while François watched him sharply.

A new expression appeared on the thick features—one of total confusion. He had never had an opponent like François before. He lunged again—and missed. A wave of agony swept over his face. With a low growl, he stopped in his tracks, staring about in puzzlement.

Politely, François stepped back, once more waiting for his opponent to recover his breath. The crowd roared in fury. "Kill him! What are you standing there for? Kill him!"

François shook his head. With an impatient gesture of his arm, he tossed his knife to the ground. A gasp went up from the onlookers. Unarmed, what advantage did he have, even against an exhausted enemy?

Armand saw the blade fall, and his eyes lit up. With a roar, he threw himself toward his tormentor. His knife flashed in the sunlight as he lifted it high above his head. The fight was his, after all! His face showed his joy—and his surprise.

Just before the blade reached François' head, he leaped aside, landing on one foot. The other foot shot out, high in the air. This time he didn't hit at Armand's shoulder. His aim was true—and forceful. Straight in the middle of Armand's chest the blow connected. It knocked the air from the big man's lungs and threw him across the circle. He fell to the ground with a thud. His knife flew from his hand, landing point down in the dirt.

The crowd went wild. Grabbing the knife, a gray-haired hag pushed it into François' hand. "Kill him! You won fair and square! Kill him now!"

Francois refused to take the blade. "No. He has to live."

Juliette stared at him in surprise. He was hardly out of breath, though he'd been leaping around for almost a half hour. But it wasn't François' endurance that surprised her. If ever a man deserved death, Armand did. Hadn't he threatened to rape her? Quickly, she pushed her way to François' side. "Why, François, why?"

He gazed around at the milling crowd, his eyes

steady. "What would I prove by killing him? That I'm smarter than he is? That I'm better trained in hand-to-hand combat?" He glanced down at the unconscious form. "He'll be sore for a while, but he'll recover. Juliette, I can't kill him. He's the best they have!"

Her smile was hard. "Good! Kill him then, and they'll all go back where they belong."

François ignored her words. He turned to an ancient hag. "Do you know this man?" She nodded. "Then take care of him. He's a good man. We need good men in the fight for freedom."

The old woman nodded and crouched beside Armand. Shrugging off the excited adulation of the delirious crowd, François drew Juliette aside.

She felt certain she would explode, she was so angry. "François, how could you? He'll only try again when he recovers!"

Francois shook his head. "No, little Juliette! Not at all. No woman is worth two fights. He'll just find another."

Her face grew livid. "So that's what you think! So I'm just another female to you! Well, you're wrong! I'm—I'm—" She sputtered in frustration. When he didn't respond, she inhaled deeply and started again. "I don't understand you, François! You let your parents die without seeking revenge. You see me attacked over and over again, yet you never blame the beasts who try to rape me! What kind of man are you?"

His eyes grew suddenly sad. "I don't know, Juliette. But I can't kill these poor creatures, no matter what they do. How can you blame a beast that is so mistreated it lashes out at its owner? How can you blame the poor for their fury? Juliette! Think what they have had to endure!"

She stamped her foot in anger. "Think what we are

being forced to endure! You claim you love me! How can I believe you? Is this the kind of life you want for the woman you say you love?'' Her eyes flashed, holding his with the intensity of her rage.

He stepped close to her then, grasping her firmly by both elbows. His voice was low—and filled with burning fury. ''Don't you ever set yourself up as a judge of my feelings! I've told you I love you—and that will never change. If I didn't love you, I'd let you share the fate of the other selfish aristocrats!'' He spit the last word out as if he hated even to use it.

Juliette glanced about her nervously. Had someone heard what he said? Would they now turn on her? But no one was paying the least attention to the argument. The mob that had been so fickle during the fight had settled back to drinking and carousing. Armand had recovered consciousness and was lying with his head in the old hag's lap. Even he wasn't looking at François.

The meaning of François' outburst penetrated Juliette's consciousness. Turning back to him, she stared up into his face. ''You mean you'd let them kill me? As they killed Helene?''

His face softened. ''Never. I'd die before they hurt you! Oh, Juliette!'' It was there again. All his longing—his tenderness. She felt her anger drain away, replaced by joy that he had survived the fight. It had been a battle to protect her. He had risked death to save her life!

All of her resentment vanished. How could she be angry with François? She loved him so much! His arms circled her waist, and she melted against him. Her lips were ready for his kiss. And when he lifted her up and carried her into the shadows, she knew her body was ready for his caresses.

* * *

They were on their way the following morning. François carried a bag of food that Armand had forced upon him. Contrary to Juliette's expectations, there was nothing Armand wasn't ready to do for the man he had tried to kill the night before. Juliette watched the big man with disgust. He was practically groveling, he was so thankful to be alive! Silently, she determined not to accept any of his largess.

By sunset, after a day of walking without food or water, she had changed her mind. When François offered her food, she took it eagerly. François chuckled. "It upsets you that Armand gave us some of his food? How did you expect us to eat?"

"It isn't Armand's food! He stole it from some helpless landowner! François, how can you be friends with a man who wanted to kill you?"

"He didn't, though, did he? It shows how big a man he is that he could be friends after I humiliated him. I think at the time he would have preferred to die."

"Die? Why, in God's name?"

"He'll bear a lot of ridicule because of last night. He's always been the strong man in the province. Now he's been defeated. He'll have a lot of fights to win before his reputation is reestablished. But I made it clear why I left him alive. We'll never win the battle for freedom if we just vent our anger by killing each other."

"We!" Juliette spit out the word. "You speak of them as if you were one of them! How can you be so disloyal?"

He gazed into her angry face, but he didn't answer. She knew why. They had been over the same ground many times during the journey—and always reached the same conclusion. He could never convince her of what he considered her error in supporting the nobility and the status quo. She was unable to make him realize how unforgivable it was for him to defend the peasants.

François was stuffing the remainder of his food into his sack when he looked up. "Did you hear something?"

Juliette nodded. She was staring at the bushes, her eyes wide with fright. Someone—or something—was creeping through them. Her anger forgotten, she crouched behind François. A rustling in the underbrush told her the attack was near.

A snarl ripped the silence, and a body hurtled toward them from the bush. It landed with a growl on François shoulders, forcing him back against Juliette. Crying out in fright, she tried to move out of the way, but she was pinned to the ground.

This time, François' knife flashed wildly in the cold moonlight. As suddenly as the attack had been launched, it was over. Panting, François stared at a tear in his coat.

Juliette looked down at the beast that lay at his feet. A dog! A wild, hungry dog had been attracted by their food and had tried to steal it from them. Juliette looked into François' eyes. "Did he bite you?"

François shook his head. "Fortunately, no. At least, I don't feel anything. Help me look, anyway."

They searched his arms and face carefully, but his skin hadn't been punctured. Juliette looked once more at the animal. "Do you think he was mad?"

"I don't know, but I'm glad I didn't get any bites, anyway. The sickness one gets from a mad dog can't be cured." He bent down and studied the open jaws. "No, I don't think he was mad. His mouth isn't foaming." He rose quickly, lifting her by one arm.

"Come, we'd better not stay here any longer."

"Why not? The beast is dead, isn't it?"

He looked into her eyes. "Do you want to eat its meat?" She shook her head. "Then hurry! Someone else might!"

He pulled her past the bushes from which the dog had emerged. But he wasn't quite fast enough. Suddenly, a man sprang out of the darkness. With a growl almost as fierce as that of the dog, he leaped toward the fleeing pair. His arm shot out—and Juliette felt herself caught between two unrelenting forces. François struggled to pull her free. Her dark attacker tried to keep her in the small clearing.

Once more François' foot shot out, catching the stranger by surprise. With a roar, he released his hold on Juliette's wrist. In that instant, François tightened his grip and ran with her into the night. She lost her footing once and tumbled to the ground. Screaming for him to stop, she struggled to regain her balance. "François! Stop!"

Impatiently, he lifted her to her feet. Then he was off again, pulling her behind him. She was panting from the exertion, but he didn't permit her to rest. Every bush they passed seemed to harbor danger, and though no other attack occurred, she felt relieved when at last they reached the open road. Space opened up around them. Wherever she looked, she could see clearly, even in the pale light of the moon.

François slowed his pace, his ear cocked toward the woods through which they had run. There was no sound behind them. Whoever it was who had attacked them hadn't bothered with pursuit. Juliette felt her wrist fall free of François' grip. "What happened? Why were we attacked by the man?"

François settled beside her, but he made no move to

stop. "I don't know. We're getting close to Paris, and food is very hard to get. It was probably some hungry man searching for something to eat." He looked down into her face. "I lost the bag. If he finds it, he'll have quite a haul for his night's hunting."

"The dog—do you think it was his?"

"Oh, no!" He chuckled wryly. "When a man's hungry, he doesn't keep animals for pets. He might have been hunting the dog when we got in the way." François smiled grimly. "He might have thought we were going to eat it ourselves."

The thought made her stomach turn. "I couldn't ever do that!"

"You would, if you were hungry enough."

She didn't pursue the thought. She'd had more than enough of his concern for the poverty of the peasants. Once more her life had been threatened by the animalistic behavior of the rioters, and his sympathy had gone to her attackers. When she spoke again, her voice was cold. "How far are we from Paris?"

"We're close. Another day or two and we'll be in the city."

Juliette stumbled. She was so tired! The run had used up what little reserve she had after a day of walking. "François, please, do we have to go on right now? I need to get some sleep."

He stopped then and gazed into her pale face. "No. We'll go into the field and rest." Her shoulders drooped. He smiled gently. "Juliette, we can't sleep beside the road. It's too dangerous!"

She tossed her head in anger. It was dangerous everywhere! She would never feel really safe until she was inside the walls of Versailles.

François located a spot hidden from the road yet open enough so no one could attack them suddenly.

Sitting down, he pulled her down beside him. She made no protest. Long ago she had grown accustomed to sleeping on the bare dirt.

Without glancing at François' face, Juliette settled herself on her side. He lay next to her, cupping her body with his own. She lay silently. His nearness set her body tingling, but she was determined not to let him know of her emotions. She had to remain near him, for protection and for warmth. But she wouldn't give him any chance to touch her intimately again.

As she grew drowsy, her hand closed around his ring. Soon she could take it off forever. A vision of François fighting the dog flashed through her mind. He still wore her locket. She wondered if he would remove it when she was gone.

Her fingers rubbed against the smooth gold of his ring. Maybe she wouldn't actually throw it away, though she'd no longer need it. She'd keep it as a reminder of—how frightening the journey had been.

His hand touched hers and closed around the ring. "Good! It still can be of help to you, even in Paris."

"You've been in Paris?" she asked coldly.

"Yes. I have friends there." His voice was still warm and gentle. "I still have your locket, Juliette. I'll wear it all my life, even if you leave me."

She couldn't restrain her irony. "You'll wear it until one of your *friends* steals it!"

He pulled her closer. "No. Before it's taken from my neck, I'll be dead."

She didn't answer. What was there for her to say? Watching the violence around them, she felt certain that day would come. Living by his wits among undisciplined animals, François was doomed.

CHAPTER TWELVE

As they approached the city, the road became crowded. Juliette gazed ahead apprehensively. Something was going on in the narrow streets. She tugged at François' hand. "Can't we go around the city? François, I don't want to go into that mob!"

He leaned close to her ear. "Trust me, Juliette. You need to be clean before you try to enter Versailles. Do you think they'd do anything but throw you out the way you look now?"

She glanced down at her dress. He was right. She was filthy. And she smelled as badly as any peasant.

The sharp report of rifles brought the mob to a sudden halt. Then, with screams of excitement, they surged forward again.

Frantically, Juliette pulled and pushed her way toward the bank of the River Seine. She felt relief when François made no attempt to keep her on the thoroughfare. When they broke free of the crowd, she settled herself against an ancient tree. "Please, François! Let's wait here for a while. I don't want to go through another Macon!"

He nodded. "No, I don't want you to. That's why we have to stay together." A deeper roar reverberated through the crowd, followed by a puff of smoke that slowly drifted above the roofs of the dilapidated houses. "Cannon!" François looked eagerly toward the source of the sound. Beyond the buildings towered

the Bastille, cold, timeworn stone battlements
silhouetted against the blue sky. "Juliette, I have to
know what's happening!"

She looked at him in dismay. "You want to go in
there?"

"I have to! If something is taking place, I should—"
He gazed anxiously toward the city.

Juliette felt her heart sink. He was determined to get
himself killed! She felt an overwhelming sorrow as
she gazed into his stern face. Despite the trials they'd
endured, and in total contradiction to his insistence
that he was just one more pawn in the peasants' revolt,
his features reflected a nobility she couldn't ignore.
With each day of intimacy, she had come to know him
better and to fear for his life more. It wasn't so much
because of his association with the revolutionaries; she
felt sure many would survive to an old age. It was his
untarnished idealism. Nothing he saw dissuaded him
from his faith in the integrity of the common man. All
the proof she presented to show that the peasants were
bloodthirsty and vengeful he brushed aside. He refused to see what, to her, was so very obvious.

She looked down at the river, surprised, in an
abstract way, that it was still filled with water and not
with blood. She wondered how many people had been
killed in the city already. Gazing at François' tense
back, she wondered when he would find a bullet—or a
knife—to end his dream. It would come, of that she
was certain. With a sigh of resignation, she rose from
where she had settled on the riverbank. "Do you want
to go now?"

"Yes. But I can't leave you here. If you won't
come with me, I'll stay." The disappointment in his
face pleaded for her understanding.

She nodded. "All right. I'll go with you." He

grinned boyishly. "Just one thing, François." Her voice was low. "Try to stay out of the fighting, at least until you've delivered me to Versailles. I don't want to get this close to safety and then not reach it."

The corners of his lips turned down. "No, Juliette, I won't risk your life now." He reached for her hand. "Come on! The firing's starting again!" The sound of gunfire was followed by a roar of voices. "Listen! What was that?"

Grabbing her hand, he pulled her back into the surging mob. It was no easier to find a place on the crowded road than it had been to get free of it earlier. More than once, Juliette found herself pushed toward the river, and she grasped François' sleeve to keep from falling. Everyone about them seemed infused with some new spirit. They all were eager to reach the city, eager to join in whatever violence was taking place within its gates.

Juliette tugged at François' arm. "Let's wait! Please! We'll be trampled to death!"

He put his arm around her waist, using his own body to protect hers. "No, you won't! Come on, we've got to get inside."

It was then the word came back. It flew from mouth to mouth as if carried on the wind. When Juliette heard it, she looked up in alarm. It couldn't be true! But the call was repeated again, louder. Soon the entire crowd was shouting, "The Bastille has fallen! The Bastille has fallen!"

She stumbled, and François stopped to help her regain her footing. A heavy woman with a basket jabbed her in the ribs. Juliette cried out in pain. With a curse, François shoved the woman out of the way and guided Juliette to the shelter of a doorway. Sighing in relief, she leaned against the wooden casement. Her eyes went up to the high walls of the ancient fortification.

"François, is it true? The guns and cannon! Surely the attack was repulsed!" She trembled. Paris was worse than Lyon—or Macon!

The crowd roared loudly, and then the cry was again repeated. "The Bastille has fallen!"

Juliette shivered. All Frenchmen knew of the Bastille. It symbolized oppression—and willful imprisonment. Yet, for a mob of shopkeepers and workers to storm and capture it seemed impossible!

François braced his body to protect her from being crushed by the ever-moving crowd. Twisting backward, he gazed up at the Bastille. When he looked at her again, his face was pensive. "Juliette, have you really thought through what you plan to do now?"

She gazed up at him, searching for the cause of such a strange question. "Of course I have! I want to get to Versailles as quickly as possible! I'm tired of filth and slime—and rape and riots. I want to go where things are proper and settled. I want to be ready to marry Roger when he returns from India."

"Are you sure he went to India?"

She frowned. "What do you mean by a remark like that? Certainly I'm sure. He told me he was going!" She paused. No, that wasn't quite right. Bouchard had told her. "But why wouldn't he do what he said he was going to do?"

François looked down at his dusty shoes. "Juliette, I've refrained from saying anything about duDeffand because I was sure you'd misunderstand. But it has to be said. I know he has spent the last few months at Versailles. I can't let you marry him without at least trying to tell you what kind of man he is."

The shouts of the mob grew louder. Suddenly, François and Juliette were picked up by the flow of bodies and pushed forward. Frantically, Juliette clung to François' arm, praying that he could guide her to safety once more. But he had no control over where they went. Like leaves on the river, they were swept through the street. Each time they passed a doorway, François grabbed at the supports, trying to stop their tumultuous forward movement. But only when they were opposite the entrance to the tall stone prison was he able to pull her to a place of shelter.

Pandemonium was all around. Those people who had just entered the city were struggling to cross the moat. Those who had accomplished the capture were already storming out, guns and boxes of ammunition held high over their heads. Juliette pressed her body into the narrow shelter François had secured for her.

Once more he gazed into her eyes. "Juliette, what kind of man do you think Roger duDeffand is?"

She remembered the bored, languorous face, the pastel suit, the long curl tied with a bow. "My father said he was a wealthy man—and most respected at court. As his wife—"

"What makes you think you'll be his wife?"

She felt her anger rising. "What are you suggesting? He wouldn't dare treat me like a common——"

His hand cut off her words. "Juliette, you forget, I love you. But you also seem to have forgotten that I *have* loved you." She started to protest, but he stopped her once more with his hand. "No, don't even think of these last few times. You and I—loved each other—before you ever were engaged to duDeffand. Did you tell him of our little game in the meadow?"

She felt tears of anger rise to her eyes. "No! Why should I? What business is it of his——?"

"What business? Juliette, you're not that stupid! You know a man like Roger duDeffand will want a virgin for his bride! Why should be marry you? What force will you use to compel him?''

''I won't have to force him to marry me. He's already asked for my hand! And, as for my not being a virgin''—she stood speechless for a moment. Then, with sudden inspiration, she continued—''There are ways to—deceive him about that!''

He smiled wickedly. ''So you plan to start your marriage with a lie! Do you know how? Do you know what to do? Who, do you think, will be trustworthy enough to share your terrible secret? And where will you find the information you need? Oh, Juliette, maybe, if Bouchard were still alive. But without her? Don't——''

His words were lost in a sudden roar from the mob. A new surge of humanity burst across the moat, carrying before them a tall, dignified-looking man dressed in the uniform of an officer. François gasped. ''The Marquis de Launay! They've captured the marquis!''

The cry of the mob changed now, divided almost equally. Cries of ''Try him!'' and ''Kill him!'' fought for control of the will of the mob. Once more Juliette and François were pulled into the street. For a time, they were almost next to the marquis. Then, slowly, that part of the crowd shoved its way ahead.

Listening to the voices around her, Juliette realized there had been fatalities during the raid. Close to a hundred people had fallen before the moat was stormed. A ragged man fell in beside her. Timidly, she touched his arm. ''How many prisoners——?''

He spat out the word. ''Seven!'' Then, as if reconsidering, he continued, ''But the Bastille is ours!'' His face wild, he pushed his way toward the captured marquis.

The irony of the entire situation overwhelmed

Juliette. One hundred people dead to rescue seven! And most of the seven were probably aristocrats, incarcerated on *letters de cachet*. What a revolution! What insanity!

She glanced at François' determined face. What had he been about to say when the crowd interrupted him? She looked angrily away. What a thing to suggest! How could he pretend Roger would reject her now that she was finally in Paris? In her memory, his smooth features gathered strength, his kiss seemed to have been gentler, his lust became love. Roger duDeffand became the romantic hero François could be no longer.

Suddenly a scream went up from the crowd ahead. The pikes and sticks that had floated over the heads of the mob moved furiously up and down. Everyone was shrieking and yelling, as if there was a madness that consumed their minds.

A stillness totally out of keeping with the noise that had preceded it set Juliette's heart pounding. No one made a sound. Even the wind seemed afraid to whisper. Pausing in confusion, François and Juliette strained to see what had happened.

Suddenly a cry went up that made Juliette's hair stand on end. As it reached its peak, one pike was lifted up into the air. Balanced at its tip was the head of the Marquis de Launay. Blood ran down the staff and dripped from the ragged edges of the severed neck, but the recipients of this gory shower accepted it with shouts of joy.

Juliette grasped François' arm as she screamed in terror. She could see that his face had gone pale, and he was staring ahead in horror. Then the sunlight grew dark. She was aware only vaguely of an arm circling about her, catching her as she collapsed. To the very last moment of consciousness, she heard the cries of triumph from the murderous revolutionaries.

The room in which Juliette awakened was far better than any of the hovels in which she and François had taken refuge during their long journey from Chalon. She was lying on a real bed, with four posts and a soft mattress. There even was a pillow under her head.

What struck her most, however, was how clean everything was. The walls were whitewashed, the coverlet that lay over her was spotless. Open casements let in the noise of the mob, still undiminished in volume, but they also welcomed the glowing rays of the afternoon sun. As Juliette listened, the sounds of the cries seemed to change. Loud voices were demanding the destruction of the Bastille.

She turned her head and looked at the figures standing at the foot of her bed. Immediately, François was at her side. "Thank God you're all right! I didn't dare leave you until I could tell you where I was going."

She looked at him with new appreciation. Once more he had caught her in time to save her from certain death. She couldn't change her feelings about his political views, but she had to admit her indebtedness to him. Nothing that happened would ever change her appreciation for his protection.

He looked very different from the way he had been when last she saw him. He had bathed and changed into fresh clothes. His hair was clean and combed into a braid at his back. His cheeks still shone from the scrubbing he had given them. He took her hand gently. "Juliette, if you consent, I'll leave you here while I go to discuss—things—with my friends. I'll have everything arranged for your move when I return." He paused, studying her face solemnly. "Are you sure you want to go to Roger?"

Her eyes were steady, hiding her inner trembling. "Of course I am! Are you going to leave your murderous friends?" She saw him start to protest, and she brushed his words aside. "Roger has his faults, I know. But at least he's a loyal follower of the king!"

He looked down at her fingers. "Juliette, my dear, do you really know the man? Have you the slightest idea of what kind of person he is?"

She struggled to keep her expression from changing. "Of course I do! He's generous—and very thoughtful! He proved that while I was at the Abbey Villeurbanne. Never a day passed that he hadn't prepared some surprise for me, delivered by his coachman—or by one of my maids."

François smiled grimly. "Is that all you want from life? Little gifts and new dresses?" He paused. "In the time you spent with his friends, is that all you learned about him?"

Juliette remembered Helene's words after her advances had been rejected. No, that wasn't all she knew about Roger duDeffand. But it was all she'd talk about to François.

He leaned over, his face close to hers. "Do whatever you wish. But remember this. If ever you change your mind—if ever you have had enough of—that kind of life—I'll be waiting for you. I love you, Juliette de Condillac. I always will."

He stepped back then and, with a half salute, said his good-bye. She reached out to touch him once more before he left, but he moved too swiftly. Repressing her disappointment, she turned her attention to the portly woman who stood quietly watching her from the foot of her bed.

A smile broke the solemnity of the round features. "Hello! I'm Madam Germaine, an old friend of François'. I hope you'll forgive me for listening in on your conversation with him. I didn't realize——''

Juliette smiled. Here, in the middle of a hostile city, she had found a second Hermione! There was no doubt about the woman's resemblance to Juliette's nurse. She was equally plump, equally light on her feet despite her size, and her expression showed just the right mixture of affection and reserve. She moved up from the foot of the bed like a mother hen rushing to rescue a lost chick.

"It's all right, Madam Germaine, it isn't what you think. He's only a friend."

Madam Germaine grinned slyly. "If you wish. It's none of my business, anyway." She smiled warmly, the little joke forgotten. "Come, my dear, you need a bath. I'll go order the tub brought in. I can't have filth like this in my house!"

Juliette chuckled. She even sounded like Bouchy! Angry as her words were, her smile was reassuring. Embarrassed nevertheless at having soiled a clean bed with her dirty clothes, Juliette rose and stood gazing out the window until the tub was brought in. Madam Germaine directed the placement of the tub and then brushed the servants from the room. Juliette began to remove her dress. "I'm sorry I soiled your bed. You should have at least removed my dress before you let them put me down."

Madam Germaine chuckled. "And you with nothing underneath? For shame! No, now that you're up, I'll just take all the bedding off and send it down to the kitchen to be scrubbed. It'll be fine after a day of airing in the sun."

Juliette looked at her dress as it fell to the floor. "I hate to put this back on, but it's all I have. It's too bad. It was a beautiful dress, once."

"It might be again, but not for you. I have something not quite as good quality, but neat and clean. It''—the woman paused, her expression clouding—''belonged to my oldest daughter, Francine.''

Juliette climbed into the hot water. Her legs tingled as they sank into the steaming tub. She had caught the tone of Madam Germaine's voice, but she felt uncertain as to how she should answer. When she was settled in the bath, she looked up. ''I'm sorry—'' Her voice trailed off. It wasn't polite to inquire as to how someone died.

Madam Germaine paid hardly any attention to Juliette's remark. She was staring out the window. ''She was such a lovely girl! And so good! She died in the Bastille, three months ago.''

''The Bastille! What happened?''

''She was imprisoned on a *lettre de cachet*—by the devil himself.'' She paused. ''All because she wanted to protect her sister from the horrors she had suffered herself.'' Again she stared at the window. ''It still hurts to think of it all. But I'm proud of her. Not even the baron could make her his slave.''

Juliette felt vaguely uneasy. More than anything, she wanted to drop the subject, but some little demon inside her refused to let it lie. ''The baron?''

''Yes, Baron duDeffand! Vile beast! He saw her as she went to church one Sunday, and he had her kidnapped right off the street.'' Madam Germaine's voice was bitter. ''When he let her go, she was bleeding from his attack. It was terrible! He forced himself into her—'' The wrinkled face twisted in pain. ''He's an unnatural man!''

Juliette felt herself tremble. It was Roger duDeffand the woman was speaking about. Her baron! Yet she couldn't say the words that would have stopped the diatribe.

Madam Germaine continued, her voice breaking

with emotion. "He sent her home to bring her sister. I guess he thought she was in such fear of him she wouldn't dare disobey. But she did. When she got home, she told Henriette to hide, and then"—tears were flowing down the leathery cheeks—"when she knew the child was safe, she went up to her room and waited. She didn't come out again until the soldiers appeared, with the *lettre*." Madam Germaine was spreading out the dress on the freshly made bed. "I never saw her again—until they sent her body home for me to bury. He seems to have forgotten about Henriette, God be praised."

Juliette murmured a few words of condolence. She was too shaken to hear more. When Madam Germaine changed the subject, she breathed easier. The motherly woman had taken over the task of washing the filth out of Juliette's hair, and as she worked, she spoke of her life in the city.

"My husband is a very successful baker. He's made all of the pastry for Her Majesty's parties from the day she arrived in Paris! He's at Versailles now." Her voice dropped confidentially. "He doesn't know about—François and—how I feel."

Juliette looked up in surprise. "You mean you sympathize with the rioters?"

Madam Germaine took a towel and began to dry Juliette's dark curls. "How could I do anything else. A government deserves to fall when it can produce a man like the Baron duDeffand."

Juliette avoided the subject during the remainder of her stay with the Germaines. The first two days she spent resting and playing with little Henriette, a light, playful child of ten who seemed untouched by the fears that disturbed her mother.

The third day she ventured into the streets. A rumor

spread excitement throughout the city. A miracle was about to take place. King Louis himself was coming into the town to declare his acceptance of the new government of the people! Juliette wished François could enjoy the triumph with her. The king's move made everything different.

As the royal carriage approached the corner where Juliette stood with her hostess and Henriette, the crowd screamed with delight. *"Vive le roi! Vive la revolution! Vive le roi!"*

Juliette joined in the glad acclaim. A meeting ground had been established between the revolutionaries and the monarchy. Everything was right with the world once more.

The gilded coach was surrounded by men on horseback, but only one of them attracted Juliette's attention. He was in pale pink this time, and the suit contrasted oddly with the tricolor sash all the attendants wore. DuDeffand! She would know him anywhere. Quickly, she looked away. But she found her nervousness reflected in Madam Germaine. The frightened woman had already tucked her daughter under her arm and was hurrying away from the procession.

Juliette followed. Why had she been afraid to let duDeffand see her? She knew without a doubt. Now that the revolt was over, she could, if she wished, marry François and return to the country. That was what she wanted. She would even forgive him for his support of the dissidents, since the whole affair was over!

Madam Germaine looked nervously over her shoulder. Then, clutching Henriette close to her side, she turned up a narrow alley. Juliette ran beside her. "What's the matter, madam?"

"Henriette. I think he saw her. I must save her from

him." They reached a church, and she hurried inside. She dropped her voice to a whisper. "Henriette, go back to Madam Bonnet's. She'll understand. I'll send for you when it's safe."

Henriette nodded. All the playfulness had gone from her face. She looked like a small, very old woman. Standing on her toes, she kissed her mother's cheek. "Don't worry, *maman*. I'll be all right. And he'll forget again, as he did before!" Then the child was gone, slipping quietly out through a side door.

Juliette watched the drama in silence. When the child was out of sight, she took Madam Germaine's arm and returned to the street. As they stepped into the sunshine, a man detached himself from the shadows and moved toward them. Then he vanished into the crowd.

Madam Germaine smiled. "Good! He's lost her, and we're of no interest to him. She's safe again. He's one of the baron's men."

Juliette looked back nervously. He wasn't in sight. Relieved, she scurried beside her hostess. When they reached the bakery, she looked back once more. A figure merged with the shadows, but not before she recognized him. It was the same man. He had followed them even after Henriette was no longer with them.

She felt terror grip at the small of her back. Roger hadn't gone to India at all! He was in Paris, as François had said, and now he knew where she was. The man who had trailed them had been following her. He wasn't the least interested in the child, Henriette Germaine.

CHAPTER THIRTEEN

"Open up! Open up in the name of the king!"

Juliette leaped from her chair. They had come, as she knew they would! She was the one the man had been following!

Madam Germaine rose sedately. Juliette could see the fear on the woman's face. "Don't worry, Juliette. They're looking for Henriette. When they see she isn't here—" Her voice trailed off. There was no way of knowing what would happen then.

Juliette cowered behind her chair. If, in truth, the men were searching for Henriette, what was to stop them from taking Madam Germaine a prisoner in order to force the release of the girl? And if Francine had been as mistreated as the woman claimed, why hadn't they complained to the king? Surely he wouldn't allow one of his courtiers to behave so abominably.

Madam Germaine scurried to the door and pulled it open. A tall officer entered. His face was handsome in a cruel sort of way. His eyes were dark and piercing, his chin square and very firm. A muscle rippled in his cheek. He saluted smartly. "Madam Germaine! A thousand pardons for disturbing you on such a special occasion. However—" He let his eyes roam about the room. When he saw Juliette, he smiled, a look of mock surprise on his face. "Mademoiselle de Condillac!"

Juliette had regained her composure. She recognized him now. He had been in attendance at the abbey, but he had disappeared sometime during the fire. She looked at him coldly. "Yes, captain?"

He smiled disarmingly. "I would not have expected to see you here! The baron said he thought he recognized you and sent me to find out if you truly were alive—and safe—after all!"

She didn't smile. "Yes, I'm safe. And I appreciate the baron's concern. Give him my thanks."

He laughed humorlessly. "But, surely you don't wish to remain here! He has missed you and wishes now to make up for all the hardships you must have endured." He paused dramatically. "We thought you were dead!"

Still she remained aloof. "Well, I'm not, as you can see. Please deliver my thanks to him and tell him I've changed my mind. I'm perfectly content where I am, thank you."

Madam Germaine gasped, but Juliette didn't look in her direction. The officer's face grew grim. "Mademoiselle, I wouldn't survive long were I to bring such a message to the baron. You must come with me! I'm sure you can tell him anything you want to say far more effectively than I could. No man would refuse to listen to a woman of your beauty."

She felt a glow of pleasure. Maybe he was right. It was rude of her to be so abrupt. After all, the baron had done nothing to make her lose her confidence in him. Everything she'd heard—including what Helene had said—could be only rumor. She took a step around her chair.

Immediately, Madam Germaine was in front of her. "Don't go, Juliette! Please. He's one of them! He'll surely harm you!'' Her voice dropped to a whisper. "He'll throw you in prison! You'll never see the sun again.''

Juliette hesitated. Maybe her hostess was right. After all, this wasn't Roger—it was a servant of his! Then she brushed the fear aside. "Please, madam, it's all right. I'm not a daughter of the bourgeoisie. He can't treat me—'' She stopped. There was no need to be unkind. Proudly, hiding her uncertainty, she held out her hand. "Your name, sir?''

The officer saluted. "George Dumont, mademoiselle!'' Taking her hand, he brought it to his lips.

She turned back to Madam Germaine. "Please don't worry. I'll be all right. And thank you for your kindness—and concern.'' She hesitated. "I'd appreciate it if you'd tell François I'm fine and will be back as soon as I have things settled with Roger.''

Madam Germaine chewed at her lips nervously, but she made no further attempt to stop Juliette. She stood silently, her eyes wide with alarm, her fingers pulling frantically at the hem of her apron.

Juliette gazed at her for a moment. Then, impulsively, she leaned forward and planted a kiss on the wrinkled cheek. "Tell François I've made up my mind. Please tell him to wait for me.'' Then, hiding her uncertainty in a proud smile, she took George Dumont's arm and swept from the room.

The carriage came to a halt. Eagerly, Juliette pushed aside the curtain. She'd been restrained from looking out as they rode through the streets after Dumont warned her there still were rioters about. He'd been most apologetic. "I hope you'll understand, mademoiselle. They can be dangerous. I wouldn't want anything to happen to you now, just when you've reached safety.''

A heavy iron gate, decorated with crowns, was slowly opening. Versailles! Despite her determination to return to François, Juliette felt a surge of excitement.

The horses started up, throwing her back into her seat. The curtain slipped from her hand and fell closed. When she pulled it open again, she was past the guards.

The next time the coach stopped, it was in front of a tall building. Juliette felt a wave of disappointment. They hadn't gone past the ornate gardens she'd been told existed within the walls of the royal city. They'd hardly gone far at all. Then she heard the handle turn. Before she returned to François, she would make certain she received a grand tour.

Dumont stood before her, his arm up to assist her descent. Juliette gazed about her with unconcealed curiosity. The building seemed strangely austere to be the residence of a baron!

The carriage moved quickly away. Without a moment's hesitation, Dumont led her through a heavy door and up a narrow staircase. Somehow this wasn't right! Surely there would be more ornamentation in the Baron duDeffand's quarters! Alarmed, she pulled her hand from Dumont's arm. ''Where are we going? Where's the baron?''

Dumont smiled reassuringly. ''He doesn't know you're here yet. I thought you might want to surprise him.''

She nodded uneasily. She'd visualized a straightforward confrontation with her affianced. She'd even decided on the words she would use to tell him of her decision. Then she shrugged her shoulders. Nothing that happened would change her decision to return to François. Maybe, if the baron were in a good mood because of her teasing, he'd take the whole thing with less irritation. Without further questioning, she let Dumont lead her up the stairs, down a narrow hallway, and into a spartan room.

When the door closed behind him, Juliette was already at the window. She swung about when she heard him turn the key. He was standing before her. The gentlemanly smile was gone, replaced by an evil leer.

Before she had a chance to understand completely what was happening, his arms went around her waist, crushing her to his chest. His lips pressed against hers.

Outraged, she pulled away. "What are you doing? I demand that you let me go! Where is the baron?"

He smiled arrogantly. "My dear mademoiselle, don't be so simple! The baron doesn't know you're here! He doesn't even know you're alive. He thinks you died in the abbey."

She stared at him in disbelief. This couldn't be happening! It was too outrageous! Her voice was cold. "Let me go, or I'll scream."

He chuckled wickedly. "Do you think anyone would listen? Don't be a fool! You're in the barracks. Women are always coming here to please the soldiers, and many scream, especially if they're enjoying the attention of some of our more—virile—men. Go ahead—scream. It only makes my pleasure the greater."

As he spoke, he grasped the neck of her gown and jerked it from her body. She screamed wildly, clawing at his shoulders, but her fingers passed harmlessly over the heavy wool of his uniform.

He swore when he saw her petticoats, but he tackled

them systematically, throwing her to the floor so he could pull them off more easily. Her chemise suffered the same fate as her dress. Torn by the force of his lust, it was ripped from her body, the buttons bouncing on the floor.

When he began to unbutton his breeches, she broke away and ran for the door. Fumbling madly with the handle, she tried to throw it open. But the door was locked, and the key was not in place.

He took her without bothering to undress himself. His eyes registered his surprise when his first thrusts met with no resistance. "Bitch!" His voice was venomous. "Did the baron take you before you left your home?"

She tried not to answer, tried to inure herself to the pain of his thrusting, but she was not successful in either attempt. Automatically, her head moved from side to side.

His laugh was cold and hard. "So you gave your prize to someone else!" He pushed farther into her body. A cry ripped through her throat. Never had she imagined she could endure such pain.

He poised himself above her, holding her fast to the floor. "Is it that François you spoke of? Is he the one?"

She sobbed, her body tense with anticipation of pain to come. Viciously, he pushed down against her. This time her scream was muffled by his lips as they closed over hers.

Once more he pulled back. "Is it? Is he the one?"

When she didn't answer immediately, he thrust once more, tearing at her tender tissues with the violence of his fury. He laughed then and rose to his knees. "He's the man. Well, the baron will want to know who it was who despoiled his bride."

Suddenly Juliette found her voice. "You—beast! You're contemptible!"

He roared delightedly. "Contemptible, am I?" With a sudden motion, he rolled her over onto her stomach. Roughly, he slid his hands under her hips and pulled her to her knees. "What's more contemptible than a whore who pretends to a virgin?"

She could feel him against her and she screamed again. Then, with a grunt, he pushed himself forward. A burning pain seared through her body. She screamed once more, and then she lost consciousness.

When she awoke, she was alone, lying on a cot, her naked body covered lightly with a rough blanket. She tried to sit, and the pain returned. Her entire abdomen ached, and each movement of her legs brought a sharp distress. Her glance fell to the floor where he had taken her. It was still wet from her blood.

Grimacing with the agony of each movement, she forced herself to her feet. One by one she gathered up her clothes and put them on. Then she lay back to recover her strength. The exertion had weakened her, and she did not wish to faint again.

As soon as she recovered, she was back on her feet. She had no idea how much time had passed since his assault, though from the sky it appeared to have taken place some hours before. Dawn was breaking. She had been unconscious through most of the night. He might return at any minute, and that possibility spurred her into action.

Agonizingly, she worked her way across the room. The door was still locked, but now she had more time to tackle the problem. Long ago, or so it seemed, when she was a child, she had learned how to open locks with a hairpin. It had served her well when Bouchard locked her in her room as punishment for lying. It served her better now. Carefully, she worked at the lock until she heard the click that told her it was open.

The pain made her stumble, but she didn't allow herself to fall. If she could reach the gates, she would talk her way out. She determined she would promise the gatekeepers anything, if it was necessary, to get them to open up and let her return to the city.

As she descended the stairs, her strength returned. The pain was still there, but it was eased by her joy at the success of her getaway. By the time she reached the ground, she was walking upright once more, though she still moved slowly. Some pride deep within her refused to permit her to show her pain to the common soldiers she would encounter as she made her break for freedom.

She was at the gate when a carriage pulled up. She backed away, waiting for the gate to open, but she couldn't move quickly enough. A head leaned out. Roger duDeffand!

His voice was light with surprise. "Juliette de Condillac! Is it really you?"

Fearful, she nodded. He stared at her in obvious confusion. "My dear! What happened to you?" He seemed to notice her expression for the first time. "Have you been attacked by rioters?" The carriage door swung open. "Climb in, my dear! Tell me what's taken place! How did you come here? I thought you were dead!"

When Juliette couldn't mount the steps of the carriage, Roger climbed out and helped her inside. Then he settled himself beside her. She felt her fear and terror slowly melt away. She hadn't expected such kindness.

The story of the attack on the abbey spilled out.

Roger interrupted her once, his voice filled with anger. "He lied! Dumont told me you were killed along with your uncle!"

Juliette sobbed. "He found me! He found me and—" Again she broke into tears. Now the horror of Dumont's assault returned to her in all its terror. Should she tell Roger what happened? She hesitated, unsure what effect the tale would have on her rescuer.

Roger looked at her sharply. "He raped you? The bastard! My own man! No wonder he told me you were dead. He wanted you for himself." His eyes narrowed. "He'll regret this."

Juliette felt her fear lift. It was all right. Roger understood. He didn't blame her for her misfortune.

They were passing the gardens. Despite her discomfort, Juliette leaned forward and gazed through the window. Before her stretched the elaborate mazes of which Helene had spoken more than once.

Far in the distance, Juliette could see fruit trees, but what impressed her most of all was the magnificence of the fountains that spotted the landscape. Then she looked ahead—and gasped in awe. The *Cour Royale*, with its imposing *chapelle*, towered above her on the hill. It was far beyond her wildest dreams. Nothing she had ever seen equaled its beauty.

Roger leaned close to her ear. "My quarters are to the right, at the end of the *cour de chapelle*. They've been in the family for generations, ever since Louis the Fourteenth! I find them most satisfactory. They provide the utmost in privacy and elegance."

He signaled for the carriage to stop. "Let me point out some of the loveliest places of interest."

As they sat side by side, Juliette heard a thundering of hoofs. A horseman was approaching from the city. She felt a momentary disappointment. Despite her tender body, she felt drawn to her companion. He was so kind—so considerate of her misfortune! He leaned away from her and waved his arm in salute to the rider. *"Hola!* Rider! News?"

"Terrible news." The rider pulled his horse to a halt. "The price of bread went up again today, and the riots have resumed. I ride to Monsieur Germaine. His wife was killed by rioters who robbed his shop just this morning."

Juliette sat stunned. Madam Germaine dead? It was hard to believe such a kind woman was gone.

Roger settled beside her, his face solemn. "I told Louis it was useless! They won't be satisfied until they've destroyed all of France! There's only one way to deal with such insurrections! Death is too simple!"

Juliette felt the length of his leg press against her own. In these peaceful surroundings it was hard to believe the fighting had started again. Yet, it couldn't have been a fabrication, designed to convince her to stay in Versailles. No man would ride to tell another of his wife's death were it not the truth!

Her mind raced in confusion. Henriette! What would happen to the child now that her mother was gone? With a sigh, she put that worry to rest. Madam Bonnet, whoever she was, would surely care for the little orphan until her father could come to claim her.

Then her greater fear returned. François! If the fighting had started again, he would be in the middle of it. And, with Madam Germaine dead, he would have no way of learning what had happened. He might think all the residents of the bakery had been murdered.

She pressed her hand against her fluttering heart. François would think she was dead! He would never come searching for her! And she dared not return to the streets without him. Her hand went to her ring. It had carried little weight in Macon. It would be even less of a defense in Paris.

She gazed up into Roger's intent face. At least she had found him before she was cast adrift! Now she would have to consent to their marriage. There seemed to be no other alternative. But she wouldn't hurry into this new alliance. Maybe, if she waited, François would learn of her whereabouts and come searching for her.

Then she remembered. If the fighting had resumed, she wanted nothing to do with François! They were enemies once more. Her heart cried out in loneliness. Her dream was once more shattered by the demands of people she knew not at all and cared for even less.

CHAPTER FOURTEEN

In the days that followed, Juliette often wondered how she could have misjudged Roger so completely. He was the picture of propriety—and consideration. He settled her in a suite close to his own, provided maids who cared for her injuries and did everything in their power to speed her return to health. She was surrounded by luxury far in excess of anything she had enjoyed even at the abbey.

He visited her every day, bringing reports on the renewed violence in the streets. She had a special chair set for him at the foot of her bed so she could see him without straining, and he headed for it as soon as he entered her room. He reported on Dumont, and what he told her filled her with satisfaction. A man stripped of his rank and returned to duty as a foot soldier would think twice before again assaulting the honor of a gentlewoman!

A week passed, during which she gradually grew stronger. The ache in her body vanished, and once again she greeted the morning with pleasure. Only one thing ruined her happiness. She couldn't put François out of her mind. The memory of her decision to remain with him obliterated all thoughts of the hardships she had endured on the journey. If only she could see him once more, she would accept her life with Roger without further regret.

On the eighth day of her illness, Roger arrived, as

was his habit, just after her lunch. She had felt well enough to dress and was sitting on the balcony, gazing down at the garden. She rose when he entered. "Roger! I'm glad you've come! It's such a lovely day!"

He bowed quickly over her hand. "Mademoiselle! I'm delighted to see you've recovered."

A happy smile lit her face. "Recovered—and ready to live once again." She paused, suddenly shy. They had not mentioned their upcoming marriage during her illness. Now she felt it was time to settle the entire issue. Taking courage, she lifted her eyes to his. "Have you made any plans for our wedding? I know it's sooner than you intended—but——"

His expression stopped the words in her mouth. He was looking at her with amusement mixed with outrage. Before she recovered herself, he had her hand once more in his own. Mockingly, he bent over it. "Wedding?" His voice was muffled. He was laughing! At her! "Why, what for, mademoiselle? Surely, you understand my position. The Baron duDeffand cannot marry a common woman!"

She bristled angrily at his words. "Common? Sir, you forget——"

"I forget nothing! It would be impossible! I can hardly pass off your little escapade with Dumont, can I? Surely, you understand it cannot be ignored, no matter how generous I might wish to be." He was pacing before her, his face working in anger. "But, even were I to forgive you that episode, I surely can't ignore your own deception."

She gazed at him in surprise. Before he continued, she already understood. His voice was harsh. "Dumont was contrite enough about his own actions, of that you can be certain. But he also informed me that he had taken no prize. You had been deflowered long before he touched you. How can you suggest that I marry a woman who, knowing she was to be my bride, robbed me of her most valuable asset?''

Juliette drew back in alarm. Roger's face showed none of the polite good humor he had evinced on his previous visits. It was flushed with fury, and a small muscle over his right eye twitched angrily.

There was nothing she could say. For the first time since she accepted his assistance, she wondered if he had lied to her about Dumont. Maybe he hadn't been punished at all.

Roger moved angrily to his chair and threw himself into it. Startled, she settled herself opposite him. He hadn't bothered to give her the courtesy of seating herself first. He valued her as a lady not at all! A cold fear gripped her. "What—" She waited until the quiver in her voice was under control. "What are you planning to do with me?''

He looked at her with mock surprise. "Do? What do I need to do?'' His voice was heavy with irony. "Aren't you satisfied with your present status? Surely, it's better than if I sent you out on the street like the common whore you are!''

She recoiled in horror. She didn't have to take such mistreatment! How could he speak to her in such an insulting manner? She'd go back to——

Where? There was no place for her to go. François had not followed her, nor had she any assurance that he was even alive. Why was she deceiving herself? François was probably dead. And even if he weren't, she wanted none of him! He was a traitor!

Suddenly a new cunning possessed her. Glancing at Roger through the corner of her eyes, she smiled seductively. "You intend to keep me here as your mistress?''

"The thought has passed through my mind. It's a shame to waste all the training you received at the abbey, and you are really quite lovely." He paused. "No, you're more than lovely. You are far more beautiful than you were when last I saw you. You can still be an asset to me here at court." His expression hardened. "We must, however, clarify our relationship. I expect you to obey me and to cater to my demands. If you stay with me, it will be due to my kindness. Not even the queen would expect me to care for you after what you have done. The least you can do is show your gratitude by pleasing me."

The memory of Madam Germaine's story chilled Juliette. Could she agree to obey a man with such bestial desires? Then the terror of her rape in Dumont's quarters set her trembling. What more had she to defend? She'd already been taken in the most degrading manner possible—and she had survived.

Roger pulled a cigar from his jacket and lit it with a candle. "Well, Juliette? Do you need more time to think about what I have said? All right! I'll return in an hour. If you agree, I have some duties for you to perform tonight." Rising, he took her hand once more into his own. His smile mocked her, but his manners were impeccable. When he left the room, he closed the door softly behind him.

Juliette rose and returned to the balcony. She was far too agitated to sit still any longer. What should she do? If she left the palace, where would she go? She shuddered. She knew what would happen to her, sooner or later. She would become open prey for the wild rioters who had taken over the streets—or for soldiers like Dumont. Either way, she would end her life as Helene had, ravaged by an angry mob.

But would staying in Versailles be any better? She looked about her. There was no doubt as to the answer to that question. She would have luxury—as long as she complied with duDeffand's wishes. She would eat well, dress magnificently, attend parties given by the king and the queen.

True, she would have to submit to Roger's demands. But they certainly could be no worse than what she had already gone through with Dumont.

Her spirits lightened. There was always the possibility that she could manipulate Roger into being more considerate of her than he indicated he planned to be. If she obliged him in every possible way—if she made him indebted to her because of her skill in the social aspects of her duties, maybe she could demand some consideration in their private relationship. She would have to play her hand carefully. If she succeeded, her life would be far from unbearable.

Roger returned, as he had promised, within the hour. He accepted her decision with no show of pleasure or disappointment. Still, gazing at his impassive face, she wondered if he didn't feel some interest in her that he worked to conceal. She wished he would show it, wished he would take her immediately, as a confirmation of their new understanding. But he simply kissed her casually on the hand. "You're a good girl, Juliette, despite your foolish behavior." He paused. "I've invited a few guests for an evening of entertainment. You'll be my hostess."

She shuddered. So soon? Was it starting so soon?

His look quieted her fears. "Mademoiselle, calm yourself!" His voice was unruffled. "You're to be my mistress, and I intend to keep you for myself, at least—" He stopped. When he continued, his voice was cold and distant. "We have a small company that will be performing the music of Herr Mozart's *Il Sogno di Scipione*. His Majesty is looking forward to the performance.'' He looked at her intently. ''You will dress modestly, for Her Majesty has become quite domestic in the last years.'' He sighed. ''These days, one must keep one's amusements to oneself! It isn't like the old days at all, when Marie Antoinette lived only for pleasure!''

Juliette breathed a sigh of relief. Her worst fears had been unfounded. Whatever he intended, Roger wasn't going to put her at the disposal of his friends. She would be allowed to maintain some pretense of dignity.

The opera went off most satisfactorily. Juliette, dressed in a plain velvet gown of the richest gold, received the king and queen with all proper respect. She was quite awed at their presence, though they weren't at all as she had expected them to be. Louis was a small man, quite retiring, who showed none of the aggressiveness she had always assumed he possessed. Marie Antoinette was equally surprising. She dressed most simply, more like a shopkeeper's wife than the queen. Juliette found it easy to imagine her spending the afternoon with Madam Germaine, discussing the problems of raising children!

During the performance, Juliette sat beside Roger, her head high. Obviously, none of the other guests knew of her degrading position, for they treated her with all due courtesy. The queen even complimented Roger on her charm before she said her good nights.

When the last guest was gone, Roger led Juliette up to her chambers. All the way up the steps, she prayed he would leave her alone, as he had every previous night. But that was not his intention. He entered her room at her side and waved the maids away. ''I'll care for your mistress tonight. You may attend her for her bath in the morning.''

When they were alone, he settled himself in his

chair. She stood before him, no longer embarrassed at the thought of his odd lack of manners. What difference did such a small thing make when his intentions were—what they were?

He cleared his throat. The tic in the muscle of his right eye was acting up again, giving her the impression he was winking at her. He stared at her in silence. Then he cleared his throat once more. "Take off your clothes."

She stared at him in surprise. His voice was cold and businesslike, as if he'd ordered her to bring him a kerchief. "Sir?" Her voice shook and she cursed her inability to conceal her nervousness.

"Take off your clothes!" His voice was angry now, Clearly, he did not appreciate any delay.

With trembling fingers, she undid the buttons of her gown. Carefully, she placed it over a chair. Then, one by one, she removed the full petticoats. Last came her new chemise. As she removed each garment, she caressed it gently. She loved her new clothes. They were, to some degree, her compensation for the humiliation she expected from him.

When she stood naked before him, she folded her hands over the soft down on her mount of Venus. His laugh was bitter. "Drop your hands. What place has modesty between you and me?"

Flushing, she did as he commanded. For one moment, her eyes met his, and then she turned away, her face red with embarrassment. He was studying her with the intentness of a man examining a valuable statue! Never in her life had she felt so bare! Never had she felt so strongly her position in his life. She was his possession—his thing—to do with as he wished.

When he spoke, she jumped in surprise. "What a

pity!'' His voice was gentle. ''You're far more beautiful than I believed you to be when I arranged to marry you.''

His face grew suddenly red. With a curse, he slammed his fist furiously against the arm of his chair. ''What a *crime*!''

She felt herself begin to tremble. What was he going to do? Why was he whipping himself into such a fury?

He settled back in his chair, his face once more calm. She smiled in relief. When he spoke again, his voice was even and devoid of all emotion. ''Come here. I want to look closer.''

Obediently, she stepped before his chair. The examination he gave her made her blush with shame, but she made no sound of protest. When he questioned her about her experiences and about the episode with Helene, she answered honestly, her eyes lowered, her heart burning with humiliation. At last, tired of the inquisition, he rose and began to disrobe.

She watched him timidly, her eyes filled with fear. He'd asked her questions she'd never thought to answer except in confession. Now he gazed at the bed as if trying to decide what his next move would be.

Despite her embarrassment, she couldn't take her eyes from his body. With his fancy clothes off, it was clear he was a well-built man. His chest was broad and solid, with a growth of hair in the middle. His stomach was flat and very firm, his legs long but quite muscular. And his desire was obvious. His questions—and her answers—had done much to arouse his libido.

He caught her glance and smiled. ''So you find my body enticing? Good! Your appetites have been sufficiently aroused through your experiences. Who knows? Maybe, in the long run, I'm better off this way. It really would be a shame to waste such a lovely body on childbearing. I'm sure you'll give me far more pleasure as my mistress than you ever would have provided as an innocent virgin bride."

She didn't answer. What did it matter what might have been? Gazing at him, she prayed he wouldn't be the brute Madam Germaine had claimed he was. Her experience with Dumont had shown her just how vicious a man could be.

Gently, Roger led her to the bed and indicated she should sit on its edge. His voice was surprisingly tender. "Well, my lovely child, you aren't a virgin, that I know. But I suspect you still have much to learn. Helene obviously had little opportunity to teach you her skill, and since I was saving you to be my bride, the others kept their distance. So I'll have to tend to it myself." He smiled. "It might be by far the most pleasant part of our relationship."

She didn't respond. There wasn't anything for her to say.

He continued in a confidential tone. "You show ignorance in two aspects of love. One, Dumont touched upon briefly, though in his usual coarse manner. The other— We'll begin with it." He rose and stood before her. You must learn the proper use of your lips and tongue in the act of love. We'll start with that."

She resisted when he directed her to use her tongue to lick the drops of liquid that glistened before her. But when she realized he was determined, she complied. To her surprise, they were sweet. When he directed her to take him into her mouth, she made no protest. She found it difficult to hide the pleasure she felt as the smooth skin touched her lips.

When he realized she took pleasure in the act, he settled himself on the bed, abandoning himself to the ecstasy she stirred with her uncertain movements. "Ah, I was right, you'd have been wasted as a wife!" Slowly, he began to move his hips, until his passion overwhelmed him and he shuddered with the force of her active tongue.

He lay still for a moment, breathing heavily. Kneeling at his feet, she felt a momentary disappointment. Was this to be all? Was he going to keep her for his own pleasure—and give no thought to hers?

He rose suddenly, pressing her back against the bed. "Now I'll show you what your reward is for so delightful a service! I know very well that to keep a mistress attentive, a man must see that her desires are not neglected."

She lay beneath him, aware only of the fire he lit when he touched her body. The shame she had felt when she first disrobed was lost under his caresses. A moan escaped her lips, and she felt a heat move from her thighs through her abdomen.

With a cry of ecstasy, she pushed her hips forward. She wasn't aware of her hands holding his head, or of the swiftness of her breath. A dizziness overwhelmed her. She lost all touch with the bed beneath her. Her only consciousness was centered at the point where his tongue touched her. Trembling with a passion she had never experienced before, she gave herself to his ministrations. All her reserves were dropped. What he offered so freely, she accepted with cries of bliss. She was intoxicated with her own responses. She was content to move when he directed her, remain still when his hands held her firmly. Her body responded to his touch—and she moved and moaned, echoing the excitement that pounded in her veins.

He made no protest of love—spoke no words of endearment. But his body and mouth said more to her than words ever could. She accepted his advances with eagerness, aware only that he gave her endless pleasure. And, before the night was over, he held her close to him, cradled against his body, united with her as Dumont had united. But this time there was no hint of pain. This time there was only delight—and a surprising, wonderful, mind-destroying ecstasy.

CHAPTER FIFTEEN

Juliette yawned and stretched her arms over her head, exposing the round swell of her breasts above her coverlet. Today was the day of the queen's ride, and she had been invited to attend.

Despite her general ennui, Juliette couldn't deny the honor bestowed upon her by Marie Antoinette. The queen was most selective in her choice of companions since she had become addicted to the domestic life.

Turning on one side, Juliette felt for Roger's body beside her. When her hand encountered only the sheets, she opened her eyes and stared about the room.

It was, by far, the most beautiful boudoir she had ever occupied. The walls were papered with scenes of court life and elaborate paintings of the gardens, all done by Monsieur Reveillon before his factory was destroyed by the mobs. The drapes were of the finest satin, and, when they were opened, she gazed through windows onto the gardens of Versailles. She herself had chosen the material for the upholstery, a rich velvet that stood out proudly against the white and gold finish of the ornately carved wood. In one corner was her wardrobe. Close to the bed was a chest for her shoes. Her chaise longue was close to the window so she could rest on it and view the garden. At the foot of her bed was a chair especially reserved for Roger.

It was on the chair she found him, gazing pensively at her. He did not return her smile when she caught his eyes.

Languorously, she threw back the covers and stretched her legs toward the corners of the bed. The smooth mound of her stomach looked soft and inviting, and she felt again the power her beauty gave her over this man who ruled her life. He cleared his throat. "You make things most difficult for me, my dear, most difficult."

A tiny wrinkle appeared on her smooth brow. "Difficult, Roger?" Lifting one leg, she bent it gracefully and stretched it up into the air. She smiled at his reaction. She had learned her role well, and she reveled in her ability to arouse Roger through simple motions. She had abandoned all hope of ever seeing François again. Madam Germaine was dead, and he must have died at the same time.

With her acceptance of François' death, she immersed herself in the life Roger had opened to her. The old Juliette, the child who dreamed of living her days on a farm with her young lover was gone. In its place was a woman who was fond of jewels, of fine clothing, and of the excitement of court life. She had to live her life as best she could, and, as Roger's mistress, that meant she had to please him—and him alone. Gazing into his eyes, she knew she had succeeded beyond her imaginings.

He rose and moved his chair to one side of the bed. "Yes, Juliette, difficult." He gazed at her speculatively. "Tell me, my dear, are you happy with your life?"

"Oh, yes, Roger!" Her words were positive, yet she didn't feel quite as certain as she sometimes had. She rose and knelt on the bed. She wore no nightgown, for Roger preferred her that way, yet she felt no embarrassment at being naked before him in broad daylight. His many hours of visual examination of her charms had eliminated such modesty long ago.

"Then why are you permitting our relationship to change?"

Her eyes opened wide. "You know?"

"Of course I know. I'm no fool!" His voice was suddenly harsh. "Had you expected to hide it from me?"

She gazed at him in confusion. Hide it? Of course not! "How can one hide a swelling belly?"

"Good! At least you aren't totally ignorant!"

She flushed. "Roger! I come from a farm. Certainly, I recognize the body changes that occur when a woman becomes pregnant!"

"Aha!" He rose to his feet and began to pace about the room. "So you admit it! You're pregnant!"

Something was wrong with the conversation. It was not supposed to have moved in this direction! Confused, Juliette stared at her stomach. There was, as yet, hardly any sign of the child growing within her, yet she knew it was there. "Of course I admit it. How can I do otherwise?"

He stopped his pacing. Facing her, he pointed his finger directly at her abdomen. "And where is my charming whore going to keep her brat after she whelps?"

Juliette felt as if she had been slapped in the face. She was accustomed to the epithet *whore*, for he called her that most of the time. But always, in the past, there had been a playfulness and a certain amount of affection in his voice. He expressed only anger now. Anger—and disgust.

She crouched down on the bed, as if, by hiding her body, she could protect herself from the venom of his words. No appropriate retort came to her mind, though she searched frantically for something to say that would straighten the conversation out and put it on the right path. His reaction had taken her totally by surprise. "I—I thought you'd be happy." She spoke quietly. Too quietly.

"What?" His voice was louder now, and she trembled. He was growing angry. She hadn't wanted to arouse his ire. He became so unpredictable when he was in a temper.

"I thought you might be pleased. You haven't married anyone else, and you've spoken often of your desire for an heir." She forced herself to speak slowly. There was no reason for her fright. He was only angry because she spoke too quietly for him to hear her. "My nurse said it's best if a child has a youthful father—and you're—" She paused. Somehow, it didn't sound right when she tried to say it.

His response startled her, nevertheless. He circled the room restlessly. When he returned to the bed, he stood before her, his face red with fury. "Damn the stupidity of all women! Juliette, have you no mind at all? Yes, I want an heir! But I must have a wife *first*!" His voice was heavy with sarcasm. "Tell me, my love, do I have a wife? Are we married. Did it all happen when I was drunk?"

She shook her head. "Oh, no! But—" Her voice grew quiet again, and a tremor caused her to pause more than once as she continued. "I—thought we— might"—the rest of her thought poured out quickly, before her fear could stop her words—"get married, now that I bear your child!"

She had dreamed of this moment many times since she had discovered her condition. Her need for acceptance had overcome her ability to see life as it was. She would tell him, she dreamed, and he would cry out in delight and fall into her arms. Then, together, they would prepare for the marriage ceremony that would make the child she bore within her legitimate. Never in her imaginings did she visualize what was now occurring.

He stared at her without speaking, his face working in growing anger. Then with an explosive curse, he threw his arms up into the air and strode across the room to the window. Pulling the drapes open, he stared out into the barren garden. Juliette let her eyes follow his. Winter had come, and the grounds were wet from rain and melted snow. Trees that had been filled with flowers when she arrived were now barren. Only the fruit trees that peeked from behind the right wing of the palace were green.

When Roger turned around, his face was hard. There was none of his usual indulgence in his glance. "Juliette, you will listen to me now, for, clearly, you haven't the wit to understand by yourself. Answer me, what are you to me?"

She lowered her eyes. She knew what he wanted to hear. This was a question he asked her almost nightly. "I'm your beautiful whore."

"Good! At least you know that much. Now I will tell you about whores. They do not raise children—nor do they get married! A whore is a female of convenience. Her major asset is her beauty." He paused and stared at her white body. "Let me spell that out for you. Beauty in a woman means a slender, shapely body, clear skin, well-formed breasts."

She gazed at him in silence. Her mind was in a turmoil. Why did he persist in acting so strangely? How could he fail to understand that she was different now?

He cleared his throat and spoke again. "Now, tell me. When a woman is with child, do her breasts remain firm and smooth—and well formed?" She shook her head. He continued without waiting for her to speak. "Right! They sag. They fill with milk! They become distorted and swollen and ugly."

She stared at him in disbelief. Ugly? She had always thought of full nursing breasts as beautiful! Why, she understood even the queen had insisted upon nursing her own children because she took such pleasure in the natural way of life! Still, Juliette didn't answer. There was nothing she could say that wouldn't increase his anger.

Roger snorted furiously and swung around to face her again. "Tell me, when a whore is pregnant, is she capable of pleasing her master at his command?" Again, he gave her no chance to respond. "No!" The word was like a shot. "She's ill, she suffers from the vapors, she's too bulky! She fears for the safety of her brat!"

She winced at his repetition of the word. The child she bore in her stomach was his! It was not a brat! Still, she was afraid to speak out. Maybe, once he had let his anger spill from him, he would become more reasonable.

He turned back to the window and stared out at the rain. When he didn't immediately return to continue his outburst, she felt her spirits rise. He was cooling off! Now he would see the reasonableness of her situation.

When he looked at her again, she knew her hopes were unfounded. His face no longer was livid, but there was no smile to soften its cruel angular hardness. Slowly, he walked to his chair and sat down facing her. "Juliette, let me explain." His voice was calm again, but she saw no hope for her plans in its cool detachment. "As you know, you're my mistress. You were to have played an entirely different role in my life, it is true. Had you been pure when you arrived at Versailles, you would have borne my child to fruition, and I would have been most pleased with you for giving me one so quickly.''

He leaned forward intently. ''You chose otherwise. We won't go into that again. I'm sure you know it all by heart. So then, since you are a lovely female, and a peer, I made another place for you. You couldn't be my bride, but you could be my mistress. And you have, until this moment, filled that role to my utmost satisfaction.''

She smiled tenuously. Was he softening at last? When he continued, she knew her hopes were shattered. ''There is one other part of my life of which you know little. I enjoy more—strenuous—pleasures with females from the masses.'' Juliette thought of Francine Germaine. She had not, obviously, been the only girl Roger had defiled. ''Their ability to please me is short-lived. Usually, they provide me with replacements. When they don't—'' He paused. She knew what happened. They were thrown into prison, to rot away—or to die of consumption.

The expression on his face had grown sinister. She looked at him with unconcealed fright. So this was the Roger duDeffand poor Francine Germaine had encountered!

He rose again and paced before her. ''If you wish, I can try to use you in that capacity, though I can't see your usefulness. There, as in a bride, I prefer virgins.''

He paused and stared at her solemnly. When he didn't continue, she rose up again to her knees. ''You don't want the child?'' Her voice was questioning. How could he reject his own issue?

''Not at all!'' The red was returning to his face. He

breathed deeply, forcing himself to become calm once more. "No, Juliette, I don't. Isn't that obvious?" There was no passion in his words at all. He spoke as if he were turning down an offer of a vegetable. "If you choose to have the brat, you must prepare to vacate my apartments. I will need to find a replacement for you."

She stared in disbelief. "You are throwing me out?"

"No. You are leaving!" He paused. "You can stay, of course, if you get rid of the brat now, before it disfigures your body. I'll permit you the days needed to recover from the abortion." He showed no change in his expression. "I understand you might be useless for a few days afterward. But, then, that is no more than happens during your monthly flow, so I would not be inconvenienced too severely."

She tried to speak, but her tears threatened any moment to spill from her eyes. She didn't want him to see her cry.

He sat on the bed beside her. "Juliette, I confess I am fond of you." He patted her hand gently. "I would much prefer you to get rid of the brat and remain as my mistress. I have many reasons, but one important explanation is the time I have invested in training you. I would not wish to have to repeat it with another, at least not so soon." He lifted her hand and gazed at it for a moment. "After all, you've only been truly adept at your trade for a few short months."

She knew he was right. The first month of her life in Versailles had been spent in learning the skills that pleased him—and in overcoming her natural modesty. Now she accepted his demands without question, and she no longer felt ashamed at being naked in his presence—even when he remained fully dressed.

He put her hand down on her lap. "Think about it, child. Where will you go with your brat, if you insist upon bearing it? Will the queen care for you? You know she won't! She's made it quite clear how she feels about bastards! Will the king? Never! He's too weak to stand up to his wife! No, you'll have to go out into the streets. Your child will have to fight for his life with the mobs of Paris—if you live long enough for him to see the light of day!"

Juliette hoped he would not continue. She could see the mobs easily, whenever she closed her eyes. They were cruel—vicious! Neither she nor her child would have a chance with them. Yet, she had been so sure he would be pleased by her news! She had dreamed of a quick wedding and then of an entirely new life starting for them both. How could he be so callous as to ignore the child she offered him?

"Well?" His voice was harsh. "What's your decision? Do you plan to keep the brat? Or will you be content with what you have?" He touched her hand lightly. "I'll confess it will please me mightily were you to choose to remain with me."

She resisted the urge to pull free of his fingers. He spoke as if he was being kind to permit her to—do what? She spoke quietly. "What can I do? God controls all life—and birth."

He rose to his feet, laughing heartily. Even when he caught her eyes, he continued, throwing his head back in delighted abandon. "Oh, Juliette! Did they teach you nothing at the abbey? What did Helene do with her time? She was told to see if you were a virgin— and to make certain you remained one. But I never told her to deny you pleasure—nor to keep you in childish ignorance! She was attentive to you, wasn't she?"

"Helene—" Juliette still could not speak of her encounter with that strange woman—nor of the death that had ended the life of pleasure. "No, she never told me anything about reversing the will of God!"

"Oh, come now! Enough of such nonsense! The will of God, indeed! It was the foolish carelessness of either myself or Dumont, assuming, of course, that the blame can't be placed on your friend François."

Juliette felt her belly. No, she wasn't far enough along. This could not be François' child.

Roger strode toward the door. "Take your time. Make the decision by tonight. I must know if I have to search for a replacement."

She held out her hand to delay his departure. "Roger"—the question was too difficult a one to even ask—"if I—decide—to—" She blushed and lowered her eyes.

"Get rid of the brat? You want to know what you will have to do? Ask Angela. She's performed that service for me in the past. She's actually quite skilled at it." He threw open the door and was gone.

Juliette remained on her knees, her mind in a turmoil. How could she do as he wished? But, if she didn't, she'd be out on the streets of Paris. Could she endure such a life? She rose and pulled the chain that summoned her maids. It was time to dress for the ride. The queen would be ready at the appointed hour, and she wasn't accustomed to waiting.

The pleasure she had expected to experience during the preparation for the ride didn't materialize. As Angela combed her hair and Julie buttoned the back of her gown, Juliette's thoughts were on the question she could not ask. She hardly saw her image in the mirror when, dressed and ready, she stood motionless under her maid's final fussing. Angela patted her curls. "My lady, you look ravishing! It's a good thing the king isn't going on the ride. He'd have eyes only for you." She held up the hat that was to crown Juliette's curls. "The queen would become quite jealous."

Juliette looked up. "What did you say?"

Angela chewed uncomfortably on her lower lip. "Madam, you're worried. Is there anything I can do to help?"

"Yes." As the word came out, Juliette heard it with alarm. Was she now going to ask the fateful question? It was as if another person were speaking. "Angela how does one—remove—destroy—?" She felt as if she were about to cry. "Oh, Angela!"

A knowing smile wiped away the concern of the girl's face. "Ah! You wish to—cleanse your body of a growth that is displeasing to the master?"

Juliette nodded. "No—yes— Oh, Angela, I don't know! What would have to be done?"

"It really is quite easy. I can do it in an afternoon, and then, for a few days, you'll be weak and a bit sore. Don't let it frighten you. There's no problem. It is at least as safe as childbirth itself." She stepped away and looked at the hat. "You wish me to make plans?"

Juliette turned away. She knew now she could never consent to such an act. She would have to endure the hardships of the street. She would have to risk the safety of herself and her child. If she let Angela have her way, there was still a danger. She couldn't deny the child a right to be born. She couldn't go against God's will, no matter what threats Roger used to control her.

Without answering Angela's question, she picked up her riding crop and walked to the door. As she touched the handle, she turned. "No, Angela. I'll tell him when the ride is over."

The chase was surprisingly difficult. The rain and snow had combined to make the ground slippery, and the horses seemed uneasy on their feet. Juliette, her thoughts on her coming eviction, fell farther and farther behind. She looked up when the queen called loudly, "Juliette! Are you riding with us?"

Juliette's heart began to pound. It wasn't good to offend the queen! Spurring her horse to a gallop, she leaned forward in her saddle. Eagerly, the beast leaped ahead. His hind legs landed on a hidden stone and slid from beneath him. With a shriek, he fell to the ground, throwing Juliette into the air. She screamed and reached for support, but her fingers closed on empty air. Then the ground rushed up, and she lost consciousness.

"Angela!" The woman stepped beside Juliette's bed. Something in her expression had changed. She seemed unwilling to look into her mistress's face. "What happened? Why do I ache so much?"

Angela smiled sympathetically. "You fell from your horse. Remember?"

"Yes." Juliette let her body relax. Never had she felt so weak. Her entire abdomen was filled with pain. "I hit my head, didn't I? Why does my stomach hurt so?"

Angela stroked her brow, wiping the beads of sweat that had formed with a light, soft cloth. "The master felt it was wise to take advantage of your unconsciousness. It is far easier if the woman isn't aware of her discomfort."

A frown creased Juliette's brow. "The baron? Why would he take advantage of my unconsciousness? What ha—?" She gazed into Angela's knowing face. There was no need to ask the question. She knew what had happened to her, knew why her abdomen ached so unmercifully. Roger duDeffand had, in fact, taken advantage of her accident. He had denied her the right to make her own decision. While she was unable to resist, he had directed Angela to perform the abortion. The child she had decided to keep was hers no longer.

She closed her eyes. A sadness like none she had ever felt before filled her soul. She had been lost when Bouchard died. She had felt alone when she stood at her father's grave. But this was worse than both losses put together. She was empty—useless. The life that had been pleasant before was suddenly worthless.

Angela leaned close. "Don't worry, mademoiselle, I did a good job. I damaged nothing. If you wish, someday, you can have another child."

Juliette shook her head. She would never go through this kind of torment again. "No. You must show me what to do to avoid it—happening again."

The girl nodded. "Later, mistress. When you're well again. Now you must sleep."

When Angela left the room, Juliette stared up at the ceiling. The light caught on the ornate crystal chandelier, but the sight brought her none of the delight it had in the past. Her dream, her hope, her baby was gone. Her fists clenched at her sides. Roger had won—this time. He had proven his power over her. She was, once more, his whore. But things would never be the same again. Now, gnawing within her heart, was a bitterness she would have to fight hard to conceal. She would do as he told her, she had no choice. And she wouldn't go out into the streets, not now. There was no reason to do so.

She would remain his possession. But she would hate him as long as she lived.

CHAPTER SIXTEEN

"It's time, my sweet, for you to branch out a bit!"

Juliette lay quietly beside duDeffand, her bare body still beneath his touch. "Branch out? What do you mean?"

He propped himself on his elbow and gazed into her still face. "You seem too lacking in inspiration. It occurs to me you might need a bit of a change."

"Are we moving? I've heard from Angela rumors to that effect."

"Yes, we are moving. Louis has informed me that he is going to Tuileries within the week, and we will go with him. That isn't what I was speaking of, however. You seem lacking in enthusiasm. The eagerness of your caresses is fading." He touched her thigh. "Have you pains there still?"

"No. I'm fine now." Her voice responded to his question, but her mind remained detached. "There's no pain anymore."

"Well, then, I was right. You need some new experiences to renew your interest in life!" He rolled onto his back and stared at the ceiling. "I've been considering a few surprises. For one thing, I am contemplating a gift that should put things right once more."

Juliette held her body immobile. There was no gift he could give her that would compensate for the child he had taken away.

When she didn't answer, he raised his knees and

arched his back. Then, resting again on the bed, he yawned and stretched his arms over his head. "You aren't curious?" His voice grew sharp. "You aren't still fussing over your little accident, are you? It seems to me it was quite fortunate!"

Still she made no response. He had told her, without her even asking, that her fall had resulted in her losing the child. Not once did he change his story. But she knew the truth. Angela had told her. The effect of his lie was not to comfort her, but to prove beyond a doubt his untrustworthiness.

"Well, I suppose I should expect some reaction. You're far younger than any mistress I've ever had before." He sat up beside her. "So, my dear, I will be patient—for a time." He frowned. "However, you must understand that even I have my limits."

She looked into his eyes without flinching. There was nothing he could do to her now that would hurt more than what he had already done.

He lay back on the bed, once more fastening his eyes on the ornate chandelier. "I've arranged for you to get an entire new wardrobe as soon as our move to Tuileries is complete. Isn't that nice?"

She nodded. "Yes, Roger, it's very nice. Thank you." She knew his present deserved more, but she could not rouse herself to any enthusiasm.

Once more he was sitting up, his eyes fastened on hers. "Juliette!" His voice was angry. "Enough of this self-indulgence! An accident is an accident! There's nothing that can be done about it! I was pleased at the time, for it meant I didn't have to change my life. But if you continue to behave in this selfish manner, you'll find yourself on the streets yet!"

She felt a momentary fear. There was no doubt he

meant what he said. She considered the terror of the streets once more. The visions that came to her mind were not new. Often, in the days since her accident, she had considered running away. But each time she had been forced to admit she hadn't the courage to confront the mobs alone. She couldn't leave, no matter how much she hated Roger.

He leaned over her, his face hard with anger. "You have to change now—to show gratitude for my generosity. If you don't please me—" He paused dramatically. "If you can't renew your interest in my pleasure, we will forget the gift—and you may prepare for your life in Paris—alone. I have no use for a whore who pouts like an angry wife."

She gazed up into his flashing eyes. There was no way she could bring back any of the emotion she once had felt in his presence. But she could pretend if she had to. She knew her trade well. He had seen to that.

Once again, she considered the streets, and the weakness within her cried out in protest. Such a life she could not endure. Without the child, there was no reason for her to put up with such discomfort—and danger.

The sparkle that came to her eyes was forced, but it grew as he watched. She masked the anger in her heart with seductiveness. She concealed the hate she felt toward him with a warm smile.

With a snort of pleasure, he lay back on the bed, his eyes closed. She recognized the motion. He expected her to show her contentment by pleasing him.

Repressing an urge to do him harm, she touched him lightly. As her fingers slid down his hard stomach, a smile touched the corners of his lips. She performed them all—every skill he had taught her through the months of her stay in his chambers. He moaned in delight as she moved above him, and when his eyes met hers, she smiled mechanically and moaned in response. But she felt nothing. When, at last, he lay spent beside her, she stared up at the ceiling.

As was his habit, he dropped immediately into a deep sleep, his even breathing broken occasionally by a tremulous snore. Slowly, so as not to waken him, she moved away until no part of her body touched his. She lay staring toward the windows. Outside, the moon reflected against the white of the falling rain. She had felt nothing at all. He had taken his pleasure without once stirring her responses.

The hard stone that had once been her heart had not been touched by his caress, even when she had willed it to react. He muttered in his sleep and rolled onto his side. Turning, she stared into his quiet face. She had obeyed him—and he had been satisfied. As long as she continued the pretense, he would be content.

Her thoughts wandered back to his earlier promise. Now, she was certain, he would give her the wardrobe he had spoken about. And when the dressmaker came, she would demand only the best.

The best— Her fists clenched beside her. The best had been denied her. For the rest of her life, she would have only second best. She knew now that for a whore, the best in life was unavailable.

She felt a twinge of pain when she thought of herself as a whore. Yet, now, for the first time since she had moved into Roger's apartments, she knew she deserved the name. She was, in truth, a whore. Silently, she began to plan her new wardrobe. Since she was a whore, she would make certain that she was well paid for it.

* * *

As soon as she entered her suite after the morning's ride, she knew something was different. The furniture was not changed. It was, in fact, almost a duplicate of the equipage found in her suite in Versailles. Even the chairs had been covered to suit her taste. The wardrobe was new, made to hold her elaborate gowns, and a new, large mirror fit neatly into the pattern of the painting on the wall. Roger's chair sat at the foot of her bed, as one had in her first suite in the country palace.

There was, she knew, only one major difference. At Versailles, her suite had been above his. At Tuileries, they were side by side, with a door adjoining their bedrooms.

Her attention was now drawn toward that door. The drape that hung over it had caught in the breeze from the open window, and it floated out into the room. The movement surprised her. Most of her drapes were too heavy to move so easily in a light wind.

Curious, she walked toward the drape, intrigued by its unusual pattern. One panel seemed to have been changed since last she saw it.

The wind died down, and the drape fell back against the wall. Everything appeared normal. She took hold of the drape and pulled it out, stepping behind it to the door that connected her room with Roger's. The drape fell behind her, and she turned in surprise.

She was in a small alcove, staring out into her room as if it were a stage. Through the flimsy material of the single panel, she could see every detail of her bed.

She glanced down. The transparency stopped just below her chin. From that point on, the material was heavier. A person standing as she did would be invisible to anyone lying on the bed—or walking about the room—unless they knew exactly where to look.

There was a knock on the door and she quickly slipped out from behind the curtain. Had it been there when she first entered the room, months before? She couldn't say. Probably it had. She just hadn't noticed it before. There certainly had been no workmen in the room since her arrival.

Angela and Julie entered. "Mademoiselle"— Angela's smile seemed particularly motherly—"it's time for you to dress for the party." Juliette couldn't restrain her smile. Angela treated her much as Bouchy had when she was a child. She wondered if it was because of the abortion. Maybe the girl still felt her guilt for her part in the deed.

Silently, Juliette stepped to the center of the room. Julie began to unbutton her dress while Angela pulled the costume from the wardrobe. It would take quite a length of time to get her hair done properly, and she knew Roger was counting on the effect of her disguise.

When she was totally naked, she stood before the mirror, her arms out from her body. She was aware of a lethargy, a feeling of uninterest, that never left her, no matter what she did. Years ago, when she was a child, she would have thrilled at such a dress-up occasion. Now it was just one more thing to do to fill her empty days. There were moments when she felt a renewing of her earlier excitement in living, but then she would think of the child that had been taken from her, and her spirits would fall.

When her costume was placed before her on the bed, she felt a momentary pleasure. It was particularly seductive—and daring. It showed her body in a most delightful manner. Made entirely of transparent silk, it was shaped in the form of pantalettes, with a loose covering on her body and long sleeves that were gathered at her wrists. A low neckline cut way below her full breasts. Angela pulled it over her body.

Angela clasped a girdle made of gems and bright bits of gold and silver over her hips. The ornament held the tissue cloth against her body and made it flare out over her thighs. It also concealed the dark hair that crowned her femininity, but it concealed nothing else.

Two plates were affixed over her breasts, held on with silver cords. Like her girdle, they covered the variations of shade in her body, but did nothing to obscure her firm, youthful shape. The gossamer material floated around her hips like a spider web, emphasizing her narrow waist and firm stomach.

Angela combed Juliette's hair loosely about her shoulders, covering it with another bit of the fine material, in which gems had been stitched. Roger had insisted on the costume, informing her it was exactly the dress worn by women in Arabian harems. She had immediately decided not to like it because he chose it, yet, despite her knowledge that it would please him, she could not refrain from smiling when she saw her image. She did look extraordinarily lovely.

She turned slowly. There had been a time when she dreamed of growing up into a beautiful woman like her mother, but even that didn't delight her. When she thought of her parents, she remembered that such a role was forever denied her. Gazing at her image, she wondered that her looks didn't reflect the barrenness of her heart.

She gazed dully into her jewel box. How could she have ever been delighted by such simple pleasures? Now nothing made her ecstatic. She was simply thankful when there was enough to do to keep her from thinking of her broken life.

Her eyes fell on the ring François had given her.

How long ago was it? Lifting it from the box, she held it in her hand. Almost two years! She had forgotten its existence!

"Do you wish to wear that, too, mademoiselle?" Julie leaned forward, unable to conceal her curiosity.

Juliette held the ring out before the woman. "Where can I put such a simple thing? It's far too big for my finger."

Angela began to fumble in the box. At last she pulled out a long gold chain and held it up before her. "Mademoiselle, you could put it on this, and wear it around your waist. It would be most seductive—and unusual. Its simplicity would make it quite remarkable."

Turning her hand, Juliette let the ring roll into her palm. It felt heavy—and warm—and comforting. She gazed at it with a growing sense of pleasure. She had faced troubles then. She had even feared for her life. But she had felt so aware—so alive! She had experienced passion, and terror—and love. Touching the ring with her thumb, she tried to remember how those emotions felt. But her heart refused to respond. It had been dead for too many months.

Still, she was reluctant to put the ring down. There was a magic in it that promised to penetrate her shell of isolation. Gazing at it, she wondered whether François had worn her locket when he was killed. She hoped he had. She wanted no one else to wear it, unaware of its value to her. Sighing, she held the ring up in her fingers. "All right, if it would give you pleasure."

Angela took the ring with a forced smile. Juliette was aware that the woman felt great sympathy, that she even had an affection for her mistress. But Juliette did not dare to allow herself to recognize such a warm compassion. It might break through her reserve and open the wells of sorrow that lay buried in her heart.

Maybe Angela even regretted her part in Juliette's loss of her child. But Juliette refused to broach that subject, even in the most intimate of moments with her maid. Now, she lifted her arms and let Angela string the chain around her waist under the light gossamer. She had tied the ring on one end, and when she knotted the chain, the ring hung down over Juliette's navel. She stepped back with a smile. "It looks wonderful! Promise me you'll wear it all the time. I'm sure the baron will find it most intriguing!"

Juliette turned toward the mirror. Angela was right. The ring did add a bit of intrigue to the entire costume, and the gold chain around her waist was particularly charming. She nodded. "I'll see. But if he objects, don't be unhappy. It's hard, sometimes, to predict how he'll react."

His reaction was entirely favorable. He raised his eyebrows when he saw the ring, but he seemed totally taken by her appearance. In fact, he even remarked that the chain around her waist increased her seductiveness.

As for the effect of her costume at the party, nothing could have pleased him more. None of the gentlemen in attendance could take his eyes away from her body. Armored as her heart was from all emotion, Juliette still felt a slight stirring of pleasure at such appreciation.

She danced with every man present. With each she flirted outrageously, glancing up from lowered eyes, smiling, fluttering her eyelids. And she took delight in seeing that each one would have liked to have her on his arm as he left the dance. Only one thing bothered her. Roger wasn't around to see her triumph. He was off in a corner with the king, and only once did she see him gazing in her direction. And at that time, it was the king's expression she noticed. He was looking at her with obvious appreciation.

As the evening wore on to its close, Roger came to Juliette and took her arm. "Juliette, need I say I have been most pleased with you all evening." She nodded, a quiet smile on her face. He patted her hand. "You have made me very proud." With a tilt of his head, he gestured toward the king. "I've been speaking with His Majesty, as you might have noticed." She nodded. She had wondered what could have kept him from the festivities for such a long time. "He's shown an interest in you that is most gratifying."

"He wishes to dance with me?" A small spark lit Juliette's eyes. This was a dream she had had as a child.

"Yes, my dear, he does." Roger paused and gazed at her thoughtfully. "He might have other thoughts as well. A glass of punch, a walk in the garden. You'll satisfy me most thoroughly if you accept his attentions graciously."

She nodded. Often, it was difficult to understand what motivated Roger. Why, now, was he making such a fuss over asking her to dance with the king? Surely he knew she was more than willing to be gracious to her monarch! She turned and gazed across the dance floor at Louis.

As if drawn by her glance, he left the side of the queen and stepped onto the floor. Immediately, the dancers paused to make room for him to pass. When he stood beside her, the music started up and the dancers resumed their graceful movements. He bowed ever so lightly from the waist. "Mademoiselle, may I have this dance?"

She nodded, a fixed smile on her face. Back when she was a child she would have given anything for this moment. Now it stirred her emotions very slightly.

When the dance was over, she looked about for Roger, but he was nowhere in view. Louis placed her hand on his arm. "Mademoiselle, Roger spoke to me of the importance of realizing one's own inner strengths." He paused. When he spoke again, he had walked with her toward the door that led into the garden. "He has made what I recognize as a valuable argument for a more liberal life than I have, until this time, led." They had left the ballroom and were strolling arm in arm past the sweet-smelling roses. She inhaled the fragrance with enjoyment. She loved the flowers. Their ever-changing beauty reminded her of her father's farm.

"Mademoiselle"—the king seemed nervous— "Roger has recommended you most highly and has informed me of your eagerness to give me pleasure. I've considered it with great seriousness." He had reached the door to duDeffand's wing, and he was grasping the handle. "I find his arguments most persuasive."

She found her voice at last. "Persuasive, Your Majesty?"

"Yes." He began to mount the stairs, her arm firmly in his own. "He claims a man who has not experienced his manhood fully is often incapable of decision-making." His laugh was short and bitter. "Certainly, no one in the court can doubt it fits my description. The prince himself is better at making up his mind than I am!"

Juliette tried to protest, but he brushed her words aside. They were turning up the second flight of stairs. He stopped suddenly. She felt a wave of relief. He was going back, at last. He had not meant to head for her quarters.

But he didn't turn and descend. Instead, he faced her solemnly. "To make the matter simple, Roger has said you have offered your—services. I understand your position, and I assure you if you show discretion, you will be well rewarded"—he paused again—"especially, if it results in my increased manliness."

She looked at him in confusion. Maybe he was just making a fool of her because of her daring costume! Surely, when she reached the door to her room, Roger would be waiting there, and all three of them would share a laugh.

Louis led the way up the final staircase. When he reached her door, he opened it politely. Helplessly, she stepped inside. It was really happening. Roger had said she needed variety. Now she knew what he meant. He was giving her to the king—at least for the night. And he knew she would not refuse. How could one say no to the king?

Trembling with repressed anger, she stared about her. Maybe, at the last moment, the king would change his mind! But Louis had slipped out of his clothing with a nervous restlessness, dropping each piece on the floor as he removed it. When he stood un- clothed, he settled himself in Roger's chair, his hands resting loosely between his legs.

He looked up. "Mademoiselle, duDeffand told me you perform most delightfully. He says you have a dance that fits your costume, and talents worthy of a sheikh's harem queen. I have always had a fantasy of being seduced by such a woman. Tonight, you will be Salome, and I, Herod. Dance for me, Salome! Dance for me!"

There was no disobeying. Her eyes cast downward to avoid his gaze, she began to gyrate sensuously.

As she passed close to his chair, he reached out and tugged at her girdle. There was no doubt as to his demand. Without missing a step in her dance, she reached down and released the clasp. As she passed her chaise she dropped the girdle on its cushion.

Louis crowed in delight. The next time she approached him, he pointed at her breastplates. It wouldn't be long, she knew, before she was entirely naked. Still, she couldn't refuse. The silver plates dropped beside the girdle.

When Louis slipped the gossamer from her shoulders, she glanced away. She was far too overcome with shame to face him. Roger had won—there was no longer any doubt. She was a whore, a courtesan in every sense of the word. He even dared to give her to another without asking her, and she obliged without a fight. Silently, she cursed the fear that kept her from dashing into the streets of Paris. But even as she berated herself, she knew it was more than fear that held her in Roger's power.

She would face assault in the streets, too. But there she would have nothing to compensate for her loss of respect. She watched the gossamer drop to the floor. Here she received beautiful gowns, jewels, and gifts for her loss of virtue. On the streets, her only reward would be pain—and hunger.

The king rose and moved to the bed, his eyes fastened on her naked body. She knew what she had to do. Slowly, she moved around the bed so as to approach him from the side. As she climbed up beside him, she glanced up. The curtain over the narrow door to Roger's room moved slightly.

With a blush of shame, she lowered her head over the king's supine body. But the vision of the moving drape remained in her memory. She knew now where Roger had gone. He had entered his room to wait for her arrival. And now he stood behind the curtain—

watching! Her shame was complete. There was no lower point for her to reach. He was giving her to another—and watching to make certain she performed to his satisfaction.

When she awoke, she was alone. Rising, she stepped to the window and gazed at the sun as it rose over the palace roof. When she turned, her eyes rested on her chaise. There, beside her girdle and breastplates, was a magnificent necklace. She hurried over and lifted it in her hands. This was the king's way of showing his appreciation.

Quickly, she hurried to the mirror and held the necklace around her neck. Never had she seen anything so beautiful! Diamonds sparkled in the sunlight, reflecting in rubies and emeralds of a size she had not imagined existed. And all were placed in a design of impeccable excellence.

There was a light tap on the door and Angela and Julie entered. Angela spoke as she closed the door. "Are you ready to dress now, mademoiselle?"

Juliette nodded. "Find me a gown that's appropriate to wear with this new bauble." Lightly, she tossed the necklace to her maid. The gasp of delight that escaped both women pleased Juliette more than any praise from Roger ever could. She smiled quietly as she settled herself before her dressing table. She was a whore, as Roger claimed. Of that there was now no doubt. But at least she had the satisfaction of knowing she was an excellent one.

CHAPTER SEVENTEEN

Despite Juliette's resolve to take satisfaction from what little joys were given her, there was no pleasure for her in the necklace, nor in any of the other gifts she received in the weeks that followed. She wore her new jewels only when Roger insisted, and, when she had them on, she avoided the eyes of the other women, knowing they had to be aware of her shame. Yet, filled with guilt though she was, she had no heart for struggle.

Louis had changed considerably during the months at Tuileries. At Versailles, he concentrated on politics. In the city palace, he seemed to give up entirely. No longer did he make any concerted attempt to maintain control. He kept up a secret communication with Mirabeau, from whom he received one kind of advice. He received another kind from his courtiers, particularly from Roger. And in the meantime, Marie Antoinette was pursuing her own plans to save the crown—and her royal skin.

Louis devoted most of his time to his hobbies. He spent hours working in his room on various locks, some of which he had invented himself. When he wished to spend time out of doors, he worked in masonry, repairing walls and building new structures, with the help of artisans assigned to the palace. Occasionally, when his other entertainment lost its charm, he visited Juliette's chambers. Sometimes, he demanded her services. But at other times, when she was in Roger's arms, she would notice the curtain move and she knew Louis was watching.

The king had been quite taken by the chain around her waist, so much so that he insisted she continue to wear it, even though Roger would have preferred not to see it. Juliette did as her monarch demanded, and even in her apathy, she was pleased that she could keep François' ring near her again. Each time she felt it press against her abdomen, she remembered the time when she had loved—and been loved. Once she had been alive. She took comfort from the memory.

Despite a busy schedule of public parties and private assignations, Juliette seldom felt an interest in what was happening to her. She learned to take whatever came with stoicism, knowing it would, eventually, pass and be replaced by something else equally uninspiring.

One result of Roger's decision to share her body with the king was a lessening of her contact with him, and for this she was most grateful. She had not forgotten his cruelty, and she found it no easier to pretend pleasure in his presence long after the pain of the abortion was forgotten than it had been in the days immediately following her unfortunate "accident."

Still, she knew her duties. When he visited her, she made him most welcome. She had not forgotten the threat he held over her head.

During one of his increasingly rare nights in her bed, she glanced toward the curtain and realized it was moving. Startled, she raised herself up on one elbow. "Roger—look. Someone's watching us!"

He stroked her smooth stomach. His voice showed no surprise. "Well, so there is! Maybe we should find out who dares to invade our privacy!" He spoke loudly, as if he were reciting lines in a play.

Juliette felt a shiver run up her body. Obviously, Roger knew who hid in the corner. He had planned it before he entered her chamber! Suddenly uneasy, she dropped back onto the bed. "Oh, it's all right. Since you already know who it is, we can just let him stay there."

Roger rolled onto his stomach and lay watching the curtain, which was beginning to move convulsively. "No," he was reciting again, "I insist you go and expose the knave. Now!" The last word was sharp, and she knew its meaning. He was through with giving her a choice. She had noticed the change in his speech often enough to recognize a command.

Silently, she rose to her feet and moved toward the swaying curtain. She looked back once, but Roger was still lying on his stomach, his head propped on his hands. He was smiling with pleasure. There was no misunderstanding his behavior. He had planned this as a new form of erotic entertainment. Only she, among the three actors, had not been given the opportunity to learn her lines in advance.

She turned back to the curtain. It really didn't matter. There was little danger of her taking a wrong cue or ignoring one when it was given to her. Her duty was obvious. She was to throw the curtain aside in assumed horror, expose the watcher, and take him across the room to her bed. She expected Roger would defer to this new companion, maybe watching from his chair—maybe replacing him behind the curtain.

As she approached the door, she crouched playfully. With a leap, she grasped the curtain and pulled it aside. There, stripped of all his clothing, stood the king. He had been watching the scene with growing excitement, and his hands were performing the duties usually provided by her talents.

She felt a shock. Louis didn't belong here, in such a shameful position! He was the king! She had grown to know him during their talks together, and she recognized him as basically a quiet, reserved man, much like her father had been. He had none of the fierce eroticism that came so naturally to Roger. Louis was happier with a new lock than with a new woman.

Yet, he was as much a prisoner in Tuileries as she. Bored with the inactivity, unable to cope with the tremendous political forces surrounding him, he had at last abandoned himself to sensuous living.

Juliette watched the cowering monarch with revulsion. The whole of France was depending on the political adeptness of this man, and he was wasting his time in games suited only for lechers like duDeffand! What hope was there for her world? France was lost for sure!

"Juliette! Bring the culprit over here!" Roger's voice was filled with excitement. The king shrank back in mock terror. More of the erotic script had been devised, she was certain, in the king's fertile brain. Instead of being the seductive Salome, she was to play the outraged mistress, out to punish a trespasser in her boudoir.

This was the worst humiliation of all! She was accustomed to acting the submissive one. But to assign the role to Louis! To turn the king into a simpering fool, cowering eagerly beneath her reluctant hand, begging for mercy while clearly anticipating erotic chastisement—that was more than Juliette could bear!

She was almost relieved when the script suddenly changed. Once he reached the bed, Louis took charge—in his usual timid way. Nevertheless, Juliette became the main focus of attention. He made it clear she was to take them both to please his curiosity. So far had she fallen into the corruption Roger had inflicted upon her that such a demand roused no resentment. She submitted meekly, as if she had been the one caught behind the curtain. It seemed only proper that, even in a game designed to humiliate another, the final humiliation be hers.

She let herself be moved about, let her body be taken without protest. She even moaned with assumed ecstasy when she realized such a response was expected. But, when the two men fell exhausted to the bed, she lay between them with no more awareness of pleasure than could have been felt by the pillow at her head.

Immobile, she remained as they left her until she was sure they were both asleep. Then, careful not to disturb them, she slipped from the bed and hurried across the room and into Roger's quarters. Once there, she summoned her maids and ordered a bath. But even soaking in the steaming water, the depravity that ate at her soul would not wash away. As she rose to dry her body, she knew she never again would feel completely clean.

"Oh, Count deEpnay! What a sly fox you are!" Juliette tapped the count lightly with her fan. They had just finished a minuet, and she was following Roger's requirement that she be the flirt with every partner, even with an ancient man like the count.

DeEpnay was obviously flattered. A red flush tinted his neck and forehead, creeping in behind the snowy whiteness of his goatee. His eyes sparkled with what Juliette felt sure was a memory of the time when he might have backed up his seductive words with action. But those days were past for the count. After a few lascivious suggestions accompanied by winks and gestures, he staggered to a chair and settled himself on its cushions.

Juliette watched as he made himself comfortable. Then, opening her fan, she waved it frantically. "My goodness! I suddenly feel terribly overheated!" The fan fluttered madly. "My dear count, will you excuse me? I feel the need for a moment in the fresh air."

A look of disappointment flitted across his face. Then he smiled wickedly. "Ah, you wish to meet someone? Go ahead, I'll serve as your cover. I haven't forgotten the pleasures of youth!"

She curtsied without answering and headed for the rows of glass doors. There was no one she planned to meet. Quite the contrary, she had become bored with mock flirtations. She needed a few moments to herself before she returned to the dance floor—and the next companion Roger had chosen for her.

Without glancing back, she slipped through the door into the garden. Immediately, a cool breeze touched her heated brow. Resting against the stone balustrade, she drank in the refreshing scent of early May flowers.

A new feeling had grown within her during the days since her strange night with Roger and the king. She had found herself thinking back on her idyllic days on the farm, when she and François had spent hours lying side by side in the meadow, talking about themselves, about their future, about his studies—and about France. He had told her then of the ancient Romans, whose empire had covered all of Europe, and of how the magnificent government, created through generations of conquests, had fallen into decay.

He had described graphically how the rulers had ignored the signs of inner disintegration. They had played their games, watched life-and-death struggles between gladiators, reveling in a power they did nothing to sustain. And, gradually, their world had crumbled around them.

This, she felt certain, was what was happening to France. She looked back through the sparkling glass at the ornately dressed dancers. In one corner, the king was bending over some new woman, a silk kerchief dangling from his pocket. Sitting on the throne at the end of the large hall, the queen was deep in conversation with three men Juliette had seen only once before. They had arrived secretly from Austria, with new plans for the salvation of the monarchy.

Juliette shuddered. What was it about this night that made her more aware of the danger in which she lived? Pensively, she strolled away from the glowing windows into the darkness of the garden. A sudden thought brought an explosive laugh to her lips. It was close to her birthday! How many years had passed since that wonderful celebration with François?

She paused in dismay. Only two years! Two years from the day when she had been a happy child. And in that time she had grown old—and disillusioned. She was eighteen—but she felt as if she were a hundred! Her life was over before it had had a chance to really begin!

The heavy scent of roses pushed its way into her consciousness. Roses— She and Bouchard had placed roses on her mother's grave when she was a child. Often, when she had felt particularly lonely, she had taken one bud and pushed its stem into the mound as she poured out her sorrow to ears that could no longer hear. She inhaled deeply. Maybe the strength of the fragrance was a message to her. Maybe it was time for her to end her unhappy existence.

She turned again and gazed back at the chain of windows strung across the base of the building like some magnificent necklace, spilling light onto the edge of the garden. She didn't ever again want to return to its brittle fantasy.

Her bare arm brushed against a sharp branch that marked the beginning of the hedge-maze. Instinctively, she pulled back with a cry of alarm. She hadn't realized she had gone so far.

Sinking onto a stone bench, she contemplated the moonlit complexity before her. What should she do? The music of the dance was faint, and, far in the distance, the cries of the city could be heard. Should she go to the mob and give herself up to their cruelty? Her life would soon end if she did that. But it would end in pain and agony. She couldn't face such a future—even for a short time. She would have to take her life by herself.

A small voice within her heart suddenly came alive. In phrases straight from Bouchard's mouth, it reprimanded her for such sinful thoughts. How could she dare to consider taking her own life? And how did she suddenly learn enough to condemn the political moves of men and women trained for such matters? Who was she—a simple country girl—to judge her king?

And why did she take her present life so lightly? Wasn't she well dressed and fed the best of foods? Didn't she have many pleasant games with which to while away the hours? What had she expected of life that could equal all of this? François? He was a traitor—and, besides, he was dead. Then she should stop her foolishness and be thankful for what she had.

Overcome with shame, she lowered her head and stared at her lap. How could she have been so ungrateful? Even Roger's treatment of her was better than being torn apart in the streets! After all, he never beat her, and she was well rewarded for everything she did. She was not being realistic. He had scolded her for this sin before, and she had ignored him. She was again indulging in meaningless self-pity.

"Juliette!" The voice was so faint she thought at first she had imagined it. "Juliette!" She turned and gazed into the darkness of the maze.

"Who is it? Who calls my name?" So Roger had discovered her and had sent one of his friends out after her! It didn't matter. She knew the appropriate words for the game of hide and seek. And her wish to be alone had passed. She rose and moved toward the quiet voice.

"Juliette! I'm over here, in the maze!" Something in the tone sent tremors down her back and brought tingling life to her arms and fingers. She stumbled forward, her arms extended. She didn't even dare admit what she was thinking. It was too wild—too impossible!

Her hand was grasped, and she was pulled into an alcove. She felt strong arms go around her body and firm lips press against her own. The kiss was the magic that released her heart from its frozen void. She was a child again, pressing with excited wonder against the body of her lover! She could feel the pounding of her blood as it surged through her veins. She was alive—really alive! Her heart had not died! It had only been waiting for this moment! It had been sleeping until François' kiss could awaken it again.

His lips slipped from her mouth to her cheek and from there to her ear. His words burned into her brain like flames of fire. "Juliette! Oh, my dearest! Thank God you're alive!"

"François! Oh, François!" She could hardly speak his name, she was so overcome with emotion. Her fingers sought his face and touched him gently, as if afraid he would vanish before she could grasp him firmly.

Slowly, her voice returned. "Oh, François, I left a message with Madam Germaine, and when I heard she was dead, I thought you had been killed, too! Oh, I've missed you so!"

His hands were stroking her back, running over her hips and then moving up once more to her shoulders. As they moved, her consciousness moved with them. She was trembling with mixed joy and surprise. It had been so long since she had felt the touch of love on her body!

"François! Where have you been? How did you escape the fire at the bakery?"

Even in the dark, she could see his expression change. "Oh, my dear, it's been a sad time." He took her hand in his and began to play idly with her fingers. "I fear I've not been altogether right about the revolution."

She felt a momentary joy. "You understand now? You realize the people can't be given power?"

"Oh, no! Not quite. I just realize there's much education needed. We can't give untutored men power over others without first teaching them how to handle government." He paused. "I realize the time for rousing speeches and letters is over. Now it's time to become a teacher. I've been traveling from town to town, trying to help the peasants understand the responsibilities that accompany power."

"That isn't en—" Suddenly aware of the ease with

which they could fall into an argument, she bit her lower lip and stood facing him in silence. When she spoke again, her voice was soft. "Oh, François, it doesn't matter. I don't care if we don't agree about politics! Not any more! What matters is that you're here—and I love you!"

"You love me—still?"

"I love you"—she listened to the longing within her heart—"and I want you—now!" As soon as she spoke the words, she blushed. Did he still love her, even after she had given herself to duDeffand? So far, all he had said was that he was glad she was alive!

Gently, he stepped away and spread his cape on the ground. Then, tenderly, he lowered her beside him. "Juliette, I've searched all over for you! When you weren't in the prisons, I began to hunt through the streets. Then I met a man who said he had seen you transported to the palace at Versailles. Whenever I could get away from my duties, I've searched for you. I even hunted through the soldiers' bastion. I thought you might be a prisoner there." He pulled her close, pressing his lips against hers with a burning passion.

A dizziness threatened to rob her of consciousness. This was too much all at once! He was alive—and he loved her!

He kissed her lightly on the neck. "Oh, my love, I've missed you so! Thank God you still have room in your heart for me!"

It was like a cold knife cutting through her passion. He'd spent agonizing days and nights searching for her. He'd been true to her, had longed for her love. And what had she been doing? She blushed, the heat of her ecstasy gone. How could she dare to touch him now? How could she take advantage of his trust and fidelity after all that had happened to her?

He seemed not to notice her sudden withdrawal. His

lips pressed against her neck and she felt again the force of his desire. Deep inside, her body responded. She wanted him so! More than anything, she wished she could wipe away the past months and be his pure, innocent love once more.

Abruptly, she pulled away. She couldn't change the past. How could Roger duDeffand's mistress dare to pretend she deserved honest love? It was impossible! She couldn't defile his affection with her routine compliance. She was unworthy! All she deserved was what she received from Roger and the king. A prostitute had no right to accept honest passion!

He felt her pull away, and he tried to grasp her close once more. His voice was low in her ear, whispering words of longing. But the magic spell was broken. Listening to his plea, she heard the echo of a dozen other male voices, all begging for a moment of her time—for a kiss, and embrace. She was a fallen woman! François—glorious, wonderful, idealistic François—deserved far better than that!

"Why? Juliette, why do you push me away? You can't deny your love. Not now! I can hear your heart. I can feel the rush of your breath! I love you. I want you with me always!"

She slipped from his arms. "No. I—" She knew he wouldn't listen to her explanation. He would want her anyway. He would cast aside her fears with one kiss. But he wouldn't change the reality of her life. The time would come, she was sure, when he would think on her days in the court—and he would hate her for her acts. She wasn't worthy of the love of a good man—not anymore. If he really understood what she had done, he would despise her. And she couldn't endure the thought of his rejection.

She tried to pull away. "No, François. I can't! I belong here now. I can't return to the streets with you!"

She tried to make her voice hard, tried to conceal the pain that cut through her soul, destroying her moment of happiness. "Go away, François! I want to stay where I am!"

His lips were on hers again. This time he didn't ask her to help him. He pressed her to the ground and slipped gently between her thighs. She tried to make her body resist, but it would not listen to her mind. It wanted him. With all the passion that had remained frozen within her for so long, it wanted to be loved.

As he moved within her, she tried to tell herself it wasn't the same as it had once been. She tried to pretend that François was like duDeffand and the king. But her heart knew she lied. With him there was no thought of skill—or playing a game. Her passion grew within her as he held her close. Her love—and her love alone—directed her response.

Her entire body was alive with ecstasy. Her fingers tingled when they touched him. Her legs pulsed with pleasure as they wrapped about his hips. Her body knew this was real. It was not like the pretense she maintained for Roger.

But, in the end, it was her mind that admitted this was different. She felt as if she were floating beneath him, held to the earth by the pressure of his body against hers. She stretched her hand and touched the stars. It was as it had been before. Her body knew him, and it would not be denied the ecstasy of his presence—nor the joy of feeling her own passion swell within her once more.

They lay together in silence, resting from the force of their ardor. Then, gently, his hand touched her cheek. "Juliette, I love you. You must come away with me!"

The coldness closed around her again. She had allowed herself the luxury of responding to his passion. But it hadn't changed anything. She was still a whore, still unworthy of his love.

"I can't, François. Every day I hear stories of the fighting that continues in the streets. Where could we go for safety? We would be pursued by the mob and by duDeffand. Where, in all of France, is there a place for us to hide?"

He kissed her fingers and drew her up so they sat together on his cape. "Do you believe you are safe at Tuileries?"

She nodded. "The king is here. Surely, of all the places in France, the king's abode is most secure. Who would dare to storm Tuileries and attack him?"

"Who would not? Oh, Juliette, you see very little of what is happening in the city! The king and queen glut themselves on pleasure while their people starve! Oh, they donate some crumbs occasionally to salve their consciences. But that isn't enough, anymore! Big changes are necessary. The temper of the mob is changing. There will come a day when even Tuileries will not give him the shelter he needs!"

The tears she had suppressed for so long forced themselves down her cheeks. "Oh, François! Why did you come? Why did you hunt for me? It's too late! I'm one of them! I'm too weak to endure the thought of pain and hunger. I want nothing but to end my days as one of the king's playmates, being light and entertaining on command—and feeling nothing! You've come too late. Too much has happened to me!"

His finger touched her cheek like a brand of fire, drying the tears. "Dearest, don't speak of the past. I've found you again. We're together. That's all that matters."

She let herself sink into his embrace. He was

wrong, she knew it. But it didn't matter. For the moment, she'd pretend. For a little longer she would enjoy the fantasy. Then she would go back to the dance.

"Listen, Juliette. The king is in danger. Everyone who stays at Tuileries is being observed—and guarded. The crowd grows more angry every day. Soon they will be out of control. You must come away with me—or you will suffer the same fate as the king."

She leaped to her feet. Now he was being foolish! It was almost a relief. It would be easier for her to leave him when he spoke in such a ridiculous manner!

But she had no opportunity to tell him of her disbelief. As she rose to her feet, she heard the sound of footsteps on the walk. Someone was coming!

With a jerk, she pulled François to his feet. "Quick! You must go! Roger will kill you if he catches you here!"

She felt François kiss her lightly on the lips. His voice was a whisper again. "I'll be back, Juliette." Then he was gone, blending into the shadows like a ghost.

She stood for a moment, staring around her, but he wasn't in sight, nor could she hear the approach of whoever it was who had interrupted their meeting. The night was suddenly very still. The wind failed, and its whispering voice through the branches of the maze was stilled. Behind her, she could hear the rhythmic beat of the music.

She looked down. François' cape lay where he had placed it. For a moment, she considered picking it up and carrying it to her room. But instead she kicked it into the bushes. Maybe it would not be found until morning, and then it would not be quite so incriminating. There was no point in picking it up. It would only be taken away from her.

She stood still, waiting for the ice to re-form around her heart. Then, with a calmness dictated by despair, she walked across the garden toward the shining windows. Now she heard a scuffling behind her, but she didn't turn around. There was nothing she could do to assist him. Only one thing gave her hope. She was sure she would hear a cry of triumph if Roger caught François. And the night remained silent.

By the time she reached the ballroom, she had settled once more into her cocoon of despair. She had thrilled at François' touch, it was true. But it was over. Even if he escaped, he could never return. Roger would set guards around the grounds to make another invasion such as this impossible.

Yet, despite her sadness, a small voice inside her sang with delight. He loved her. He didn't hate her for what had happened in the last year! But most of all, he still wore her locket! She had touched it, had felt it hit against her neck as he lay above her. Wherever he was, he was hers, just as she, despite all the corruption to which she had been subjected, would always belong to him.

CHAPTER EIGHTEEN

"What's the matter? Is the prince ill?" Juliette's voice was petulant. For a week there had been no games in the sunlit gardens! The middle of June, and the queen was acting as if it were midwinter!

"No, Juliette, not at all. But the queen has been busy. So has the king. You know how little time either one has had for social affairs in the past few days." Roger didn't bother to stand beside her. Twisting in his chair, he turned just in time to catch her eyes. "Don't worry your pretty head! Everything will be taken care of—in due time."

"In due time!" Juliette stamped her slippered foot. "I wish we'd return to Versailles! I miss the canals—and the oranges!"

"We'll miss a good deal more in a few days." He leaned back and stared at the chandelier. "Why don't you do some embroidery? We'll have things settled soon enough."

"Settled?" Juliette felt suddenly alarmed. "What's the matter? Please tell me."

He shook his head. "No, my dear. You have no head for such things!"

"What things? Come now, Roger, I dislike being treated like a stupid child!" She stood facing him, the sun crowning her hair with a brilliant halo. She looked particularly lovely—and delightfully innocent. She caught the look on his face. He liked the country girl costumes the queen advocated.

He turned his chair to face her. "If you insist. But you know you don't like politics."

"I prefer politics to being bored!"

"Have it your way, my dear." His expression grew sober. "You know the Constituent Assembly has abolished feudalism all over France, don't you?"

"Of course! That happened before I ever left for the abbey!"

"No, it didn't. It happened just last week. Before, only individual provinces had made such a move. Now it's the law of the land."

"So how does that change things? Most of the peasants have been acting like uncivilized beasts for the past three years."

He smiled at her description of the mobs. "Yes, you're right. But it still does make a difference. Because the damn-fool Assembly has pushed things even further!"

Juliette felt a growing alarm. Roger was very upset. For him, that was unusual. He generally stayed out of the politics of the court. "Is the Assembly making the serfs into landowners?"

"Very close to that, my dear. They've nationalized the Church lands and opened them up for anyone who has the money to buy them." He paused dramatically. "Anyone! Can you imagine that!"

"The Church? But surely the cardinal has had something to say about such a terrible thing!"

"Nothing at all! Oh, not because he didn't want to speak! The Assembly just wouldn't listen to him! And the worst of it all is that the king was persuaded to go along with it! There's talk now of putting the clergy on salary. Imagine! How can the Church perform its duties if its people are required to please the government instead of God?"

Juliette frowned. "I thought the king wanted to

limit the power of the Church. Fran—I heard once that he tried to levy taxes on the ecclesiastic societies, and that he was very upset when he didn't succeed.''

Roger glanced at her sharply. Then, as if he had decided not to begin any arguments, he remained silent. She was certain he had caught her slip, and she wondered how much he had heard that night in the garden. The subject had never come up, though she had longed to question him. Had François escaped? Had he been caught—and did he lie dead in some untended grave? The pain of not knowing tore at her heart more than any cruel truth possibly could.

Yet, she dared not bring up the subject: Roger had made it clear he would kill the man who had deflowered her if he ever found him. If she asked about François, he would know who he was searching for. Since Roger continued to treat her as if nothing had happened, there existed the possibility that he was unaware of her encounter in the garden. If she mentioned it, he would know for certain. Then, he would probably send soldiers to make sure François was killed— and then banish her to the city to fend for herself.

When he didn't speak, she braved another question. ''Why are you so concerned about the Church?''

''Oh, I don't give a damn about the Church! But what happens to it does influence what happens to France—and to the king. If the Assembly has the power to force the Church to comply with demands such as this, the power of the king is gone, too.''

''But that's impossible! He's—'' She searched for the proper words. ''How can France exist without the king?''

''The Assembly seems to think France would get along very well. Or, if not minus the king entirely, at least with a king who held no power. It's suggested that the new government should be so arranged as to split executive and legislative powers between the king and the Assembly. Equally! Can you picture His Majesty seeking approval for his decisions from a pack of shopkeepers and impoverished bourgeoisie?''

Juliette visualized quiet, mild-mannered Louis. Yes, she could easily imagine such an arrangement. She even suspected that Louis would find himself more comfortable with such companions than he was with men like Roger and the other aristocrats. How often the king referred to himself as a ''simple man''! How often he made remarks that he would have been better off as a working husband of a dutiful wife than as king of the realm!

She spoke timidly. ''He might feel more comfortable with the Assembly than he is with the queen's countrymen.''

Roger smiled bitterly. ''You're right, dammit! And his actions have proved it! He's signed every new law they pass! According to the new rules under which France is to exist, the clergy is under a civil constitution. Principles underlying the administration of justice have been radically changed. As of a week ago, judges are to be elected by the proletariat! Have you ever heard of anything so insane? How can a judge rule properly when the men who stand before him are the same ones who pay his salary?''

Juliette didn't answer. She feared any response would only increase Roger's irritation. But when he sat without speaking, she decided to risk a question. ''If he's consented to all the changes, why has he been behaving so strangely?''

''Because he no sooner signed the legislation into effect than he regretted his actions. He waited to listen to us until it was too late! Now he has changed his mind and regrets his acts. I think, however, we've finally worked out a solution.''

Juliette raised her eyebrows. "You have a way to save the king from having to enforce laws he himself approved?"

"Not only I, but a number of his wiser counselors." He looked at her solemnly. "What I say to you must not be repeated to either of your maids." She nodded. "The king is leaving Paris—tonight."

"Tonight? All alone?"

"No. He, Marie Antoinette, the children, and a few loyal friends are heading for Montmedy. Her Majesty the queen has friends there who will protect us until the trouble is over. Then, while he is gone, the legal government of France will take over, invalidate the ridiculous laws put into effect by the Assembly, and clean up the rioting throughout the land. When everything is safe once more, the king will return."

"But"—Juliette hesitated to speak, but the question disturbed her—"isn't the king in danger if he puts himself at the mercy of a foreign power? Isn't he better off with his own people?"

Roger's lips twisted into a sneer. "You've been on the streets. Is *any* civilized human being safe there? Anyway, it's been decided. We're going with him to make certain he remains well protected."

Juliette turned once more toward the garden. François had said the king wasn't safe in Paris. Maybe this was the right thing to do, even though it seemed outrageous. She let her eyes drift over the sunlit garden. What a shame it would be to leave Tuileries at such a lovely time of year! The nineteenth of June, and every flower in the garden seemed to be in bloom. As she watched, a flock of birds settled in a tree close to her window and began to chatter loudly. Impulsively, she threw open the casement. The warm breeze ruffled her hair and floated the curtains far into the room. The fragrance of a thousand flowers assailed her nostrils.

She turned her back on the breeze and faced Roger once more. "What a shame! Tuileries is so lovely!" Her regret rose from more than her appreciation of the palace. It seemed to her she had spent most of her life running from one place to another. Ever since her sixteenth birthday, she had been traveling, searching for security. It had not been found in the abbey, nor in Lyon, nor even in her home at Chalon. Versailles turned out to be insufficient protection against the mob. Now Tuileries was to be abandoned. "When do we leave?"

"Early in the morning. It's all been arranged. We take nothing with us but the clothes on our backs." He rose and walked to the window, his voice dropping to a conspiratorial level. "It's imperative no one knows of our plans. Tonight I'll sleep in your bed. We'll slip out at two. The carriages will be waiting near the gate."

Juliette felt suddenly cold. This sounded more like an escape from a prison—maybe even from death— than an unobtrusive move of the court to less troubled surroundings. Maybe François had been right after all! Maybe the danger was greater than she had ever believed it could be.

Before Angela and Julie were called in to prepare Juliette for bed, Roger helped her pick the gown she would wear for the journey. It was a pale green linen, with long sleeves and a simple neckline. At the cuffs and at the throat was a loose ruffle of white. Over her head she pulled a white cap. She grimaced as she gazed at herself in her mirror. Such caps made women look like domestics! But the queen was in one of her pastoral moods, and Juliette knew better than to go against Her Majesty's wishes.

When everything was chosen, she hung the garments at one end of her wardrobe so she would have an easy time finding them in the dark, for Roger informed her they would light no candle when they awoke. Then she rang for her maids.

She sat patiently as they prepared her for bed, answering most of their friendly compliments with a quiet nod. They left with an exchange of knowing smiles. It wasn't often the baron came to Juliette's chambers so early in the afternoon.

As soon as the girls had left the room, Roger settled himself again in his chair. "Juliette, I think you might be pleased to know I didn't have to argue with the king to convince him you should be with us. He was as concerned for your safety as I."

A warm glow filled her body. It had been a long time since Roger had spoken kindly to her. For a moment, she even forgot her resentment of the way he had arranged her life. "Thank you." Her face glowed in the late sunlight. "There are many times when I feel so very—useless."

He reached out and took her hand. "I've regretted, particularly in the last few weeks, that you were—that you didn't come to me as I had hoped you would. Our children would have been strong—and very beautiful." The tenderness in his voice cut her to the heart. How could he speak so, after all he had done?

"But you—" There was no point in starting a fight. She'd leave the past behind. If only he'd do the same!

But Roger was in the mood for reverie. He touched her cheek lightly. "Times are changing, Juliette, and maybe, with them, some of the old morality. I have heard of a number of gentlemen who have married their mistresses." Abruptly, he walked over to her desk and drew out a deck of cards. "Let's play that variation of whist you've devised for two people."

Relieved, Juliette settled in a chair across from him. She'd expected him to want her body—as he usually did when he visited her. But evidently he was too per-

turbed for such entertainment. As she immersed herself in the game, she felt a weight lift from her shoulders. He had no right to pry open the lock that secured
her heart from further pain! That was far too cruel,
even for him! But his desire to play whist pleased her.
It would keep his mind busy and allow her to maintain
her control without any further hurtful assaults on her
isolation.

She won the first game with surprising ease. Curious, since he usually was the victor, she glanced into
his face. His brow was furrowed with a deep frown,
and he glanced regularly at the window across the
courtyard. Suddenly, he rose. "Juliette, let's get ready
now. Then we can play until it's time to go. I feel
much too restless to sleep."

Putting down her cards, she went to the wardrobe
and began to pull on her petticoats. He helped her button up the dress and tucked her curls under her cap.
When she was dressed except for her cape, they resumed their places at the desk.

They played many more games, stopping only to
light a lamp when the sun set. Juliette won most of
them, for Roger's thoughts were clearly elsewhere.
After what she thought was about their tenth game, he
rose to his feet and picked up her cape. "It's time,
Juliette. They're gathering at the Avenue de la Bour-
donnais. We must move immediately."

Juliette glanced at the clock Roger had given her as
a present for her birthday the year before. One
o'clock! If anyone had listened to the planning, they
would be in for a surprise. They were leaving an hour
earlier than she had expected.

They slipped quietly down the stairs into the night.
The moon was hiding behind a heavy bank of night
clouds, and the darkness was absolute. Roger held her
around the waist and guided her along the building un-

til, ahead, they saw the waiting carriages. Juliette looked around. "Are there no more?"

Roger pressed his finger to his lips. "Two are all the king dared to take. The cart behind it is filled with food—and some of their majesties' most treasured possessions."

As she allowed herself to be guided to her carriage, Juliette became aware of the strange quiet that surrounded her. The hoofs of the horses were padded with rags, as were the wheels of both vehicles. A man rode on the back of every horse, leaning forward to minimize the noise the beast might make.

Once more, before she entered the carriage, she leaned close to Roger's ear. "Do all those who are staying know we're going away?"

"Only the men of the council. They'll keep the others quiet until they're sure the king is safe. Some of them will probably leave then. There's no reason for the mob to bother anyone but the king."

"But that's not true!" Juliette felt her anger rise. He was the same as he always had been. Interested only in his own welfare. She wondered what he had done to procure his position as the king's guard. Maybe that was what her involvement with the monarch had been all about!

She felt certain of that when she settled herself in the carriage. Louis grasped her hand and squeezed it furtively. Then the journey began. He settled the princess on his lap. Juliette realized that all four members of the royal family were dressed as she was, in simple, ordinary garments.

Marie Antoinette smiled across at her. "You understand, don't you, that we must travel as common citizens. For the duration of the journey, we are all equal. The safety of your king rests in your ability to remember what I have said."

Juliette nodded. "Yes, y— madam." She sat silently, gazing at the dark windows of the palace. Over and over she repeated the words *yes, madam: no, madam; very fine, madam*, until they flowed easily from her lips. She had no desire to be the cause of problems to her monarch.

The first day of travel was uneventful, though there were moments when all six passengers held their breath in fear. Yet, they managed to pass through the empty streets without being noticed. Royal guards stood at the gate, and they opened swiftly when Roger spoke to them.

Once out of the city, the rags were removed from the wheels and the horses' hoofs. The carriage and cart looked more normal. The extra men who had kept the horses quiet during the trip through the city disappeared. Juliette wasn't certain where they went, but she assumed they returned to the palace.

Now the travelers, riding in simple black carriages, looked to be most unremarkable. For all any observer could tell, a Parisian locksmith and his family were moving north to settle in Champagne.

They stayed the first night at a small inn. Conversation at the dinner table was monopolized by Louis, who spent the entire evening describing a new lock he had invented. Marie Antoinette paid little attention to her husband, but she fussed over the children with such intensity that Juliette felt certain no one could ever suspect her of being the queen.

Evidently, no one did. The journey was renewed the following morning with no interference from local authorities, though there were plenty of them about. When the carriage passed a large contingent of soldiers, everyone inside held their breath. But the soldiers went on their way with not even a glance at the frightened travelers.

The second day of travel ended just south of Varennes, at a small, poorly appointed roadside inn. As on the previous evening, Louis dominated the dinner conversation. He seemed more confident now. He laughed more often, patted the children's heads, and even kissed the queen's cheek. Juliette felt oddly uneasy when Louis ordered a large tankard of wine. His drinking had often been a problem in the palace. Here, it was a definite danger.

Marie Antoinette rose, and Juliette immediately followed. "It's time the children were in bed, Louis. I trust you will join us shortly. We have much distance yet to cover."

Louis nodded, bringing the wine once more to his lips. Roger leaned close and whispered in his ear. Petulantly, Louis slammed the tankard on the table. "Waiter! Some cheese and apples!"

There was a scuffling near the kitchen door, and then a sturdy lad appeared, his brown breeches covered with a large white apron. In his hands he held a platter on which was heaped shiny red apples surrounded by an assortment of cheeses. He placed it before Louis and stepped back toward the wall. The king looked up at Marie Antoinette. "Sit down, my dear, and have some fruit and cheese. It would be good for the children, too. Come, now. This is no time to be angry!"

When the queen resumed her seat, Juliette joined her. Without thinking, she took an apple from the platter and bit into its crisp meat. Roger touched her arm. His face showed his disapproval. Lifting the dish, he held it out toward the king. "Would you have some, your—" He flushed. "Your taste for fruit is well known, and these are beautiful apples!"

A hush fell over the table. Anxiously, Juliette looked back toward the serving boy. Had he been close enough to hear? Had he noticed Roger's slip?

The heavy features of the lad remained unchanged. He stared dully ahead, and, watching him, Juliette decided he was too stupid to notice fine nuances in a conversation. Still, it was unnerving to have Roger make such a mistake.

The lad moved slowly to the kitchen door and vanished from her sight. With a prayer, Juliette turned her attention to the princess. They were so close to freedom! A few more hours and they would be in the protection of the Prussian army.

Despite her decision that all possibility of danger was past, she listened for some sign of disturbance from the kitchen. But none came. It was all right. The danger—if there had been any—was past. She smiled with relief.

Nevertheless, she felt her spirits lift when Louis leaned forward over the table. "I think we will do well to continue on our way without resting here. This place makes me uneasy. Roger, get the carriage ready. We'll be on our way within the hour."

CHAPTER NINETEEN

Juliette huddled in her corner of the carriage, her half-closed eyes on Roger's broad shoulders. His obvious apprehension worried her. He hadn't approved of continuing the trip, even though the remaining distance was slight, and he had even argued with the king in an attempt to delay the ride until morning. "Your Majesty, we risk much to move now. The men will soon be unable to see their way, and the horses may be injured. We may encounter highwaymen. But most dangerous of all, we mark ourselves as unusual travelers. What reason is there for a simple locksmith and his entourage to rush away from an intended rest just at nightfall?"

Louis had refused to listen. As he watched Marie Antoinette hurry the children into the carriage, he had gazed into the red clouds that streaked their way across the sky. "It feels wrong here. We can sense such things. Hurry, Juliette, you can help Marie get settled with the children."

Juliette had immediately scurried into the carriage, but the queen had had no need for assistance. She had held Marie Theresa in her arms, and she had seated young Louis beside her, with his head resting on her arm. He had already dropped off into sleep.

The men had climbed into their places and then, with much rattling of harness and reins, the carriage had begun to move. No one spoke. Juliette was praying fervently for a satisfactory end to their journey.

Looking at the queen's half-closed eyes, she felt certain more supplications than hers were being made. Even the king sat with his hands folded and his eyes lowered.

Only Roger showed no interest in supplication to God. He was leaning forward, his hand holding the dark curtain aside, his eyes focused on the road ahead.

The king opened his eyes and looked across the carriage. "I find it difficult to believe that this is happening. For the king of France to run for shelter and protection from his own people! It isn't right! I should have stayed in Paris."

"Louis! You must stop worrying!" Marie Antoinette opened her eyes and looked into her husband's face. "This is the only thing for us to do! The only thing! Can you stay in a place where your children's lives are in danger? If we are to help France, we must survive!"

Louis nodded, but Juliette could see he was still concerned. His capacity for indecision seemed undiminished. Yet, this time, she could understand his emotions. She, too, felt reluctant at leaving France, now that they were almost at the border. Once the king crossed into Prussian territory, he admitted defeat. Maybe even his own army would desert him.

Her own personal emotions were confused. She longed for safety as none of the other occupants of the carriage could, for she had been fleeing for so long. Yet, as she left Paris, she had felt a great loss. François had last appeared while she was in Paris. Now her chances of finding him were gone.

Despite her sorrow at losing any opportunity to again contact her lover, she could not deny her pride at being one of the few chosen to seek safety with the royal family. She had no doubt it had been her closeness to the king that had made her presence in the carriage possible, but she felt no shame as she thought of the past. Certainly, she had not sought the king's affection. It had been forced upon her. If he chose to reward her in this manner, she was willing to accept the honor without embarrassment.

She had done little talking throughout the entire trip, for her thoughts had been on François. Each mile they covered increased her fear for his safety. Was she never to see him again? She had decided Roger could not have caught him that night. Had her lover been killed, Roger would have taken great pleasure in informing her. His silence proved François was still alive.

Abruptly, Roger settled back in the coach, as if he had been pushed by some unseen force. His lips were pale, his face white. Juliette touched his arm. "Roger?"

He cleared his throat. "Men—ahead on the road."

Louis was instantly alert. "What shall we do? Can we avoid them by cutting across some of the fields?"

Roger shook his head. "No. Fences line both sides of the road, and there's a bridge ahead." He inhaled deeply, as if seeking confidence. When he spoke his voice was firm. "I'm sure we can bluff our way past them. There are eleven men in our party, counting the liverymen and the coachmen. I see only four men on the road."

Juliette gazed around the carriage. Little Marie Theresa was sound asleep in her mother's lap. Prince Louis, too, was dozing, his head on his mother's arm. Louis and Roger both had been looking out the window, immersed in their own secret thoughts.

Had it been Roger's slip that gave the king's identity away? She doubted it. His had not, unfortunately, been the first such error. They had stopped to rest their horses and to refresh themselves at least three times during the journey, and each time someone had forgotten the need for caution.

Once, Hariette Avignon, one of the women in the other carriage, had referred to the little princess as "Your Highness," instead of calling her Theresa, as her mother had instructed. Another time one of the men, Henry D'Arcy, had bowed to the queen. True, it had been a small error, quickly corrected (he had pretended he had been searching for a loose thread on her skirt), but it had unnerved everyone, anyway. How many other such slips had occurred? She didn't know. Probably many that no one—except some outsider—would have noticed.

Searching back over the past two days, Juliette could not think of one time she had made such a dangerous mistake. She was accustomed to being constantly alert. None of the other travelers had had such experience in the past.

"Roger, can you tell what manner of men they are?"

He shook his head. "They aren't dressed in rags, which can mean more danger than if they were. A roaming band of peasants out to raid a prosperous caravan might be easily overcome." His face was solemn. "Your Majesty, I fear the worst."

The steady sway of the carriage changed as the horses slowed to a halt. The queen opened her eyes, startled into wakefulness. "Louis, are we there at last?"

Roger lifted his hand to his lips. "No. We've been stopped by some men on the road. I'll go see if I can get us moving again." He opened the door and stepped out before anyone could stop him.

Juliette slid over in her seat and stared out at the cause of their delay. There were not four men, as Roger had said, but ten. They had taken hold of the horses' bridles and were arguing with the coachmen. Their voices were loud and coarse—and not at all understanding. Roger walked to one man who stood alongside the road, as if supervising the actions of the others. "Sir!" He reconsidered. "Comrade! What seems to be the trouble?"

The man he approached was short and heavy of build, with a youthful face. Startled, Juliette realized he probably was no older than her François. Maybe he, too, was a student who had joined the revolution through his idealism.

The young man began to speak, but she was unable to hear his words. Fretting slightly, she turned to look at the royal couple. The king was already climbing down, his face firm and settled. Marie Antoinette sat quietly, her arms around her children. There was no sign of fear in her eyes. Juliette felt a momentary shame at her own fright, but her shame vanished quickly. She knew the terrors that could be inflicted upon helpless travelers. Neither the king nor the queen had ever experienced what she had been through.

When Louis stood outside the carriage, he turned back to his wife. "Marie, you had better wake the children. They need time to collect their thoughts before they are accosted by the highwaymen."

Little Prince Louis was instantly alert. He sat close to his mother, his eyes wide with alarm. Like the noble child he was, he wasted no time in useless fretting. For a child of seven, always in ill health, he was behaving most admirably. His sister, Marie Theresa, still little more than a baby, began to whimper. Immediately, Marie began to rock her back and forth, quickly calming the child. Juliette watched the domestic scene with growing concern. How terrible it would be if the children were not to reach safety after all they had endured!

A loud voice broke through her reverie. "Out! Everyone out!"

Without answering, Louis took the princess from his wife's arms and stood her on the ground beside him. Then he reached out one hand and helped the prince down. Last of all, he assisted Marie Antoinette out of the carriage. Juliette expected to be forced to get down by herself, but he held out his hand for her as well.

Now she could see that all the men were armed—and that there were more than even the ten she had counted. The carriages were surrounded. And, as Roger had noted, all the men who stood about were well dressed, either in uniforms or in plain dark clothing. One of the men directed Louis to join the other men, all of whom stood on one side of the road. The king moved reluctantly away from his family, glancing back at them with undisguised concern. At last, evidently annoyed by the delay, one of the highwaymen nudged him with the muzzle of his rifle.

Now only the four women and the two children remained near the carriage. Juliette began to tremble. The memory of Helene's fate, which had faded during her months in the palace, returned with vivid intensity. One of the men grabbed the children and pushed them toward the captured men. The women were all alone. A feeling of panic made Juliette's heart beat quickly. Now it would start! They would keep the men away, and, one by one, they would rape the women.

Instinctively, her hand went to the ring, which she had transferred to a chain on her neck for the journey. It had been an almost automatic action. Long ago, François had told her she wasn't safe in the countryside without it. As she clutched it, she saw the eyes of the young stout man follow her hand.

He was beside her immediately, pulling her hand

away from her neck. The ring hung exposed, catching the golden light of the setting sun. *"Diable!"* The voice was harsh—but filled with amazement.

She looked at the youthful face. He met her eyes. "This ring—it is yours?"

"Yes." She spoke confidently now. "It was given me by François du Quesnay, a student at the cathedral in Lyon."

He looked at it carefully, an expression of surprise on his face. "Mademoiselle, what are you doing here? In this carriage? With the royal family?"

She hesitated. Was it a trap? If she failed to quarrel with his remark, would they then know the woman beside her was the queen? She opted in favor of caution. "I don't understand your questions. I'm traveling with my sister, Marie and her children. Her husband is a locksmith and has decided to move from Paris, where it is most difficult to carry on a business. These men are workers in his shop—or in the store he operates. Of course, they bring their wives with them."

The young man watched her face as she spoke. When she finished, he bowed slightly. "I'm Pierre Monage. I, like your François, am a student who has taken up the cause of freedom. I cannot understand the reason for your subterfuge, but you only confirm my suspicions." He paused and looked at her troubled eyes. "Don't worry, young lady, you are not guilty of disclosing the identity of your companions. We knew they were on their way to exile. We just were not certain which road they would be taking. It seems I and my men are the fortunate ones who will bring the king back to Paris."

He turned to the queen. "Madam, please, resume your seat." Politely, he held open the door and held out his arm to assist her up the step. When the queen and the two children were settled, he helped Juliette inside. There was a delay before the men joined them, and then the door was shut. Juliette sagged back in her seat, her mind overwhelmed with despair. It had all been for nothing!

Roger touched her hand lightly with his. "I heard them talking. One of the lackeys who kept the horses quiet as we left the city was apprehended. It was not difficult to get him to talk. They were on the alert at every crossing town."

"But we traveled swiftly! How could news have preceded us?" Juliette thought of the short rest stops, of the hurried meals. Certainly no one could have moved faster!

"One man on horseback travels far quicker. We had no chance. Under the circumstances, I'm surprised we got as far as we did."

Juliette looked across at the royal family. The four sat nobly, already resigned to whatever lay ahead. They reproached no one. Even the little princess was quiet, as if she understood the seriousness of the situation.

No one, not even the children, attempted conversation on the journey back into captivity. They were all too discouraged for such frivolity. Louis held the prince close to him, one arm protecting him from the terror that the future would bring. Marie Antoinette cradled the princess. The child had already fallen into a fitful sleep. As Juliette watched, the queen, too, began to snore lightly.

Lulled by the steady sway of the carriage, Juliette felt herself dozing off. She felt a desire to dream for just a little longer. All too soon reality would intrude upon her once more.

The journey to Varennes had taken two days. They made it back to Tuileries without stopping, except to change horses.

CHAPTER TWENTY

Roger threw open the door to Juliette's chamber without bothering to knock. "Juliette!" His voice was strident. "I must see you before I leave."

She rose from her chair near the window. There was, as usual, little to see in the great square that stretched before the gates of the temple where the royal family and its supporters had been imprisoned after the abortive attempt to escape. "Yes, Roger. You have, then, decided to join the fighting?"

"Yes. Any true son of France would do the same! We've received word that any man confined with the king will be permitted to leave if he joins in the defense of France against the invaders."

Juliette nodded without answering. She was aware that the Assembly had declared war on Austria. There had not, in actuality, been an invasion. Yet, once the fighting began, the Prussians had joined with Austria to launch an attack that completely overwhelmed the ill-equipped revolutionary army. Even in the court, where little was said about the situation, at least in the presence of the royal family, the courtiers were fully aware that the fight was going badly.

Juliette pulled her cape closer around her shoulders. Throughout the entire winter the halls and rooms of the temple had been cold. She had endured the discomfort with firm stoicism, but it had pained her to see that the children, especially young Louis, suffered from the chill.

Roger cleared his throat. "I've decided at last. It's one thing to take the royal family to Montmedy while other loyal Frenchmen deal with the problems of the country. But for another monarch to invade our land while our king remains in Paris—that calls for warfare." He gazed out through the thin curtain that did little to keep out the chill spring wind. "We can solve our internal problems ourselves. All we need is time. The devil take any foreigner who tries to tell us what we should do!"

Juliette smiled sympathetically. It surprised and pleased her to see Roger showing some real concern for his country. Yet, she was not at all sure he was right in his choice. "Are you sure the thing for you to do is fight? You have always been far better at diplomacy."

"The time for diplomacy is past!" He stamped indignantly about the room. "Had the Prussians stopped as soon as they repelled the revolutionary army from their borders, I would not consider fighting beside the rabble army. But I've had my fill of foreign intervention! The queen is showing her true colors at last. She never has been French, despite her protestations to the contrary. Even her abandoning her mother tongue when she married Louis was only a deceit. She's an Austrian! Her sympathies lie with her fatherland. She's convinced the only way to save her throne is by encouraging the Prussian advance."

Juliette nodded, suppressing a smile. Roger was so out of character when he paraded around in such a military manner! He was a fop, a dilettante! He was at home in silks and fine linens, not in the rough uniform of a soldier. Despite his determination, he had no place in the army.

But, then, neither did many of the ragamuffins who had been fighting since the beginning of the war. As soon as the army began to lose, thousands of peasants had swarmed to defend their land, using sticks and stones when guns weren't available. Clearly, their effectiveness was minimal. The Prussians had continued to move forward, drawing ever closer to Paris.

At first, none of the aristocrats had paid much attention to the fray. It seemed to be just another idiocy of an irrational Assembly. But then, one by one, the more militant courtiers had begun to slip away. First some of the soldiers who guarded the king left for the battlefield, joining other loyal soldiers throughout the country.

Roger was among the last to decide to leave. He had spent many frustrating hours arguing with the king, trying to convince him the queen was wrong in her pro-Prussian sentiments. Often, he had left the king's chambers so filled with anger he had been unbearable. But all of his struggles had been useless. In the months since the king's return to Paris, he had grown increasingly distrustful of his own people and more willing to believe the queen's words.

Juliette touched Roger's arm and brought his pacing to a halt. "Roger, what will happen to us? Surely, the people can't expect the king and his family to remain in this place much longer! It has been a most unpleasant winter, and I suspect summer will be no better. Why can't we move back to Tuileries, at least?"

He shook his head. "I have no voice in the Assembly, nor, I fear, does any member of the king's court." He flipped her ring up with his finger. "You seem to have some special influence with at least some of the revolutionaries. You might do better than any of us!" His voice was derisive once more. The time for friendly communication was over.

The sympathy Juliette had felt moments before vanished. There was no dealing with Roger! He had changed, that was true. She doubted that he continued his escapades with virgins picked off the streets, for his opportunities were gone. And his interest in the welfare of France seemed unexpected to her. Still, when he reverted to his scornful speech and his digging remarks, she knew he still considered her as disgraced as ever. Even though the wild parties were past, she was still his whore. She would never be anything else.

Nor did she want to be. Even if he changed. Even if he decided to ask her to be his wife, she would not consent. She would rather live her life as a spinster than wed a man like Roger. Forever, between them, would stand the memory of his cruelty when he forced her to give up her child.

Her face a mask, she rose to her toes and kissed his cheek. "You look marvelous, Roger! Have you said your farewell to the king?"

He snorted angrily. "What would be the value of that? He'd only protest that I was fighting on the wrong side." Juliette shook her head, but he gave her no time to answer. "Oh, yes, he would! I know him too well. He's convinced now that we were stopped at Varennes because of traitors in the ranks. If he sees that I plan to fight for France and not for the Prussians, he'll be certain I was the one who betrayed him. Then you might not be safe. He's already uneasy about that ring of yours." Once more he flipped the ring with his fingers. "I told him I was going to fight for his safety, and he interpreted it as meaning I'm going to fight with the enemy. Let him think what he will."

"But, surely, he must understand. He and the queen were not mistreated after we returned to Paris!"

"It all depends on what you consider mistreatment!

Marie Antoinette is outraged because we are all confined to the temple, instead of being returned to Tuileries."

"Yet, I can't believe she thinks France's salvation lies in our losing the war to Austria!"

"Ah, but she does, and even worse, she is conspiring daily to bring their victory about." He touched the ring once more. "I do honestly believe you should remove that trinket. I don't know for certain what it means to you, but I do know the queen is uneasy about it—and you. Despite it all, I fear for your safety. And now, if the king learns I am fighting for France, you might be in serious trouble."

She tossed her head rebelliously. His concern only irritated her. "What can he do? If he believes we're already prisoners here, he can hardly incarcerate me!"

Roger nodded, evidently determined to ignore her impatience. He also seemed unwilling to abandon the question of her ring, though he seemed willing to pursue its personal implications. "Maybe you're right. Yet, he might begin to suspect you're aligned with the revolutionaries. He saw the effect your ring had on the men who halted our trip." He paused, his expression so strange Juliette could not decide what he was thinking. "If things go wrong here, you may have to use your charm again. It's possible a time may come when it will not be wise to be known as a supporter of the crown."

She looked at him in surprise. What a strange thing to say! Surely, of all places in France, this still was the safest! "That sounds outrageous! Roger, no matter what you think of the queen, she is the wife of our monarch! And no one would dare hurt the king of France!"

His voice was quiet again. "I hope you're right.

Anyway, take care of yourself. And be alert! The climate within the court changes almost as much as the weather.''

She gave him a farewell kiss that reflected her duty, for there was nothing more she could offer. With a strange expression on his face, he gazed into her eyes and then, abruptly, he slipped from the room. Like the other men who had deserted the king to fight in the army, he left by a rear gate. No one could pass through the front gates without being seen by the queen.

Juliette settled herself once more in her chair. In a while, it would be time for her to play with the princess. The women took turns entertaining the young child with games such as hide and seek, *Sur le Pont*, and any other they could invent.

Despite the cold of the winter, Juliette had had very little trouble adapting to the new surroundings. She wore warm dresses and even wrapped her feet in shawls to protect them from the chill of the floor. Much of her time was spent with the royal children, for the confinement was hardest on them. She spent an hour each day with the queen, usually sewing on some bit of embroidery. The rest of her time she was alone—unless, bored with contemplating the empty square before her window, she joined others in entertaining the children.

Prince Louis had been sick much of the winter. Even Christmas, usually a time of fun for the children, was spoiled by his being confined to bed. He seemed to improve, however, as spring approached, and now he once more was on his feet. Her heart ached for him when she saw his pale face and slender body. He badly needed a chance to run in the sunlight, but there were no grounds around the temple. She thought of the meadow where she and François had played. That was the kind of place young Louis needed. But a king's son couldn't have advantages available to the least of his subjects.

Slowly, Juliette rose and left her chamber. The latest game of hide and seek had already begun. Down the hall from her door, she could hear the princess counting loudly. *"Une, deux, trois, quatre, cinq—"* There was no need to enter the nursery. She'd fit into the game with no problem if she just found a place to hide.

Juliette tiptoed down the hall in search of a suitable spot. Ahead loomed a doorway—the entrance to the king's quarters. Silently, she stepped behind one of the stone pillars that guarded the opening. It was a satisfactory place for her to hide from a small child. Out of sight, yet easy to locate.

A high-pitched child's voice called out that the count was over, and then Juliette heard the patter of tiny feet on the cold stone of the hallway. The child's call echoed through the empty corridors, emphasizing the isolation in which the girl lived. Juliette felt a pang of sadness. The baby had no real understanding of what was happening to her. Once in a while she asked about some courtier who was no longer around, but most of the time she accepted her changing environment without question.

She's one of the real victims of the queen's scheming, Juliette thought. *The poor dear doesn't know what's going on. It's surprising how well she retains her good humor. Still, I know she misses some of the friends she used to have at Tuileries.*

It wasn't that any of the courtiers had abandoned the royal family. They were as firm loyalists as ever. But many, like Roger, had finally withdrawn their support from Marie Antoinette. It was commonly agreed that the entire attempt to escape to Montmedy as well as the readiness of the Prussian army to respond to the French assault was the result of the queen's scheming.

Marie Theresa discovered Juliette behind her pillar. "I see you! I see Juliette!" Shouting excitedly, she raced toward the nursery. Juliette, surprised by the child's appearance, was slow to follow. The little princess never tired of winning the race to safety.

When she reached the goal, the princess was jumping excitedly. "You're it, now! You're it! Juliette's it!"

Juliette smiled indulgently and took the child's hand. "I'm it. But first, help me find the rest of the ladies!"

Together, the two moved out into the corridor. The first person Juliette found was Hariette, but she made no attempt to race to the goal. The plump hand of the little princess felt warm in her own, and at least it was entertaining to search the halls for the other players. When she hid, she had little to keep her mind busy— or to keep her thoughts from roaming.

She had, she knew, done too much thinking of late. The face of young Pierre, the leader of the men who had stopped the royal escape, had reminded her so much of François. And when she thought of François, her mind became terribly confused.

François! The youthful idealist! The enemy of cruelty and persecution! She wondered how he bore up under the knowledge that the revolutionists he supported were presently keeping his king in a veritable prison.

When she sat at the window, her thoughts were on her lover. She had searched the crowds that swarmed about the carriage as they reentered Paris, hoping she would see his slender figure and sensitive face. Once she had even thought she had located him in the mob. But the second time she looked, he was gone.

"Mademoiselle!" Marie Theresa tugged at her hand. "You're not looking! You have to help me look!"

Juliette glanced down at the petulant child. "I'm sorry, Marie, I was thinking."

"Well, don't think! You're not supposed to think! You're supposed to play with me!"

Juliette nodded and continued the search. When, at last, she had found all the players, they returned to the nursery. She stepped to one of the windows and gazed out into the late afternoon scene. A few men were strolling across the square, evidently in rapt conversation. Paris, glorious, lively Paris, was as still as a tomb. "I'm glad Papa didn't live to see this!" She spoke so quietly she was sure no one heard her. "It would have broken his heart to see the king living here. And he would have been miserable to think that France was losing a fight with Prussia!"

"Juliette!" Marie Theresa called imperiously. "Hurry up! It's your turn to count!"

Juliette obediently lowered her head, covering her eyes with her hands. "*Une, deux, trois—*" She listened to the patter of slippers as the ladies who were playing ran from the room. Then, at last, she heard the scraping of a chair. The princess was hiding in the room. She would be sure to look there only after she had caught everyone else.

She took her time searching. Each time she passed a window, she paused and gazed into the square. She was growing tired of this royal prison. She wondered if release would come before the Prussians entered Paris.

Quickly, she abandoned such a thought. The Prus-

sians would never get that far into France! Now that
the revolutionaries and the loyalists were united behind a common cause, the fighting between them
would be over. Together, they would surely win the
fight with Prussia and Austria.

As she passed through the corridor, she paused at
the narrow window and looked again into the street.
Below, she could hear the tramping of many feet. A
tremor of fear passed over her body like a chill. Was
the rioting starting again? She leaned out as far as she
could and gazed down.

Below her a line of soldiers marched past. She'd
seen many such in the days following the outbreak of
the war. At first, they had been ill-equipped, but
gradually their armaments had improved. This one
was properly dressed and armed. Their uniforms were
worn but clean, and their rifles shone brightly in the
setting sun.

Suddenly, her eyes fell on one man, his face out-
lined by the low rays of the sun. François! He was well
in her view, his finely chiseled features so out of keeping with the weapon he carried. Before she had a
chance to consider her act, she shouted his name.
''François!'' Her voice was shrill. Frantically, she
lowered it, afraid he might ignore such a shriek.
''François!''

She could see his eyes searching the building and
then, suddenly, they met hers. He made no attempt to
nod or to call out in response. Instead, he fastened his
gaze on hers and held steady until he was out of sight.

She remained immobile, listening to the fading beat
of the march. He was alive. He was still alive! And he
remembered her! Trembling, she lowered herself to
the floor and continued on with the game. François
loved her still! Suddenly, the dark halls were bright

with the glow of her happiness. He was safe! He hadn't been killed by Roger—or by the palace guards back in Tuileries!

When the game was finished, she returned to her quarters. She needed to be alone, needed to have a chance to think. But even as she headed for her chambers, she knew nothing had really been altered. Yes, François was alive. But he was on his way to war, and she could not follow him. He might just as well be dead! It was too late to change things. Seeing him did nothing but arouse her longing and remind her that now and for the rest of her life she was alone.

Juliette opened her eyes in alarm. Something was causing a noise to which she was not accustomed! Sitting up, she listened eagerly. It was coming from the square. Slipping into a robe, she pulled slippers onto her feet. The summer had been all too short. Short— and chilly, at least in the temple. Now fall was here again, and it appeared that the court would be required to spend another winter in the icy prison.

Rubbing her eyes, she moved toward the window. Immediately the sound became clearer. The square, usually almost empty, was crowded with people, all shouting and cheering loudly. She stood quietly, trying to tune her ear to their words. "Hurrah! Hurrah for France! *Vive la Republic!*"

She wished her room were closer to that of the king and queen, for they faced out directly onto the square. She could see it only if she leaned way out. Still, there were some advantages. The fence that surrounded the temple came close to the wall at the sides of the building. In the front, there was far more room. If she looked down from her window, she could call to a passer-by.

Suddenly a lad appeared and began to race toward

the square. Leaning out, she shouted to him, "Please! Boy! Please tell me what has happened! Why are the people cheering?"

To her relief, the boy stopped and gazed up at her. "Don't you know? We're beating the Prussians! We're winning the war!" He was gone before she could thank him.

With new enthusiasm, Juliette rang for Angela and began her toilet. She was eager to join the others in celebrating. Angela shared her joy. "Maybe things will be better now." Angela fluffed Juliette's curls up over her head. "Maybe we can return to Versailles."

Juliette smiled happily. "Oh, I hope so! I long for a chance to ride across the fields again!" She rose and gazed at herself in her mirror. She still looked as beautiful as ever, even though she had begun to feel dull from the monotony of her confinement. Now all the months of tedium were forgotten.

Eagerly, she hurried into the corridor and up toward the queen's chamber, where she could see a number of the other women gathered. When she reached them, she called out eagerly, "Hariette, Marie, have you heard? We're winning! The French forces are winning!"

Her announcement brought forth none of the cheers she had expected. The women stood silently, their eyes lowered. Suddenly, behind them, the queen appeared. Lowering her eyes, Juliette curtsied. "Good morning, Your Majesty."

The queen's face was red. "Did I hear you speak with joy at the thought of the revolutionaries winning the fight with Prussia?"

Juliette knew why her announcement had been so ill-received. Still, she was too proud a Frenchwoman to deny her words. "Yes, Your Majesty."

"But don't you see the folly of such pleasure? We'll

be safe only if the Prussians reach us and rescue us from this prison. Otherwise, I fear for our lives."

"Oh, Your Majesty! No loyal Frenchman would harm a hair on the head of any member of the royal family!"

The queen's expression softened. "True, no loyal Frenchman would. But how many such are there in the crowd outside? Not many, I'll warrant!"

Juliette shook her head. "Oh, but Your Majesty! There are thousands! Surely you've heard of the Girondins! They want to do all they can to preserve the royal family—and the monarchy. All they ask is a compromise between royal and plebeian authority."

"All they ask! All they ask is that the entire world be swept up in their revolution! They seek this same turmoil for the whole of Europe! Is that being loyal to France—or to her king?"

Juliette held her tongue. There was little point in arguing with the queen. Marie Antoinette had grown more and more distrustful of the French people during her months of confinement. She had complained about the poor appointments in the temple and had more than once requested that they all be moved back to Tuileries. But no one had listened to her, not even when the prince took sick. Now, after more than a year in the stone prison, she had given up all hope of leaving—unless her relatives from Prussia rescued her.

Juliette waited to be sure the queen had no more to say. Then, timidly, she made her peace. There was nothing to be gained by incurring the queen's wrath. Roger had told her to watch out for herself, and she could best do that by maintaining open channels to both the queen and the king. "Forgive me, Your Majesty. I'm afraid I was taken up by the enthusiasm of the mob. It won't happen again." To herself, she added one phrase: *At least not in your presence.*

Marie Antoinette smiled sympathetically. "I understand, my dear. This confinement is difficult for us all. Let's forget all this foolishness and plan something that will make this Christmas more enjoyable than last year's." She took Juliette's arm. "Maybe if we think up some new games that will interest Louis, he will begin to perk up. I worry about him so!"

Juliette thought furiously. It was difficult to make up new entertainment for the bored children. She was as bored as they. As she followed the queen into her quarters, she thought once more of the news she had just heard. Maybe the queen was right. Maybe the only way she would ever be free again was if the Prussians opened the doors for the royal prisoners.

But there was always a better possibility. Maybe, now that the French were winning, they would be able to cooperate in the governing of the country. Maybe life would return to normal and the king would be allowed to move back to Versailles. Silently, Juliette prayed for that form of release. Because only if victory brought such rewards would life for her—and her friends at court—be worthwhile.

CHAPTER TWENTY-ONE

"Open up, in the name of the Republic!"

The pounding on the massive front doors of the temple called a halt to the game of chase the court women were playing with little Marie Theresa and young Louis. It was much slower than when Louis sat out, for, as usual, he was not feeling well. He coughed if he ran too fast, and he had to stop often to recover his breath if he pushed himself too hard.

He had almost caught up with Juliette, however, for she had been moving slowly ahead of him, and so, when the pounding began, he hurried to her side. The guards at the door unbolted it and began to pull it open. Juliette pushed the prince behind her skirt and began to back up the stairs toward the nursery. She didn't know who was at the door, but she wanted no harm to come to the child. He had been sick through most of Christmas and was on his feet for the first time, well near the end of January.

She was startled when Louis pulled free of her skirts and stepped toward the door. "No. I don't want to go to the nursery. My father has told me there is trouble afoot, and I must know what is happening. After all, I'm the son of the king of France! Someday, I'll reign in his stead."

Juliette looked down at the fine young face. She knew where he had learned such proud words. The queen had been with him constantly during his illness, and the king had spent an equal length of time at his bedside. And the king was so sad these days. Very probably, he had spoken of his own death and of the prince's assumption of the throne.

Nevertheless, Juliette had to admit the child was right. He was the crown prince, and he would be king someday. Difficult as it was in such troubled times, he had to learn to face whatever trials beset him—in a manner befitting his position. She let him move slightly ahead of her. "Yes, Your Royal Highness. Forgive me for treating you as a child."

He nodded proudly and moved toward the door. It stood open, and ten soldiers had entered the stone hallway. Louis paused at the inner portals. Juliette could see the newcomers gazing at the lad with ill-concealed amusement. But Louis paid no attention to their behavior. He drew himself up to his full height. "I'm Louis, the dauphin of France. Is there something I can do for my people?"

Despite the seriousness of the times, Juliette had to fight to repress a smile. The child was so brave! His words gave indication of such inner power! Except for his childish voice and the smallness of his stature, he might have been impressive, for his words certainly were. But as it was, he served only to further amuse the ruffians who waited behind the palace guards.

Juliette looked into their faces. These were not royal guardsmen. They were commoners decked out in worn uniforms that might well have been stolen from the backs of dead soldiers. Their hair was ragged and unwashed. All ten men had shaggy beards. But it was more than their dress that made Juliette uneasy. The men showed no respect for the boy at all. They hardly looked at him! Their eyes roamed over the visible portion of the corridors as if in search of booty. They looked more like robbers than soldiers.

The man closest to the prince stepped forward.

"Yes, there's something you can do for your people!
You can get Louis!'' When the child looked surprised,
he repeated himself, reluctantly. "You can get the
king.''

Juliette wanted to question them further, but she felt
a hesitancy about taking the position of authority from
the prince. She looked down at the boy's face. He was
studying the man with an intensity all out of keeping
with his age. At last he spoke.

"Wait here. I'll tell him you've come.'' He turned
without glancing at her and headed for the stairs.
Juliette followed obediently. Behind her, she could
hear the start of an altercation. Evidently, the ten newcomers wanted to follow the prince into the temple,
and the guards at the door would not let them pass.
She breathed a sigh of relief. At least animals like that
could be kept at bay!

Once he was out of sight of the door, Louis began to
walk faster. He pulled Juliette along, hurrying up the
steps and past the nursery until he reached the chambers where his mother and father resided. When he
reached the door, he knocked forcefully, but his small
fist made almost no noise on the heavy wooden panel.
Juliette reached up and raised the knocker.

Immediately, a lackey opened the door and peered
out. "What do you want? Their majesties are not to
be disturbed.''

The prince didn't even bother to look up at the man.
Pushing his way through the half-opened door, he
stepped inside. "They'll see me.''

Immediately, the lackey stepped out into the hall.
The prince was right. Never had the king and queen
refused to see the lad when he came calling. Juliette
was about to turn and leave, but Louis held tight to her
hand and pulled her inside with him. "You must stay
as a witness to what the soldiers said. I don't think

Papa was expecting anyone today,'' he said.

They passed quickly through the second door and into the queen's parlor. As soon as she saw the royal couple, Juliette curtsied. Clearly, the prince was right. The king was in a comfortable suit he often wore when he joined in the games with the children. Marie Antoinette was in her long robe. They had obviously expected to spend the day in private relaxation.

The prince hurried into his father's arms. "Papa, there are strange-looking soldiers at the door. They say they've come to get you." He climbed on the king's lap. "I didn't know you were going to meet with the Assembly today."

The king helped the child settle on his knees. "I didn't either, Louis. I don't think that is their purpose. Remember what I spoke to you about the other day?"

The boy's face grew sober. "Yes, Papa. But———"

"I fear this is it. Be brave, my son, and care for your mother." He embraced the child, kissing him on both cheeks. Then he placed the boy on the floor and headed toward his dressing room.

Marie Antoinette was on her feet. She took her husband's arm and held it tightly. "No, Louis. Don't go! Tell them you are above their judgment!"

Slowly, the king turned toward his wife. Juliette could see his expression, and what she saw frightened her. Never before had she seen him look quite as he did now. He had always been so insecure—so indecisive. But there was no uncertainty in his face now. His eyes were sad, it was true, but his jaw was set firmly, and his shoulders were square and proud. She had seen him almost this calm on that terrible night when they had been captured near Varenness.

She felt a wave of despair. Why was Louis a king only when the situation was hopeless? Why had he, in all the days since their return to Paris, neglected his duties in favor of playing with his son and daughter? Why hadn't he tried to tackle the problems that beset his country? Why had he let others do the work he had to do?

There were, Juliette, knew, no answers to those questions that had not already been given many times before. Louis had said of himself that he was a better locksmith than a king—and he had spent his life proving his words to be the truth. It was too late to change things now.

Gently, he took his son's hand and placed it in that of the queen. "Stay with your mother, my son. She will need you."

Juliette had the feeling she was eavesdropping on something very private. But with his next gesture, Louis brushed such a thought aside. "Ah, Juliette. Stay with the queen, my dear—and with my son. They will need your strength in the days to come."

He turned then and entered his chambers. When he emerged, he was dressed in a simple, but beautiful, suit. She gazed at him in awe. Something very important was about to happen, but she was not sure what it was. Marie Antoinette patted her cheeks with a kerchief, but Juliette realized her eyes were dry.

"Louis—" She touched his arm with her fingers. "Must you?"

"Yes, my dear. We both know it. But don't be discouraged. We may return." The queen gazed mournfully into his face. "No, you are right, that is most doubtful. We must assume we will never see each other again. If the rumors we have heard are true, my time has run out."

The prince was gazing up at his father with wide, solemn eyes. "Papa, is this what you were telling me about?"

"Yes, my son. You soon will be king of France.

Oh, my boy, rule wisely. Rule far more wisely than your father ever did!''

''But how will I know what wisdom is?''

Louis touched the lad's head lightly. ''Ah, my son, by those very words you tell me you already know. Follow your heart, my son—and love France.''

He moved slowly toward the door. As he reached it, the lackey swung it open. Juliette realized the man had been listening to all that went on. Suddenly, the prince's voice cut through the stillness. ''Papa, may we walk with you to the door?''

Louis turned. ''Yes, my dear. I would be honored to have you at my side.''

He waited while the queen and the prince walked to the door and then the three moved down the hall together. Juliette followed behind. She had not been told to wait, yet she was unsure of her role in the drama that was being enacted before her.

They moved slowly down the staircase. When they reached the entranceway, Louis paused. Deliberately, he kissed his wife on both cheeks. Then, with equal solemnity, he said his farewell to his son. Juliette heard a bustling behind her. Hariette was coming down the hall with Princess Marie Theresa beside her.

Everyone waited as the little girl's hand was placed in that of her brother. Then Louis picked the baby up and held her in his arms. From her position behind the queen, Juliette was sure she saw tears in his eyes.

At last, he put the girl down and walked toward the hallway. When he reached the portal, he paused and brought his hand to his lips. Deliberately, he blew them each a kiss. His voice was low. ''Good-bye, my dears. God be with you!''

As if they had practiced their part in the ceremony, the queen and her two children responded. Then they stood quietly as the king turned and walked into the

center of the formation made by the ten waiting soldiers.

In response to the king's regal bearing, the men
raised themselves up and stood more proudly than they
had before. The rifles they shouldered were held more
upright. Their heads were erect and facing forward in
an almost military manner.

Juliette watched the scene with growing horror. She
had heard the same rumors everyone else had heard,
but she had refused to believe them. How could the
people of Paris be so foolish as try their own king for
treason? Yet, she knew that was exactly what was
happening. The king was being carried off to a
court—a court of revolutionaries. There was no doubt
what the decision would be.

The day was spent in helpless waiting. It had been
morning when the king walked out the door of the
temple, his head held high as he was led through the
square and off in the direction of the Assembly.
Juliette had spent the morning in prayer. She still
couldn't believe that everything that was happening
was true. He was the king of France! How could they
dare to put him on trial?

A servant brought her lunch—and a letter from
Roger that had been smuggled into the temple during
the hubbub that had occupied the morning hours. She
opened the envelope eagerly.

Dear Juliette,

*I write you to warn you of a terrible change that is
taking place in the militia. The stronger the French
force becomes, the more audacious they grow. I have
news that the revolutionaries, with no assistance from
any of the elite loyalist army, have overcome the Bel-
gian army and are occupying that country. They also
have invaded the Rhineland and Savoy, as well as the*

*county of Nice. All this without aid from the loyalist
forces. In Nice, the feudal regime has been abolished
by the invading forces, though they still have nothing
constructive to propose in its place.*

*The result? Starvation follows the army like a
haunting specter. Wherever we go, farmers have deserted their lands and have joined the revolutionary
forces. Ground is not being tilled. Cattle starve for
lack of fodder. Every place they go, the soldiers raid
for food and, in most cases, they are backed up by
rioting peasants. The land is devastated. France is on
the verge of ruin.*

*I hear frightful things about Paris. The demon
Robespierre seems to have taken control of the Assembly in the absence of any better leadership, and
that bodes ill for the country—and for our king. Please
show my letter to His Majesty and urge him to take his
family and leave the city by any route he can find. I
believe sincerely that his life is in danger.*

*Keep the bed warm for me. When I return, I will
need your comfort.*

Roger.

Juliette read the letter twice, tears welling in her
eyes. When she finished, she folded it and placed it in
the top of her drawer. There was no use showing it to
the queen. It had come too late to be of any help.

Pensively, she settled herself in a chair and gazed
out the window. What was happening to the king?

She remembered his words to her and rose to her
feet. She had no time for self-pity. The queen needed
her.

She was at her door when she had second thoughts.
Quickly, she returned to her drawer and withdrew the
letter. It was far too dangerous a letter to keep.
Swiftly, she walked to the fireplace and threw it in.
She waited until it disappeared in flames.

As she hurried through the halls on her way to the

queen's chambers, she thought about Roger. He had changed during the trials that had torn at the foundation of the government of France. He had changed, and yet he was the same. He had joined in the fight for France, but he still thought of her as his whore. In that, she thought bitterly, he would never change.

Her musings turned from Roger to François. She had thought of him often since seeing him pass on the street. She wondered how he reacted to seeing his fellow fighters turn to pillage of their own lands. Did he still have his idealism? She doubted it was possible. Too much had happened.

Maybe he had already returned to Paris. Some soldiers had. Silently, she prayed that he was not among them. She felt certain he would be heartbroken were he to hear of Louis' trial. "It's an outrage!" Her voice rang hollowly in the halls. She hadn't realized she spoke aloud.

But what she said was true. François would fight to defend his king, just as she wished she could. But there was nothing she could do. Nothing—except wait.

She reached the queen's door and knocked. As she entered, the street sounds began to grow. Something was happening—at last. Voices far in the distance were shouting the name of the king.

Her heart leaped. Maybe they were returning him amid a cheering crowd! Maybe he had outwitted his prosecutors and was returning in triumph!

Quickly, she rushed to a window. The royal quarters were on the second floor, directly above the entranceway, and from the windows it was possible to see not only the square, which was now named the Place de la Revolution, but also many of the roads leading to that large open space.

She searched the square swiftly. Something had

been changed. When she saw the scaffolding, her heart fell. It had not been there in the morning.

The cries of the populace grew louder. Slowly, people began to spill into the Place de la Revolution from all directions, but especially from the road leading to the Assembly. Juliette glanced toward the queen.

Marie Antoinette was standing immobile at the window, her hands clasped in prayer. Her lips moved steadily, but her eyes were open, staring directly at the wooden structure in the center of the square. Beside her stood Prince Louis. His face showed his fatigue, but he made no protest of exhaustion. He bore himself with pride, his head high. Once in a while he glanced up at his mother, as if seeking reassurance. But when she failed to return his glance, he resumed his position stoically.

Now, at last, the largest part of the mob was entering the square. Juliette watched in amazement. The enormous space was becoming crowded with a shouting, surging, screaming multitude. There seemed to be no order to what they did or said. Shouts interrupted shouts, and all the words were buried in the sheer volume of noise.

Then, slowly, a rhythm developed. It began quietly, and then it grew louder and louder until the entire square rang with the cry "Death to Louis! Death to the king!"

Nothing seemed to stop the sound, nor to dim its terrible meaning. "Death to the king! Death to Louis!" The words beat into Juliette's consciousness, repeated over and over again with a rousing regularity that hammered against her brain: "Death to Louis! Death to the king!"

Once more she glanced at the queen. Marie Antoinette's hand had tightened into a fist, but otherwise she had not moved. Beside her, little Louis had grown even more pale. Juliette searched his face. Was he about to faint? But the child shook himself and lifted his head high. She could almost hear him thinking, *I am the dauphin. I must not falter!*

The pathos of his position tore at her heart. More than anything, she wanted to rush to the child and take him in her arms. She wanted to protect him from the horror taking place before his eyes. But she knew she could not touch him. She would only insult his dignity—and break down the fine reserve that held his fear and loneliness in check. And that she could not do. He would need all the strength his small soul could muster to see him through the terror that lay before him.

She noticed then that Marie Theresa was not in the room. "Madam"—her voice was hushed—"should I get the princess?"

"No. She's too young to understand. It is horror enough that our son must see what is taking place today."

Juliette turned her eyes back to the Place de la Revolution. It was filled to overflowing. People spilled out from its edges into all the streets, even pushing against the gates that surrounded the temple. Still, there seemed to be no focus for the energy that was being released. The small wooden platform was almost invisible in the crowd. Everyone was yelling—screaming the terrible words over and over again: "Death to Louis! Death to the king!"

When the prince spoke, his voice seemed tiny compared to the volume of the crowd. "Mama, are they going to kill my father?"

The queen put one hand on the boy's shoulder. "Yes, my son. They are. He told you what they were considering. Then we only feared it might happen. Now it is reality.''

"But I don't see him, Mama. Maybe he has managed to escape!''

The queen shook her head. "No, Louis. The time for escape is past. We tried that—and failed. The king of France—and his family—must not run away again.''

"Yes, Mama.'' The boy paused, a small break in his voice. "Mama, do they have to shout like that?''

Marie Antoinette's face grew stern. "My dear, we must learn to face even such cries of vengeance. Your father has always loved France. He has cared for the people of France all of his life. These are the people you must rule after he is gone. You must know how vicious they can be so you never will underestimate their treachery—as your father did.''

"But my father didn't underestimate them! He told me that Robespierre was a cruel man who was hungry for power. He told me Robespierre would even kill us all if he could.'' The child paused, as if considering his own words. "Can he do that, Mama?''

"If he can kill your father, he can kill anyone.''

Louis took a deep breath. "When I become king, I will have Robespierre executed! He is a bad man!''

Marie Antoinette gazed lovingly at his proud head. "It may be some time before that can happen, my son. It may never happen. You and I may follow your father to satisfy the raging mob.''

Juliette looked at the small, peaked face of the prince. He was obviously frightened, but he held himself under tight control. He bit his lip nervously, and then, lifting up his chin, he gazed straight into the square. "Yes, Mama. But if we do follow Papa, we will die proudly, like him.''

Juliette could no longer restrain her tears. They

flowed freely down her cheeks as she stared out into the raging mob. If she could judge the king's behavior by what had happened earlier in the day, the prince would not be disappointed. Silently, Juliette prayed that Louis would have strength, that he would not break before the eyes of his son.

Suddenly, the shouting of the crowd increased in volume. From one corner of the square, a cart was half-pushed, half-pulled through the surging mob. People jostled one another in an attempt to see the single occupant of the fragile vehicle, and Juliette could see that some were even crushed by the force of the masses.

She followed its progress as it moved slowly through the mob to the center of the square. When it reached the small wooden scaffolding, it came to a halt. For the first time, Juliette realized that only one thing stood on the platform. A solid block of wood with a half-circle depression in its center rose above the crowd.

Juliette gasped as a roll of drums drowned out the screams of the mob. Then the lonely figure in the cart was pushed down onto the steps and from there up toward the high platform.

Juliette closed her eyes. Surely, this could not be happening! If she held her eyes closed, when she opened them again, the entire nightmare would be gone!

But when she looked out once more, nothing had changed. Nothing—except that now she could see clearly the lonesome figure as it stood on the steps, almost at the top of its climb. His hands were tied behind his back, but he seemed unconcerned with this discomfort. He walked firmly, as if he didn't know the terror that lay ahead.

He stepped onto the platform with a firm tread. She

could see him now, and she breathed a sigh of relief. He was not going to shame his son! He stood for a moment, facing the windows of the temple. Even though he was too far away for her to see his face, Juliette knew he was searching for the figures of his wife and son in the windows.

The crowd had gone completely mad. The people were screaming and shrieking, waving their arms and crying ever louder: "Death to Louis! Death to the king!" But he seemed not to notice their cries. Nothing in his carriage indicated the slightest fear. Juliette pressed her fingers against her ears, but the sound could not be shut out. She wondered if she would ever be able to forget it as long as she lived.

Now, as if he were preparing to say his prayers, the king knelt on the platform. He looked once more toward the temple windows and then, as if he were suddenly tired, he lowered his head onto the block.

The executioner had mounted the platform beside him, a black hood over his face. Slowly, he raised the ax into the air.

Suddenly, Juliette became aware of a commotion at the gate. Some of the courtiers in the temple were trying to force their way out to the king. But the press of the crowd held them back. They couldn't even move through the gates, though it appeared that they were not locked, and the guards who were assigned to watch them seemed to have gone.

Juliette felt a scream rise to her throat, and she squelched it. She could not be weaker than a boy of eight!

The crowd had grown silent. A loud roll of drums sounded across the square. Then, suddenly, the ax fell.

Nothing covered the thud of the blade as it hit the block of wood. But the screams of the crowd hid the sound—if there was any—of the king's head as it dropped to the platform. Juliette could see the red blood spurt from the severed neck.

Pushing back her fright and nausea, she looked once more at the little boy. Prince Louis stood straight, his head high. A spasm seemed to pass through his body as the head rolled onto the platform, but he let out no cry.

Juliette found herself repeating the age-old cry of succession: *The king is dead—long live the king!*

It was true, the king was dead. Would the last part of that cry have any meaning? Would "long live the king" apply to this fragile child who stood so proudly before her?

Curtsying, she quickly left the room. She could stand no more of this torture.

That night neither Juliette, nor anyone else, slept at the temple, for it had suddenly been turned into a house of death.

CHAPTER TWENTY-TWO

"Une, deux, trois—" Juliette hurried down the great stairs, a feeling of deep satisfaction suffusing her thoughts. It had been six months since the king was executed, and this was the first time the young prince had been persuaded to come out of his seclusion and join in the games with his sister. Juliette had been influential in convincing the lad that his sister needed his companionship, and she was aware that the queen was grateful for her efforts.

As she reached the great corridor at the foot of the stairs, Juliette recalled the king's departure. It had taken them all a long time to recover from the trauma of watching him die. Marie Antoinette still expected to follow him any day, and that presentiment hung over the life of all the prisoners like a heavy cloud.

Only the presence of the princess kept the spirits of the women from sagging completely. The little girl was far too young to understand what was happening around her. Her desire for games and fun kept everyone who cared for her at least putting on a front of cheerfulness. And Juliette learned in those sad months that a pretense of happiness did serve, eventually, to create increased well-being.

Her eyes swept the corridor in search of a hiding place worthy of the young prince's acumen. She felt a desire to make him search hard enough so his preoccupation with death would be broken. The princess needed an easy game. Louis deserved something more challenging.

One of the men guarding the door shifted in position, and Juliette turned in his direction. Behind the front pillar, just inside the entranceway! There she would be hidden, and Louis might not think of such a place right away.

Quickly, she explained her plan to the guard, and he moved to one side to let her pass. Only after she was in the entranceway did he think of his duty. ''Ma'am, don't try to get outside!''

She smiled. ''Don't worry. There'd be no place for me to go.'' As she settled into her hiding place, she looked at the young guard's strong, broad back. In the months he had been on day duty, he had come to know them all, and to be far more kind than he had been at first. She wondered if he had changed his mind about the revolution. Maybe, now that he knew the royal family, he regretted the murder of the king.

In the distance, Louis' childish voice finished the counting. His slippered feet padded along the stone corridor as he began his search for the ladies. One by one he located them, each time running swiftly back to the nursery to count them out. At last, only the princess and Juliette remained hidden. By this time, little Marie Theresa was giggling delightedly, making it impossible for Louis to pretend any longer that he could not see her. When the little girl was permitted to reach the nursery safely, Juliette felt a pang of sympathy for the prince. At only a few months more than eight, he was already acting like a grown man!

His voice cut through the laughter that followed Marie's success. ''Well, I've found everyone! It's Georgette's turn to be it, now!'' Juliette suppressed a smile. She knew that once more he was teasing his small sister.

The princess rose immediately to the bait. "Oh, no, Louis! You haven't found Juliette yet!"

The boy's laugh sounded over his sister's giggle. Juliette felt a glow of pleasure. He had been somber far too long. "Yes, I know I haven't found her yet"—his voice was clear and bright—"but I've found all the rest of you who haven't the sense to seek a good place to hide!"

The ladies tittered foolishly. Even Louis' snort of disapproval seemed to delight them. Then the slap of his shoes on stone floor told Juliette he was on his way to the stairs.

At that moment the door behind her swung open. Two burly soldiers stepped into the entranceway, their passage immediately blocked by the two guards. The young man who had stepped aside to let her hide held up his gun to challange the newcomers. "What do you want? By what orders do you barge into the temple?"

The first man to enter the hallway rested his hand on the muzzle of the rifle. "My name's Andre. We've come for the prince."

Juliette felt a shock of horror. The prince! Why would they take a mere child? Could they actually be so cruel as to murder him, as well as his father? She gazed at the youthful guard. What would he do? Could he let the prince be taken away without challenging his captors?

The young guard dropped his gun to his side. "By whose orders?"

"Orders of Robespierre!" Andre's voice was sharp.

For a moment the young guard was silent. Then, without a further word, he stepped back. "Proceed."

Juliette looked at him in horror. How could he be so heartless? But the young man did not look at her. He stood quietly at his post, his eyes focused straight ahead, as if no one were with him in the hallway. A strange silence filled the corridor. Despite his freedom to enter, Andre seemed reluctant to move ahead.

In that moment, Juliette became aware of the beat of Louis' shoes on the stone steps. He was on his way down to the great corridor. Soon he would walk right into the arms of his enemies!

Before anyone could stop her, she slipped around the pillar into the main corridor. He was halfway down.

"Go back! Louis, go back!" Her voice was high with terror. She intended to explain, but she had no chance for further speech. A big hand reached out and clamped itself over her face, cutting off her cry. As she was pulled back into the entranceway, she saw Louis turn and run back up the staircase.

She was lifted into the air and tossed to the floor, like a rag doll. As she landed, she reached out to the wall for support, and by sheer force of willpower kept from falling. Her anger was far too great for her to be afraid.

"What do you want with Louis?"

A crooked smile broke through the gray, unshaven face before her. "You think we want to execute him?" Andre's voice was heavy with sarcasm. "How suspicious of you! Why would you think such evil thoughts?" She glared into his face but refused to answer. At last he continued. "Considering the queen's fondness for intrigue, Robespierre has decided we can no longer trust such a valuable hostage in her care. Why, she might be foolish enough to try to smuggle him from the country! And that would be treason!"

"Treason? For seeking safety for her own child?" Juliette glared into his face. "You can't mean that! He must stay with his mother! He's a delicate boy! He won't survive unkind treatment."

"Who speaks of mistreatment? Did I?" Andre

turned to his companion, who leered back malevolently. "We have no desire to injure the lad. Why, we'll give him far more care than he can get in this cold prison! He'll live among people who will show him what it means to be a citizen of France." He looked at her solemnly. "Now, young lady— *citizen*—tell us where the boy is, so we can be finished with this chore."

She stood her ground, gradually becoming aware of the danger of her position. "No!" Her voice broke, and she paused to regain her composure. "Kill me if you will, but I won't betray my king!"

"Your king?" Andre turned once more to his companion, and the two men guffawed mirthlessly. "What makes him your king?" He looked back into her flushed face. "Ah! The king is dead—long live the king! Right? Well, king or no, the boy goes with us. And, as for killing you, my sweet, there are far better things to do with a lovely woman!" He turned again to his companion. "How about it, George? Think we have time for a bit of rutting?"

George shook his head. "Better not. You know Robespierre expects us to return quickly." He paused and glanced at Juliette. "Of course, we can always come back for such play later."

Andre grimaced angrily and dropped Juliette's arm. "Damn Robespierre! Sometimes I think we've exchanged one master for another! Can't we just tell him we had a problem finding the boy?"

George stood silent for a moment, his eyes focused on Juliette's face. She returned his stare with all the courage she could muster. His answer would decide her fate, for she was determined to fight violently if they tried to attack her. And, if they succeeded in having their way, to die by her own hand.

His eyes dropped to her throat. The ring she had received from François hung around her neck. Before she could back away, his hand shot out and grabbed the trinket. His voice showed his surprise. "Where did you get this?"

Instinctively, her hand rose and hit his fingers. As she felt his grip loosen, she backed out of his reach. "Don't you touch me!" Her voice was filled with unconcealed hatred.

"Answer me! Where did you get that?"

When she saw he made no attempt to approach her again, she told him what he wanted to know. His next question surprised her. "Why are you here? What are you doing in the service of the queen?"

She was too angry at the thought of his intentions to think before she answered. Her voice rose in fury. "None of your business! Leave me alone! Go away!"

He pursed his lips and stared at her in silence. When he spoke again, his voice was quiet—and almost respectful. "Well, will you at least help us get the prince?"

"No!"

He studied her again, as if deciding whether to believe her words or the symbol she wore around her neck. Then, abruptly, he turned and led the way into the corridor. Andre followed. Before she could call out, they were halfway to the stairs.

She started to run after them "Stop! You can't go in there!" They paid no attention. At the top of her voice, she shouted the warning: "They're coming to take the prince! Hide him! Don't let them find him!"

George turned as if to silence her, but Andre motioned for him to continue. "Let her go! She isn't worth our time. There are better wenches any place in Paris!"

George laughed in response, and his laugh sent a

shiver of fear down Juliette's back. Once more she called out, "Hide him! Hide Louis!"

By this time the men were on the stairs, and they turned to glare down at her. She tightened her jaw to conceal her fear. It looked as if they might still return to her side just to quiet her.

A noise behind her turned her around in terror. The big front doors were opening once more. The young guard stood to one side as the entranceway filled with soldiers. Frantically, she tried to remember how many men remained in the temple. Four—maybe five—and all of them elderly. All the younger men had left either to join the loyalist forces in the fight with Prussia, or to serve with Leopold in his attempt to rescue his sister, Marie Antoinette.

One of the newcomers stepped into the corridor and looked up at Andre. "Hey, Andre! Need any help?"

Andre paused. "Yes. Two of you check the back door on this floor, just to make sure our little bird doesn't fly the coop. The rest of you come with me."

Juliette leaned against the stone wall as the soldiers filed past. One reached out and grabbed at her breast, but she dodged out of his way. Each one made some ribald comment as he approached her, but she refused to listen. She felt overcome with despair. If Andre hadn't thought to send the two men to the kitchen, Louis might have escaped! Now, there was no hope at all.

Once more Andre and George resumed their climb. With the other soldiers right behind them, they had reached the top of the steps when they halted as if suddenly frozen in their boots. Juliette looked up at the balcony. What she saw made her jaw fall open in amazement.

A small procession had arrived at the banister. At its

head was the queen. Beside her, his hands folded loosely in front of his chest, was young Louis. On the other side of the queen walked little Marie Theresa. Behind the three were the rest of the ladies of the court and the five elderly men.

The queen looked down over the balustrade. Her voice was as calm as if she were directing one of the princess's games. "Juliette, come up here, my dear. You've done well to warn us of this latest outrage against the crown!"

Juliette moved forward as in a dream. The magic of the queen's serenity reached down and quieted her fears.

The same magic that held her in a spell also mesmerized the soldiers. They stepped aside as she passed. Some even bowed slightly. Not one made any attempt to impede her passage.

When she stood behind the queen next to the other ladies, Juliette looked into Andre's face. He was staring at Marie Antoinette with unconcealed awe. He made no attempt to speak. An unnatural silence filled the room. Clearly, this was not at all what Andre and his fellows had expected.

All the aggressive militancy they had shown earlier was gone. They had thought they would be greeted by weeping females, that was obvious. Juliette realized they probably had been prepared for an attempt at escape. But the queen had taken them entirely by surprise. They had no response to such evidence of nobility.

"You have come for your king?" The queen's voice was mellow.

Andre shook himself as if he were coming out of a trance. "Yes, Your Majesty." He seemed then to realize what he had said. Roughly, he looked around at his comrades, daring them to make something of his slip. "Yes, citizen Marie."

Juliette could sense his confusion. There was too marked a difference between himself and the woman who stood before him. This was, in all probability, Andre's first contact with royalty. It was, most certainly, an experience he would never forget. Despite the seriousness of the situation, a faint smile touched Juliette's lips. Such a title was just too inappropriate for the queen. She would never be a *citizen*!

Young Louis stepped forward. He, like his mother, appeared to be icy calm. His head was high, his features composed. When he spoke, he lowered his voice in an obvious attempt to sound more mature. "Then you are looking for us. We will come with you, of course. We are ready."

His voice sounded frail in the large chamber, but his pride was great. Standing close behind him, Juliette could see there was no tremor in his small body. If he expected to be killed, he was not going to show his fear. He was a king. In that moment, he showed his true dignity.

He reached up and formally kissed his mother's cheek. Then, gently, he took his sister's face in his hands and kissed her lips. He stood for a moment, gazing into the tiny features. When he spoke, his voice wavered ever so slightly. "Be a good girl, Marie. Obey your mama."

His voice cracked, and he stopped speaking. He stood with his back to the soldiers and turned his eyes up toward his mother's face.

As Juliette watched, the two gazed deeply into each other's eyes. Love, pride, courage, strength—all were transmitted from mother to son in that glance. Louis' stature seemed to increase as he remained locked in communion with his mother. Then, with the manhood instilled through his mother's iron will, he turned and faced his captors. "Lead on. We are ready."

Silently, the men stepped aside to allow the child to pass. Louis moved slowly down the steps, his head high, his back stiff. At the door to the entranceway, he paused and looked up at his mother. "Courage, Mother! Remember me!"

The soldiers had moved quietly around him, and they closed ranks, shielding him from view. Then the great front doors opened and the jailors filed out, taking their tiny prisoner with them.

Juliette stood motionless behind the queen, expecting that at any moment the woman within the royal exterior would faint from the agony of such a parting. But Juliette was wrong.

The queen waited until the door was closed and then, without a word, turned and led the princess back to the nursery. Gently, she settled the child in a rocking chair. When she spoke, her voice was calm and filled with tenderness. "Marie, listen to Mama. You must stay with your ladies, and play with them. Mama will be going away soon, like Papa and Louis. Remember, baby, we love you. And remember always that you are a princess."

Marie Theresa smiled. "Will they play hide and seek like Louis did? I like it better the way Hariette does it! She never finds me!"

The queen rose to her feet. "Yes, my dear, they will play with you any way you want them to." She turned to Hariette. "Take care of the child. Don't let her forget who she is. I'll see her again before I go, but I have no idea how soon they will come for me."

Hariette curtsied, her eyes brimming with tears. "Yes, Your Majesty. But, surely, they won't—" She could not continue.

Without answering, Marie Antoinette turned and left the room.

Juliette watched the proud figure move slowly down the hall. There had been no break in the queen's control. Tears welled in Juliette's eyes. Never before had she felt so much pity for the proud woman.

A month of relative quiet passed before they came for the queen. Each day the women gathered to share news of the little prince. There had been no execution, though they had expected the worst. To everyone's delight, the messages they received through the cook, who spoke daily with the tradesmen, made it clear that Robespierre had no intention of destroying the boy. He had placed the child with a cobbler, where the prince was expected to learn to behave like a commoner.

Juliette felt aghast at such mistreatment of a noble child, but she realized he was, at least, still alive—if what they heard was true. She was careful not to let the queen know of her worries. Marie Antoinette had enough on her mind as it was.

Someone in the court spotted the escort for the queen as it approached the temple, and so the lady was ready when they arrived and met them at the head of the stairs. She had spent the entire night before with her daughter, and Juliette realized some warning had been given of Robespierre's intentions.

Even the queen, however, was shaken when two groups of soldiers arrived. Some waited for Marie Antoinette to descend the stairs and fall in place in their procession. The others proceeded to round up eight of the courtiers, including all five men and three of the women closest to the queen. They were escorted out separately and led off toward the Assembly.

It happened so quickly, there was little time for anyone to protest, and when the queen questioned her captors regarding her friends, she received no answer. She was ushered away with great speed, but Juliette had time to run to the window and see that the queen was not led off in the same direction as the others.

The remaining inhabitants of the temple gathered in the royal apartments, where the windows permitted the best view of the Place de la Revolution. There was nothing they could do but wait. Even the cook, their usual source of information, had nothing to tell them. He had received the tradesmen earlier in the day and had learned nothing new from any of them.

At noon, he carried food up to the princess and to the frightened ladies. Juliette felt no hunger at all, but when she realized her fright and preoccupation were upsetting the princess, she tried to be more cheerful and to eat at least a bit of the food. When Hariette offered to take the child into the nursery, the other women, including Juliette, agreed thankfully.

A shout from the street brought them all to attention at the windows. At last, something was happening!

The yelling continued for a long time before the crowd appeared. It was a large group of people, somehow surrounding a long, heavy scaffold of some sort with heavy beams that reached far above a solid wooden base.

Juliette felt a tremor of premonition. As the mob rounded the corner, something bright caught the sun. She closed her eyes. She was sure what it was they carried.

The mob reached the center of the Place and came to a halt. Shouting and groaning, they began to shove their burden into an upright position. Juliette opened her eyes and watched. It was just as she had expected it to be. They had brought a guillotine and set it up in the square.

Once the terrible machine had been erected, the

crowd faded away until it stood alone in the middle of the large space, its blade shining cruelly in the rays of the sun. Silently, Juliette and many of the other women began to pray. There was no doubt that soon someone would be brought out and sacrificed on the massive object.

The afternoon dragged on, and still no one appeared. Juliette began to feel a faint hope stir in her breast. Maybe the queen was safe after all! Maybe they had brought her to see the prince! She turned from the window, feeling a need to gaze on some more pleasant scene.

"Look! The crowd is coming back." The woman who spoke pointed toward the far corner of the square. Juliette returned to the window. She could not ignore what was taking place.

Many people arrived, some in groups, others alone, but they did little to fill the square. Whatever was going to happen wasn't as satisfying to the mob as the king's execution had been.

Juliette was the first to see the cart. It moved slowly out of the street that led to the building where the Assembly met. As it drew closer, Juliette felt herself grow weak. There were eight people riding within it. All had their hands tied behind their backs. All were gazing at the windows of the temple with steady, almost frozen faces.

Juliette began to tremble. Up until now she had assumed that the executions were to be reserved for royalty. But the sight before her proved her wrong. Five elderly, helpless men and three ladies, simple companions of the queen, were facing death! Why?

The rest of the afternoon was a nightmare. One by one the men were led onto the platform, forced to prostrate themselves on the bench, and then held, as their heads were severed from their bodies. The crowd went wild, screaming and shouting each time the ax fell. Juliette felt a jolt each time the blade dropped and another head rolled into the large basket that had been placed beneath the platform.

When the men were all dead, the women followed. One woman, whom Juliette had always thought to be a foolish creature, broke down as she was removed from the cart. Her screams of fear tore to shreds the small courage of those who had still to face the terrible death. Juliette crossed herself as the poor woman's head flew from her body. *May I have more strength when my time comes! Please, God, don't let me act like that!*

When she opened her eyes, she was alone. The others, unable to endure any more, had rushed from the room. Juliette looked out into the square. The cart was moving away, loaded now with corpses, and the crowd was thinning rapidly.

It was over. In the next few days, she felt certain, all of the rest of them would follow. She watched as the red of the setting sun blended with the dripping blood that clung to the sharp blade. So that was what François' glorious revolution had turned into! A bloodbath! Innocent men and women were being killed for no reason whatsoever—except to satisfy the bloodlust of a raging mob.

She stared once more out the window. A woman approached the guillotine, a small baby in her arms. With a scream, she reached up and wiped some of the blood from the blade and smeared it over the hands of her baby. Juliette stared at the scene with increased horror. They loved it! These people—whom François was willing to die for—were blood-hungry beasts!

The following morning Juliette hurried to the kitchen as soon as she awoke. She wanted to arrive before the tradesmen, for she hoped desperately to get an explanation of what had happened. When she reached the big, cheerful room, she realized only one man remained. She stopped him before he had a chance to scurry away. "Sir—" She paused, aware that he was frowning. "Citizen, please, why were those people killed yesterday? What had they done?"

The man paused and turned his scarred face toward hers. Scratching his cheek, he looked first into her eyes and then to the floor. "They ain't the first, ya know."

"Not the first? We've heard of no other killings!"

"Executions, citizen, executions! An' it warn't thought wise ta let ya know." He paused. "But now I guess it don't matter no more." He studied his filthy boots with concentrated attention. "There's been more. All the aristocrats in the prisons have been killed—or almost all. It's gettin' ta be quite the way ta spend the afternoon. They're erectin' guillotines in lots of squares, ta take care o' all the heads!"

"You mean there will be more deaths?" Juliette felt herself shake.

"Oh, lots more!" Now, at last, the man had warmed to his speech, and he no longer seemed aware of his audience. "Robespierre says there ain't no other way ta handle the aristocrats. They can't be trusted, they can't. Every chance they get, they try ta destroy the Republic! Besides, lots of 'em are bein' executed for crimes they committed against citizens—honest citizens, like me!"

Juliette thought of the three women whose heads had fallen the day before. What evil had they perpetrated against others? They were quiet people, gentle with the princess, friendly with all they met. Their only crime had been to be born aristocrats. She looked into the man's face. "Do they intend to kill us all!?"

The man suddenly looked up, as if aware for the first time that he was telling more than he should. His face clouded. "I don't know, citizen, I don't know. Ya better ask the soldiers." He was gone before she could question him further.

Juliette turned to the cook. "Have you heard news of the queen?"

He nodded. "They've put her in a prison—alone. I suppose they'll try her later, like they did the king. As for the others, the mob seems to demand many deaths every day. The guillotine that creature spoke of will take many lives——"

"Then we will all die, won't we?" Juliette's voice was low.

"Yes, I'm sure of it. It's only a matter of time."

Juliette was quiet for a moment. Then, with a sigh, she touched the cook on his arm. "Thank you."

Silently, she walked to her room. The halls of the temple seemed unnaturally quiet, and she realized that the little princess must still be sleeping. She wondered, sadly, if the mob would be cruel enough to cut off the baby's head, too, as they were obviously intending to behead her mother. Poor little Marie Theresa! She was such a charming, light-hearted child!

As she passed the nursery, Juliette peeked inside. Two of the ladies were sitting over the little girl's bed, humming a lullaby. They lifted their heads at Juliette's greeting. Then, their shoulders sagging with despair, they returned to their song.

CHAPTER TWENTY-THREE

"Mademoiselle, wait!" Juliette paused at the door of the kitchen and glanced back at Monsieur Vidot, the king's personal cook. He hurried to her side, an apple in his hand. "The greengrocer had only one, and I persuaded him to give it to me for the princess. Maybe it'll make her food a bit more appetizing."

Juliette raised the lid on the single bowl in the center of her tray. Inside, hot gruel was still steaming. Vidot was right. Anything would improve such a dinner. She watched as Vidot placed the apple in one corner of the tray. "I wonder why the man still comes around. None of the others do anymore, do they?"

"No." Vidot made a face. "I think they're afraid to associate with royalists." He snorted angrily. "But I think he comes mostly to see what is happening here. He always asks questions. I wouldn't be surprised if he were under orders to spy on us."

"Oh, Vidot! You're becoming all too suspicious!" Juliette forced an amused smile. "Not everyone hates royalists!"

"Everyone who deals with us does! But I tell him nothing! He'll get no news from me he can bring back to that devil Robespierre!"

Juliette shrugged her shoulders. "It doesn't really matter, does it? They can come in here whenever they wish and take us all! Even the servants have gone to the guillotine! I expect any day soldiers will arrive for the last of us.'' She rested the tray on the back of a chair. ''Ten! That's all that are left from a whole courtful of people!''

He took a small ribbon from the table and placed it beside the dish. ''Here, maybe that'll brighten it up a bit. As for your ten left, don't forget most of the men left to join in the fighting. There were only about fifty of us when His Majesty was—taken.''

''Well, I'm glad my maid, Angela, got away. At least, I assume she did. You haven't heard anything about her, have you?''

Vidot held up his hand. ''Yes, come to think of it! This morning, when I got the apple, the greengrocer told me a visitor would be coming to see you later today.''

''Me! Oh, no! She mustn't come here again! She might not get away this time! Oh, Vidot, what am I to do? I had to work so hard to persuade her to leave in the first place!''

He shrugged his shoulders and went back to the stove. ''Nothing we can do about it. I tried to tell him to warn her not to come, but he wouldn't let me speak on it any further. The message, that was all! Then he went back to talking about the problems he had procuring fresh vegetables and fruits.'' He waved his hand toward the door. ''You'd better hurry. The gruel will taste no better if it's cold.''

Quickly, Juliette hurried into the corridor. She walked swiftly past the silent, empty rooms until she reached the nursery. There an air of false gaiety persisted, despite the fear that lurked in everyone's breast.

Hariette and the other six women who remained were busy playing a new game with the princess. It involved something about counting and leaping from one large tile to another. Little Marie Theresa's light, carefree laugh rang out as Juliette opened the door and entered.

Hariette hurried to a table and held a small chair as the princess seated herself. Immediately, her eyes fell upon the bright apple.

"Oh, Hariette! Look! Juliette has brought me an apple!"

Quickly, Hariette took the fruit from the tray. The princess's face broke into an angry pout. "Give it to me! I order you!"

Hariette held the apple out of the child's reach. "No, Your Highness. First you must eat your gruel. It's good for you, even if it isn't very tasty, and you know your mama would want you to be healthy. You may have the apple when your dish is empty."

Marie Theresa pouted, crossing her once-pudgy arms over her frail chest. She had not adapted easily to the tasteless food Vidot was able to provide. Far too often, it remained untouched on her plate, even though she was hungry.

The offered reward, however, produced the desired results. Petulantly, Marie Theresa began to spoon the mush into her mouth, her grimaces clearly showing her dislike for her repast. Each time she slowed down, Hariette held the apple up, and the meal was resumed. When she had emptied the dish, the child grabbed her treat. Without bothering to offer her thanks, she grasped it in both hands and hurried to the window. Munching it with obvious enjoyment, she gazed into the street.

Juliette exchanged a glance with Hariette. They both knew they should be more strict with the child, for she was becoming quite an ill-mannered little thing. But none of the women had the heart to reprimand her. What purpose lay in making the child unhappy, when her life was sure to end any day under the blade of the guillotine?

Juliette glanced at the window. At least the child had been spared the daily view of mayhem that was visible from the front windows. Her room looked out on the street, where she could see people rushing toward the square but could not tell what they were hurrying to see. No one had given her any explanation of what was happening, nor had she pressed to learn where the crowds hurried as they sped past. She simply took pleasure in watching them go by.

According to Hariette, the princess had asked once why the halls were so empty now, and she had accepted without question Hariette's explanation that most of the people had moved to be with the king and queen. The poor little orphan did, at times, show impatience at being kept from her parents, but at least, so far, the women had managed to calm the child down at such moments.

Marie Theresa rarely spoke of her parents or her brother, but once in a while she upset her companions by some unexpected remembrance—or complaint. It wasn't that the women weren't prepared with an answer. They had all agreed on what was to be told to the little girl. It was just that each time they had to explain, they were reminded of the imminence of their own demise.

Suddenly, Marie Theresa turned from the window. "Hariette, you never told me where Camille went! I don't like her to leave me! Why didn't she ask permission before she left?"

Hariette met Juliette's eyes. Camille had been a regular participant in the child's games, and the princess had taken particular pleasure in the way she squealed as she ran toward the goal when her hiding place was discovered. She had been among the last to be taken off to the guillotine.

Juliette caught the plea in Hariette's voice. "Your Highness, Camille wanted to say good-bye. I know she did. But your mama had sent orders for her to come immediately, and you—you were asleep. She made me promise to kiss you good-bye for her and to beg your forgiveness for leaving so suddenly." She paused dramatically. "Please forgive me. I've been so busy, I just completely forgot!"

The little girl stamped her foot. "Juliette! You really must stop being so absentminded! What will Mama think when I tell her how you've behaved?"

Juliette lowered her eyes. "Whatever punishment she metes out, I'll deserve, Your Highness." She looked into the pouting face. "Please, don't ban me from playing with you for the rest of the day!" Despite her feeling of humoring the child, there was a ring of honesty in Juliette's words. The little girl, playing at being grown up, had taken to banishing from her presence anyone who displeased her. Usually, she would forget her orders a few hours later, and everyone would be back together again. But, when she didn't, it presented some problems. There were too few people left for one of them to be denied access to the others, even for a period of a single day.

Marie Theresa gazed into Juliette's troubled eyes. "Well, will you promise to be good from now on?"

"Yes, Your Highness." Juliette curtsied very low.

"All right, then!" The little martinet turned back to the window. "But don't do it again!"

Juliette could feel the relief of all her companions and realized she, too, felt pleased at being allowed to stay with the others. It was frightening to know the next time soldiers came you would be taken away to die. But even worse than facing their inevitable execution was the delay. Days had passed since Camille had gone to her death, and no one knew when the rest of them would be called. Together, in the presence of the happy, innocent little princess, they were able to push their fears aside. Alone, denied the companionship of the others, the wait would have been unbearable.

The princess finished the apple and tossed the core onto her tray. Immediately, Juliette picked it up and headed for the door. As she grasped the handle, she turned. "Your Highness, I will be downstairs with Monsieur Vidot for a while, preparing the menu for your dinner. I request permission to be absent from some of the afternoon games."

Marie Theresa smiled grandly and waved her hand. Juliette grinned in amusement. The little dear was so precious, especially when she acted the grand lady! "You have my permission!" The girl's expression changed from that of a grand dame to one of an unhappy child. "Please, Juliette, this time see if you can get him to give me some sweets! I haven't had any sweets in ages!"

All of the women smiled indulgently. The princess had learned the expression from her mother, but it had not appeared in the child's vocabulary until quite recently. It was as if she were trying to remember her proud parent by copying her mannerisms. Juliette curtsied. "I'll do what I can, Your Highness." Before further demands could be made, she left the room.

She ran through the empty halls, closing her ears to the ghostly whispers of long-dead friends whose heads had rolled in the square before her very eyes. Once the corridors of the temple had rung with laughter and good feeling. Now they were empty—filled with the spirits of those who had already paid the penalty for being born aristocrats. The rustling of her skirts whispered that soon all this torment would be over.

She stopped once to listen, certain she had heard some quiet voice call her name, but when she no longer moved, the sounds vanished. Nervously, she hurried on. Her greatest fear lay in being alone in the empty corridors in the dark, for it was then that the ghosts came out to haunt her.

Had it not been for the princess, she realized, the remaining women, herself included, would have been far less courageous. Somehow, they conspired to keep the child happy, and in doing so they kept their own resolution strong. None of them dared to face the inevitable moment when the child would either be left alone or would stand beside them in a cart on the way to her death. Because of this cowardice, they continued the pretense that everything was going to be all right, hoping, always, deep in their hearts, that their show of normalcy would, somehow, turn out to be real.

As she passed through the cold, empty corridors, Juliette let her thoughts wander back to François. It had been more than a year since he marched off to war, his musket flashing in the evening sunlight. Despite her hopes, she had little faith that she would ever see him again. Of one thing she was certain: he had not returned to Paris. She was sure he would have made every attempt to contact her once more if he had.

This afternoon, thoughts of Roger intruded on her reverie. She hadn't heard from him since the one letter had arrived, too late to save the king. Now, soon, it would be too late to matter. They would all be gone.

Impatiently, she brushed the fear of her own death aside. Soon enough it would demand to be heard. Now, she was determined to spend her time with more pleasant memories.

As she had done many times since the queen's removal from the temple, Juliette allowed her mind to wander back to her childhood. Stopping at the top of the stairs, she closed her eyes and let the sensations overwhelm her. Immediately, she was transported back to the meadow behind her father's home. She could see the willow branches drooping over the grassy slopes and hear the breeze as it whispered through the swaying branches. Beside her, the little brook gurgled past, laughing its way over the sun-warmed stones. Before her, just out of reach of her hand, stood François, his young face solemn as he announced his undying love.

She leaned against the stone balustrade, her hands touching her damp cheeks. "Oh, François! At least we had our love! At least we didn't let our opportunity pass us by!"

She stepped forward and dropped to the step with a start. Reality rushed back, drowning the pleasure of the past. Poor little Louis had had nothing! And the tiny princess would die before she even knew what life was all about!

Shaking herself, Juliette ran down the stairs into the kitchen. Daily, it grew harder to keep reality from intruding upon her dreams. She tightened her jaw. What difference did it make? Soon the guillotine would put an end to her life—and to the few dreams that remained.

Monsieur Vidot greeted her with a smile. Taking the tray, he put it down on the table. "No one's come yet. Maybe Angela reconsidered and realized it was too dangerous." He put a wine glass on the table and filled it with ruby liquid. Food was growing scarce, but the cellar was still stocked with fine wines, and the revolutionaries made no attempt to remove them.

Juliette picked up the glass and brought it to her

lips. "I'll wait awhile, anyway. It always cheers me to talk with you." She put the glass down. "Have you any sweets? Little Marie Theresa begged me for some again, just now."

He shook his head. "Did she like the apple?"

"Oh, she loved it! But you know children. She would love a piece of sugar candy. Is there any way we could get some?"

He shook his head. "I ask every day. I suppose they find it unnecessary to cater to the wishes of a small child they intend to destroy."

Juliette took another sip of her wine. Why did the conversation always turn to death? Why couldn't they learn to ignore it until it faced them directly? She knew she was as guilty as any of them. The guillotine lay heavy on her thoughts. When she was weak, the memory of her friend, pleading to be freed as she was dragged onto the platform, returned to haunt her. Then, shaking with terror, she would pray for strength to face her own death like a noblewoman—without sniveling.

Suddenly, she heard a light tap on the street door. Angela! She rose to her feet, her mind a confusion of emotions. She would be happy to see her friend and servant again—but at the risk of the girl's life, such pleasure seemed high priced.

Vidot pulled the door open and spoke briefly to the newcomer. A voice answered that sent a tremor through Juliette's entire body. That wasn't the voice of her maid! She felt a faintness that threatened to overcome her, and she leaned against the table for support, closing her eyes to keep the room from spinning. Surely, this was her imagination playing tricks on her once more!

The door shut with a firm click and footsteps moved

across the room. She opened her eyes timidly, fearful that they would disclose someone else than the one her heart insisted had arrived. A voice she could never forget whispered gently in her ear. "Juliette! Oh, Juliette! Thank God you're still alive!"

"François!" It was a whisper—a prayer. "François!"

His arms were around her, holding her close. Frantically, she grasped his shoulders with her fingers, testing to make certain he was real. She was afraid he would fade away suddenly and be gone, leaving her alone in the middle of the kitchen.

But he didn't vanish. His body pressed against hers, his lips sought hers and held them. His hands clung to her back, enclosing her in a passionate embrace. It was not a dream at all!

She opened her eyes and looked at him again. "Oh, François! You're not a dream! You're alive—and you've come to me at last!" She was trembling so hard she was afraid he would think her ill. Her head still felt dizzy, and she held on to him for support.

He turned to Vidot. "How many are left?"

"Ten, counting the two of us. The princess—" The kind face wrinkled in unconcealed pain. "Must she be——?"

François shook his head. "No. You can rejoice over that, at least. I bring news that the Assembly, on Robespierre's recommendation, has decided to keep the princess alive—and to leave her here with at least one female attendant. You, too, will be allowed to remain, to feed and care for them." He turned back to Juliette. "However, I realize I have arrived just in time. From the moment I saw you in the window of the temple as I headed out to fight, I've tried to arrange my return to Paris. Only last week did I finally get the proper releases."

Vidot stood awkwardly beside the stove. At last, he picked up a large pot and headed for the pantry. "François, let's talk awhile before you leave. I haven't seen you since you used to come to visit Germaine, the baker!"

François nodded. "In a few moments. I have something I must say to Juliette." Vidot disappeared into the pantry and began to shuffle pots and pans noisily about.

Juliette turned to François. She was sure of what he had to say, and she knew her answer, yet she could not stop him. She wanted to hear him ask her, even though she intended to refuse.

He took her arms and held her close. "My dear, you must come away with me—now. I've little influence left these days. The Assembly pays little attention to the leaders they respected a year ago. Why, even Lafayette has been thrown into prison and condemned to the guillotine! The power these men wield has gone to their heads!"

Juliette reached up and touched his lips with her fingertips. "Please, François. I couldn't go with you when you found me at Tuileries. Have you wondered why I refused? Why I was afraid of the streets, even with you beside me?" She didn't wait for his answer. "It wasn't just my worry about the riots then—and it isn't now. It's me. You don't know what I've become since I came to live in Versailles! Oh, François—" Her voice broke. Even now she could not face his disgust. Her eyes lowered, she turned her face from his burning eyes. "I don't deserve your love any more now than I did then! Oh, François! I have lived such a terrible life! I deserve to die! I don't have a right to your love anymore!"

His lips stilled her words. Despite her shame, she clung to him passionately. If only she could wipe away the stigma of the past! If only she could once again be the innocent child he had loved in Chalon!

His lips drew away from hers, but he didn't release her from his embrace. "Juliette, my dearest, I've heard all I wish to hear of such foolishness. Do you think I've been blameless these past years? How can you forgive my eternal faith in a mob that has turned into raging butchers? It's I who should beg for your understanding, for I was the one who kept faith with the revolution long after you realized its terror. Oh, my darling, we both need compassion. We both need to forgive—and forget. Don't deprive me of your love now, when I need you more than ever!"

She felt a sob tear through her throat. It couldn't be true! How could he want her now? But his arms remained close about her, his warm breath still touched her cheek. She could smell the heady fragrance of his desire. It was true, after all. He loved her, in spite of all she had been through.

Suddenly, she remembered where she was, remembered the danger they all faced. "The princess! You're sure she's safe?"

"Everything I've heard indicates they intend to keep her alive—and healthy. The prince is doing well, too, though I'm sure he isn't happy living as a cobbler's son. Robespierre is determined to raise the boy as a commoner, though he seems unconcerned with the princess." He leaned back and gazed into her eyes. "Juliette, we mustn't stay here any longer. You must come with me now, before the solidiers return for their last victims. Come, Monsieur Vidot will give your good-byes to your friends."

She nodded. Now that it was time to go, she was overcome with a strange lethargy. Go? Would she really be permitted to leave this stone sepulcher that had been her prison for over two years? François seemed to sense her hesitation. He lifted his head. "Vidot! Please, come out!"

The cook appeared in the pantry doorway.

François settled her in a chair and sat down beside her.

"Monsieur Vidot, Juliette is coming with me. I wish I could assure you there would be no more killings, but I have no such information. Probably, at least once more they will come—and very soon. But I do have some confidence that the princess will be saved—and that you and one woman will remain here with her. I know I've told you that already, but it tears at my heart that any of you must die."

He turned back to Juliette. "My dear, say your farewells to Monsieur Vidot. I dare not let you take the time to return to the princess. Besides, I can take only you. Why torment the others by letting them know you're going free."

She gazed into his face. It had changed since they were children. It was stronger and filled with a brooding regret she had not seen, even when he returned to her home from his burned-out estate. A maturity that had been missing in the idealistic youth gave a dignity to his clean features. And he loved her! It was difficult, still, for her to believe such a wonder.

Then, hanging around his neck, she saw her locket. It peeked over the open neck of his shirt, a bright spot of gold against his darkly tanned skin. With a small cry of delight, she reached out and touched it. He gazed into her sparkling eyes. "Yes, my dear, I still wear it. I've worn it constantly since that day when you gave it to me." He reached up and touched the spring that held it closed. "See. It holds your curl as a reminder of your love." He smiled gently. "Now do you believe me? Now will you come without any further argument?"

She nodded. Her hands moved to her own throat and touched his ring. "See. I wear it, too. It's given me help—and strength—many times these last few months."

Vidot cleared his throat. "Pardon me, François, but wouldn't it be better if you took the princess with you? Surely it isn't safe to leave her here, in the middle of Paris!"

François shook his head. "No. I understand your concern. But we'd get only a short distance before we'd be caught." He gazed steadily into the troubled face. "Haven't you wondered why you still receive food and why the same man arrives every day?" Vidot nodded. "It's because the tradesman is a spy for the Assembly. They'd know immediately were the princess to leave here."

He rose to his feet. "Come, Juliette. We must go."

Tearfully, she kissed Vidot on both cheeks, begging him to say her farewells to her friends. It broke her heart to think she was deserting them when they needed all the support they could get, but, at the same time, she realized she could be of little help. All that would happen if she stayed would be that one more head would roll at the feet of Lady Guillotine.

Juliette blinked as she stepped into the sunlight. Holding François' hand, she let him lead her through the great iron gates into the street. There were very few people about. The executions had taken place that morning, and little was left to entertain the populace on such a hot summer afternoon.

As they reached the shade on the far side of the street, she gazed up at the barren stone walls of the temple. She felt herself tremble uncontrollably, despite the warmth of the day. The great stone blocks were dark with soot and years of weathering. The windows were narrow and tall, like slits in a battlement.

Her eyes searched for the nursery, and then she remembered it was on the other side of the building. There were no watchers to look down on her escape, except the ghosts of those who had left the building through another door for the short journey to the guillotine.

"François, won't the soldiers punish the others when they see I have gone?"

"I think not." He touched her ring. "There is a rumor among the people that there has been a spy for the Republic in the temple. They'll understand your leaving now, since, supposedly, your work is done."

"Me? A spy? How could they get such an idea?"

"My ring, my dear. Remember it was noticed by a man who came for the prince?" She pursed her lips thoughtfully. "Don't say it wasn't. I was told of it as soon as I arrived in the city. You seem to have thrown quite a scare into a soldier named Andre. Remember him? He was convinced you were in the temple on some assignment from Robespierre himself."

Juliette remembered how abrupt she had been when the soldier questioned her as to her purpose in the temple. So that was why he had become suddenly quiet— and why he'd left her alone, after threatening to return. She touched the ring. Once more it had saved her life.

"Come, we mustn't stay here." François tugged at her hand. Obediently, she followed. He'd insisted on her removing her petticoats before she left. Otherwise, he had approved her costume. Somehow, in the months since the queen's departure, she'd felt no desire to return to elaborate court clothing. She and all the rest of the women had continued to wear the simple gowns of the bourgeoisie chosen by Marie Antoinette. As she walked through the streets, Juliette realized what a fortunate choice of gown it was. She blended easily with the few people they passed.

François spoke quietly. "Remember. You address everyone as *citizen*. And you respond when addressed in that manner."

She nodded. "Yes, citizen François."

He grinned, his face suddenly boyish. "Ah, my love, you're as charming as ever!" His face sobered. "Thank God we're together again."

They passed through the gates of the city without encountering any real trouble, though they had a moment of panic when the guard studied her face with sudden interest. "Pale, ain't she, citizen?"

François had pulled her close. "Yes, citizen, that she is. She's been sick, she has. Caught some illness from one of the prisoners when she went into the jail to gather a few trinkets left behind by the latest fodder for the Lady. Took her over a week to get back on her feet. I'm takin' her home, now, before she gets sick again."

Juliette listened silently. The Lady? Suddenly, she realized François was referring to the guillotine. So it had come to that! The people were speaking of that machine of torture as if it were alive!

The guard had lost interest in Juliette's skin. He questioned François about some of the latest executions and then, carelessly, he swung open the gate and stood aside to allow the two travelers to pass. As she stepped on the bare road, Juliette felt a weight lift from her heart. She had been too frightened to believe she would actually escape the city alive.

Then the memory of the journey with the king returned. It had ended at Varennes. There was still a strong danger that she would be caught. She was being premature to think she was safe.

As soon as they were out of sight of the gate, François led the way north. They traveled silently for most of the afternoon, for the walk was hard on Juliette. She had been too long in the confinement of the temple, and her legs were no longer up to a lengthy journey. Many times, François supported her, when she seemed to lose her balance or when she tripped on some impediment in the path.

As the sun began to touch the horizon, he pointed to a small building in the middle of an empty field. "We'll stay there for the night. Then, tomorrow, we'll go the rest of the way to Calais." He caught her as her ankle twisted beneath her and she almost fell to the ground. "Can you hurry a bit more, my love? I want to hold you again before I put you on the boat for England!"

"Put me on the boat? You mean you aren't coming with me?"

"No. I have one more chore I must fulfill. Then I'll be yours for the rest of our lives. Please," he touched her lips to halt her questions. "I'll tell you all about it later. I can't now. It wouldn't be safe for you to know."

She quickened her pace. The thought that he would leave her again increased her desire to possess him once more. When they reached the hovel, she felt a momentary disappointment. She'd dreamed so often of lying once more in François' arms! But, in her dreams, the reunion always took place in beautiful surroundings. Often, she'd imagined herself running to him down the hill that led to their own private place in her father's meadow. At other times, she had fancied him slipping into her soft bed in the temple. Never had she visualized rekindling their love in an abandoned pigsty!

But, when she entered the cramped hovel, she knew the surroundings didn't matter—not now—not ever. Even the lingering odor of the beasts that had previously occupied the shelter didn't upset her. The dirt had been covered with a thick layer of cloth, quite fine to the touch, and much had been done to make the odor less disagreeable.

They sat side by side for a moment, and then his fingers fumbled with the buttons of her dress. "Please, Juliette, let me love you now. Tomorrow, we'll reach Calais, and I'll have to let you go again."

Impatiently, she took up the task. His hands followed hers as she pulled her dress from her shoulders until, naked, she lay back and watched as he removed his breeches and worn shirt. Then, with a deep sigh of pleasure, she slipped into his arms.

She wasn't aware that the ice that had sealed her heart was gone. She wasn't aware that she was repeating his name over and over again. Her entire consciousness was filled with his nearness—with the touch of his body on her own—with his passion.

As he pressed between her thighs, she realized how long she had waited for him to come to her. She breathed his name and let herself float into his embrace.

She felt no desire for further words. Her entire awareness was locked in his person. She was whole again, after years of being incomplete! She was whole again—united once more with the only man she had ever loved.

CHAPTER TWENTY-FOUR

Juliette tried to penetrate the fog that closed around her as the small boat pulled away from the shore. Somewhere, alone on the empty beach, François was waving his hand in farewell. She had fought against his sending her away all through the remainder of their journey to Calais, but he had been adamant. In the end, he had won through the sheer strength of his love.

They had waited in the brush in an isolated cove, and only when the small fishing boat pulled onto the beach did she realize they weren't alone. Other refugees slipped from concealment to take their places beside her in the fragile craft. Juliette was one of the last to climb aboard, but François as last settled her in the prow and pressed a small piece of paper into her hand. "Give this to Lady Ellen. She'll be waiting at the dock for you." He gazed lovingly into her troubled face. "Don't look so sad, my dear! I'll be joining you within a month!"

A month! When he had said it, the time had seemed long enough. Now, alone among a crowd of strangers all huddled together against the chill of the foggy channel, a month seemed like eternity.

Juliette crouched down, using the side of the boat as a shield against the breeze. What a tragic group of people! Everyone was silent, as if they no longer dared to speak out loud. No one seemed adequately prepared for the cold passage. Beside her, a slender lad of about fifteen huddled against a girl who appeared to be close to twelve. His delicate features were twisted and his eyes were glazed.

"Hello." She tried to make her voice light. "I'm Juliette de Condillac. What's your name?"

The lad stared ahead silently, his expression unchanged. The young girl smiled apologetically. "I'm sorry, he hasn't said a word since his mother was sent to the guillotine. He just sits and stares like that. He won't even eat unless I feed him." She touched his arm lovingly. "I'm Marguerite. He's Alexander."

Juliette looked from the boy's still face to the bright eyes of his companion. "How did you manage to get away?"

Marguerite lowered her voice. "It's better if we don't talk too much. You can't tell who else is aboard."

Juliette gazed about in alarm. Was it really possible that someone in this crowd is a spy for the Revolution?

Marguerite leaned closer. "Alex's folks dealt in precious gems and jewelry in Calais. My store was nearby. I sold fine cloth and lace. Then I think one of our neighbors got jealous and turned us over to the Assembly. We were accused of being traitors because we dealt with the aristocrats in both England and France."

Juliette's heart swelled with pity. "Your parents— Were they——?"

"Oh, no! My father died fighting the Prussians. And my mother's been dead since I was born." A note of pride crept into her voice. "I've managed my father's shop since I was eleven. But Alexander was very close to his mother. I guess he never expected anyone could harm her." She leaned closer. "Do you speak English?"

Juliette shook her head. "Only a very little."

"Well, we both do. We had to learn it to deal with

the customers." She looked into Alex's still face. "Of course, he doesn't say anything right now." Her voice showed her sadness and confusion.

"Have you been to England before, then?"

"Once, with my father. But I didn't see very much of it. Mostly, it was covered with fog."

Juliette smiled. The rocking of the boat was making her very sleepy. Settling back against the wooden side, she let her eyes close.

When she awoke, they were in the middle of the channel. The fog had lifted, and no land was in sight. She realized Marguerite had been watching her sleep. The girl smiled companionably. "It's nice to have someone to talk to again."

Juliette looked at Alex. He seemed not to have moved at all. The sight of his peaked face brought back the memories of her own terrors. She also had gone through much. She took the lad's hand. "Alex, can you hear me?" There was no change in his expression.

Marguerite shook her head. "It doesn't help. He just sits. I have to push him to get him to move."

Juliette thought about what it was that had kept her going through everything and stared into the boy's clouded eyes. "Alex, do you believe in God?"

Alex showed no indication of hearing what had been said. Juliette squeezed his hand lightly. "Alex, think. Did your mother believe in God?" She felt certain his expression changed, but he made no move to respond.

"Alex, you do believe your mother's in heaven, don't you?" Still no answer. Desperately, Juliette continued. "Well, then, you mustn't look so sad! How do you think she feels, seeing you so upset, when she's at peace with Jesus? Don't you see, you'll only make her unhappy?"

She felt sure she saw a light in his eyes, but when she looked more closely, he stared down at his shoes. He didn't raise his eyes again, even when Marguerite called his name.

The girl shrugged her shoulders. "Don't worry, mademoiselle. Maybe he'll think about what you said and stop his mourning. I don't know. I hadn't thought to talk like that to him. Maybe if I try it again, later, he'll think about it some more." She smiled pleasantly. "Thanks for trying, anyway."

Juliette felt depressed. Alex's unresponsiveness was more upsetting to her than to his companion. There seemed to be a bond between her and the silent lad, forged by their isolation. At least, he had Marguerite to care for him. She was alone again. Turning to stare ahead at the distant haven, she wondered if she would ever see François again.

The fog settled in, as if nature herself wished to conceal the location of their landing place. But Juliette was aware of a change in the roll of the boat. They were no longer in the channel. The mist lifted for a moment, and she saw land on both sides. They were safe! They must be traveling up the Thames River toward a dock.

A shout ahead started a bustling aboard the boat. A rope was tossed across the water, and the vessel was towed toward the shore. When it was firmly tied, a voice rang out "All ashore!" Even that welcome cry did little to cheer the passengers. A few quiet voices uttered words of thanks, but many of the people remained as silent as young Alex. Juliette rose to her feet, aware that her muscles had grown cramped from the long hours of crouching. Marguerite, her face glowing with pleasure, leaped ashore and extended a hand toward Alex.

Juliette smiled sadly. She would probably never see either of the children again. Somehow, they seemed so alone. They reminded her of the dauphin and little princess Marie Theresa.

She balanced herself, preparing to step ashore, when a hand reached out to help her. She took it and looked up. Alex! He smiled shyly as their fingers touched. Marguerite, behind him, was grinning triumphantly.

Like magic, Juliette's depression vanished. If Alex could rouse himself from his stupor, there was hope for everyone. "Thank you, Alex." She leaped to his side on the dock. "Where are you two going now?"

Marguerite began to speak, but Alex interrupted. "We're staying with Lady Ellen. She's supposed to meet us here."

"Lady Ellen! How fortunate! I'm to meet her also. François—my friend—told me she was a woman about my size, but well into her fifties, with gray hair and a face that looks like a happy parrot." Both children smirked at her description. "Let's see who can find her first!"

Juliette felt a glow of delight when Alex joined Marguerite in searching the wharf. The girl spotted the woman first, Juliette was certain, but she made no attempt to call out. Instead, she glanced at Alex.

When Alex sighted Lady Ellen, his eyes lit with joy. "There she is! I see her! Come on, she's waiting!" With a laugh he moved toward the elderly woman. Juliette and Marguerite followed close behind.

Their new hostess was charming. She took the slip of paper from Juliette and another like it from Marguerite. Then, chattering merrily, she led the way to a carriage. Soon they were seated facing one another telling tales of their escapes as they headed toward their new home.

Lady Ellen was even more considerate than François had led Juliette to expect. She told them each would have a private room on her estate just outside London. To Juliette's relief, the friendly woman spoke French fluently, and, though she was obviously pleased with the children's mastery of her language, she spoke French most of the journey. "Do you ride?" Juliette realized the question was directed at her.

"Yes, madam. Though I haven't been on a horse for the past two years." Juliette thought of her childhood. "I used to have a marvelous horse! I even learned to mount it by leaping over its rump!" She giggled childishly. "It used to annoy my nurse so when I did that!"

Marguerite laughed out loud. "I thought you were a lady!"

Alex shushed his friend nervously. "Of course she is! Ladies have fun, too!"

"They certainly do!" Lady Ellen smiled mischievously. "You'd be shocked at the games I used to play when I was your age, young lady! Many of them took place right on the estate where you'll be staying."

Marguerite laughed in excitement. "May we play them, too?"

"Well, you can do some things I did. It's a reasonably large estate for being located right outside London. We had great fun playing catch me if you can in the meadow."

Juliette thought of her days with François. She had played games like that, too. Before she ever saw the estate, she was certain she would love it.

She wasn't disappointed. She spent the first two days exploring the rolling hills with the children, ending up, on the last afternoon, at a small glen that set her skin tingling. It was in a small valley through which a stream ran. On either side were beds of green grass edged with brightly colored, sweet-scented flowers. A few large rocks provided seats for the wanderers. But what entranced Juliette the most was a large willow tree that shaded the glen. It brought back memories of the hideway she had shared with François as a child.

The two children were completely impressed. They had never seen such wide-open fields. "There aren't such things in Calais," Marguerite explained. "We always played in the streets."

Alex climbed up the next rise. At the top was a neat fence made of split logs, and on the other side was a thick, uncultivated forest. The other two climbed beside him and gazed into the woods. Juliette was the first to speak. "This must be the king's forest. Lady Ellen told me we should not, under any circumstances, venture on the other side of this fence."

"Are there witches there?" Marguerite's eyes gleamed in excitement.

"No, silly!" Alex seemed embarrassed at her innocence. "Didn't you hear? Lady Ellen said there are people in England who try to recapture refugees like us and return them to the guillotine. If you want to stay safe, you'd better do as she says."

Marguerite laughed lightheartedly. "She must be teasing! That's more like a fairy story than real! I'll bet I can go over there and not have any trouble at all!"

Juliette felt uneasy. She remembered how careless she was when she was a child, and Marguerite made her think of herself. As solemnly as she could, she faced the smiling girl. "Please, you mustn't try such a thing! If Lady Ellen says it's dangerous, you must believe her!"

Marguerite was silent for a moment. Then, with a leap into the air, she was running down the hill back to the stream. "Bet you can't catch me! Bet neither of you can catch me!" Alex ran swiftly behind her. Juliette walked slowly after them both. How like François he was! She wondered if François had been frustrated by her childishness when he was fifteen. Soon, she felt certain, the two children would stop playing games. She prayed, passionately, that they would have a more fortunate life than she and François.

The third day, Lady Ellen took Juliette into her room and fitted her into a riding dress. "I know you must enjoy riding, and I have some excellent horses. Put this on, and then you can come with me and pick one horse you can use the whole time you're here."

Juliette was delighted. The dress fit, and she had no embarrassment over the possibility that it might not be the latest style. As for a horse, she chose a filly named Gaiety, with whom she felt instant understanding. From that day on, she spent much of her time on horseback.

On the seventh day of her stay, she asked for paper and a quill pen. Carefully, she marked down each day that had passed, listing after it what had been done. Just as she was finishing, the two children called her. Leaning out her window, she gazed down into their smiling faces.

What a change had taken place in Alex! Already, he was beginning to fill out, and his eyes no longer seemed haunted. As for Marguerite, now that she was rid of the responsibility of her friend, she had become almost giddy.

"Come for a hike with us, Juliette!" Marguerite's voice was pleading. "We're going to the glen."

Juliette frowned, undecided. "Later, if you don't mind. Why don't you go ahead? I'll take Gaiety and meet you there in about an hour."

Marguerite started to protest, but Alex took her hand. "Fine, Juliette. We'll see you there!"

Juliette watched as they started on their way. How carefree they were! One would never guess they were fugitives from the guillotine!

She was late in leaving the stables, so she spurred Gaiety with a feeling of urgency. As she approached the glen, she slowed his pace. It was a gorgeous day! The fragrance of freshly cut hay, spiced, occasionally, by the perfume of a flower teased her nostrils. Above, birds circled the sky, crying loudly to one another as they swooped near the ground.

As the trees closed above her head, Juliette noted how blue the sky was against the dark green branches. She had thought she would never enjoy life again, and here she was, surrounded by all the beauties of the earth! Only one thing was lacking to complete her happiness—François' companionship! For the tenth time since starting her chart, she counted again the twenty-three days left until he would be with her again.

She reached the cove without encountering either child. When they weren't beside the stream under the willow, she felt uneasy. "Alex! Marguerite!" Maybe they were hiding behind one of the bushes, hoping she would leave them alone for a bit longer! Unsure of what to do, she settled on one of the rocks to await their return.

A rustling in the bushes behind her brought her to her feet, her heart beating swiftly. Cautiously, she moved closer to Gaiety, who was placidly munching grass. If someone were out to cause her trouble, she would be ready to make her escape.

Alex stepped through the brush. His face was pale with fright, and he hurried to her side. "Oh, Juliette! I'm so glad you're here! Marguerite and I were playing hide and seek, and I'm afraid she hid on the other side of the fence. I've looked all through the glen, and she isn't here.''

''Have you called her?'' Juliette felt a wave of impatience. ''Why did she have to disobey?''

Alex frowned. ''I'm sorry she's being a problem. But she's had a rough time. On top of everything, she had to look after me all the way across the channel!''

He was right; Juliette knew it. Marguerite was just expressing her natural childish ebullience. ''Maybe if I call, she'll answer. We can't let her stay over there. I'm sure Lady Ellen wouldn't have warned us if there wasn't some real danger.'' She climbed to the ridge of the fence. ''Marguerite! Please! It isn't safe for you over there! Please come back!''

She waited a moment, but there was no answer. Then a rustling of leaves under the shadows of the trees caught her attention. Cautiously, Juliette gauged the distance to the spot. It wasn't far. If she had to, she would run there and bring the girl back. But first she'd try calling again. ''Marguerite! You must come! You don't want to be taken back to France, do you?''

Still no answer, but the bushes moved once more. With a sigh of annoyance, she slipped over the fence, followed quickly by Alex. There was nothing to do but fetch the child! She headed directly toward the movement. ''I'm coming to get you, Marguerite! It's very naughty of you to be so perverse! Maybe you'll be confined to your room after such foolishness!''

Still no response, though the bushes shook even more violently. Suddenly the brush was agitated wildly, and a figure rose up before her. She stared at it in amazement. Roger! He was holding Marguerite in his arms, one hand clamped over her mouth.

Juliette looked at Marguerite's captor in confusion.

''Roger? What are you doing here? Why are you hold-ing Marguerite like that?''

He chuckled. ''One question at a time, my dear. What am I doing here? What you evidently are doing—seeking refuge from the Lady.'' He paused and gazed insolently into her face. ''Now, the next question is, what am I doing holding Marguerite like this. Well, the answer to that is quite simple, too. I was walking through the woods, as I often do, when this child ran into me. I was ready to carry her back where she belonged when I heard your voice. Keeping her beside me seemed like an excellent way to get you to come and speak to me, free of Lady Ellen's protection—and you see, it worked!''

Juliette looked back at the fence and then into Roger's eyes. It didn't make sense. If he was a refugee as she was, why didn't he just come calling on her—like a gentleman? ''She's your bait? You wanted to lure me out here? Why?''

''Why? You see, my dear, I have a little deal with Robespierre. I keep my estates and my life in ex-change for—other, less fortunate and less wise indi-viduals. I'd heard of three new guests at Lady Ellen's estate, but I had no idea one of them was you!''

Juliette felt her skin begin to crawl. Roger was ac-tually cooperating with the revolutionaries! All of his wealth and comforts he owed to the king—and now he was betraying his peers. He removed his hand from Marguerite's mouth and reached for Juliette's arm.

Marguerite spoke loudly. ''Run! Hurry back over the fence where you'll be safe! Hurry!''

Neither Alex nor Juliette moved. Roger stifled the girl's shouts. ''My dear, you seem to have some very troublesome companions. And they don't even appear to be nobles!'' He looked into Juliette's eyes. ''You're afraid of me! How foolish! Surely you know I would never harm you! I was certain you were dead, or I would have bartered with the Assembly for your head as well as mine! Now that I've found you—well, you certainly have no need to live on another's charity''—he looked at her dress—"or to wear other's cast-off clothing. I am well paid for my services. These two, for example, will add considerably to my fortunes—and in British coin! I live quite well, I can assure you.''

Marguerite tried to bite his fingers and he shifted his grip. "Surely you know I'm honestly fond of you, my dear. You may even recall my conversation just before I left Tuileries. Times have changed. If you wish it—No, because *I* wish it, we will publish our banns and get properly married! In truth, Juliette, I'm most delighted to see you!''

She watched him appraisingly. "What do you intend to do with the children?''

"Why, turn them in, of course! Why not?''

She gazed thoughtfully at Marguerite. If only he would put her down! Then both children might be persuaded to run back to safety. As it was, he could just as well have had a rope around Alex. He would never leave Marguerite in such peril. She took a step toward the fence. "Why not? Because if you turn them in, I'll never come to you!'' She watched his expression closely. To her relief, he showed definite disappointment. "But, if you let them go, I'll come with you right now!''

Alex grasped her hand. "No! You mustn't go with him! He'll send you back, too! We'll go! You run back to safety—quickly!''

Juliette smiled. If she played her game right, none of them would have to go. Impatiently, she brushed Alex's hand away. "No, Alex. I didn't know Roger was here. I never told you about him, because I thought he was dead. But now—'' She looked into the sensual face of the man before her. ''Now that you're here, of course I'll go with you! Oh, Roger, how I've longed for us to be married!'' She pouted seductively. ''But, please, for my sake, let the children go! Just this once! I'd hate to have our reunion ruined by their misfortune! And, after all, they're not even aristocrats!''

His smile turned into a leer. ''I've missed you, Juliette. No one else is as skilled as you! I was a good teacher—but you were an excellent pupil!''

She touched his arm, letting her fingers snake up to the small of his neck. ''Help me put the children on my horse, so they'll be gone. Then we can leave together. Please—for me?'' She was rubbing against him now, teasing his ears with her breath. ''Please?''

Abruptly, he strode toward the fence. Immediately, she grasped Alex's hand and pulled him behind her. The boy's face showed his confusion. ''Mademoiselle, what are you doing? You can't go with him! You can't want to be with him! He's a traitor!''

She didn't look at the lad. If she succeeded, she could explain later. If she didn't, he would forever after think of her as partner to Roger's perfidy. She held her breath when Roger stopped at the fence. If he put Marguerite down now, he would destroy any chance for all three of them to get away. When he lifted the girl over the fence, Juliette sighed in relief.

Gaiety was still chewing on the grass, but she looked up as they approached. Juliette spoke nervously now. So much depended on what happened in the next few moments. ''Put Marguerite in front of the saddle. Then you can lift Alex up and put him behind her.''

Roger slipped the girl onto the horse's neck. As he turned to pick up the boy, Juliette untied the reins from the bush and handed them to Marguerite. Then, quickly, she moved behind the animal. He was standing close to a rock, and she stepped up on it, leaning far over as if concerned about getting Alex settled in his seat. She lifted one hand then, ready to hit Gaiety's rump.

Roger stepped back. In that instant, Juliette grabbed frantically for the back of the saddle. With a leap, she pulled herself up onto the horse's back, at the same time shouting loudly. Startled, the animal broke into a gallop. The children, surprised by the sudden move, leaned forward to hold more securely onto the reins. It was that forward movement that gave her the room she needed. Her legs trailed behind, for her skirt wasn't wide enough to permit her to straddle the horse. She clung frantically to the rim of the saddle. If only she could hold on until they were up the hill, she might safely take the time to mount properly.

As soon as he realized what was happening, Alex grabbed her wrists in his hands and held on with all his might. She felt herself slide, but his grip held her safely. They were out of the grove and up the hill— and Roger could not equal their speed.

At the top of the hill, Marguerite reined the horse. Quickly, Juliette slipped to the ground. This time, she pulled up her skirts so she could swing one leg over the horse's rump. When she was mounted safely, she spurred the beast to a trot. She could hear Roger in the distance, his voice raised in angry curses. But his anger didn't matter. They were safe—at least for the present.

They finished the trip back to the stables in silence. Juliette could think of nothing to say to the children that her actions had not already made clear. Only when they were walking through the gate that led to the cook's garden did Marguerite turn to Juliette. "Thank you, Mademoiselle! I'm sorry I caused you such trouble."

Alex grinned. "We sure showed him, didn't we! He's not going to get us!"

Marguerite took Juliette's hand. "You were wonderful! You really had him fooled!"

At the door to her room, Juliette paused. "Marguerite, promise you won't leave the estate again! Maybe, for a while at least, we'd better not even go to the glen."

They both nodded solemnly. Then, hand in hand, they walked back into the garden. Juliette watched them depart. She was certain they'd be careful every time they went out. But that might not be enough to protect them—and her—from Roger. Not after such a humiliation! He would be sure to seek them out now.

CHAPTER TWENTY-FIVE

"Juliette, you must tell me who the man was." Lady Ellen's gentle face was shadowed by a frown of worry. "Don't you see he might be stopped if we knew who he was?"

The leering eyes of Roger duDeffand seemed to stare at her from the shadows of the library. "All right, I'll tell you. But I can't believe it's true. He has few scruples, but he has always loved his king. I can't believe he'd betray his own kind!"

When she spoke Roger's name, Lady Ellen's eyes lit up. "Very possible! He's been in London for a bit over a year, and, come to think of it, many of the disappearances of our guests have taken place since his arrival! What exactly did he tell you?"

"He said he made an agreement with Robespierre for his own life in exchange for those of others. And he said he was paid in English coin for his efforts. I felt he was quiet proud of his acumen!"

"I must tell the others to watch him." Lady Ellen's tone was calm, as if she were discussing a foolish child instead of a dangerous man.

"Then you know him well?"

"He has a most unique position among the refugees. Now that he's suspect, I wonder we didn't notice before. Where all the others, like you, are fearful to move about, he has always traveled freely all about England. We've all recognized him as a rather ignoble person, but we had the picture quite backward. We thought he was collecting money—large sums of it—from aristocrats seeking freedom. It never occurred to us he might be making it by turning traitor.''

Juliette felt suddenly uneasy. "I might be wrong. He might have told me those tales just to frighten me and get me to come with him.''

''That's why we'll just watch him—for the time being. Don't worry about it, my dear. Just promise me you'll stay close to the house. François would never forgive me were I to lose you.''

Juliette had no difficulty complying with her hostess's request. In the weeks that followed she spent most of her days strolling through the garden—or sitting in a swing reading a book. The children, too, refrained from any wandering. They'd been thoroughly frightened by their near escape, and neither showed any signs of impatience at the new need for watchfulness. Alex was constantly alert, even when they frolicked near the large mansion, and even Marguerite seemed less carefree in her games.

Ten days after the close call with Roger, Juliette was sitting in the swing, basking in the warmth of the sun. A light breeze lifted a strand of her hair and flipped it under her nose. Brushing it aside, she sneezed loudly, starting a wild chattering among a flock of birds that had settled nearby on a grape arbor.

Suddenly, Marguerite leaped onto the swing and threw herself into a seat beside Juliette. "It's Alex's turn to hide. Is it all right if I count here?" Without waiting for a response, the child began. "One, two, three, four———''

Juliette looked quickly around the garden. Alex was running through the bean patch, searching for a plant large enough to conceal him when he crouched. At last he crawled among the raspberries and disappeared from her view. Marguerite finished her counting and lifted her head. "Is he hiding?"

Juliette avoided glancing in the direction of the brambles. "Yes." Immediately, Marguerite was off the swing, leaving behind the fresh scent of sun-dried clothing. Juliette returned to her reading.

A door opened in the cookhouse, and Gwen, the cook emerged. Juliette waved her greeting and returned to her book again. When Gwen appeared beside her on the swing, she looked up in surprise. "Is something wrong?"

Gwen shook her head. "Oh, no, ma'am. Something very right. I've been worried about the children. It's fine for them to have a holiday, but it isn't proper for them to spend all their days in indolence." She continued quickly, as if she were afraid she might have offended Juliette. "I mean, for common folk like them. They're used to working. It isn't good for them to get lazy."

Juliette felt mildly puzzled. "Have you thought up some work for them to do around the house?"

"Oh, no, ma'am, the mistress wouldn't think of it! But they're orphans, you know, and they're fond of each other. The mistress has been searching for a place where they could stay together."

Juliette remembered that Lady Ellen added to her hospitality by assisting her guests to find permanent accommodations. She had known it would come—yet she hated to think of being separated from her new young friends. "You mean they're going to leave us?"

"Soon. Please don't say anything to them yet. It isn't quite settled. But I know the Goodbodys, and they're lovely people. They'll treat our two little cherubs very well."

Juliette felt a warmth toward Gwen. In some ways the busy woman resembled Bouchard. She was stout, gentle of feature, and cheerful most of the time. But it was the fact that she had taken the two children to her heart that made Juliette like her the most. She slipped a marker in her book. "Will they be going soon?"

"Any day. I came out to call them in to change. Even though they're children, Lady Ellen will want them to talk the whole move over with the Goodbodys before it's finally decided."

"Then they're coming over today?"

"No. Lady Ellen is taking Marguerite and Alex shopping with her. They'll stop in at the Goodbodys' store. It'll give the young ones a chance to see where they'll be working before they make up their minds."

Juliette watched as the children went inside. Then, aware that she could only wait, she returned to her book. The day dragged slowly by. Once, when she looked up, a small rabbit was perching on the edge of the swing, his ears back, his eyes wide with interest. As soon as she moved, however, he leaped off and hopped quickly away. Idly, she followed his retreat. When the children returned, she'd show them his hole. Very possibly, having always lived in a city, they might never have seen one.

The sun was low on the horizon and a slight chill was in the air when she heard the voices of the returning shoppers. Eagerly, she hurried around the house. Two lackeys were carrying in Lady Ellen's bundles. They lady herself, and the children, were already at the front door. Juliette ran up the path. "Did you enjoy your trip?"

Marguerite jumped up and down in her eagerness to talk. "Oh, yes! And we met the nicest people!"

Alex smiled shyly. "They are nice. A lot like my

parents. And they have a wonderful business! Just the kind I'm going to have when I grow up."

Lady Ellen looked steadily into his face. "Would you like to live with them—and help them in their store?"

Juliette glanced quickly at the two happy faces. They had been pleased before, what with the trip and the shopping, but they lit up with delight at their hostess's words. Lady Ellen continued, "They have no children—and no close relatives. They have offered to take you in and raise you as their own. Mr. Goodbody has even promised that if you work well with him, he will leave the business to you, Alex, when he dies."

Alex stared ahead in silent contemplation. When he spoke, his expression was serious. "I have held a dream that we would be able to start up our own shop back in Calais, but I realize it is impossible." He turned to Marguerite. "If you like them, I'll say yes."

It was decided then, and plans were made for the children to move to their new home within the week. Marguerite was so excited she paid little attention to Juliette's rabbit—or to the hole where it hid. "I'm going to work again!" She sounded actually ecstatic. "I was growing tired of holidays."

Juliette felt left out of the general happiness. She had found nothing dissatisfying about the days of leisure. Alex's and Marguerite's delight at finding work filled her with a sense of guilt. And it renewed her sense of isolation.

The Goodbodys came to pick up their new charges a week later. The children waved until they were out of sight, and their cries of farewell rang in Juliette's ears long after they were gone. She felt let down, depressed. Their cheerful laughter and pleasant games had helped to fill the time.

Lady Ellen, standing beside her, touched her arm

gently. "Don't be unhappy, my dear. They had to find a home sooner or later. I know Gwen worried about them getting lazy."

"I don't think they could. But I'll miss them."

"Maybe, when the trouble in your country is over, you can trade there. I'm sure Alex would be proud to serve you." Lady Ellen brought one finger to her lips. "I doubt you'll have time to be lonesome. François is due in a few days, and you have a visitor coming."

"A visitor? Is it duDeffand?"

"Yes!" Ellen held out her hand to stay Juliette's protest. "Please, you must see him. Now that he is suspect, we need to know all we can about his procedure. None of us want to have our efforts subverted. France will need her leaders when the terror is over."

"But what help can I be?"

"You can let him talk—and you can report on his technique. We need to know how he persuades people who are safe to return to certain death. Of course, we have our suspicions. We think he offers them safety for people they love in exchange for their lives. But we aren't certain. We do know that few relatives of those who return ever arrive here, so we're sure that, if that's his method, he does not follow through on his promises."

Juliette lowered her head. She felt ashamed to admit her relationship with a man who could be so despicable. However, she did agree to the meeting. Somehow, she felt it was her duty.

As was Juliette's habit, she ate lunch in the kitchen, where the children had always joined her. Gwen was cordial enough, but she seemed uneasy now that the two young folk were not there to serve as a buffer between her and someone she clearly considered her "better."

The strain made the lunch far from pleasant, and

Juliette determined she would not repeat the arrangement. She liked Gwen too much to make her uncomfortable.

Lady Ellen, as usual, had driven off for London as soon as the children were gone. The constant absence of her hostess disappointed Juliette. She was convinced they could be good frineds, if only the older woman spent less time in the city.

As it was, Juliette found herself completely alone. Gwen's clear intention of remaining on her side of the invisible barrier that separated ladies and gentlemen from working people seemed to include all of the help. The maids were polite—but distant. None of them spoke except when their duties occasioned direct contact with their guest.

Roger's visit had been arranged for the last day before François' årrival, not because Juliette preferred it, but because he had left town for a short time. The close proximity between her meeting with Roger and the arrival of her lover made her quite uncomfortable. What if François came back early? She knew she would feel terribly humiliated were he to arrive while duDeffand was still in the house.

Lady Ellen showed no such concern, and, since Juliette could do nothing to change the arrangement, the meeting was not called off. Nevertheless, concern for what might happen caused Juliette to spend a sleepless night. What little sleep she did have was spoiled by dreams filled with terror. She couldn't forget that he had threatened the safety of the children if she would not consent to joining him—as his wife.

"Lady Ellen, how kind of you to let me call!" Roger bent low over his hostess's hand. When she showed little response, he turned to Juliette. With the same gallantry, he took her slender hand in his and lifted it to his lips. "My dear! I can't say how delighted I am to know you're alive! You startled me completely when I saw you in the forest!''

His hand felt clammy under Juliette's fingers. Repressing a shudder, she pulled her arm back. ''Won't you come in? Lady Ellen has some tea in the library.''

At the door, Lady Ellen paused. ''I'm sure you two have much to discuss. I shall join you in a half hour.''

Juliette repressed her apprehension. She was safe, she knew, as long as she remained in the house. ''I'm sure there's nothing we might talk about from which you would be excluded.'' Lady Ellen shook her head. ''If you insist. We'll look forward to your joining us later, then,'' said Juliette. Opening the door, she led the way into the room.

All four walls of the library were lined with books, some in English, some in French, that had belonged to Lady Ellen's husband. It was not, however, a sterile room designed for study alone. A deep, comfortable chair stood before the fireplace, which glowed brightly with flames set by one of the lackeys. Beside it, a smaller chair appeared to have been placed for Juliette's convenience.

When she was seated, she looked into Roger's face. It surprised her to realize how little she had seen of him in the woods. Her fear had blinded her to the changes that had taken place. Now she could see that he had grown stout since his days in Tuileries, and she understood why he had failed to catch her when she fled with the children.

If anything, he was more a fop than ever. His features had the same droop that had repelled her when she was a child, but there was an increased dissoluteness in his expression. He had not changed in his self-indulgence—nor in his willingness to take advantage of anyone who was helpless.

She found it difficult to look at him without remembering the shame to which he had subjected her. It seemed impossible that she had taken his mistreatment without fleeing, yet she had no trouble recalling the fear that had held her. It had all gone, now. She chose life because she knew she would be living it with François. But, were Roger to put her in an untenable position, she would have the courage to resist him now—even if it meant her death.

As she waited for him to speak, she tried to remember when the fright that had held her for so long had vanished. It had happened in the temple, when her concern for her own safety was forgotten in her anxiety regarding the safety of the royal children. Lady Ellen had said Roger used his victims' interest in others to convince them to return to France with him. She would have to be careful not to let him know of her worry over François—or the two royal orphans.

"Juliette, my love!" She winced at his cordiality. "I have news for you about your homeland."

She nodded, determined to conceal her interest, no matter what he said.

"You will be glad to hear that Princess Marie Theresa is fine. Since I had no idea I would see you, I can't bring her greetings, but I'm sure she sends them. Young Louis has not fared as well. The last I heard, he was quite ill and has been placed under the care of a court-appointed physician."

Despite her resolution, she could not repress her curiosity. "Do you know who remains with the princess?"

"Ah, yes, I should have thought! Of course you know her. Hariette—and the cook. What was his name? Ah, yes, Vidot! That's all! The rest are long since gone."

The casualness with which he spoke of the death of seven people made her shudder. Still, she had to learn more. "You say the prince is ill. Do they still keep him with that cobbler?"

"Oh, you heard of that, did you? No. He's been brought to more suitable surroundings. But I fear for his life. He never was very strong, you know."

"The queen?"

"Oh, she took the walk from her cell some time ago! A proud woman, Marie Antoinette! Never wavered once! Makes you proud to be a Frenchman!"

Juliette gazed at him in horror. How could he speak so callously? She felt no need to respond. He had answered her questions. Now, if there was to be any further conversation between them, it would have to start with him.

When he realized she was going to remain silent, he leaned forward. "I find myself still amazed at the good fortune that brought us together last week. I had no idea you were alive, much less in England! You startled me completely." She lowered her eyes. "I fear I behaved most rudely. But I trust you will understand. When you appeared so suddenly, I quite lost my mind. I said the first thing that came to my mind in hopes it would frighten you into staying with me. I had not realized you had matured so." He inhaled deeply and stared into the fire. "I trust you were not upset by my little joke about sending the children to France."

"A joke? I'm afraid I don't understand."

"Well, you see, I am well acquainted with the families here in London, and I hear of many new arrivals. I knew, of course, that a young woman and two children had come to stay with Lady Ellen. I also know there are many unscrupulous men who prey on those of us with relatives in France—and who aren't above kidnaping a child or two to increase their reward."

He paused and turned to face her. She could read him so clearly. When he was lying, he always gazed at her in a most straightforward manner, as he did now. "I knew Lady Ellen must have warned the children to stay within her grounds, and so, when I saw the little girl running into the woods, I decided to give her a scare that would keep her safe. Your precipitous escape denied me the opportunity to explain."

"Then you wouldn't have asked me to stay with you?"

"Ah, that's another thing! All I said is I have no arrangement with Robespierre—or with anyone else—for returning refugees to France. As for wanting you, my dear, I want you very much!"

She shook her head and folded her hands in her lap. She would let him speak. She couldn't stop him without leaving the room. But when Lady Ellen returned, she would excuse herself and repair to the garden. She had had more than enough of his deceitful ways.

He pulled his chair closer to hers. "Now that you understand what happened the other day, and you aren't afraid of me any longer, I wish to present my case in a more mature manner. Juliette, my love, we've spent many pleasant days—and wonderful nights—in each other's company. I recognize that in the past I have treated you shamefully, but it was only because I was not fully aware of my need—of my love—for you. I know now how much you mean to my happiness. I want you to marry me."

She looked into his dark eyes. He was lying, she was sure of it. Still, the words satisfied a longing that had been dormant in her heart ever since he had laughed at her suggestion that they wed and make the child she bore legitimate. She had wanted to hurt him then. Now— She could get some satisfaction even at this late date.

She rose and moved toward the fireplace. "No, Roger. I have no desire to marry you. Once, when I carried your child, I would have been delighted at such a proposal, though even then I didn't love you. But now I have no desire to affiliate myself with a man like you. I have no wish to carry your name—or share your wealth."

He studied her carefully. Unnerved by his gaze, she lowered her eyes to the floor. There had been a time when his glance—or his touch—would have aroused her to soaring passion. Now she felt only revulsion at his nearness. When he rose and stood beside her, she drew back.

His voice was low. "Is there nothing I can say that will persuade you? I have much to offer, and there are few men better equipped to appreciate your unique talents. After all, much you know you learned from me."

She began to tremble. Despite her determination, she knew his power was not all gone. "Please, Roger, I'd rather not talk about it anymore." She glanced toward the door. When was Lady Ellen going to arrive?

He stepped back and stood before the fire, his legs braced apart, his hands clasped behind his back. "You're very sure of yourself, aren't you?" The pleading was gone from his voice. It was hard once more—as she remembered it from the past. "I wonder if you would feel the same were I to present you with a small souvenir I picked up on my last trip to the continent?"

A small presentiment of doom teased at the back of her mind. He looked too smug—too sure of himself!

Something in his posture told her he felt in full control of what was happening. Silently, she determined not to rise to his bait.

When she didn't answer, he reached into his pocket. Cupping his hand, he gazed at its contents. "I picked this off a revolutionary when he struggled to keep me from effecting a rescue. I decided I had to bring it to you—if for no other reason than its sentimental value."

Juliette felt herself go white. There was only one thing small enough to be held in one hand that would interest her. Still, she was firm in her resolve not to let him see her emotion. She glanced into his eyes and realized he was already conscious of her curiosity— and he was playing the game out to its dramatic climax.

He moved his hand slowly before her like a snake mesmerizing its victim. "Aren't you interested in what I have?"

Deliberately, she shook her head. "No. It makes no difference to me! What sort of trick are you trying to play?"

Slowly, he lifted his hand up to her face, its contents concealed by his fingers. Then, suddenly, he opened his palm and a small gold pendant dropped toward the floor.

Instinctively, she reached a hand out to catch it, but it never touched her. He had one end of the chain tight between his thumb and his forefinger.

There was no doubt that he knew the power of what he held. Dangling before her eyes was her own gold pendant—the one she had given to François. She stared at it in horror.

"Take it, my sweet. Open it up. You might recognize its contents."

Trembling, she touched the small lever that held the lock. Inside was a small curl, tied with a tiny ribbon. It was hers. This was, indeed, the locket she had given to her lover.

"You haven't asked me how I knew you would be interested in this little bauble." He let it fall into her hand. "Ah, well, it doesn't matter. I'll tell you, anyway." His gaze, fastened on her face, was filled with anger. "I saw you, my sweet innocent darling, in the arms of a ragamuffin from the streets! Remember? Oh, well, you might not. You lay in so many arms." He began to pace restlessly. "You gave yourself to him in the garden at Tuileries! As he was skulking away, the locket caught the light. I've never forgotten it. I swore then I would kill that man, whoever he was, for I knew he was the one who stole your virginity from me."

She had lost all her defenses. The shock in her face did nothing to conceal her agony. "You murdered him?"

"Murdered? No. I'm not as crass as that! I simply denounced him to the Assembly. They handled the business quite expertly." His eyes caught hers and held them. "It's only because I'm sure your lover is dead that I offer to marry you. The fact that he enjoyed your favors is, of course, distasteful to me—especially since he took your most precious possession—your innocence." He inhaled deeply. "However, that's all water under the bridge—unimportant now, except as history. I have, at least, taken my revenge." His eyes flashed. "He was the man, wasn't he? When did he do it? Was it after I spoke to your father—or before? Did the old man know?" Juliette shook her head. "Well, at least that gives me some comfort. I would resent having spent the time and money on you that I did if I thought your father had deliberately deceived me.''

She raised her head. ''My father was an honorable man!''

''It's a shame he had such a dishonest little daughter! But, never mind! It only shows me how much alike we are. You belong with me, my dear. Your mind is just as devious—and you take as much pleasure as I in spending money.''

Juliette couldn't answer. She held the locket tenderly in her hand, as if, through it, she could touch François. Tears filled her eyes. Why, oh why had she let him stay in France? She should have insisted on remaining with him—or in his going with her. How could she have been so foolish as to let him go? With a sob, she drew the chain to her lips.

His hands grasped her shoulders, but he made no attempt to kiss her. Instead, he led her to her chair and lowered her into it. She felt herself reel dizzily. Resting her back against the chair, she let the darkness close over her consciousness. When she again became aware of her surroundings, Roger was sitting opposite her. She averted her face. She had no desire to look again at the destroyer of her happiness. In her mind one thought was repeated, over and over again. Why, oh why, had she been saved—only to lose her François?

''My dear''—his voice was solicitous now, as if some other person had delivered the death blow to her joy—''it grieves me to see you so broken. Surely, after all these years, you've grown away from your childhood infatuation!'' She made no answer. When he lifted her to her feet, she tried to pull away, but his arms were too strong. ''Come, you must let me care for you—and make up for all the unpleasantness you've had to face!''

He walked her to the door and reached for the

handle. She struggled once more to break away, but his grip tightened. Frantically, she prayed for Lady Ellen's return. If no one came to stop him, he would take her away—in broad daylight! And she was too weak to resist!

The door swung open and Lady Ellen, backed by two of her strongest lackeys, blocked their way. With a muffled curse, he dropped her arm and turned from the angry face of her savior. When he turned back, his greasy manners had returned. "Ah, Lady Ellen, Juliette is feeling quite faint. I fear I brought her bad news. I was taking her out to where she could be brought to her room."

There was no acceptance of his explanation in Ellen's face. With a snort of anger, she pushed past him and took Juliette's hand. "Are you all right, my dear?"

"I'm fine—now. Thank you for coming."

Roger cleared his throat. "If she now has a companion, I'll take my leave. Juliette—I'll return in three days for your answer. Think on it. Your life can still be pleasant." She didn't bother to look up as he left the room.

When she heard the door close, she fell into Lady Ellen's arms. "Oh, Lady Ellen, he's gone! François is dead!"

One of the lackeys lifted her, then, and carried her up the stairs to her room. When she felt her head touch her pillow, she turned her face from the light and burst into tears.

"Do you feel better today, my dear?" Lady Ellen's kindly face peered around the door.

Juliette pushed herself into a sitting position on her bed. "Come in. I know you loved him, too."

Lady Ellen approached, a tray in her hands.

"Here's some food. You've been closed up here for a whole day! It isn't good for you! My sweet young friend! If there's one thing you learn as you grow old, it is that life goes on. You will recover, even though now it seems impossible."

The pillow behind Juliette felt damp but no more tears left her eyes. There were none left for her to cry. "Maybe you're right. But I won't remain here to face the chance of running into Roger duDeffand. I want no more of his cruelty. He asked me to marry him, you know."

Lady Ellen raised a hand in protest. "You can't!"

"I won't. I couldn't do that. But I've been thinking about what he said, and it's brought my thoughts into focus. There's no future for me as I am, now that François is—dead." She forced the word through her lips, though it tore her heart to say it. "I've decided to join a nunnery." Her upraised hand stemmed Lady Ellen's objection. "Please. I've made up my mind. But there is a particular one I wish to join—in Prussian Netherlands."

Lady Ellen pointed to the tray. "Please, eat now. You can think more on that later."

Juliette obediently took the spoon in her hand and brought some soup to her mouth. The rich taste of fresh vegetables perked up her appetite. For a time she ate in silence. When the bowl was empty, she put down her spoon. "Thank you. I didn't realize I was hungry. But my mind is not changed."

"Take a little time. It can heal many grievous wounds."

"What comfort or healing can I get from time? It will change nothing! He's gone! Tell me, when did he say he would return?"

Lady Ellen lowered her eyes. "Today."

"Has he come? No! He won't, either! Oh, I have feared for him so long! And always he came through safely. He was such an idealist! He was so good! I used to feel certain he would get himself killed. And now, when at last he saw the revolution for what it is—now I lose him!"

She brought her hands to her face and held them there until she recovered her poise. "Please, Lady Ellen, will you book passage for me? I have a pin I wore on the dress I had on when I came here that is of some value. Take it to pay for the passage. I won't be allowed to keep it when I take the vows."

When Lady Ellen nodded, Juliette rose and brought her the brooch. "Thank you. You may wait, if you wish, until tomorrow. But I would like to leave before Roger returns. I do not wish to see him again."

Lady Ellen nodded and silently left the room. When she was gone, Juliette lay back on her bed. Patiently, she folded her hands and repeated a prayer for peace. There was no more happiness for her in this world. But she had her life still ahead of her. God willing, she would devote it to helping others.

CHAPTER TWENTY-SIX

The heavy gate clanged shut as Juliette stepped from the garden into the mother superior's study. The journey from England had been uneventful, but she had been torn with inner turmoil that did not abate even when she reached her final shelter. She looked at the smooth, round face of the leader of the Sisters of Charity. There was no passion on the calm countenance. A faint hope touched Juliette's heart. Others had found peace here. Surely she could, too.

"Juliette de Condillac. That is your full name?"

"Yes, Mother."

"And so you wish to join us. Have you always been inclined toward the ascetic life?"

Juliette paused. "No, Mother." She realized there was nothing to be gained by lying. Widows were accepted into the service, and she was, in one way, a widow.

"What is your reason for seeking the shelter of our walls?"

"I wish to find peace—and to serve others."

A faint smile touched the thin lips. "I have no doubt we can fill the second desire you have voiced. As for the first—" She looked directly into Juliette's face. "Peace is in the soul, my child. It is not the property of one special place. Many women who live their lives in the middle of trouble are full of God's peace."

Did that mean, Juliette wondered, that there were some nuns who never reached that beatific state?

The mother superior studied Juliette for a moment. Then, with a real smile, she settled in her chair. "Let me tell you our conditions. You may join us as a novitiate immediately. As such, you must devote your time to prayer and fasting—and to the purifying of your soul. A priest will attend you daily for your confession. You will speak to no one except him—not even to the nuns who bring you food and water."

Juliette nodded. "Yes, Mother."

"Most novitiates take their vows after a month in preparation. However, some take longer. We have a limit, however. After one year, if you haven't proved yourself a fit member of our society, you will be permitted to join the lay sisters, who help in the orphanage and the hospital—but you will not take the vows unless you are ready. We want the handmaidens of the Lord to be happy in their duties."

Juliette nodded.

"I will say my thoughts now, for it is important to your future. I am filled with compassion when I look into your face. Your passions are strong, I can see that, and your determination to take the vows is strong, too. I don't know if you will be able to destroy the evil within you and free yourself of human frailties. However"—she rose from her seat—"I see no reason not to give you an opportunity to try." She clapped her hands loudly.

A door opened on one side of the room. Juliette turned to see a young nun, not much older than she, step in. She stood quietly, her hands folded before her. The mother superior beckoned her forward. "Sister Theresa, this is Juliette de Condillac. She has requested permission to enter as a novitiate. You will care for her during her time of trial." She turned to Juliette. "Sister Theresa has taken a vow of silence within the walls of the convent. She speaks only when she is on duty with the children or the ill. Please respect her condition.''

Juliette nodded. When Sister Theresa started for the door, Juliette followed. She felt an impatience to begin her purging process because the temptations of the flesh had caused her trouble enough. Yet she missed François with passionate longing. Hopefully, after a day or two of prayers and fasting, she would quiet the demon that burned in her heart.

She was led to a small, bare room that opened up onto the garden. As she passed through the opening, Juliette realized it had no door. In the summer, the warm breezes and the sweet fragrance of growing things would caress her nostrils. But when winter came, she would have nothing to protect her from the icy winds.

The cell itself had only two items in it. One was a thin mattress. The other was a large crucifix. Sister Theresa motioned her to sit, and she dropped to the mattress. She waited there while her guide disappeared and returned, after a period of absence, with a thin wool robe.

Following silent directions, Juliette removed her gown and let it fall to the floor. She stood nude for a moment in the fresh, clean air. Then she realized Sister Theresa had covered her eyes and was looking away. Abashed, Juliette pulled the robe over her naked body. She had forgotten. Bouchard had always tried to teach her that nudity was a sin. Somehow, until now, she had never truly understood.

When she was properly covered, Juliette picked up her robe and handed it to Sister Theresa. The young nun smiled gently and signaled that it was time for prayers. Then, with a nod, she stepped into the garden. Juliette was alone.

She remained alone for the remainder of the day.

She had been shown where the outhouses were, but otherwise she had no guidance as to what she should be doing. Remembering the mother superior's advice, she knelt in prayer before the crucifix.

A contemplative mood did not come easily. Instead of prayers, memories flooded her brain. Glancing out through her doorway, she saw the chapel, directly across the garden. The sight sent a shiver of fear down her back. It was made of the same gray stone that had built the Abbey Villeurbanne. And the last time she had seen that edifice her uncle's body, garbed in a macabre red riding suit, had been carried in through a narrow door.

The thought of that moment brought the whole terrible past back with a rush. She hadn't thought to ask if he had been buried in his red suit. Now she considered the possibility. No, certainly not. He would have been covered properly with his robe of office! Somewhere in the distance female voices began a chant. The monks at the abbey would have had many such prayers to say in order to get their leader into heaven, for his sins were manifold.

The thought filled her with guilt. She hadn't prayed for him—or her parents and Bouchard—since she reached Versailles! During those terrible days, she had lost most of her faith. Deliberately, she turned back to the crucifix. She would make up for her neglect now. She would even pray for the forgiveness of poor Helene!

The days that followed flowed quietly one after the other in silent progression. Each morning she rose determined to seek out her oversights and misdeeds so she could make amends for her sinful past, but when she thought back on all she had been through, she found little to regret. True, she had lived a sinful life at the court. But it hadn't been her choice. If anything, her sin was being afraid of suffering. She had stayed with Roger only because she could see no sense in living on the streets.

She prayed for her unborn child who had been taken from her through Roger's perfidy, but she felt no responsibility for that sin. She had been a victim as much as the infant had. However, one sin rested heavily on her shoulders. During her days in the court, she had abandoned her faith. She had lost her belief in God entirely, and for that she felt ashamed. But the severe priest who came to hear her confession would not allow her such indulgence.

"Juliette! It is common for men and women who lose their faith to feel they might make amends by overzealous praying when it is, at last, recovered. Think on your God. He demands your faith—but he is also forgiving! The two thieves who died at his side on the cross repented just before their souls left their bodies, yet we have God's own word that they went directly to paradise. You can't balance the scales for your soul. That has been done for you—by your Lord Christ. Pray for His guidance in the future and let the past—all of the past—be forgotten. His love will wipe your sins away. You do not need to spell them out to Him."

Despite his admonitions, she could not let the past go. It was a full week before she found the days in Versailles pass from her conscience.

Though she concentrated daily on her relationships with others, her dreams kept returning to François. Often, she wakened in the night, her body wet with passion, and she knew she had felt again the closeness of his body to hers, the throbbing of his love as it echoed her own. When consciousness returned, she brushed the dream aside, returning her attention to what she had decided was her appointed task. It wasn't until she

SO WILD A RAPTURE 353

had been in the convent for a full month that she was forced to face her own self-deception.

She was summoned, as she had been told she would, for an interview with the mother superior. The kindly woman greeted her with an understanding smile. "My daughter, for many young novitiates, one month is enough. They come here with serene countenances and hearts that have already found peace. But this is not true for you. I have received reports that you spend your days in self-inflicted penance. The sisters report that you have twice crawled on your knees around the garden, repeating your rosary. Yet, I understand you moan in your sleep at night and wake often to seek the coolness of the garden air. These are not the acts of one who has found peace with her God."

Juliette kept her eyes directed on the floor. "No, Mother." She could not keep a note of panic from her voice. "Please don't send me away! I'll be all right in a while! Please!" Her hands raised in supplication, she fell to her knees.

Gently, the older woman lifted her to her feet. "My child, you do me a disservice when you kneel before me. I am neither your king nor your God, and they are the only two before whom man should kneel. Rest easy. I have no intention of sending you away from our shelter. I'm sure you will make an excellent nun—and a kind teacher—once you have settled your spirit. However, I forbid you to fast for more than ten days at a time. You will do no one any good if you starve yourself before you reach your understanding with your Lord."

"But surely mortifying the flesh can bring me relief from the torment I now suffer!"

"Some think it will—but not I. It has been my experience that all such behavior does is muddle the mind and weaken the spirit. We need strong women to help with our nursing duties, not frail creatures destroyed by their own impatience. Take the time you need. Haste will only frustrate you further.''

Juliette bowed her head and turned toward the door. A call from the mother superior brought her to a halt. "Juliette, one more thing. I have received a message in the past week from a Lady Ellen in England. It is our custom to dispose of all messages from the world outside. However, in your case— I wonder if it might not hasten your reconciliation with God were you to receive this one communication.''

Juliette did not raise her head. She knew Lady Ellen's objections to her decision, and she had no desire to hear more of it. "No, Mother. Your rule is wise. I prefer to follow all of your regulations.''

Silently, she continued from the room. She didn't look back, even when she heard the sound of tearing paper.

Summer passed into fall and fall into winter, yet little change took place in Juliette's troubled mind. The cold of the nights served only to make sleep more difficult, so that even when her mind was at rest, her body was wakeful. Yet, despite the low temperatures, she often woke from a troubled sleep with her body bathed in sweat and her veins pulsing with a desire she seemed unable to put aside. She knew then that her sleep had taken her back to the meadow near Chalon to commune with the spirit of her lost love.

She would rise then and crawl before the crucifix, staring into the tormented face of her God. Surely, now that François was dead, He would help her end her own torment through prayer.

Despite her hardships, she persisted with a determination that eventually had an effect on her superiors. The snows of winter were melting, and crocus peeked through the white ground cover when the mother superior once more summoned Juliette to her office.

"My child"—the woman's voice showed her compassion—"I hear much of your devotion. Sister Theresa reports that you show improvement, and the father informs me your mind delves less into the past than it has in the months gone by. I know you still fight your particular demon, but we can understand this. I suspect much would be easier for you were your hours filled with labor. Am I right?"

Juliette let a hint of a smile touch the corners of her lips. "Yes, Holy Mother."

"Good! Then it is decided. We have made you wait long enough. You seem to understand that your present unrest is God's way of testing your inner strength—and of increasing your faith in your heavenly Father. You will return to your cell and prepare for the ceremony. I believe you will be a true and worthy bride of Christ."

Juliette bowed her head. At last! She agreed with the holy mother that she would find surcease from her occasional temptations once she busied herself with the needs of others. She wanted nothing more than to be allowed to devote her life to the caring of those in need.

The mother superior spoke once more. "Sister Theresa will prepare you. You will spend the next two days in silent prayer. If, during that time, any thoughts come to you of other vocations, you must speak, for God uses that time to cleanse the mind. If, at the end of the two days and nights, your purpose is firm, you will be robed in a bridal gown, and the marriage will take place. Then you will assume the robes of the Sisters of Charity and serve your husband and God, Jesus Christ, by caring for the neediest of His people."

Once more, Juliette nodded. "Yes, Holy Mother."

With a new confidence she walked back to her cell. Her tiny feet, still slippered in the shoes she had worn in England, were hardly aware of the wet ground. As she reached the entrance to her cell, a line of nuns filed past on their way to the hospital. Her heart soared as she watched them move slowly down the path. Soon she would be in their ranks! In caring for others she would be closer to François than she could ever be—until that glorious day when she joined him in heaven.

CHAPTER TWENTY-SEVEN

A beam of light cut across the garden and touched Juliette's face. Startled, she lifted her head and gazed around her. In the two days of special devotion prior to her entry into the order, all of nature had joined her in celebration. The remnants of snow that had spotted the grass had vanished, and the entire cloister was filled with color. Jonquils and crocus shouted their delight at the coming of spring, and a blue sky above them was filled overnight with birds returned from the south.

Juliette crossed herself and rose to her feet. It was time to get ready for the ceremony. Silently, she crossed the yard to the outhouses. When she returned, she stopped at the small stream that passed through the center of the cloister and rinsed her face and hands.

A new excitement filled her breast. Soon she would take the vows that would open the door to a lifetime of service. Her days of loneliness would be over! Already she was aware of a new sense of kinship with the silent nuns who passed by her cell in the morning on their way to work. They were a unit, working as one mind for the good of others. Soon she would take her place among them.

Sister Theresa detached herself from a group just leaving the chapel. Juliette waited as she padded over the grass, her bare feet dark from dirt that had splashed from the soggy ground. Juliette realized she, too, would be expected to renounce shoes as a sign of physical dependence on comfort, but she had no doubt she would be equal to the requirement. Her bare legs had survived the winter with no harm, even though she had often been very cold. By next winter, she was sure, she would be strengthened enough to survive as easily as did the others.

"Come, Juliette, you must decide on your new name, for in renouncing the world, we also abandon the titles the world has given us." Sister Theresa led the way into Juliette's cell. She had finished her period of silence and spoke now when it was necessary. A beatific smile lit her slender face. "I'm so happy for you! Soon you, too, will wear the wimple and gown of the order of Charity! And today you will become the bride of Christ!"

Juliette was thankful she was behind the gentle sister, for her response was not one of pure joy, as she was certain it ought to be. Far back in her mind a small demon whispered regret that she should have found a bridegroom so lacking in human passions. Quickly, she wiped the wicked thought from her consciousness. Her face resumed its peaceful expression.

In blocking her willingness to acknowledge such a base fantasy, Juliette knew she was going contrary to the word of the mother superior. She had been told to report any such departure from the singlemindedness required in a novice, but she was hardly aware of her wrongdoing. So dedicated was she to achieving her purpose, she could not accept the possibility that she might not have the mental and emotional characteristics needed for success in the cloistered life. Closing her eyes, she prayed nothing would interfere with her reaching her chosen status. Her life then would be so neatly planned—so settled.

She glanced at Sister Theresa's straight back. Would they become friends, once she was part of the nunnery? She hoped so. One thing had not changed in her year of preparation. She still felt lonely—isolated from others. She had not felt alone when she was with François.

She crossed herself, pushing the name from her mind. Maybe she would feel alone for the rest of her life!

Sister Theresa gestured toward the crucifix. "Pray for a while more. I will return with your gown."

Juliette knelt obediently before the crucifix, her eyes lowered to avoid direct contact with her guide. Guilt over her unruly thoughts increased the intensity of her penance. The mother superior had told her that one vagrant thought would prove her unworthy of a life in the convent. Deep inside, she knew she was not one of the chosen. But her will refused to listen. She had to be a nun! She couldn't face the world alone! Silently, she vowed to keep her problems to herself from this day onward. Not even in confession would she admit to any hesitation or self-doubt.

Sister Theresa appeared beside her, a delicate lace gown in her arms. Juliette rose and let her fingers run lightly over the exquisite pattern. She had been told the story of the gown. It had been hand crocheted by one of the novitiates many generations ago, to be worn when she wed her affianced. Then war had taken her groom from her side. When she entered the convent, she brought the gown with her and wore it during the ceremony of joining with Christ. Then, as was the custom, it became the property of the convent. Every novice since that time had worn the gown that had been made for a more carnal ceremony.

At noon a priest appeared in Juliette's cell and administered the last rites. She was henceforth dead to the world and reborn in the kingdom of heaven. Then, purified and clean, she watched as he left her cell. Following the teachings of the sisters, she closed her eyes as she removed her novitiate's robe and slipped into the wedding dress, thus avoiding the possibility of sin through the viewing of her own nakedness. Beneath the gown she wore a plain, unornamented chemise. From this day onward, it would remain on her body, even when she removed the robe of her order to bathe.

The wedding gown clung softly to her body, fitting smoothly over her firm young breasts and hugging the slender waist. Despite her recognition of the evil of such an act, she could not refrain from a momentary satisfaction at her delicate appearance. The year of fasting and prayer had done nothing to spoil her beauty.

Her long black curls fell softly over her lace-covered shoulders, and her green eyes sparkled with excitement. She touched her hair lightly. François had loved it so! She could still bring back the delight she felt when he ran his fingers through her tresses and pressed his lips against her brow.

Guiltily, she let her hand fall to her side. It was good that her hair would soon be cut off and her head shaved! She would cover her head with the coif of her order—and never again would the silky strands of her hair seduce her mind into dreams of carnal joys!

The thought brought no pleasure to her mind. Instead, a sadness settled over her, threatening to bring tears to her eyes. Frantically, she pushed them back. She wanted no such telltale evidence of her lack of self-control!

Her supplications were interrupted by the sound of a bell in the chapel. It was time! Rising, she crossed herself and padded quietly from her cell, resisting the impulse to lift the hem of the gown so it would not trail on the dirt.

She had moved only a short distance from her cell when Sister Theresa stepped to her side and placed a cluster of jonquils in her hand. Juliette accepted the gift without a smile. Silently, she moved ahead of the double line of nuns who were to accompany her to the chapel. She knew this would be the last time she would walk anywhere without someone at her side. The thought gave her comfort. She had no desire for a continuation of her solitude.

She passed through the cloister into a small herb garden that separated the nuns' quarters from the mother superior's rooms—and from the great gate that led to the outside world. As it came into sight, two figures appeared before it—a man and a woman. Then the mother superior and some of the older nuns blocked Juliette's view. Impatiently, she tried to brush the vision of the intruders from her mind. They had both seemed familiar—and she had no desire for the outside world to interfere with her life after such a long period of preparation. She had no further use for earthly companions. She wished now only for the companionship of God—and of her bridegroom—her Lord, Jesus Christ.

Nevertheless, she was aware that the gate opened. The two figures were ushered ahead of the mother superior through the door that led to the entryway.

The bell in the chapel rang again, and she increased her pace ever so slightly. She had such a short distance to go. Once she had taken her vows, she would speak to anyone who asked to see her. But first she wanted to complete her duty.

Two older nuns opened the door to the entryway as she approached. Resisting the impulse to glance in the direction of the mother superior's study, she moved steadily forward. The nuns behind her took up a chant, and she let the prayer filter into her mind. It voiced a longing for peace—for rest. Juliette listened intently. She hadn't noticed it before, but now she became acutely aware that many of the songs the women sang had similar messages. Could it be she was not alone in her restlessness?

Inexorably, she moved forward. Now she was past the door behind which three voices were raised in obvious excitement. Juliette suddenly recognized one—Lady Ellen! Despite her decision to remain calm and imperturbable, she felt frustrated at the sound. Why, at this time, did Lady Ellen still persist in her opposition to the convent?

The door behind her opened and strong footsteps echoed through the hall. Was it Roger? Had he finally forced Lady Ellen to bring him here?

"Juliette!" It was the voice of the mother superior. "Juliette, there is someone here to see you."

Juliette kept her eyes pointed toward the floor. She had come to a halt when the mother superior spoke, but she declined to turn toward the intrusion. "Please, Mother, let me leave my past behind."

"Juliette! You must listen. Unless you face your past now, I will not permit the ceremony to proceed. I am convinced you have made an error in your decision to enter the order. You must turn and meet your visitors. Then, if you still wish it, they will witness your entry into the order of the Sisters of Charity."

Reluctantly, Juliette turned toward the door. Her eyes had been focused on the floor as she walked, and she did not raise them. They moved swiftly over the floor between her own feet and those of the man who stood beside the mother superior.

When she saw his worn boots, she felt a start. This was not Roger! She lifted her head quickly, aware that her heart was beating with renewed excitement.

She found herself gazing into a pair of dark brown eyes. "François!" It was only a whisper.

"Juliette!" His voice was thick with controlled emotion. "Oh, my darling, I almost lost you!"

With a small cry she covered the distance between them, but before she could embrace him, the mother superior took her arm and led her into the study. François and Lady Ellen followed close behind.

When the doors were closed, Juliette fell into her lover's arms. As his lips closed over hers, the emptiness that had tormented her fell away. The loneliness was gone. She stayed pressed against him until, at last, he drew back and turned to the waiting women. "Did this foolish girl refuse to read the letter from Lady Ellen?"

Ashamed of her stubbornness, Juliette nodded. "I thought she was writing to try to convince me to return to London."

François looked down into her flushed face. "She wrote to tell you I had been delayed. I sent a message as soon as I could, but it arrived too late for you. I can tell you now what I was doing. We tried to free the dauphin from his prison. Unfortunately, though we didn't know it at the time, the boy was already dead."

Juliette squeezed his arm with her fingers. "Roger told me he had turned you over to the Assembly. He took your chain and showed it to me. I still have it— unless the mother has thrown it away." Her eyes pleaded with the leader of the convent to reassure her.

"I still have it—and your ring—and your dress. We keep all such things until we are sure the novitiate has become a member of our order. You are not the first to leave at the last moment."

Juliette looked into François' eyes. "Then Roger didn't turn you over to the Assembly?"

"Am I minus my head? No, my darling—but he did cause me much delay. I caught him returning one of the people I had helped escape, and I confronted him with his perfidy. He took my words as an affront to his honor—which they were—and attacked me with a knife. He left me for dead on the sand near Calais. Fortunately, someone found me and nursed me back to health. I didn't notice until later that the chain was gone." He touched her cheek tenderly. "I had no idea he had used it to convince you I was dead."

Her thoughts were past that deceit. "You were injured? Where? Are you well now?"

"Yes, my little worrier. But it took close to ten months for me to get back on my feet. I had lost a great deal of blood. But it doesn't matter now, does it, my love! Not even Roger can hurt you now. It seems that victim I tried to take from him settled the score most effectively. Roger was denounced to the Assembly and imprisoned for embezzlement. I have heard nothing since, but I know there is no love in the revolutionary government for men who take money on false pretenses."

Juliette turned to Lady Ellen. "Have you room for us in your house?"

François spoke before Lady Ellen could answer. "We'll stay with her for a time, my dear, but things are looking up for France. Robespierre has fallen from power. The reign of terror seems to be over. I heard last week that the guillotine has been taken down from its position in the Place de la Revolution. The nation is returning to sanity. Soon we will be needed to help rebuild our land."

She was hardly aware of what he said. Her eyes were on his face. It was so beautiful! "Wherever you go I will go, too." Her voice was hushed. "I ask only that you never leave me behind again."

François turned to the mother superior. "Mother, is it possible for us to be married—now?"

The woman stood silent for a moment. When she raised her head, her eyes were alight. "I will send for the priest. You can be married here, before you leave my study. Then," she smiled, "your bride will have to return the gown she is wearing. It will be needed for others who join us."

As they waited for the priest to be summoned, Juliette slipped her tiny hand into François' firm grip. A miracle had filled her life with joy. He was alive—and he would soon be hers. Gazing into his dark eyes, she knew she would never be lonely again.

HISTORICAL ROMANCE
FROM
PLAYBOY PRESS

LOVE'S GENTLE FUGITIVE $1.95

ANDREA LAYTON

A runaway to the New World, ravishingly beautiful Elizabeth Bartlett tries to escape her secret past—only to learn that shame and degradation are the price for her freedom. Frightened and vulnerable, she is rescued from brutal slavery by the one man who could return her to England and disaster.

WILD IS THE HEART $1.95

DIANA SUMMERS

Born into wealth and privilege, Aurelia was sheltered from the gathering storm of revolution. But with the fall of the Bastille, her golden world was shattered forever. Swept into the dark currents of political intrigue, she must use her dazzling beauty to survive as she becomes wife, mistress and courtesan to the most powerful men in France.

MOMENT OF DESIRE $1.95

RACHEL COSGROVE PAYES

In London's seamy underside, where the teeming masses knew only of deprivation and hunger, Mellie's survival depended on her expertise at an exclusive brothel. In all those nights of love, not one man kindled a fire in her except one: a mysterious nobleman whose mission was shrouded in secrecy. Their one night of passion ignited a raging fire of forbidden love, hate and revenge.

DANCE OF DESIRE
$1.95

BARBARA BONHAM

In a country seething with the terror of the Inquisition, young Micaela rose from poverty to become one of the most famous flamenco dancers Spain has ever known. Devastatingly beautiful, she was sought after by men of power, wealth and position. But her heart belonged to the one man she could not have—the dashing Javier, escort to the powerful Duchess de Vallabriga.

PASSION'S PRICE
$1.95

BARBARA BONHAM

In a heart-rending story set against the harshness and isolation of the vast prairies of 19th Century America, a lovely young widow and a lusty family man struggle in vain against a forbidden but powerful attraction for each other.

PROUD PASSION
$1.95

BARBARA BONHAM

In a breathtaking tale that captures the turbulence of an era and the stormy emotions of its characters, lovely Odette Morel flees the brutal excesses of the French Revolution, endures the hardships of an ocean voyage to America and faces unthinkable dangers in the frontier wilderness.

ORDER DIRECTLY FROM:
PLAYBOY PRESS
P.O. BOX 3585
CHICAGO, ILLINOIS 60654

NO. OF COPIES		TITLE	PRICE
_____	E16455	Love's Gentle Fugitive	$1.95
_____	E16450	Wild Is the Heart	1.95
_____	E16481	Moment of Desire	1.95
_____	E16470	Dance of Desire	1.95
_____	E16399	Passion's Price	1.95
_____	E16345	Proud Passion	1.95

Please enclose 25¢ for postage and handling if one book is ordered; 50¢ for two or more but less than $10 worth. On orders of more than $10, Playboy Press will pay postage and handling. No cash, CODs or stamps. Send check or money order, or charge your Playboy Club Credit Key # _____

TOTAL AMOUNT ENCLOSED: $ _____

Name _____

Address _____

City _____ State _____ Zip _____